Those Other Women

Those Other Women

A Novel

Nicola Moriarty

HARPER LUXE

An Imprint of HarperCollins*Publishers*

THOSE OTHER WOMEN. Copyright © 2018 by Nicola Moriarty. All rights reserved. Printed in the United States of America. No part of this book may be used or reproduced in any manner whatsoever without written permission except in the case of brief quotations embodied in critical articles and reviews. For information address HarperCollins Publishers, 195 Broadway, New York, NY 10007.

HarperCollins books may be purchased for educational, business, or sales promotional use. For information please e-mail the Special Markets Department at SPsales@harpercollins.com.

FIRST HARPERLUXE EDITION

ISBN: 978-0-06-279183-2

HarperLuxe™ is a trademark of HarperCollins Publishers.

Library of Congress Cataloging-in-Publication Data is available upon request.

18 19 20 21 22   ID/LSC   10 9 8 7 6 5 4 3 2 1

Those Other Women

For the Crestwood Girls (Bec, Kate, Ally, Shell, Caro, and Carla). The kind of women who always lift one another up.

Prologue

*S*he wrapped it up in a blanket and she walked. She walked until her heels were rubbed raw and blisters appeared on the soles of her feet. She left the city and she continued on through the suburbs, past darkened red-brick bungalows with neatly mowed lawns and curtains drawn tight. She put one foot in front of the other until she found a national park. Hectares upon hectares of dense bush. Towering scribbly gums and wattle trees spread wild. She pushed her way through shrubs that scratched at her ankles and branches that lashed at her cheeks. Distant howls mingled with the honeyed sounds of owls hunting possums and snakes. Deep inside, she chose a spot near the slow-moving waters of a narrow creek. The ground was hard but she raked at the claylike soil with her fingernails, scraping and digging and pushing the dirt aside until a small cavern was formed. Serenaded by a chorus of frogs and cicadas she placed the small bundle inside and covered it over with dirt and twigs.

And then she ran.

The Imposter

Mum! MUM!" The two children screamed at her as she stole five minutes to creep into the bathroom and lock the door. Her kids had been arguing all morning and this was the one place she could demand privacy. Although she knew some mothers couldn't even find peace in there. Recently she'd seen a photo on Facebook of a toddler's fingers wriggling under the bathroom door, vying for its mother's attention.

But she'd laid down the law from day one with her kids. *You don't need to watch me poop. I don't care how lonely you are. I don't care if you want a Vegemite sandwich right this second. I don't care if you're desperate for me to see the exact scene of* The Trolls *movie that's on at the moment—one I've seen fifteen times before. Right now, in here, it's Mummy's time.*

She leaned against the toothpaste-smeared sink, signed into her secondary account on Facebook, and flicked across to the group. Just being logged in under the fake persona made her breathe a sigh of relief. A gentle calm washed over her. She may have joined with an ulterior motive in mind, but now, this was her alternate reality. Here she was someone else. Here she could shake off everything that defined her. Mother. Wife. Constant caregiver. Her surrounds melted away, the soggy bath mat underfoot, the plastic toys stacked on the edge of the bath, and the streaked glass of the shower screen that beckoned to be wiped clean.

Did she feel a level of guilt about lying to these women?

Yes, of course she did. But it didn't last.

PART ONE

Poppy

Chapter 1

Poppy pulled into the driveway of the tall, gray, Harris Park town house she rented with her husband. It was a gorgeous summer's evening, and as much as she was loving the warmer months, she wasn't enjoying the way the back of her blouse was sticking to the car seat. It was too hot to cook, so she'd picked up Chinese takeaway on her way home from work. Wontons instead of spring rolls because they were Garret's favorite. Steamed rice instead of fried because she was "making an effort" to choose healthier options. Beef in black bean sauce plus battered honey chicken because she wasn't making *that* much of an effort. Harris Park was only twenty kilometers west of Sydney's center, but the drive home from her office in North Sydney usually took more than an hour thanks to traffic. She was ravenous.

She climbed out of the car and immediately realized that the beef and black bean sauce had spilled out of the container and soaked through the paper bag. Poppy carried it carefully out in front, trying not to get the sauce on her white shirt. On the way to the door she noticed that the leaves on the row of hedging lilly pillys they'd planted down the side of the driveway had shriveled to a crispy brown in the summer heat. She wondered if they would be salvageable.

She struggled to get the keys in the door while holding the leaking bag of Chinese and was momentarily irritated with Garret for not hearing the jangling sound and coming to give her a hand. When the lock finally yielded, she stepped inside and felt an odd sensation—something was different. She ignored it, though, keen to get the Chinese food through to the kitchen before it dripped.

"Hope you didn't start cooking," she sang out as she stepped out of her heels and padded through to the kitchen in stockinged feet.

Poppy stopped short at the doorway. Garret was sitting at the table, staring up at her, hands clasped in front of him. Beside him was her best friend, Karleen, hands identically clasped. The two of them looked like they were on a panel ready to interview her.

Poppy grinned at them. Her birthday was approaching next month. They must have been planning something special for her. Later, she hated that she could have been so naive.

"Karleen! I didn't see your car out front. There's enough if you want dinner," she started to gabble, holding the soggy paper bag out in front, "provided I haven't lost too much from the split container."

"Poppy, sit down, would you?" Karleen motioned toward the bench seat opposite.

Poppy wasn't overly taken aback. That's what Karleen had always been like. Abrupt and commanding. But Garret's silence started to worry her. Plus, the fact that he wouldn't meet her eyes.

Poppy dumped the food on the table and sat. "What's up, guys? Is something wrong?"

"You have to understand, Poppy," Karleen said, her voice even more emphatic than usual as she reached across to put one hand over the top of Poppy's, her curly hair bouncing around her face, "we're not doing this to hurt you."

"Sorry, what is it that I'm supposed to understand?"

Karleen continued as though Poppy hadn't spoken.

"And that's why we want to be as up-front and honest as possible with you."

"Sorry," Poppy repeated, "what exactly are you telling me?" She looked to Garret for clarification, because so far he'd remained quiet, had let Karleen do all the talking.

But he continued to stay silent.

"It's not the kind of thing we can control, Poppy," Karleen went on. "We didn't mean for this to happen. We just fell, you know?"

A cool burning sensation was making its way up Poppy's arms. It crept up her neck, it flushed her face.

"You fell?" Poppy tried again to catch Garret's eye, but he wouldn't look at her, refused to meet her gaze.

"Yes," said Karleen. "We fell . . . in love."

"What? Don't be ridiculous! This is a joke, right?"

"No, Poppy, this is very, very serious. We've been sleeping together. We can't lie to you anymore."

Poppy snatched her hand out from under Karleen's. She glared at her friend, willing her to tell her that it wasn't true, that it was all a joke—a nasty practical joke—but a joke nonetheless. But instead Karleen simply held her gaze unflinchingly and Poppy was the one who had to break eye contact. She looked down at her trembling hands and saw black bean sauce under her fingernails. She stood and walked over to the sink, turned on the tap, and started scrubbing at her fingers, digging under her nails with the dishcloth. A large black blowfly landed on the draining board next to her, twitched its wings, and inched toward some crumbs left behind from breakfast. She automatically crouched down to fetch the flyswatter from the cupboard under the sink and then stopped. An image of her chasing a fly around the kitchen while Garret and Karleen waited for her to react to their news crossed her mind and she couldn't tell if she was on the verge of tears or laughter. It all just felt so absurd. She straightened and saw that the fly was gone.

Karleen and Garret.

Garret and Karleen.

Her best friend and her husband, announcing that they were in love. But Garret didn't even like Karleen that much. Sure, they got along okay, but more as a matter of convenience, the way any husband gets along with his wife's best friend. But he also whinged about her to Poppy. Complained if she talked too much when the three of them went to the movies together. Said she had terrible taste in restaurants when she booked dinner for them at the new Mexican place on Arthur Street.

So what, now Poppy was supposed to believe he'd all of the sudden fallen in love with her? It didn't make any sense. Or had his complaints about Karleen been a ruse?

Karleen appeared behind her then, wrapped one arm around her shoulder, and reached out the other to flick on the kettle. "Here, Poppy, I'll make you a cup of peppermint tea," she said, as if tea was going to fix everything.

Poppy squirmed out of Karleen's hold and backed away from her, placing one hand on the smooth rounded edge of the laminate bench to steady herself. Inside, she was tumbling. Tumbling and rolling and falling and crashing. Inside, she couldn't breathe.

But on the outside, she remained still. She couldn't find the right words, didn't know what to say. So instead she simply watched as Karleen casually went through her cupboards to grab the mugs and tea bags. In truth, Poppy understood that the only reason Karleen knew her kitchen so well was that she was her best friend, but now it felt like her familiarity in Poppy's home was a result of her relationship with Garret, and that betrayal felt much, much worse than the sexual deception.

For a moment, Poppy saw herself spinning around on the spot, snatching hold of one of the blue-and-white herringbone-patterned mugs Karleen had pulled out of the cupboard, and swinging her arm as hard and as fast as possible to crack that mug against Karleen's skull.

Of course, she wouldn't actually do that. But God how she wanted to. Poppy turned away and caught sight of her own reflection in the window above the kitchen sink. Her neat blond hair, parted in the middle and scraped back into a short, low ponytail—the same way she wore it every single day. *Boring. I look like a boring, middle-aged woman who gets up every morning, does her hair the same way, wears the same smart office wear, goes to the same job, comes home in the afternoon, watches the same television shows, goes to bed at the same time only to get up and do it all again.* Now she wished she could smash the mug against the head of the woman in the window instead.

She felt irritated then. Irritated that she was directing all her anger at Karleen or inward at herself when Garret was the one who'd cheated. When Garret was the one who'd betrayed his marriage vows. And she felt frustrated. Frustrated that she didn't get to tell him it was over. That she didn't get to throw his clothes on the front lawn. It was all too much to take in. Too much to process in one hit.

Maybe it would have been easier if it had happened like a scene in a movie. If she'd sprung them in bed together. Found them with the sheets a tangled mess around them. Karleen scrambling to find her bra. Garret gathering the bedclothes around himself, covering up his junk self-consciously. The telltale sticky wet patch between the two of them. At least that would have given her some satisfaction—the chance to be self-righteously indignant. The right to yell and scream and kick him out. It would have spurred her into action, instead of this weird, polite, tea-drinking confrontation they'd concocted.

Poppy gripped the benchtop harder. She looked over at Garret, who was staring resolutely down at the table.

"How long?"

Karleen didn't hesitate to step in with an answer. "Four months."

"I'm not asking you, I'm asking my husband," Poppy snapped.

"He'll only tell you the same thing."

She kept her back to Karleen. "Here?" she asked, her voice rising as she spoke. "Did you fuck her here in this house, Garret? In our bed?"

"Poppy, please," Garret whispered.

She pushed past Karleen and strode out of the room. She took the stairs two at a time, opened their bedroom door, and stood still at the foot of the bed.

There were no rumpled sheets. No indents in the pillows. She leaned down and touched her fingertips to the covers, and then she realized. These were fresh sheets. They'd had sex here, today, and afterward they'd changed the sheets. Made the bed with neat hospital corners. Was she supposed to be appreciative? She looked across at her bedside table, saw the open novel facedown where she'd placed it last night when her eyes had become too tired to continue reading. It was a thriller, which Garret had read first, and she'd rolled over under the covers and prodded him in the arm. "I'm up to the bit where you realize the guy from the coffee shop is the same one the girl is dating but she hasn't figured it out yet."

"Getting to the good stuff," he'd said sleepily.

"You want to get up to some good stuff right now?"

"Rain check, babe? Half asleep already."

She wanted to reach back through time to the previous evening, grab hold of her own shoulders, and shake. How many times had he asked for a rain check? How many times had he avoided any kind of physical contact with her, turned away from her at night? And she'd had no idea there was anything wrong. She'd thought it was a normal part of marriage. You went through dry spells. Things became complacent, you took your relationship for granted. How many warning signs had she missed?

She backed out of the room and headed down the stairs. But on the bottom step she grasped hold of the banister, sank to the floor, and let the tears fall. She cried silently, desperate that Garret and Karleen not hear her.

A moment later, a pair of feet appeared in front of her. Neatly painted toenails in a demure dusky pink. She looked up to see Karleen staring down at her, her face filled with pity. Pity that Poppy didn't want. Pity that Poppy couldn't bear.

"I really am sorry, Poppy. We never wanted to hurt you like this."

But her tone belied her words. She might have felt pity, but there was no guilt and no kindness. Why was she doing this? They'd been friends for more than thirty years. And while Karleen had never been the overtly affectionate type, had never been the friend who you giggled with late into the night or shared long lingering cuddles with—she *had* always cared for Poppy. So what had changed to turn her against Poppy in this way?

Once again, Karleen reached out to touch her but Poppy recoiled. "Don't. Why are you doing this? Why are you acting this way? Why are you being so . . . so mean?" It felt like such a juvenile question, but she didn't know how else to put it. Karleen shook her head. "I told you, that's not what this is about. We're not trying to hurt you."

Poppy looked up at her friend. "But you are! You are hurting me."

She stood and walked back to the kitchen, scrubbing at her cheeks with the sleeve of her shirt as she went. Karleen followed close behind.

Garret was still in the same place. Still staring down at the table.

Poppy sat opposite him once again.

Look at me, she begged him silently, her eyes boring into the top of his bowed head. *Just look at me.* He kept his head down, low enough that she was staring right at the golf-ball-sized bald patch on his crown. Recently she'd been trying to talk him into shaving his head so he could go bald gracefully, beat his hair at its own game. He hadn't been ready to, though, he worried that his face was too round for a buzz cut. Now that would be Karleen's problem.

And just when Poppy thought none of this could hurt any more than it already did, they delivered their ultimate blow. Karleen picked up the cup of tea she'd made earlier, placed it in front of Poppy, and said, "Poppy, the truth is, Garret *does* want children."

Poppy's head snapped back. "What are you talking about?" she asked. "No, he doesn't. Garret's never wanted kids. *Never.*"

Karleen slipped around to the other side of the table and placed one hand possessively on Garret's shoulder. "Yes, Poppy, he does."

"Stop! Using! My fucking name!" Poppy screamed back at Karleen, and now her anger did shift across to Garret. Because for God's sake, the absolute sack of a man still hadn't looked at her. *Tell her she's wrong, tell her you don't want kids. Tell her you don't want her.* She kicked her leg out under the table and caught Garret in the shin, hard. She knew it would hurt him quite a lot. He'd had shin splints over the previous few months, which meant even the slightest bump was agonizing. She was right. He let out an anguished shout and finally he did look up at her. To his credit, his expression was full of guilt rather than reproach.

Karleen, on the other hand, wasn't so understanding. "Oh, Poppy," she admonished. "There's no need for that." And her hand snuck its way from Garret's shoulder to stroke the back of his neck.

"No need? The two of you are liars. Garret doesn't want children. Garret never wanted children."

"Poppy," Karleen began, but Garret finally cut in. "Give us a minute, would you, Karls?" He shifted sideways, letting her hand fall from the back of his neck while reaching down to massage his shin under the table.

"We agreed we would do this together, as a team."

Poppy snorted. A team? Karleen couldn't stop digging the knife in.

"I know, but I need to talk to Poppy . . . alone."

Karleen huffed and left the room. A moment later the front door slammed and Poppy could imagine Karleen standing out on the front porch, arms folded, foot tapping as she waited. Karleen had never been patient.

At long last, Poppy's husband held her gaze. His eyes were kind and somehow they were full of sorrow without the condescending pity that Karleen's eyes offered. "I feel awful. This isn't how I meant for it to go."

Hundreds of questions swirled through Poppy's head.

Oh yes? And how exactly did you expect it would go?

How did this happen?

When did things go wrong between us?

Why now? Why *her*?

But the one that came out of her mouth was unexpected.

"Since when do you call her Karls?"

"I . . . I don't know."

"She's always hated nicknames. Aren't you something special, then?"

Even when they were kids no one was allowed to shorten Karleen's name. She'd given one of her ex's the boot for no other reason than the fact that he wouldn't stop calling her Kazza.

Garret reached across the table and took hold of one of her hands between his own. Poppy knew she shouldn't let him touch her. He didn't deserve to ever feel the warmth of her skin again. But somehow she couldn't make her body react, she couldn't pull away. He stroked her wrist with his thumb.

"I hate seeing you like this. I hate hurting you and I never intended for this to happen. I swear to you I didn't. Karleen and I falling for one another, it was so far out of the blue, I don't think anyone could have predicted it. She wasn't lying when she said it just happened."

"And what about the other stuff? About you all of a sudden wanting kids now. Is that true too?"

Garret hesitated and then he nodded. "It is. At least, it's what I think I want."

"When did that happen? When did you change your mind? Or were you lying all along?"

"I didn't lie and it's not that I've suddenly changed my mind either. It was more gradual. It's like this, when we first got together you knew straight out what you wanted and it wasn't kids. To be honest, I wasn't fussed either way, but I loved you and I was happy to go along with what you wanted."

"But you—"

Garret silenced her with a small shake of his head. "Let me get this out. I know, I *know*. I said it was what I wanted too. And I believed I was happy. But over the years, I started to wonder, I started to have doubts."

"You never said."

"That's true and I should have told you, I should have voiced my thoughts, my fears that one day I was going to regret not having children. But I didn't, because like I said, you've always been so sure. Tell me, babe, had I brought it up with you, would you have honestly considered changing your mind?"

Everything that Poppy wanted to say clamored to have its turn. Where did she start with something like this? The blowfly returned, landing on the table between them. Poppy fixed her gaze on it and eventually she spoke.

"How am I supposed to answer that? How am I supposed to know what I might have said, what I might have done? When you never even gave me the chance?"

"I didn't ask because it wouldn't have been fair for me to put you in that position. Especially when I was still trying to figure it all out for myself. To expect you to reconsider when you made it clear from day one that you never wanted children. Babe, it was a deal breaker for you, I knew that."

Poppy finally wrenched her hand out of Garret's grip and slammed her palm down on the table, killing the fly. She wiped the remains of the dead insect on her gray suit pants. "Stop calling me babe! You don't get to call me that anymore. And you want to talk about being fair? You didn't want to put me in that position, so instead you cheated on me with my best friend! That's fucking absurd!"

"I know, but like I said, we didn't mean for it to happen. We started out just talking. That time we were all meeting for a drink after work at Platinum's Bar and you ran late. It was awkward at first, usually Karleen and I would need you to be the icebreaker between us. But she'd just had that terrible blind date with the IT guy. She was feeling down and we both put a fair few drinks away and got chatting. She told me how she was ready to start a family and she was scared she was running out of time—"

"STOP! I don't want to hear it. You think I need the details? You think I want you to describe how the two of you started staring into one another's eyes over your margaritas? Let me guess, her knee brushed against yours? Your hand landed on her thigh and you don't even know how it got there? You started confiding about how your bitch of a wife was going to deprive you of the chance to be a daddy?"

Something flashed across Garret's eyes and Poppy knew she was bang-on. *That arsehole.*

She forged on. "And next thing, I show up—completely clueless and ruin the moment for the two of you. But from then on, you're exchanging secret little glances of longing, and before you know it . . . you're fucking one another. That's how it went, right?"

"Poppy, don't do this. Karls and I, we both still love you. It tears us up that we're hurting you, it was the last thing we wanted, but it was like we didn't have a choice in the matter."

"Oh yeah, she sure looked all torn up inside."

"You know what she's like, she puts up a front, she's all business, but it's only because she's trying to hold it together."

"Business? So what, this is just a neat little business transaction to her? We switch roles, she becomes the wife, I become the best friend, the third wheel, and we go on like nothing ever happened? And you think you can sit there and tell me you both still love me? You two make me sick."

Garret reached once more for her hand but Poppy lurched backward, almost falling off the seat. "I never want to see either of your faces again."

She stood and fled. Karleen didn't try to stop her when she passed her on the front porch.

In the car, Poppy drove aimlessly. She didn't know where to go. Usually if you had a fight with your husband, the person you turned to was your best friend. But obviously Poppy didn't have that option anymore. Not that she and Garret had really fought much throughout their marriage. Was that another sign she'd missed? Did their lack of arguments equate to a lack of passion?

She couldn't bring herself to head over to her parents' place. They would try their best to comfort her, but ultimately they wouldn't know the right things to say. The same went for her brother, Nolan. He'd be lost for words, and probably would want to punch Garret in the face, which wouldn't necessarily be a bad thing. It was a shame she'd never become close with Nolan's wife, Megan, but Poppy had really only ever had the one female friend—Karleen, who had been her friend since primary school when she'd walked up to her in the playground and asked for a turn of her My Little Pony toy.

"You can play with my Cabbage Patch doll if you want?"

Boom. Just like that. Friends for life. Well, that's what Poppy had thought anyway. She thought that's how it worked. You start with your family, and then you make your friends as a child and they stick with you, and that right there is your safety net. Then you fall in love and you get married and your best friend is your maid of honor.

Her maid of honor. Her maid of honor had slept with her husband.

Eventually she pulled over on the side of the road and simply sat in the car. Hands gripping the steering wheel. Her body shuddering with sobs as she let herself completely succumb to the self-pity, not caring who might walk or drive past and see her broken form.

Her mind swung from one gut-wrenching moment to the next.

The moment she'd touched her fingers to the freshly made bed.

The moment Garret had whispered those words: *Poppy, please.*

The moment Karleen had dropped her bombshell: Garret does want kids.

She still couldn't really believe it. Not wanting to have children had been something they had agreed upon so early in their relationship. Yes, of course she had been the instigator, but Garret had never once expressed even the slightest hesitation on the matter.

"Kids are expensive," he'd agreed, "and they take over your lives."

Okay, so his reasons for being on board didn't exactly stem from the most deep-seated of desires, but regardless, he'd said he was all for it. He'd said that whatever made her happy made him happy. And not having children made Poppy happy.

She couldn't really pinpoint the moment when she'd come to that decision for herself. There was no single defining incident. No one driving reason. It was a combination of things. It was the immense relief she felt when she held someone else's baby and then she got to hand it back. It was the pride she felt in knowing her choice was the environmentally responsible one. It was the freedom she knew she had to do what she wanted, when she wanted. Knowing she could travel, knowing she could grow her career, knowing she could spend her money on an expensive outfit without compromising her hypothetical child's future education.

And lastly, it was the acute absence of any maternal desire or instinct within. When it came down to it, she simply didn't want to be a mother. And she knew she never would.

So in truth, what would have happened if Garret had brought up his change of heart instead of straying? He wasn't wrong when he'd said that not having children was a deal breaker for Poppy. But surely he should have given her the chance to at least talk it through. There might not have been any easy solution, but couldn't they have found a way to work things out?

Or did she mean she might have been able to talk him round? Change his mind back? And would that have been fair? Either way it didn't matter, because Garret hadn't given her the chance. Instead he'd found his own simple solution. Trade his wife in for a different model, a better model. Was Karleen better than Poppy? Simply because she was ready and willing to give Garret the thing his heart suddenly desired?

A thought occurred to her then. Was Karleen being so cold and hard throughout their confrontation because she believed she was actually doing the right thing? Rescuing Garret from an oppressive wife who was refusing to bless him with a family. It certainly would have made it easier for Karleen to reconcile her part in all of this if she thought that Poppy had somehow tricked Garret into agreeing to forgo children. Karleen had always been the prissy do-gooder. Never one to break the rules and becoming the "other woman" in her best friend's marriage was one hell of a rule-breaking move. But if she imagined her role as the noble savior of a man trapped in a loveless marriage, then she'd probably decided it was all for the greater good. Bitch.

Poppy tortured herself as she tried to replay any and every interaction she'd witnessed between Garret and Karleen over the past few months and saw the two of them through her new, hyperaware lens. She saw the time Garret picked a leaf out of Karleen's curls when they'd picnicked at the park. She saw the time Karleen had dropped around with tomato soup for Poppy when she was sick with a bad cold. Poppy had been laid out on the couch in her old terry-toweling dressing gown with a tissue stuck in her nose. Karleen had been wearing a short skirt and her favorite silvery top. She'd disappeared into the kitchen with Garret, and Poppy had thought nothing of it at the time. Now she wondered, had he pushed her up against the fridge and kissed her then and there, while Poppy coughed through an episode of *The Blacklist* in the other room?

The image of the two of them kissing made her double over in pain. Who knew heartbreak could hurt so physically?

Four months! How could this have been going on behind Poppy's back for four whole months? How could the two people she loved most in the world have betrayed her in this way?

In one afternoon, she'd lost her husband and her best friend. She pressed her forehead to the steering wheel and let the tears overcome her.

Poppy and Garret's separation was pretty easy. No kids, no pets, no mortgage. Separate bank accounts, one car each. And their rental lease had been due for renewal.

There was a shared savings account they'd each been depositing money into to buy a house one day, and they simply split it down the middle. Admittedly, Poppy earned a little more than Garret, so she'd probably put more money into the account than he had, but she didn't care. She didn't want to have any arguments. She didn't want to delay things any more than she had to. She just wanted to get Garret and Karleen out of her life as quickly as possible.

Garret got the sofa; Poppy never liked that pattern anyway.

Poppy got the coffee table—it was an antique from her grandmother.

Garret got the bed. Poppy got the bedroom furniture.

Garret got the coffee machine and Poppy got the kettle.

Garret got the toaster and Poppy took the blender.

And of course, Garret not only kept his best man from the wedding—his mate from high school—but he also cleaned up with the maid of honor too. How nice for him to collect the set.

It was an amicable divorce settlement with a nauseating rhythm.

And ultimately, it was the catalyst for the group.

PINNED POST

Poppy Weston—Hi all and a big welcome to any new members. A reminder that this group is still in its infancy and we're ironing out the main guidelines and trying to keep it quite small and intimate. If you know of someone who you think might like to join, please make sure they fit the parameters BEFORE you invite them as we want to keep this group a secret from the general public. Thanks!

Chapter 2

If she was asked, Poppy would argue that the news of Karleen's pregnancy and the timing of the group were completely unrelated. But deep down, she knew it was no coincidence. Of course it hurt, hearing within mere months that her ex was expecting with her best friend. It twisted at her heart and squeezed against her sides. Not because she envied them, but maybe because she felt like they'd proved her wrong. Like somehow, Karleen had triumphed in a race, while Poppy never even knew she was meant to be competing. And then there was the realization that Garret really was gone. That he'd chosen someone else over her, that this wasn't a horrible, weird blip in their relationship. He was never going to come crawling back, begging for her forgiveness.

She never would have had the confidence to start up the group had it not been for Annalise.

Poppy had been working at Cormack Millennial Holdings as head of the research department for the past six years, whereas Annalise had joined a year back as their warehouse manager. Their friendship, however, was brand-new—a result of Annalise picking up on Poppy's heartbreak after Garret and Karleen's betrayal and deciding to appoint herself as her "best friend and savior"—whether Poppy wanted it or not.

Poppy had been chatting with their marketing manager, Lawrence, in the break room just a few weeks after the separation, when Annalise walked in and lifted herself up onto the benchtop. She drummed the back of her shoes against the lower cupboard doors as though she was a teenage kid hanging out with her mates. The difference in looks between Lawrence and Annalise was almost comical: he was tall and lanky with dark hair cut neatly into a short back and sides. By comparison, she was a petite elfin creature with shocking cherry-colored locks complemented by sharp blue eyes. Rarest combination, Poppy had once read: red hair and blue eyes, something to do with recessive genes that have to be present in both parents. It was hard to look away once Annalise caught your attention.

"It's still a little while until our season starts," Poppy

had been saying to Lawrence, "but we lost so many players from last year that we need to lock down the team ASAP and start training early."

"What's the sport?" Annalise asked.

"Soccer," said Poppy. "I play on a women's side for Parramatta."

"And you need more players?"

"Absolutely."

"I can play."

Poppy was a little taken aback at her instant enthusiasm. "Oh, that would be great," she said, "but it's an over-thirty-fives team. You're not that old yet, are you?"

Annalise gave Poppy a flirty smile and winked. "I'm thirty-two," she replied, "but I can be whatever age you need me to be."

Poppy couldn't help laughing. "Um, no you can't," she said. "You'll need ID to register."

"Not a problem."

Poppy shrugged.

"Are you any good?" she asked.

"Yes."

"Screw it," she said. "If you really are serious, you're in." She hesitated. The corner of her mouth twitched and she returned a flirtatious smile of her own. "You better be as good as you think you are."

Lawrence had raised his eyebrows over the top of his purple-spotted mug. "Ooh, look at you two, scheming ways to cheat the system."

Just like that, Poppy had a new best friend. And Annalise was sweet. Okay, so Poppy admitted that wouldn't be how most people would describe her. The woman swore like a drunken sailor. She was tough, she was unforgiving, she was crude and brash. But she was also loyal, protective, funny, and within mere days she was pulling Poppy out of a dark, hollow place.

Poppy had quickly learned that her new friend wasn't one to pull any punches. Annalise wasn't interested in small talk. The first time they went out drinking together, two beers was all it took for Poppy to start tearfully spilling the entire messy story of her separation from Garret. Annalise listened. She said the right things—but she didn't comfort. It wasn't about hugs or ice cream or cups of tea. It wasn't about reassuring Poppy that things would get better or easier over time. It was about telling her to move the fuck on and providing solid, practical solutions. For instance, when Poppy whinged that she was going insane having moved back in with her parents while she searched for somewhere to live, Annalise simply said, "Problem solved. The apartment upstairs from me is up for rent. You'll love it."

Annalise's building was in the center of Parramatta

with views over the river. Poppy had grown up in the area, but she'd never lived right in the heart of the city. Now she was surrounded by life. The restaurants and cafés all stayed open late. There was a pub on the corner and a nightclub up the road. You could jog along the river, walk through the park, wander up to the movies. There were people and noise and lights and chaos, and Poppy loved it.

Maybe it wasn't the healthiest way to deal with what had happened. After all, Poppy didn't really get the chance to grieve over Garret and Karleen, Annalise wouldn't let her. She knew if Poppy was wallowing and she wouldn't allow it. She'd hear the depressing ballads wafting from upstairs, and next thing there'd be a *thump, thump, thump* from under Poppy's feet because Annalise was whacking the handle of her broom against the ceiling. A minute later, there'd be a knock at the door and she'd grab Poppy by the hand and drag her out of that place and into the world, without giving her the chance to put up her hair or change her shoes.

Poppy brought up her idea with Annalise as they warmed up at soccer training one night before the start of the season. Poppy lay on her back on the ground and hugged her knees into her chest. The day had been warm but there was a chill in the air. Typical autumn weather—summer hung on during the days, but winter was creeping into the evenings. The last rays of the sun painted stripes across Poppy's face as it disappeared over the horizon while the field lights flickered into life.

Annalise stood above her, finishing up another set of squats.

"Have you heard of the Mums Online in Parramatta and the West Facebook group?" Poppy asked.

"That's a mouthful," said Annalise. "Nope."

"I found out about it last night. Someone was posting on Facebook about a lost dog and there was a comment suggesting they try sharing it in MOP. So I took a look to see what it was, and they have, like, five thousand members."

"Wait—they call it MOP for short?"

"Yeah, short for Mums Online—Parramatta."

"MOP," Annalise repeated. "That's hilarious. Okay, go on," she said as she folded her body in half and wrapped her arms around her legs to stretch out her hamstrings and lower back.

"These five thousand members, they're all local women like us—some went to my high school, some I've worked with, women I know from . . . well, just from around the place. But if you or I wanted to join, we'd be ineligible—because we're not mums."

"So?"

"So! Doesn't that piss you off? They have events!

They have spin-off groups, like the MOP netballers or the MOP wine tasters. They share important community information about stuff we have every right to know about."

"Yeah, but I assume it's mostly parenting-related, isn't it? We wouldn't want to be a part of that. In fact, I'm not sure anyone would want to be part of something called the MOP wine tasters."

"Okay, that's true. But it still annoys me that we couldn't join even if we wanted to."

Annalise stared at her. "What you actually mean is, it annoys you that Karleen's about to be eligible to join now that your dickhead ex knocked her up."

Sometimes Annalise's ability to zero right in on the heart of the matter completely blindsided Poppy. At the same time, hearing Garret described as a dickhead by someone who'd never even met him shot Poppy through with the automatic desire to defend him. She had to remind herself that it was warranted—all Annalise knew of the guy was that he'd cheated on her and left her. Of course she should call him any and every name under the sun.

"No. It has nothing to do with that."

"Bullshit. Last week I had to pry you out of the fetal position because some idiot friend of Karleen's thought you had the 'right to know the truth' about their happy news. Now all of a sudden you're noticing mother's groups."

Poppy sat up and picked at the grass by her feet as she tried to decide if Annalise was right. Would she have paid any attention at all to MOP had she not just heard about Karleen's pregnancy? The old school friend who'd felt the need to message Poppy and warn her claimed she wanted to make sure Poppy didn't get a shock if she heard it elsewhere. But they weren't close and Poppy was pretty sure she was just excited to be the one to spread the juicy news.

"It's not the point," Poppy said eventually. "The point is, you and I are a part of this community too and we're being excluded." She hesitated before adding, "You want kids one day?" She tried her best to look like she didn't care either way as she waited for an answer.

"Nope."

"Really? How do you know? Because for me—I've always been certain."

Annalise shrugged, "What do you mean 'how do I know?' Why does there have to be a reason?"

"It's just that most women who say they don't want kids actually mean they might not want them *now,* but they do still plan to have them someday. I don't meet many who've decided for good."

"Poppy," Annalise said, "you're not something special. I'm sure there are plenty of people who feel the same way. Trust me."

"How come?" she pressed.

"Well, why don't you want them?" Annalise countered.

"Lots of reasons. The lifestyle for one thing. My career as well. But mainly because there's never been any burning desire in my ovaries for them. When I see my future, I just don't see a place for kids in it. I see myself working. I see myself traveling. I mean, I used to see this life with Garret by my side, but whatever." Poppy hoped Annalise wouldn't pick up on the touch of vulnerability that had crept into her voice when she mentioned his name. Annalise is right, she reminded herself, he really is a dickhead. He doesn't deserve your sorrow.

"So, what's your reason?"

"I'm just not a kid person, simple as that."

Poppy suspected there might be more to it than that, but she was too excited about the idea she was about to put forward, so she let it go.

"Right. In that case, I was thinking, why don't we start our own local community group? But ours could be restricted to the child-free."

"But what would be the point of it?"

"I don't know. It would be a place to connect with

other people, make new friends, I guess. Have our own wine tastings or book clubs or whatever. A group only for women who don't have kids, but not just that, they have to be the same as us—they never want to have kids. Not, 'someday maybe,' but never. Never ever." She paused. "So, would you be in?"

Truthfully, Poppy hadn't really expected it to take off the way it did. She assumed they'd get a few members— some like-minded women who wanted to chat about local area news without the baby talk. What she hadn't expected was for it to blow up so big, so fast. She was onto something. She'd hit a niche demographic.

There were plenty of women out there who felt the exact same way as Poppy about the countless parenting groups, both online and out in the real world. Women who felt left out—silenced. Their rival group gave them a place to share ideas for quiet, child-free cafés and restaurants where they could enjoy a peaceful coffee or get some work done over breakfast without any ear-piercing squeals. There were suggestions for the best time to catch a flight to decrease the likelihood of a lot of kids being on board, parks where they could walk a timid dog without worrying that a whole heap of children might come barreling up to it wanting to give it a pat.

Poppy loved the group. It was her baby and she was protective of it. They called it Non-Mums Online in Parramatta, and NOP for short as a bit of a mischievous nod to the MOP ladies. Maybe that had been their first mistake.

Now, on an unseasonably warm Saturday in April as Poppy strode through the pub and made her way out to the beer garden, she couldn't help marveling at the fact that she was about to catch up with a group of women who had all been complete strangers just a couple of months back. When Karleen had been her best friend, she'd never really considered the idea that she needed more mates. Weekends consisted of brunch with Garret, movies with Karleen, dinner with both of them—or some variation of the three depending on who was or wasn't interested in the latest rom-com someone suggested they see. Poppy hadn't realized how different her social life could be. Today she was meeting Annalise plus a few other members of their group. NOP was only meant to be an online thing, but as they became friendlier and friendlier, the logical progression was an occasional face-to-face catch-up.

The place was packed with families, couples, and groups of friends making the most of the afternoon autumn sunshine. She'd wanted to get here early and grab a good table—somewhere in the sun, the right distance from the stage so they could enjoy the live jazz band but still hear one another, but she'd run late. So she was relieved when she spotted Kellie—one of their first members—sitting at a high table in the corner of the garden. There were two other women seated opposite her—one was tall with light brown skin, huge, dangly earrings, and a stunning, colorful dress; the other sported a purple shaved undercut and a leather jacket. They looked like movie stars next to Kellie, who was in blue jeans and a plain white T-shirt. The three of them were guarding a few extra barstools as they waited.

"Nice," Poppy said as she approached the table.

"Perfect spot," Kellie replied, moving her handbag so Poppy could sit down. "Nowhere near the playground. Not making that mistake again."

The last time they'd come here, Kellie had been roped into playing the role of gate opener for all the tiny children who kept running up to the playground and realizing they couldn't reach the lock to let themselves in.

"Don't know why you kept giving in to them," said Poppy.

"It was just easier. I couldn't handle the desperation on their little faces."

"You're too much of a softy," suggested the woman

with the dangly earrings. She reached out a hand to Poppy. "I'm Carla," she said, "and this is Sophie."

Poppy introduced herself as she shook their hands.

"Oh, you're her!" said Carla.

"I'm her."

"Poppy's the one who started all of this," Carla said to Sophie.

Annalise appeared next to Poppy. "With my help," she said, elbowing Poppy. "You didn't wait for me."

"Of course I didn't," she replied. "I knocked on your door three times and I called out that I was leaving."

"Yeah, I still thought you'd wait."

"I have to ask, considering the nature of our group, why are we meeting at a pub with a playground any-way?" asked Carla. "Surely we could avoid the gate issue by going somewhere else altogether."

"It's Kellie's fault, she's mad for the jazz band that plays here on weekends," said Annalise as she took the seat opposite Poppy. "So is this all of us?"

"Yeah, I think so," said Kellie, pulling the elastic out of her ponytail and fluffing out her brown hair. "I know Viv pulled out last minute and Jess couldn't make it 'cause she and her husband are having a dirty weekend away in the Blue Mountains."

"Viv always cancels," said Annalise.

"How do you know it's a dirty weekend?" Carla said. "Could be perfectly tame, all antiquing and candlelit dinners."

"Because she put a post up on Facebook asking if anyone knew where she could buy a cheap set of handcuffs."

"Fair enough."

"So you two haven't made it to one of our catch-ups before, have you?" Annalise said, addressing Carla and Sophie.

"First timers," Carla confirmed.

"Excellent," said Annalise. "First timers have to buy the first round of drinks."

"Is that a thing? I don't think that's a thing," Poppy said.

Carla pulled her purse out of her bag obediently. "All good, I'll go. What's everyone having?"

Poppy couldn't help but be transfixed by the way the honey highlights in Carla's long dark hair caught the sunlight as she stood up. Good grief, the woman could be in a shampoo commercial.

They all placed their orders with Carla, and Sophie accompanied her to the bar to help carry the drinks back.

"What do we think of the newbies?" Annalise asked

the moment they'd left the table. "The purple-haired chick has crazy eyes."

"Annalise!" Poppy whacked her arm. "No, she doesn't."

Kellie narrowed her eyes at Annalise. "I think you're just jealous because she looks more alternative than you. You're wishing you had a purple undercut right now, aren't you?"

"Bullshit. I've already done the half-shaved look. Took me two years to completely grow it out again." Annalise cocked her head to the side thoughtfully. "I just think she has a very intense look about her."

"How about Carla?" Poppy asked. "Is it only me or does that women look like she belongs on a catwalk in Paris?"

Kellie laughed. "You sound like you're crushing on her, Poppy."

"Stop it! It's not like that. I mean, come on, she's stunning."

"It's okay, I know what you mean. I think she might be a full two feet taller than me. People like that shouldn't be allowed to wear high heels. It's not fair. Oh! I love this song, someone dance with me!" Kellie jumped up from her stool and held her hand out, waiting for one of them to take it.

"How can you love *this* song in particular?" Annalise scoffed. "It's jazz, it all sounds the same."

Kellie feigned a knife to the heart. "Sacrilege. How could you say such a thing?"

Knowing there was no way Annalise was going to oblige Kellie's request, Poppy reluctantly got up to join her. "Um, how exactly does one dance to jazz music?"

Kellie grabbed Poppy's hands and started swinging her around, wriggling her hips as she went. "One dances however one wants to," she replied. "One simply feels the music."

"One really needs a drink first," said Poppy as she tried to keep up.

Thankfully Sophie returned a moment later, precariously balancing three glasses. "Carla's coming with the rest in a sec."

Poppy relieved Sophie of one of the drinks and backed away from Kellie. "Sorry, you're on your own."

Kellie huffed as they all sat down again. "You guys are no fun."

Annalise raised her eyebrows. "My idea of fun is very different to yours, honey."

Sophie leaned right across the table then and beckoned for everyone else to lean in too. The three women obliged and Poppy noticed a bemused look on Annalise's face. Sophie's eyes darted around as though she was making sure no one else could hear them. Up close Poppy could see darker roots starting to peep through from under the purple color in her hair. She could also tell that someone must have eaten a whole lot of garlic earlier and she wondered if she ought to offer around some chewing gum.

"So," Sophie hissed, "are there any rules I need to know?"

"What do you mean?" Poppy whispered back. "What sort of rules?"

"You know, like the first rule of fight club is you don't talk about fight club, that sort of thing." Sophie was still speaking quietly, but now they all leaned back and laughed.

"We're not an underground boxing club!" Kellie was almost choking on her rum and Coke. "It's a Facebook group."

"Yeah, but there was all this secrecy and exclusivity around joining."

"Okay, yeah, it's a secret group, but it's not the Illuminati."

Sophie looked disappointed. "So there's no secret handshake? No signal I give another woman if I pass her in the shops and I want to check if she's NOP?"

"Nope, nothing like that," said Poppy. "I guess if you want rules, though, the main thing is that we don't share stories from inside the group with people outside of the group. Don't take screenshots of posts, don't re-tell stories elsewhere. But that's only because it's likely that if other people found out about NOP, they'd probably take it the wrong way."

Carla returned with the last two drinks and took her seat next to Sophie again.

"There's no handshake," Sophie said to Carla in an accusing tone. "You said we'd learn the secret hand-shake today."

"Good God, Soph, I was being facetious! I thought you knew."

"Ah." Sophie looked forlorn for a moment but quickly recovered. "Oh, before I forget, I brought busi-ness cards for you all." She reached into her handbag for a stack of cards and started handing them around.

Kellie read out the company name. "Coco's Cuts, Curls and Colours. Cute name."

"Soph, I told you this isn't the same as that business networking group," Carla scolded.

"No, it's okay. I need a new hairdresser," said Kel-lie. "Do you do balayage? I tried to get my last hair-dresser to do it for me and it looked like I'd just dipped the lower half of my hair in a bucket of bleach. It was awful. I had to chop it all off."

"Balayage is my specialty. Book in with me and I'll have your hair looking glam like that." She snapped her fingers.

Annalise took a long sip of her double bourbon on the rocks and eyeballed Carla. "How about you? What's your deal?"

"God, you're blunt," said Kellie.

"Dum da dum," sang Sophie in a menacing tone. "This is Carla's most hated question."

"It's not!" Carla said. "It's fine."

"Oh really?" exclaimed Kellie. "How come? What do you do—work in a slaughterhouse or something?"

"No, nothing like that. It's just that I don't work."

"So you study?" Kellie asked.

"Nope. No study."

"She's a lady of leisure," Sophie said, putting on a posh accent.

"Rich husband?" Poppy asked.

"Nope. I'm single."

"She's a trust fund baby," Sophie explained.

"Seriously?" said Annalise. "You're so rich that you don't have to work?"

"Yep." Carla picked up her wine and gulped it in a way that had Poppy guessing she might be a match for seasoned drinker Annalise. Poppy suspected that despite her assurances, Carla actually was feeling uncomfortable and she smoothly switched the topic of conversation to the previous night's episode of *The Bachelor*. From there, the five of them chatted about everything from Kellie's new colleague who was possibly making a move on her—and whether she ought to tell her husband about it—to Sophie's new jeans that apparently made her feel like a model, and Carla's upcoming holiday to Thailand. They kept up a steady flow of drinks, and as it grew darker, the families started to clear out and the jazz band packed up. The temperature dropped as the stars began to pop into view in the night sky above them and they all pulled on jackets and scarves.

"So am I allowed to ask 'the question'?" Carla said when there was a lull in conversation.

"What question?" Kellie asked, shivering and wrapping her thin cardigan tighter around her body. Poppy smiled as Annalise feigned irritation before wordlessly unwinding the scarf from around her neck and handing it over to Kellie, who accepted it gratefully.

"The 'why doesn't everyone here want kids' question. Or is that taboo?"

"Why would it be taboo?" Kellie shot back.

"You know, 'cause it's too personal or whatever."

Annalise groaned. "Or maybe because it's the kind

of question we all face constantly and we don't want to continually answer?"

"Yeah, or that," Carla admitted.

"Well, I don't mind talking about it," said Kellie. "I don't want kids because I have never ever been the type of person to take on responsibility for anything beyond myself. I can't imagine having the weight of someone else's life on my shoulders."

"What about pets?" Sophie asked. "Could you handle keeping a cat alive?"

"Nope. I can barely keep a potted plant alive."

"Seriously? I'd go insane without my two dogs. My fur babies more than satisfy any need I have to nurture."

"For fuck's sake," said Annalise, "why does there have to be 'a reason'? Do people ask mothers what their reason is for choosing to *have* children?"

"I guess not." Carla looked guilty. "Sorry, I didn't really think of it that way."

"Well, for me it's totally political and environmental," said Sophie. "Once upon a time procreation might have been a necessity to keep the human race alive, but now the world is far too overpopulated. Having children is a selfish act, as far as I'm concerned."

Poppy felt an unexpected surge of protectiveness toward her brother, who had three boys—twins in kindergarten and a two-year-old. While she might not want kids herself, she loved her nephews. "I don't know if that's really fair," she said. "I don't think my brother and his wife were being at all selfish when they decided to have a family." She thought about the way Nolan doted on his kids. He was an absolute natural as a father—she couldn't imagine him without them. The twins had inherited Nolan's infectious laugh and their younger brother was adorably shy.

"I'm not saying they're being intentionally selfish," said Sophie. "I just mean it in a more general way, you know, across the board. The wider population doesn't really think about the effect of a human life on the world. The easiest and by far one of the most effective ways you can reduce your carbon footprint is by cutting down on the number of children you have."

"So you want us to adopt a single-child policy like China?" Kellie asked.

"Look, I don't know what the solution is. I'm just saying that's how I made the decision to stay kid-free. More people ought to consider adopting rescue dogs like me when they get the urge to mother."

Two kids ran past them then playing a game of tag, knocking Poppy's bag off the empty seat at the end of the table.

"I thought all the families were out of here by now,"

said Annalise, hopping off her chair to grab Poppy's bag for her.

A woman appeared next to them. "Sorry about that," she said, indicating Poppy's bag. "Trying to round them up."

"All good," said Poppy with a friendly smile.

"How relaxed is this?" the woman added, seeming to suddenly take in the fact that five women were sitting around a table full of drinks and not one had a child hanging off her. "Jealous! I'm so overdue for a girls' night out without the kids."

Kellie grinned back at her. "Every night for us is a night out without the kids."

The woman looked perplexed for a moment, as though she couldn't figure out how they could possibly achieve this. Then the other shoe dropped and her face switched to embarrassment.

"You guys aren't mums? Sorry!" she exclaimed. "I just assumed because you all look around my age that you—" Her face reddened and she stopped short before rushing to clarify. "Not that it means anything, of course. Like, just because you're old it doesn't mean you should . . . oh shit, not old, I mean *older.* You're not old at all. You still have heaps of time to have kids if you want to. Not that it has anything to do with me. I'm going to shut up now. Sorry!"

"Don't be," said Annalise. "We're about to order another round and tomorrow we'll be sleeping off our hangovers with zero interruptions. We're all good."

The woman nodded fervently. "Yes, of course, of course," she said. "You're so lucky. I am super envious right now." She backed away from the table as though they had morphed into an unknown species.

"Wow!" said Carla as they all started laughing. "That was mortifying. Did you see how embarrassed she was when she realized her faux pas?"

"Why do mothers always feel the need to reassure us that we're so lucky in case they offend us?" said Kellie, shaking her head. "Thanks, love. We're good."

Poppy grinned. That mum had just proved exactly why they'd needed this group in the first place.

Bette—Recommendations, please? I'm after a public pool in the area that doesn't do pre-school swimming lessons in the mornings. The little tykes are very cute and all, but I'm always getting splashed when I'm trying to do my sidestroke, not to mention I'm sure they're all peeing in the water. I love having my morning swim as part of my exercise routine. TIA.

Dianna—Hi Bette, I can highly recommend the gym where I do yoga. It's called Mind 2 Body and it's on George Street. They have a small pool that you can use as part of your membership.

Yasmine—@Dianna, Ooh, I need a place to do yoga, I might check it out too.

Jess—Ladies, there's no better exercise than a good sex life!

Annalise—@Jess, PMSL!

Chapter 3

Mondays at Cormack always started with the weekly "managers' strategy chat." Poppy and Annalise were the first ones in Meeting Room Two— the other managers were usually slow to arrive.

Cormack Millennial Holdings was a company with a name that no one had ever heard of, because they were hidden behind a brand-new trading name almost every week. Poppy knew it was a strange business model for a company, but she loved it. Each week, her research team would scour the latest news sites and all the different social media platforms to see what new trends were taking off. It might have been Polaroid cameras or old-fashioned bicycles that had trended up because of hipsters, or a certain superfood because of the latest fad diet, or a particular toy—practically anything.

Then the procurement team would start sourcing the popular items, the marketing department would come up with a new temporary trading name, buy a domain name, and set up a quickie website, and wham bam, thank you ma'am, suddenly they were the suppliers of the one thing everyone wanted. They'd flood the market until the trend burned out and then move on to the next thing.

Last year, Poppy had realized people were suddenly going mad for this "ship your enemies glitter" start-up. So, Cormack Millennial registered the trading name "Glitter Bomb," ordered in pallets of glitter, and now, twelve months later, the warehouse staff was still finding glitter in their clothes.

Their slogan may as well be "Cormack Millennial— We jump on everyone else's bandwagon." Their CEO, Paul, came up with the concept. It was like he thought to himself, *Hmm, I really like that company and that company, why can't I do what they're doing? You know what? I think I will.*

Sometimes they had multiple trading names running at once, sometimes they would zero in on one big idea. They'd drill down. They'd lean in. Over the years Cormack had often been accused of being the leeches of the entrepreneurial world, of attaching themselves to other people's great ideas and sucking the life force out of them before dropping off and moving on. But Poppy thought Paul's business model was actually a stroke of brilliance. The job was hard work and fast-paced but it was always interesting. These days Paul sat back and let his staff come up with all the good ideas. He'd always come across as just slightly on the wrong side of arrogant to Poppy, but lately he was tipping more toward laziness in her opinion.

Annalise leaned forward in her seat, resting her elbows on the table between the two of them. "So," she said, "how many of 'em are going to ask for time off today?"

"They better not."

"They will."

Poppy knew she was right. Weekly meetings were supposed to be all about planning their next big project. But lately they seemed to be monopolized by other managers wanting to discuss their schedules, ask for time off due to family commitments. It was like there had been something in the watercooler at Cormack over the past few years. Women kept falling pregnant, one after another, and heading off on maternity leave. Then each one would return to their roles only to demand more flexible hours in order to fit around their kids. Poppy knew it was great that Cormack was a family-friendly workplace. She knew it would be hard to juggle a job and children—but she also knew there were certain mothers at Cormack who took advantage of this.

The worst culprit, though, would have to be Frankie—Paul's assistant. This was because, on top of being able to use her kids as an excuse to come and go as she pleased, she was having an affair with Paul. And that meant she could get away with murder. So to speak. Poppy didn't know Frankie's husband and she'd only met Paul's wife, Linda, briefly on the odd occasion that she dropped by the office, but her heart broke for the two clueless partners. She'd been where they were so recently.

Poppy usually liked to think she was observant, but it was Annalise who had drawn it to her attention first.

"Do you think there's something going on between Paul and Frankie?"

It was funny how as soon as something was pointed out to you, you started noticing the little details. The closed office door and the blinds shut tight. The eye contact between the two of them, those little knowing glances. When two people had a secret, they couldn't seem to help exchanging that knowledge between them with a simple look. Adding adulterer to Paul's list of faults had recently cemented Poppy's dislike of the man.

And as for Frankie, Poppy already found her irritating enough as it was. She was always guarding the door to Paul's office like he was a celebrity, and she would only grant you access if she deemed you worthy.

To top it all off, Frankie was so damn smug about her position. Just the other week, Poppy and Annalise were at the coffee shop next door to the office, about to order their morning caffeine hit. In a time when most cafés had gone full hipster—everything organic, staff with beanies and thick glasses, and seats made out of tree stumps or milk crates—the café next to Cormack was unapologetically . . . *plain*. Everything on the menu had gluten in it, there was no fancy coffee art on top of the cappuccinos, and no quirky 1950s-style names for the meals. No beards, no fedoras, no kale. Poppy and Annalise loved it.

On this particular morning as they were about to step forward and place their orders, Frankie walked in, stepped straight in front of them, and said, "Sorry, girls, I'm ordering for the boss and I don't have time to wait. You don't mind, do you?"

Before they had the chance to say a word, she started ordering. And, Poppy noted, it was two coffees she asked for, one for herself as well.

Now, as they continued to wait for the rest of the managers, Poppy opened up Facebook on her phone and started looking through the latest posts on NOP. "Hey, what did you think of Carla and Sophie the other night?" she asked as she continued to scroll mindlessly.

Annalise tipped her hand side to side to indicate she'd found them a bit iffy.

"I know what you mean," Poppy agreed, putting her phone back down. "They were okay, but they kind of stirred the pot a bit, didn't they? Like wanting to quiz everyone about why we don't want kids and bringing politics or whatever into it."

"Yeah, and what's with Carla's whole 'trust fund baby' thing? I mean, I'd love to not have to work but what do you think she *does* all day?"

"I know, right?"

Poppy's phone lit up with a notification and she picked it up again to take a look. "Speak of the devil," she said. "Post on NOP from Carla."

"What's it say?"

"She wants to know when people want to get together for drinks again."

"Is it a public post?" Annalise asked.

"Yep," said Poppy.

"Shit," said Annalise. "Doesn't she realize we have over one hundred members? You can't put it out there for everyone."

"Nah, I wouldn't worry too much. She hasn't mentioned a date or venue. I'll PM her and let her know if she wants to invite people out, she needs to make a private event and just put it out to a few people."

Lawrence came in and Poppy quickly put her phone facedown on the table. He eyeballed her as he pulled out a chair and sat down by Annalise.

"One of these days I'm going to set up a secret camera and find out what it is you two are always talking about," said Lawrence.

"What do you mean?" Annalise asked, leaning back in her seat and smiling innocently at him. "We were just chatting, nothing important."

"Don't give me that look," said Lawrence. "You have something going on. Lately every time I walk in on the two of you talking you both stop midsentence." He shifted his gaze back and forth between Poppy and Annalise. Annalise was completely capable of just staring back at him, but Poppy had trouble meeting his eyes.

"Maybe we were talking about your skills in the bedroom," said Annalise with a sly smile.

Poppy was bemused she could be so brash about it. She knew the two of them had slept together a few times and that it was all completely casual between them, but there was no way she could have pulled off that level of sass with a guy she'd slept with, let alone one she saw at work every day.

If Annalise was expecting Lawrence to be rattled by her comment, though, it didn't happen. Instead his face brightened.

"That right?" he said.

"No," she replied, "of course not. We were talking about soccer, it's out first game next Monday night."

"Oh yeah?" Lawrence looked back at Poppy. "So how's the newbie been fitting into the team at your training sessions?"

"She's bloody brilliant."

Several more managers finally started filtering into the room, cutting their conversation short.

Paul and Frankie were the last ones to take their seats. Poppy wasn't even sure why they bothered waiting for Paul to get the meeting started. These days he pretty much sat back and let everyone else keep things ticking along. Once in a while he'd throw an idea out and all the managers knew to humor him, nodding and smiling and pretending to consider it carefully before gently steering the conversation around to someone else's suggestion.

"Oranges," said Paul, who had apparently decided to kick things off with a completely random comment.

They all stared back at him, waiting for him to elaborate. He tapped the tips of his fingers together, pausing long enough to make them all feel uncomfortable. Eventually, he spoke again. "I'm thinking . . . see, now last month it was frozen berries. So this month, why not oranges? Or . . . actually, now that I think about it—orange juice, right? Frozen orange juice. Next big thing, yeah?"

The other managers all stayed quiet, exchanging awkward glances. Poppy knew she was going to have to be the one to say something.

"Could be something in that, Paul," Poppy said, choosing her words carefully. "Although, don't forget, the reason we jumped on the frozen berry bandwagon was because of the hepatitis C scare with the imported supermarket-brand berries, right? So we were filling a hole in the market, giving the consumers that peace of mind they were craving with the bright new packaging—safe, fresh Australian-grown berries! But oranges . . . um, I'm not sure if there's been anything in the news about those, has there?" She glanced around at the others.

"I mean, unless I'm wrong, of course," she added quickly. "Unless I missed something. Lawrence, you heard anything in the news about oranges?"

He gave Poppy a look, then said, "I'm not too sure, Poppy, but I'll have my team check it out."

Throughout the whole exchange, Paul stayed quiet. In fact, it didn't really look like he was actually listening, his gaze seemed to be fixed on a corner of the ceiling. His slightly silvering hair glinted under the fluorescent lights. He was right on the verge of shifting from good-looking, middle-aged CEO to past his use-by date has-been.

Frankie jumped in. "Okay, great, so Lawrence will check up on that for us, thanks, Lawrence. Now, if I could just steer us back to the agenda."

Paul seemed to snap out of it and gave Frankie one of his telling smiles. "Yes, that's right. The agenda! Jumped the gun with that one, didn't I? What would we do without Frankie here to keep us on track?"

Poppy caught Annalise's eye and gave her a subtle eyebrow raise. *Oh yes, of course,* she thought, *wonderful Frankie, running the whole damn place at ninety words per minute.*

The meeting continued on with no further mention of oranges. There were a few solid ideas that warranted further investigation. Poppy put forward the suggestion that they start looking into organic, biodegradable picnic plates and cups made from plant matter.

"People still want the convenience of disposable options, but they don't want the guilt of leaving behind a massive carbon footprint," she explained, silently thanking Sophie for sparking the thought in her mind the other night, even if Poppy had found her somewhat offensive. "There's a manufacturer in Brazil doing leaf-based plates and their promo video is about to go viral."

Most of the managers agreed she was onto something and they spent the last half of the meeting throwing around potential trading names and ideas for suppliers.

They were winding up when the inevitable happened. Jody from accounts cleared her throat and said brightly, "Oh, before we head out, I just wanted to let the team know I'll be in late the next two days. I've got a specialist appointment for Eleanora tomorrow morning and Christine is getting an award at assembly the day after."

Poppy looked across the table at Annalise. She was resolutely avoiding looking back at her, but Poppy saw her place one finger surreptitiously on the table in front of her and she bit the inside of her cheek to stop herself from laughing. *One down, who was going to be next?*

"Actually," said Anne, who was sitting to Jody's left, "Jody's just reminded me, I'm leaving early this afternoon. The mum who normally picks my kids up for me is sick, so it's on me for today."

A second finger appeared on the table next to the first. Annalise was pretending to nod along sympathetically with the others. *Two.*

The room fell quiet and everyone began gathering up notebooks and pens or pushing back their chairs when Frankie spoke up. "Oh well, not that it really affects anyone, but if we're all updating our schedules, I'm not here Friday morning." She looked around at everyone and Poppy saw her jaw clench. She probably thought it was no one's business what she was doing, but thanks to Jody and Anne's explanations, she likely felt railroaded into following suit.

Poppy was right.

"I have to take my kids to the dentist," Frankie continued. "And Paul has a very busy morning, so if you could save any issues you need to take to him until after I get in, that would be appreciated."

Annalise lifted a third finger onto the table, looked right at Poppy and waggled the three fingers. Poppy barely stopped herself from letting out a snort of laughter.

After the room had cleared, Lawrence, Annalise, and Poppy lagged behind. "All right," said Lawrence, "what was happening at the end of the meeting there? You guys realize you're not as subtle as you think you are, right?"

"Nothing," said Annalise. "Secret women's business."

"You were pissed off with the girls discussing their time off, weren't you?"

"Maybe," Poppy admitted.

"More like definitely," Lawrence said.

"Come for a chat with us down in the warehouse," Poppy replied, "you can bitch with us some more."

"You know you're both obsessed, right?"

"Can you blame us?" Annalise retorted.

Chapter 4

Once a month Poppy had a standing dinner date with her parents and brother. Annalise teased her about it, said they sounded like the perfect nuclear family. That was probably Poppy's opportunity to ask her about her own family—but to be honest, their friendship was decidedly one-sided right from the start and Poppy simply hadn't ever thought to switch the focus away from her own dramas.

Poppy was the first one to arrive. The city was the logical place for them to meet. After living on the outskirts of Parramatta their entire lives, Poppy's parents had sold up and moved over to the Northern Beaches a couple of years ago, claiming the need for a sea change. It was obvious to both Poppy and Nolan that they'd moved there to be closer to their grandkids—Nolan and Megan had bought a place in Curl Curl when they'd married.

Poppy was waiting for the day when Nolan suggested they move the monthly dinner to somewhere more kid-friendly and include the littlest family members. So far it hadn't happened. And while she knew it was selfish, Poppy couldn't help but feel a little relieved. Growing up, she'd been quite close to her brother, so she enjoyed having the chance to have Nolan and her parents all to herself during these regular catch-ups.

Plus, as much as Poppy thought Nolan's boys were pretty cute, she was still looking forward to the day when they were old enough to hold a grown-up con-versation. That's when she knew she would shine as an aunt. But for now—as babies or as little kids—she never quite knew the right way to interact.

She suspected Nolan was keeping them away for her benefit, though. Poppy's parents and Nolan couldn't seem to accept the fact that she had zero interest in ever having kids of her own. They thought it was a defense mechanism. That of course she'd want to have her own children one day and either her biological clock would suddenly kick into gear, or else it already had but she'd draped a sheet over it and silenced the chimes.

It didn't matter how many times Poppy assured them it was a personal choice. They were angry with Garret, but for all the wrong reasons. They thought he should have been patient, that he should have waited for her to be ready. Poppy knew their hearts were in the right place, but she was frustrated that they couldn't seem to trust her own desires.

At dinner they had a window table overlooking the harbor. Poppy ordered a bottle of red—the rule was whoever arrived first got to choose the wine—and started examining the menu, listening to the ambient sounds of low chatter and cutlery scraping against plates around her. It was a popular restaurant, and despite it being midweek, pretty much every table was taken. Nolan was next to turn up. He sat opposite Poppy and poured himself a glass, much to the displeasure of the nearby waiter who'd been about to pounce, especially when the wine dripped onto the white tablecloth.

In looks, Nolan was pretty much a male version of Poppy. The same blond hair with no body to it. The same pale blue eyes. They were even the same height, give or take a centimeter or two. But in personality, he was much more outgoing and chatty.

"What's new?" Nolan asked as they both perused their menus.

"What's new," Poppy muttered to herself. "What's new . . . not much," she said eventually. "Leaning toward the duck, I think."

"Exciting," he responded sarcastically. "Aren't you going to ask me?" he added.

"Huh? Oh, what are you going to have?"

"No, not my dinner choice. Aren't you going to ask me what's new?"

"I think you just did it for me. Go on. Tell me what's new?"

"Megs is pregnant!"

"Again?" Poppy realized as soon as she said it that it wasn't the right response. Nolan's face fell and she knew he'd expected her to respond with more excitement. But then his expression changed.

"Oh shit. I'm sorry, Poppy," he said. "I should have waited to say anything. It's too soon, isn't it?"

Poppy closed her menu. "Too soon? What do you mean?"

"Too soon after, you know . . . everything with Garrett . . ."

Gah, Poppy thought, *there he goes again.*

"Oh, God no," she replied. "I'm sorry, I was just surprised. I shouldn't have said that. It was only 'cause I assumed you guys were done with three. Sorry. It's great news. Congratulations. Hey, shouldn't you have waited until Mum and Dad got here? Mum won't like me having heard the news first."

"Oh"—Nolan looked uncomfortable again—"they

already know. I figured I should tell them together with Megs, so we announced it a few days ago when they came round for lunch. Sorry, I didn't think you'd mind."

Poppy waved it off. "Of course I don't mind. Congrats," she said again, and this time she held up her wineglass and clinked it against his. "Very exciting. Hoping for a girl this time?"

Nolan shook his head. "I don't really mind either way, I'm used to boys now—but I get the feeling that's what Megs is after. I don't think she'd admit to it, though. Doesn't want people to think she'd be disappointed if it comes out with a rod and tackle."

"Lovely," Poppy replied. "You won't find out beforehand?"

"Nah, we'll wait and see. Doesn't change the outcome, does it?"

"Guess not." They both turned to watch a large boat as it pulled away from the wharf out on the harbor.

A waiter materialized beside the table and reached for Nolan's napkin but Nolan beat him to it and placed it on his own lap. The waiter looked lost for a second and then he reached for the wine instead and topped up Poppy's glass. "Still waiting for two more?"

"Yes, they shouldn't be too much longer, sorry," said Poppy.

He continued to hover and Nolan cocked his head to the side to look up at him. "Ah, we're all good for the minute, thanks, mate."

He nodded curtly and swept away.

"Oh my God," said Poppy, a thought suddenly occurring to her, "have you two considered that it could be twins again?"

"We have and it's not. First question I asked at the ultrasound." He paused before adding, "Sure you're okay?"

Poppy rolled her eyes. "Okay, I get why I can't convince Mum. She's old-fashioned. 'Woman no want baby' doesn't compute for her. But why are you being dense about it? I *don't want kids*. So yes, I'm fine with hearing your happy news. I'm really glad for you."

"Oh," said Nolan. "No, I'm not dense. It's not that I don't believe you about kids, it's more that you've been through . . . well, I don't need to tell you, you know what you've been through. I just don't want you to feel like you need to put on a brave face around me."

Poppy was touched. "Thanks, Nolesy. Means a lot. Look out, here come the parents."

They watched as Therese and Chris weaved their way between the tables to join them. Therese had her blond hair blow-dried into the shape of a large space helmet, and Poppy's dad followed behind her, looking like he was having trouble seeing around it. Chris had recently decided to grow a wiry, salt-and-pepper beard and Poppy was still getting used to it.

When they reached the table, Therese took a seat next to Poppy and Chris sat next to Nolan. Therese immediately reached for Poppy's hand and held it on the table between both of her own.

"Okay, Nolan," she said, "we're ready."

Poppy was perplexed for just a second and then she caught on and pulled her hand out of her mother's grip. "Jesus, Mum, he's already told me."

"You were supposed to wait," Therese said accusingly, then she wrapped an arm around Poppy's shoulders. "Are you okay?"

I should have started with a vodka, Poppy thought. *Where's that waiter who didn't want to leave us alone before?*

On cue, she looked up to see the waiter making a beeline for their table. When he reached them, Therese allowed him to place her napkin on her lap, which he did with a considerable amount of flourish. No wonder he'd been so disappointed when Nolan had done his own. But when he tried to do Poppy's father's napkin, Chris simply batted his hands away. "I'm right, mate."

Like father, like son.

The waiter topped up Poppy's glass yet again, which

was now almost full to the brim, and then filled both Therese and Chris's glasses. He pulled out a notepad when he was done. "Are we ready to order?"

"Oh, love, give us a minute to check the menu, would you?" Therese asked.

The waiter openly sighed and glided away from the table yet again.

"What's with Mr. Impatience?" Chris asked.

"Ants in his pants," Therese suggested.

"You better open up your menu, Mum," said Poppy. "Look, he's over there watching us."

The dinner plates had been cleared after the fastest service the four of them had ever experienced. Poppy was feeling pleasantly buzzed due to her constantly refilled wineglass. Their speedy waiter was becoming a family joke and they'd had to rescue Therese's unfinished barramundi halfway through the meal when "Speedy" attempted to snatch it away while she was in the bathroom. Earlier, Nolan had lingered for so long over the last two potatoes on his plate that the waiter was—in Therese's words—almost having kittens as he waited to clear it.

Therese now steered the conversation toward one of Poppy's least favorite subjects: her disapproval of Poppy's new apartment. She didn't like that Poppy was "wasting so much money" on a place that was smaller than the town house she'd shared with Garret. Poppy wasn't entirely sure why she needed any more space, considering she was just one person. Therese also wasn't sure about Annalise's "influence," which had led her to move in there. Poppy thought this was hilarious—she was a woman in her thirties, not a schoolgirl being peer-pressured into smoking behind the school sheds.

"Remind me again, how long is the lease you've signed, darling?"

"Twelve months."

"Mmm," she said. "And you won't renew it after that?"

The question mark at the end of her sentence barely managed an appearance.

"Not sure yet, Mum. But at this stage, I'm leaning toward staying there. I love it. Love being in the middle of everything."

"Ye-e-e-s," Therese said slowly, "but it's hardly a long-term arrangement, is it? Don't you want to put a deposit down on a house?"

"But, Mum, if I do that, how will my wonderful prince come along and rescue me from my tall tower and take me back to his castle in the outer suburbs?"

"Don't be sarcastic, darling. Sarcasm is the poor cousin of wit."

"If sarcasm is the 'poor cousin' then what does that make slapstick?" Nolan asked.

Therese ignored him. "And anyway," she forged on, "what's so wrong with wanting a fairy-tale ending?"

Poppy gulped her wine, then choked and coughed as Therese slapped her helpfully on the back.

"The fact that I'm a feminist," Poppy said when she'd finished choking. "That's why a fairy-tale ending is wrong."

Therese tipped her head to the side. "I don't think I'm a feminist," she said thoughtfully. "I mean, I'm all for women's rights, but I don't think I'd actually call myself a feminist *per se*."

"If you're in favor of women's rights then you're a feminist," Poppy said firmly.

"I'm a feminist," said Nolan from across the table.

"Here, here," Poppy replied, and they clinked their glasses.

"That's how I got women to pay for dates back in my youth," he added happily.

"Oh, grow up," Poppy said. She dipped a finger in her water glass and flicked a droplet at her brother.

"Who needs to grow up?" Nolan retorted.

"Nolan!" Therese gasped. "We raised you to be a gentleman. I hope you never made Megan pay for any meals when you two were courting."

"Did she just say courting?" Poppy asked as her dad interrupted, "Or at least go dutch, Nolesy."

"She married me, didn't she?" Nolan said. "So I can't have been that bad to date."

"Slip her a fifty next time you see her, darling," Therese said to Chris, "to make up for the dinners she paid for." She shifted her attention back to Poppy. "So is that why you've this sudden fixation on not having children? Because you're going through a feminist stage?"

Poppy grimaced and Chris reached across the table and placed one hand over Therese's. "Ease up on her, love," he said quietly. Therese absentmindedly patted his hand in return but continued on as though he hadn't spoken.

"You used to be so sweet with your dolls when you were little—pushing them around in their strollers, changing their nappies, putting them up on your shoulder to burp them. You were a natural-born mother."

"And Nolan used to love playing with his garbage truck, but he didn't grow up to work for Cleanaway, did he? And I also used to pretend to be a vet and a doctor and Wonder Woman. But I didn't become any of those things. I was just playing, Mum!"

"What about Annalise?" she asked. "Does she plan on getting married and settling down with a family?"

"Nope."

"There!" said Therese, rapping her knuckles on the table and causing all of the glasses to wobble.

"There what?" Poppy asked, exasperated.

"There you go. That's what this is all about, isn't it? You were always so easily influenced, Poppy, always ready to follow. That's what's happened here. You have a new friend and she's a new person for you to follow, and because she says she doesn't want to settle down you don't want to either. Where did Annalise grow up anyway, is she a Western Sydney girl like you?"

Usually Poppy could handle her mum's exhausting but ultimately well-meaning banter, but tonight she'd had enough. Yes, she might have been a bit of a "follower" as a child—Karleen was bossy and so she'd fallen in line because there was only room for one boss in their friendship. But her mother didn't seem to understand that she'd stopped being a follower long ago.

"I don't know, Mum, I've never asked her where she grew up. What does that have to do with anything anyway?"

Nolan and even her father saw she was about to tip over the edge.

"Mum," Nolan began.

But Chris interrupted. "Therese, why don't you keep Nolan company outside while he has a smoke?"

Nolan looked surprised. He only smoked occasionally

and neither of their parents had ever approved. In fact, mostly they liked to pretend it wasn't happening. But the tone of Chris's voice had even Therese complying, and she reluctantly left the table with Nolan, heading for the balcony.

Speedy saw them leave and strode over to the table. "Would we like the bill?" he asked.

"No thanks, mate, but we will take the dessert menus." Chris dismissed Speedy with a nod of his head and looked across at Poppy. "I know you always do your best to tolerate your mum and I think it's very sweet of you. But I could see it was getting to you tonight, more than usual. Fed up?" he asked.

"A little, I guess."

"She'll get there, eventually. She just wants you to be happy and she's worried. She's mad as hell with Garret."

"But she doesn't *say* that. She doesn't even mention his name. It's almost as if she's more upset about me not having children rather than my husband cheating on me and leaving." Poppy's voice cracked on the last word and Chris gave her a look that told her his heart was breaking right alongside her own. "Ah, Popsy," he said, reverting to her childhood nickname and reaching across the table to tuck a loose lock of hair behind her ear. "I can't tell you how much I want to wring that bastard's neck for hurting you. I know your mum doesn't seem to be saying the right things, but it's just her way. She can't fix what happened with Garret, so she's trying to find something she can fix."

"Dad, my life choices don't need fixing."

"I know. But she worries that one day you'll change your mind and it'll be too late." He hesitated. "I'll talk to her," he promised.

Later that night Poppy posted on NOP.

> Anyone else have trouble convincing friends or family that you don't ever want to have kids? My mother is driving me up the wall. It doesn't seem to matter what I say or how many times I say it—she's certain I'm lying or that I'm in denial or whatever. Any tips on how to make her understand once and for all would be greatly appreciated!

Within seconds Facebook notified Poppy that several people had already commented on her post.

Nicole—*Have the same exact issue with my little sister. She has two of her own and every time I'm around her and the kids I catch her looking at me with these guilty puppy dog eyes, like she feels terrible for beating me to it. As if procreation is a race that's supposed to be won. Unfortunately, I still haven't been able to make* *her understand that she has no reason to feel sorry for me 'cause I'm actually perfectly happy.*

Marns—*For me my family got it straightaway. They were like, oh yeah, you never were a kid person, even when you were a kid! So I can't really help you but I get it must suck.*

Bette—*Honey, my family didn't accept it till I hit menopause! But here's a thought for you—perhaps your mother is craving grandchildren?*

Jess—*Don't know. Don't care. LOL. More importantly, someone in this group told me the best place to buy fluffy handcuffs recently and I can't remember who it was—but anyway, thanks for the tip! Now I'm after recommendations for a good hotel in the city to spend a night with my husband. Somewhere with a real sexy vibe if you know what I mean?*

Marns—*@Jess, when you say sexy—do you mean like mirrors on the ceiling? Or less tacky? Anyway, PM me.*

Poppy—*Jeez-@Jess, thanks for your support!! LOL!*

Viv—*You know what's absolutely ridiculous about this? The fact that it's even an issue! It shouldn't even be a flicker on their radar. For one thing, it's none of their business, and also, who CARES?! I mean it's not like you're asking them to accept your decision to join ISIS, is it? The conversation should go something like this:*

"You reckon you'll have kids one day?" "Nah, don't want to." "Fair enough. Hey, want a game of tennis?" Right?!

Viv's comment particularly resonated with Poppy. *Exactly!* she thought. She flicked a reply to her.

Yes! You're so right. Why does it matter? Did you have trouble convincing your family?

Viv's response shot back: *TBH, I'm not close with my parents, so there was no opportunity to see either way how they'd react.*

Poppy took the conversation to private message and sent her another question: *You married? Can't remember if you've mentioned a husband before.*

Yeah. Tied the knot thirteen years back.

Was your husband always on board with your choice not to have kids?

We seem to be on the same page on most things, which I guess is lucky. Yours messed you around with that, hey?

The comment surprised Poppy. She'd talked about her divorce within the NOP group before, but she didn't think she'd ever discussed the circumstances of Garret changing his mind about wanting kids. She wondered if that meant there were some secret discussions going on between NOP members behind her back.

What do you mean? She flicked back.

Oh, I just heard your partner really let you down over the whole "to have or not to have" kids debate. Sorry—shouldn't have overstepped.

It clicked for Poppy—Annalise would have been the one to share. Not because she was into gossip, but because she was genuinely pissed with Garret for what he'd done.

It's okay. I'm guessing I know who's been chatting about it. Annalise. She can't help it, she wants to stick up for me all the time and that includes the need to bad-mouth my ex at any given opportunity.

Ha! Yeah I think it was Annalise who mentioned the issues. She seems like a great friend to you. Anyway, I'll let you get on with your Tuesday night. Nice chatting.

You too.

Chapter 5

Poppy and Annalise stood together with the rest of their team in the middle of the field, facing their opposition, the Granville Raiders. After all of their pre-season training, it was finally time for the first game. Following on from another warm autumn day, the night air was now cool and crisp. Rain had been forecast, but so far it had held off and hopefully it would continue to do so until the end of the game. The referee—a boy who couldn't have been older than fifteen—had gathered them together and was listing his rules in a wobbly, pubescent voice that skated between high-pitched squeaks and low rumbles. *Poor kid,* thought Poppy, *he's probably terrified of telling a bunch of older women what to do.*

Poppy was feeling great. Annalise wasn't lying when

she said she was a decent player, and throughout their training sessions their team had been working really well together. They were in with a good chance of continuing with their winning streak from last season.

The ref flipped a coin to determine which team would kick off and then Granville's captain stepped forward. "All right, ladies, let's keep it friendly, hey? We're all mums, most of us have jobs, and no one wants to cop any injuries."

Poppy stiffened. She was about to say something but Annalise beat her to it. "Speak for yourself, mate, just because it's the over thirty-fives doesn't mean all of us have kids." She slung an arm around Poppy's shoulder.

The captain raised her eyebrows and looked sideways at her teammates, amused. "Yeah, all right, not everyone, but let's still keep it friendly, eh?"

"Are we here to play soccer or have a social?" Annalise said. "I say go hard or go home."

The captain laughed. "Righto," she said. "Whatever you say."

There were nervous giggles from women on both sides and Poppy wondered if Annalise had just set them up for a rough game. A player standing to the left of the captain caught Poppy's eye and all of a sudden Poppy knew what was coming.

Don't do it, don't do it, do not do it.

The woman tilted her head just slightly to the left, pursed her lips, crinkled her nose, and lifted her eyebrows.

BAM.

She did it. She fucking well did it.

The sympathy look. It was clear as day and Poppy wanted to slap the silly puppy-dog expression right off her face.

I do not need your pity. Poppy clenched her jaw and then checked herself. *Hold up, Poppy, you don't actually know for a fact that's what she's thinking.*

But why else would she be throwing her that look?

The two teams separated and spread out to take their positions. Poppy's place was in the goals, while Annalise as striker was going to be up front, so she squeezed Annalise's arm before heading to her box. "Hey, thanks for standing up for me."

Annalise shook her head. "I was standing up for both of us," she replied. "And now we're going to kick their butts."

"Sounds like a plan."

For the first twenty minutes of the game, Poppy was afforded far too much thinking time. True to her word, Annalise was going hard and the rest of their team seemed to be following suit. Rowena, who was an ex–premier league player, was up front with her, and while the two of them hadn't been able to put away a goal yet, they were keeping the ball in the top half at least 90 percent of the time.

"Oy, Poppy!" a voice shouted from the sideline. "Stay sharp, you look like you're about to fall asleep out there."

The voice belonged to their coach. Elle had been training Poppy's team for several years and she took the competition extremely seriously. To Elle, soccer was life. Skipping training was the sporting equivalent of blasphemy. Not pulling your weight on the field was the ultimate betrayal of your teammates. If you missed a game, you needed to be on your deathbed.

"What do you want me to do," Poppy shouted back, "run around in circles? They haven't even let me touch the ball yet."

Jen, who was in the back line, cut in. "You want us to let one through so you can feel needed, Poppy?"

"Fuck off, Jen!" Poppy shouted. "I'm well needed."

"Don't even think about letting one slip through, Jen," Elle called. "You just keep doing what you're doing."

"Jesus, Elle, I was joking!"

The best way Poppy could describe Elle was that she was a woman with presence. She was actually younger than the players—in her late twenties—and she always wore the same jersey, the same shorts, the same base-ball cap hiding her hair and pulled down low so it was hard to see her eyes. Yet she had a way of commanding complete attention with ease.

Elle was distracted then by Annalise and Rowena, who were making yet another play for the goal. They lost their chance and Poppy saw Elle burying her face in her hands. To Elle, every moment in every game might as well be the final thirty seconds of the grand finale. Any missed opportunity was a calamity. Last season Jen had taken a photo of Elle standing on the sideline midgame and posted it to Facebook with the caption "My dream is to find a man who looks at me the same way Elle looks at a soccer ball."

Poppy had to admit, she admired Elle for her passion.

By halftime they were still drawn at nil-all. Elle gathered them together for a pep talk and someone sent a bag of lollies around the group for an energy boost. A light rain began to fall and Poppy folded her arms tightly and jogged on the spot. She loved being a goalie, but if no one was taking any shots at her, it was hard to keep warm or energized.

"Right," said Elle, "what's happening out there? You guys have had so many chances to score but for some reason you're not following it through. Rowena,

I reckon you need to get out of your own head, you're overthinking. Annalise, you're the opposite. You need to slow down and *start* thinking. During training, almost all of your shots were on point. Your aim is usually incredible. You've got fucking mad skills."

Poppy saw Annalise's cheeks flush pink in a very uncharacteristic moment of embarrassed pride and her eyes shone in a way Poppy had never witnessed before. Elle continued on.

"But tonight, you're all over the shop. Actually, you know what? I'm gonna shake things up a bit. Poppy, let's take you out of goals and put you up front."

Poppy let her mouth drop open. "Elle," she said, "I'm the goalie, I'm always the goalie, you can't take me out of there."

"I can do whatever I want. Anyway, it'll give you a chance to get some action. Annalise and Rowena, I'm dropping both of you down to the back line." She went on to redistribute the rest of the team and most of them nodded their assent before breaking apart to grab drink bottles and rewrap bad knees and ankles before the whistle blew for the second half.

Annalise pulled Poppy aside. "Has Elle lost her mind? She's going to have the team in a mess, everyone will be lost. And isn't Ads our only left-footer? Why is she putting her over on the right?"

Poppy threw her hands up as if to say, *Your guess is as good as mine.* Then she said, "Hopefully there's method to her madness."

Annalise didn't look convinced and Poppy sensed she was annoyed at being made to drop back when she'd been so close to scoring so many times.

In the second half of the game things started out poorly. Mixing up their positions took them out of their comfort zones. They all had to focus more and work harder in order to play their part. Granville took advantage of the chaos and managed to break through for a shot at the goal but Jen put in a good effort and was able to save it. Another ten minutes in, they started to get used to their positions and hold their own while the rain grew heavier, cutting down on visibility. The two teams were fairly evenly matched, though, and as the time continued to tick by, Poppy was beginning to think they were doomed to finish the game without a single goal.

With about three minutes left, Annalise took out an opposing player and Granville was awarded a penalty kick right in front of the goal. Poppy held her breath as Jen prepared for the shot. *Stay light on your feet,* Poppy willed her, *keep your eyes on the ball.*

The ball went up high. It was a beautiful shot, it was heading in for sure. Jen leaped up and plucked it out of the air and their team erupted with cheers. Poppy was stunned, she wasn't even certain she would have been able to save that one.

"How the hell did you pull that off, Jen?" Rowena shouted.

"Used to play volleyball." Jen grinned. She threw the ball out to Annalise, who brought it up the right-hand side. Then the midfield passed it through right in front of Poppy, and all of the sudden she found herself with a clear run at the goal.

She started sprinting and her legs protested, reminding her that running wasn't her forte. Now she appreciated the steady rainfall that was keeping her cool, even if the pitch was becoming slippery. The ball was slick but she was managing to keep it close. Her chest tightened and her lungs burned.

She could hear Elle on the sideline screaming at her. "Take the shot! TAKE IT NOW!"

She wanted to follow Elle's instructions—Elle was the coach and so she wanted to do right by the team and listen to her. But at the same time, Granville's goalie was coming out to meet her and Poppy wasn't sure she'd be able to get the ball by her. She knew Carmen was backing her up, so she veered left, drawing the goalie over to the side, and passed it off to Carmen, who placed it neatly into the back right-hand corner of the net.

The whistle blew for the end of the match and Carmen whooped and ran over to hug Poppy, followed closely by several other teammates who tackled both of them almost to the ground in celebration.

Back on the sidelines, Elle approached Poppy and pulled her aside. "How come you didn't take the shot?" she asked.

Poppy hesitated. "Because it wasn't the right call."

Elle stared back at her and Poppy waited to be told off. But then Elle smiled. "You've changed lately," she said. "I like it."

Chapter 6

The pub was packed, and the crowd was noticeably skewed toward soccer players who'd come in for a postmatch drink. It made Poppy feel a lot less self-conscious about the fact they were both still in their sweaty soccer gear, although Annalise looked annoyingly hot in her footy shorts, her small frame swamped by a baggy Macquarie University jumper, her socks pulled up to her knees. As they searched for a table, Poppy tried tucking in her shirt, realized she looked like a schoolboy, pulled it back out again, and accepted that she would never look as cute as her friend.

She hoped a couple of drinks might lighten Annalise's mood. As much as she knew Annalise was happy with their win, she could also tell she was still disappointed about being pulled out of her favorite position as striker. When Elle had taken the time to congratulate Poppy on her goal, she'd noticed Annalise watching them with a strange look on her face. A minute later, she was scribbling furiously in a red notebook, which she quickly stashed in her bag as soon as Poppy approached. She'd considered asking her what was with the notebook but decided to let it go.

Eventually they snagged a couple of stools at the bar and ordered their first round.

"I'm calling it now," said Annalise, "we're gonna be leaving your car here overnight and Ubering it home."

"You know what?" said Poppy. "I'm all in. I want to meet someone tonight."

Annalise responded with a most un-Annalise-like squeal. "Are you serious? Yes! Wait . . . we're talking one-night stand, yeah? You're not trying to meet Mr. Perfect, right?"

"Totally talking about a one-nighter."

"What's brought this on?"

Poppy carefully considered her answer before responding. What *had* brought this on? From the minute they'd met, Annalise had been keen to play wingman, assuring Poppy it would be the best way to move on from Garret. She was a firm believer in the rebound bang as a crucial part of the recovery process, but thus far, Poppy had resisted her attempts to set her up with anyone. So what had changed? Was it the fact that she'd been taken out of her comfort zone at tonight's game? Was it the way Elle had looked at her afterward? *You've changed,* she'd said.

Had she changed? Had something shifted?

Or was she just craving an intimate touch? It was coming up to five months since she and Garret had separated. And prior to that, they hadn't slept together for several weeks. At the time Poppy had assumed it was because they were tired or busy. It hadn't occurred to her that it was because Garret was cheating. And how long before then had Garret actually still felt something for her? When was the last time someone had truly wanted her?

It would be nice to feel desired again. Although admittedly, she wasn't giving herself a fighting chance in this outfit. Too bad—if she went home to shower and change, she'd likely lose her nerve. Plus, her proclamation that it was time to hook up was already pulling Annalise out of her funk, so that was a definite bonus.

"I'm not sure," she finally said. "I think I just really want to have sex."

Annalise laughed. "Say that a little louder and you can probably walk out of here with someone in the next thirty seconds."

Poppy's face warmed. They were packed in pretty tight, but there was so much noise she hadn't been worrying about whether or not anyone could overhear their conversation. She lowered her voice. "I'm not ready this minute! We need to have a few drinks first."

"Stop stressing, I was only kidding. No one's listening."

Their first drinks were placed in front of them and they picked them up. "Cheers," said Annalise, clinking her glass against Poppy's. "Here's to getting you laid, and FYI, we're downing this in one, got it?"

An hour later they were several rounds in and Poppy was starting to feel wobbly on her stool. Keeping up with Annalise was challenging. Annalise had arranged for the bartender to keep the drinks coming and every time Poppy emptied a glass, a new full one would be in front of her within seconds.

Annalise elbowed her, causing her to almost overbalance and she had to grab the bar to right herself. "Hey, check out the guy behind you and to the left, he's not bad."

Poppy turned carefully, wobbled some more, and attempted the subtle once-over. But she had no idea where she was supposed to be looking. "Beard or no beard?" she whispered out of the side of her mouth.

"You can't seriously think I was talking about either of those two with the open-neck shirts and their chest hair showing? No, *further* left, dark hair."

Poppy readjusted and found him. She spun back too quickly and the room took a second to catch up with her. "No way," she said, "not my type."

"Really? I think he's cute."

"Then why don't you go for it?"

Annalise drummed her fingers on the bar. She looked like she was weighing it up. Finally, she said, "Yeah, I might, later. But this is all about you, remember?"

"So things are still only casual with you and Lawrence?"

"Yep. I don't do anything apart from casual."

"What, like never? What's been your longest past relationship?"

"Um," said Annalise, looking up to the ceiling. "I'm not sure exactly . . . I'd have to work it out. Hey, let's throw a post up on NOP telling the girls we're out on the pull. We can ask them for their best pickup lines."

She'd whipped her phone out of her bag and started typing before Poppy could protest. She wasn't sure she wanted almost four hundred women becoming invested in her love life. Or sex life, as was more accurate. But once Annalise had her mind set on doing something, it was unlikely anyone could stop her. Besides, Poppy was too inebriated to argue.

While she waited she waved at the bartender to get his attention. "Two more?" she mouthed at him, pointing down at their glasses. He gave her a thumbs-up. She knew it was probably time to start substituting the odd round of water for alcohol, but tonight wasn't really the night for making sensible choices.

"There. Done," said Annalise a moment later. "I'll check back in a few minutes and see if anyone has any great ideas."

"Another round is on its way. I'm going to the bathroom to see if I can dab a bit of soap under my arms and somehow fix my hair before you start throwing me at random men."

Poppy stood up and started to head for the ladies'. Annalise called loudly after her, "You know that's called a whore's bath, right?"

Poppy swung around and put her finger to her lips, "Ssshhh, woman!"

She saw Annalise chuckling happily to herself as she accepted their drinks from the bartender.

In the ladies', Poppy leaned against the basin and slow-blinked at the mirror. The bright fluorescent lights were unforgiving and her stomach began to churn. She splashed water on her face and did her best to smooth down her hair, which had frizzed up quite a bit after the soccer game in the rain.

As she focused in on her hazy reflection, she wondered if she really was up for meeting someone tonight. Maybe she'd been too brash when she'd told Annalise she was ready. Maybe she needed to wait a little longer, or at least try again when she was in nicer clothes with her hair done and feeling more confident. But then again, she had spotted a nice-looking suit sitting across the bar from them a few minutes earlier. And he had been glancing their way. Maybe she should bite the bullet. Just walk over there and at least talk to him. What did she have to lose?

Her dignity.

Her self-esteem.

Her good mood if he shot her down.

Jesus, she needed to pull it together.

Her phone buzzed in her pocket and she pulled it out to see a notification from Annalise's post. There was an unread private message on the NOP admin account showing as well. She read through the comments first.

Viv—*Good luck picking up tonight! I hope you meet someone bangin. (Pun intended.)*

Sophie—*Racking my brain to come up with a good pickup line for you to try. All I can think of is the totally cheesy ones, like "Did it hurt when you fell from* heaven?" Or "Is that a mirror in your pocket? 'Cause I can see myself in your pants!" My best advice to you is just be yourself and have fun!

Kellie—*OMG, I want to be out at a bar instead of sitting in bed next to my fast-asleep husband. You go, girl, just make sure you update us so we can all live vicariously through you. God, I miss the days of being single. P.S. FYI, I do actually love my husband! I just miss the fun of the chase!*

Jess—*@Kellie, You can actually still have all the fun of the chase even if you're married—there's heaps of ways to spice things up: role-play, bondage, bringing in a third party if you're inclined that way. My husband and I will even go to a random bar and pretend we're meeting for the first time. Feel free to PM me if you want some ideas.*

Annalise—*@Jess, FFS woman, stop hijacking posts to discuss your sex life!!*

Nicole—*When I met my partner I walked right up to him and said, I'd like to buy you a drink. Guys like it when a girl is confident. Well, he did anyway. Give that a try.*

Carla—*You two are out meeting guys? EXCITING! Which bar are you at, maybe I could come join you?*

Poppy briefly considered letting Carla know the name of the pub, but reconsidered. She had enough competition with the redheaded pocket-rocket by her side, she didn't need supermodel, shampoo-commercial-worthy Carla distracting any potential dates as well.

She remembered the private message then and went to check it but saw through blurred vision that there was nothing there. Where did it go? Had she imagined it? She jabbed at the screen, going out of Messages and back in again. Nothing new there. Weird.

Back out in the pub, she headed for Annalise but stopped short. That suit she'd been checking out was now sitting next to her and the two of them were chatting away. *Goddammit!* Poppy swore in drunken frustration. Didn't Annalise have enough options? Why did she have to make a move on the man Poppy was hoping to make a play for? There was no way she could compete with sexy, petite Annalise.

"Ah well," Poppy mumbled to herself. She'd better back off and let Annalise do her thing. She looked around for somewhere else to sit, but Annalise glanced up and caught her eye. She waved her over and Poppy shuffled moodily toward the two them.

"Hey," she said when she reached them. "So I'm thinking I might just take off."

"Fuck off," said Annalise. "You're not going anywhere."

Poppy glared back at her. "Um, I'm pretty sure you

just told me to fuck off. So I think I am going some-where."

"No, not fuck off home. I mean sit the fuck down, woman. Will's been waiting to meet you."

Poppy looked at the suit who suddenly had a name attached. Will? He seemed like more of an Aaron or an Adam to her. She wasn't sure why. He smiled back at Poppy and reached a hand out, which she accepted and shook.

"Nice to meet you, Poppy."

"You too," Poppy said slowly, a suspicious tone creeping into her voice. Why would anyone be waiting to meet her when they already had Annalise cornered?

"Your friend has given me the all clear to shout you a drink. Happy with another gin?"

"Oh," Poppy said, "no, no, you don't have to buy me a drink just 'cause Annalise is bullying you."

"You misunderstand," he replied. "I came over to ask her what you drink. A bit of a wuss move, I know—waiting until you walk away so I could check with her first—but I like to play it safe."

"Oh," Poppy said. "In that case, I'll take one. Thanks."

"So, now that I've done the introductions, I'm off," said Annalise.

Poppy shot a quick glance at her, tried to convey

everything she wanted to say with just one look: *No, you don't! You can't leave me. It's too soon, I'm not ready, I don't remember how to do this, I don't know what we're going to talk about.*

But Annalise just grinned and shook her head before leaning in and whispering, "You'll be fine, just go with it."

"But . . . but we were going to split a cab home, weren't we?" Poppy asked.

"Not anymore." She waggled her fingers at Poppy, winked at Will, and left.

Will turned his attention to Poppy. "Right," he said, "I'm guessing you haven't done this kind of thing in a while, right?"

"How did you know?" Poppy asked, instantly disappointed.

"Oh, sorry," he said quickly. "I didn't mean it as a put-down, it's just that . . ." He paused and reached toward her left hand, which was curled around her glass. He touched her ring finger lightly. "There used to be a wedding band right about here, didn't there?"

Poppy stared down at her hand. There was no longer a white mark from where the ring used to be. She'd pulled it off that first day when she'd sat sobbing in her car and shoved it in her glove box, where it had stayed ever since.

"How'd you know?"

He cocked his head to the side. "Well, I *could* say I have a sixth sense about these kinds of things and pretend it's because I'm connected to my inner emotions or whatever. Or I could just own up to the truth. Your friend gave me a heads-up."

"Oh God. What else did she tell you?"

"Only that you'd been hurt, and that I'd better not hurt you too, or she'd go all bunny-boiler on me."

Poppy laughed. "Typical Annalise."

"She seems like a good friend, really cares about you."

A plate of wedges was placed on the bar in front of them and Poppy looked up in confusion. "We didn't order these."

"Some redheaded chick ordered them for you," said the staff member. "She also told me to remind you to have some water and uh . . . she asked me to give you this." He smirked as he reached into his pocket and passed across a square foil package. "She said better safe than sorry, and then she said a whole bunch of super-explicit stuff, which I'm not getting paid enough to repeat to you. Just trust me when I say she wants you to have a fun night."

"Oh. My. God." Poppy leaned over until her forehead was touching the bar. "I am mortified." She straightened up and locked eyes with Will. The corner of his mouth twitched and next thing the two of them were falling about laughing and Will had to catch her arm to stop her from tumbling from her stool.

When they'd eventually stopped laughing, the ice was well and truly broken. Poppy hid the condom in her pocket and they shared the wedges and chatted some more—nothing quite as deep as the opening of their conversation, mostly they just asked one another about where they both worked, where they lived, hobbies, and families. Eventually the food was finished, and after switching to water, Poppy had sobered up a little. She still felt tipsy and giggly, but the room had stopped spinning. It seemed like they were winding things up. *The question was,* Poppy thought, *would they be leaving alone or together?* Her radar on these kinds of things was totally off. She couldn't tell whether he was truly interested or not.

"Just going to the men's room," Will said. "Won't be long, so don't disappear, okay?"

Poppy nodded.

"Promise?"

"Promise."

He leaned in close and whispered in her ear, "Because I don't know about you, but I don't think we should let your friend down, should we?"

Poppy felt a tingle shiver its way through her body.

Will walked away without waiting for an answer and Poppy was left trying to calm the butterflies within.

She didn't look up at first when a different guy sat on the stool next to her. She figured he was just there to order a drink, but then he started speaking to her.

"Excuse me, love, have you got a second?"

Poppy turned toward him and took in his appearance. Usually she'd take offense to a stranger calling her "love"—if someone did that to Annalise, she'd probably deck him—but there was something about the way he said it that didn't bother Poppy. He had a sort of gentle, country lilt to his voice that made it seem more innocent. More old-fashioned charm than sexist. He was clearly another soccer player cutting loose postmatch. His hair was damp, either from the rain or from sweat, and he was wearing the same navy-blue jersey with a red-and-white stripe down one side that represented Poppy's club. Although to be honest, Poppy thought he was built more like a rugby player than a soccer player.

"Only a quick one," she replied, "I'm about to head off. You guys have a win tonight?" she added.

"Yeah, three–nil."

Despite not having any personal connection to him

or his team, Poppy felt a twinge of pride, he was part of the same club after all.

"But listen," he continued. "I was grabbing a beer before when your friend was talking to that suit I think you're about to leave with."

"Mmm," Poppy said, waiting to hear where this was going. She also noted that it wasn't a country lilt she'd heard in his voice after all, it was a mild Irish accent.

"This might not be real nice to hear, but that bloke you're with, he's a real player. I've seen him go home with a different woman every week I've been here after my games. And your friend sort of sold you out."

"What do you mean she sold me out?"

"I mean she tipped him off that you'd be an easy score for him."

He hesitated, screwing up his face like he was getting ready for Poppy to slap him or something. But Poppy stayed still and quiet. She was feeling a slight sting that Annalise had described her as an "easy score." But then again, wasn't it the truth? Annalise knew full well what Poppy was after tonight, so all she'd done was try to help her along.

Giggly, tipsy Poppy was gone. She squared her shoulders and her voice was crisp as she responded. "Right. And you feel the need to tell me this because . . . ?"

"Because . . . I don't know. I just thought you might appreciate the warning."

"You warn every woman he takes home?"

"No. You're the first."

"How did I get so lucky?"

"Look, I'm sorry, I didn't mean to upset you. I just thought you seemed more . . ."

"More what?"

"More vulnerable than the others."

"What does that mean?"

"Fuck, I don't know. You just don't look like his normal type."

"Not pretty enough?"

"God no! That's not what I meant at all."

"Mate, you don't even know me. So please don't stand there patronizing me."

"Okay, fine," he said, holding his hands up in defeat. "Maybe I shouldn't have said a word, but it just didn't seem right to me. That friend of yours, I don't know how well you know her, but in my opinion I don't think she was doing you justice." He stood up from his stool to leave. "Sorry," he said, "have a good one." And he headed away back to a table with a bunch of other players.

Poppy watched him go, feeling a mix of humiliation and anger and irritation as she imagined him and the rest of his team all sharing a good laugh at her expense. All at once she was reminded of an altercation with Karleen when they'd still been in primary school together. She'd found a love letter in her school bag.

> *Dear Poppy,*
> *I think you're really, really pretty.*
> *I like you. I love you.*
> *Will you be my girlfriend?*
>
> *From B*

At the time, she'd had a crush on a boy called Ben. She'd showed the note to Karleen and they'd both squealed with delight. They'd discussed at length how Poppy should respond and whether or not B definitely meant Ben.

But two weeks later, she'd found out the truth. The note hadn't come from Ben. It hadn't come from any of the boys in her class whose name started with *B*. It had been written by Karleen. Much like Annalise, Karleen's intentions were pure. She'd wanted to make Poppy happy. She just hadn't thought it through. Ten-year-olds rarely do.

But they weren't ten-year-old girls anymore, they were grown women. And was promising some strange bloke an easy lay taking the role of wingman way too far?

All right, so Irish football dude was correct—this wasn't right, it was weird and creepy.

Meanwhile, Will was making his way back through the pub toward her. He reached her side, placed one elbow on the bar, and leaned in close. The smell of bourbon was strong on his breath as he spoke. "Well, I'm happy to call it a night and head home." He paused, leaned closer still, and added, "But I'm hoping you might join me?"

Poppy pulled back, tipped her head to the side, and stared at him, weighing him up. Was she even that attracted to him? She had been before. When she'd first spotted him across the bar she'd thought he had a cute smile. That he looked sexy in his suit with his wavy Hugh Grant hairstyle. Now he looked smug. His suit was pretentious, particularly in a pub full of sports people. His smile was more of a leer. If only she hadn't started to sober up.

"Why do you want to take me home?" Poppy asked.

"Because I think we'll have a fun night together," he said.

"But why me?"

"Why not you?"

Wrong answer, buddy.

"You have pretty eyes," he rallied quickly. "I could see them sparking from across the bar."

Oh God, thought Poppy, *he's grasping at straws here. And he knows he's losing me.* He reached a hand out to place it on Poppy's waist and brought his mouth close to her ear. "You have a great body," he whispered, "even under your soccer gear I can tell. You have just the right amount of curves hiding under there. And a fantastic set of tits." He inched even closer still, his body pressed against hers. His breath warmed her neck. "I need to know," he said, "I need to know what they look like when they're free of that . . . annoyingly constrictive sports bra." And his hand snuck its way up from her waist, his thumb brushed against the underside of her breast.

The anger dissipated and instead it was replaced with desire. Who cared why he was really doing it? Who cared if Annalise had pimped her out? Who cared if she was making a complete fool of herself and if she would hate herself in the morning?

She wanted to fuck. She wanted to be fucked—like she'd never been fucked before. By a stranger. With no chance of any kind of future between them. With no strings and no expectations.

"Let's go," she mumbled into his neck.

He took her by the hand and they weaved their way through the pub toward the exit. As they walked, Poppy could feel a set of eyes on her. She didn't want to look.

She didn't want to see the judgment, but she couldn't help herself—the gaze was boring into her. She glanced sideways and caught his eye.

She didn't see judgment, though. Or even amusement. She saw disappointment. And maybe even . . . hurt? Was he hurt? Why? She didn't owe him anything. Besides, she'd come here tonight looking for one thing and one thing only. Didn't that make her just as bad as Will? She looked away quickly and focused on what was waiting for her once they found their way to a bed. Her place or his? Didn't matter. She just wanted him inside of her. She wanted to feel desired. She needed to be touched. She craved the illusion of love.

Yasmine Hunter—Hi, Ladies! I just wanted to share some special news with you all! Are you ready for it?!! Yep, you guessed it, I'm PREGNANT!!! I know! I can't believe it either. I thought it was all over for me and John and TBH, because I thought we couldn't have kids, I'd tried to shut myself off from everything to do with them, tried to convince myself I never wanted one in the first place. And can I just say, this group has been a godsend for me during this time. I felt like I was a part of something, like I wasn't alone. Like I could move on. But now . . . Well, I guess it turns out I did still want a child, I guess all along that part of me was still there—I mean, the moment I saw the two blue lines, I was just shaking and crying . . . and oh, you should have seen John's face—he wanted it too, maybe even more than me. Anyway, I hope you guys will be happy for me to still stay a member, right? Even though I no longer "qualify," LOL! But considering the friendships I've forged with you all, I'd hope you guys wouldn't want to throw all of that away. Hey, maybe I can kind of be the neutral spectator between us and "them"—"them" being the annoying parents of the world! I could be like Switzerland!! Love you guys. Xxx

Chapter 7

Earlier on at the start of the year, in those first few weeks following the breakup, Poppy had received precisely three voice mails from Karleen. Each time, she waited until late at night, when she was sitting up in bed with some sort of alcoholic beverage on the table beside her before she put the phone to her ear, breathed in deeply, and listened to the messages.

In the first, the tinny voice was kind, much kinder than it had been during the confrontation: "Poppy, I know this has been such a huge shock for you and I know we've hurt you badly. But if you can bring yourself around to seeing our side of things, if you can understand that we simply couldn't turn our backs on love, then maybe we could all move past this and be friends. I do still love you, Poppy."

Poppy's heart had ached for the life she'd had before. For the nights she'd shared on the couch sitting between her husband and her oldest friend, watching a rented movie, passing around takeaway Thai or a pizza box. Back when those nights ended with Karleen heading home to her own place while Poppy took Garret by the hand and pulled him upstairs to bed. Back when they still made love. Back when no one had ripped the rug out from underneath her and her deepest concern about Karleen was helping her find the right man to settle down with. As much as Karleen's request was wildly unreasonable, the most ridiculous thought had crossed her mind—was there a way she could have the two of them back in her life? Of course, the idea was absurd and it disappeared as quickly as it appeared.

Then the second message came through, in which Karleen couldn't help letting a hint of her usual crispness creep through. "Poppy, I can't understand why you're not returning my calls. You need to look at the bigger picture. Garret is racked with guilt and it's not fair on him. His intention was never to cause you any hurt. We're all adults and there's no reason why we can't work this out. We've been friends a long time. Call me back. We need to talk."

And then the third voice mail, in which her voice

sounded resigned and tired: "All right, Poppy, I'll leave you alone. But please, considering the history of our friendship, I just would have hoped you wouldn't want to throw all of that away. Because I still think we should be able to find a way through all of this. So if you can find it in your heart to give us a chance, call me."

Poppy had wanted to hurl her phone across her bedroom. The acute injustice of Karleen's words was beyond comprehension. Why should it be on her to forgive them? Why should the weight of their lost friendship fall on her shoulders? She'd buried her face in her pillow, pummeled the mattress, and let loose a guttural, primal scream of pure frustration and fury. How could she have been friends with Karleen for such a long time and never realized how horrendously selfish and insensitive the woman was.

So when the post from NOP member Yasmine had appeared in Poppy's news feed and she'd read those words: *Considering the friendships I've forged with you all, I'd hope you guys wouldn't want to throw all of that away*—something inside Poppy had snapped. It was the day after her night out on the pull and she was feeling seedy from having drunk far too much. Reading someone's joyous pregnancy announcement was the last thing she was in the mood for. She snatched up her phone and marched downstairs to the warehouse, glad to escape the dry air-conditioned hell of the office above.

Now she and Annalise were sitting side by side on a pallet, hidden between two large piles of stock. Poppy had kicked off her heels to place her stockinged feet on the cool concrete floor and Annalise hadn't pulled her up on the Occupational Health and Safety rules. Annalise's feet were encased in steel-cap work boots and she'd crossed her legs beneath her. "Here," said Poppy, passing Annalise her phone. "Have you seen this post yet?"

Annalise started reading and Poppy almost held her breath as she waited. Her shoulders and back muscles squeezed together involuntarily. A part of her was scared she might think it wasn't such a big deal, that she wouldn't understand why it had upset Poppy so much.

"That's ridiculous," Annalise finally said. "I can't believe she wants to stay a member."

Poppy's body relaxed.

"I mean, you put up a reminder a week ago when we started getting requests from women who thought we were some kind of support group for infertile people," Annalise continued. "Your whole idea was to reach people who don't ever want kids, not women who thought they couldn't and then suddenly do. There's no way she deserves to stay. It's not like we're all going to get excited about her stupid baby announcements."

"Totally!" Poppy tried to keep her voice steady. She didn't want Annalise to see how emotional she'd felt about this entire situation. She was embarrassed about how much it had got to her. "She can always go and join MOP anyway, right?"

"Exactly. Don't worry about it. I'll boot her from the group."

"Do you think we've let NOP get too big? Maybe we need to be more selective with who we let in."

"Yeah, you could be right. I guess we have started to relax our approval process, haven't we? Don't let it stress you, we can get back on top of it."

"Thanks, Lise."

"All right. I've been patient but I can't stand it anymore, aren't you going to tell me?"

"Tell you what?"

"Don't be obtuse. You know what. How did it go with Will last night?"

"Oh. That. Well . . . I went home with him."

"And?"

"And . . . we made it as far as his apartment, and we'd just got out of the cab when I felt a lurch and next thing I was throwing up in the gutter."

"Oh no! Poppy, you lightweight."

"Lightweight? You're kidding me, right? We were downing doubles all night. I can't believe I didn't throw up sooner."

"So what happened next?"

"He called it a night and put me straight back in the cab."

"I'm surprised the cabbie let you back in."

"Me too."

"So are you disappointed he didn't offer to hold your hair back and nurse you all night long?"

Poppy laughed. "No, I'm not stupid. I know we were only going back there for one thing. It's a shame he didn't even ask for my number, though."

"But I thought you were only after a one-night stand, weren't you? Shit, you didn't start to fall for him or something, did you?"

"No, no, of course not."

Poppy sighed and rested her head on Annalise's shoulder. She badly needed a Gatorade.

A voice called out from down the end of the aisle. "Annalise? You about?"

Annalise grabbed hold of Poppy's arm and yanked her backward, making her pull her feet up onto the pallet and out of sight. "Shh," she said. "That was fucking Frankie. If she sees us hiding out here she'll probably run and dob us in to her boyfriend."

Poppy stifled a laugh and they waited quietly until they heard her high heels clip-clop away.

"She's going to wonder where you are," said Poppy.

"Who cares."

They sat quietly for a few more minutes before Poppy eventually stretched and started to shuffle forward to get up off the pallet. "Guess I should go back upstairs."

"You want to catch a movie tonight?" Annalise said, putting her hands out so Poppy could pull her to her feet. "I usually like to do my own thing on Tuesdays but I can make an exception this once. Plus, discount tickets. You in?"

"Yeah, why not."

Chapter 8

The cinema complex was decked out in crudely cut cardboard love hearts and red crepe-paper streamers. They were showing reruns of classic romance movies. Poppy and Annalise made their choice based on a process of elimination, taking turns striking off the least likely contenders one by one.

"*The Holiday* is a no for me, I can't handle Jack Black."

"So is *Breakfast at Tiffany's*. Used to be my fave but Garret and I watched it together on our first date."

"I'm not doing *Notting Hill* either. Never been a fan of Julia Roberts."

Eventually they found they were left with *Love Actually*. Poppy would have preferred something with some action or adventure, but this was going to have to do.

As they bought a large popcorn to share, a packet of malted milk balls, and a couple of soft drinks, Poppy wondered if she should confess to Annalise before the movie started. She wasn't entirely sure what had made her lie to her this morning, but the truth was, she hadn't stuffed things up at the forty-yard line with Will the previous evening. She'd headed down to the warehouse ready to give Annalise all the details of the previous night's tryst, just as Annalise always told Poppy about her own escapades with Lawrence. But at the last minute, she'd changed her mind and instead told the fabricated version of events.

Maybe it was the guy at the pub who'd warned her about Will. Maybe he'd got into her head when he'd said Annalise wasn't a good friend for offering her up to Will on a platter, and Poppy didn't want to give Annalise the satisfaction of knowing her technique had succeeded. But now she felt funny about her lie.

The real story was that once they'd made it back to Will's place, the cab had pulled away and Will had taken Poppy inside. She was drunk, he was drunk, and she hadn't slept with anyone apart from Garret in more than nine years. So she couldn't say it was sexy or sweet or romantic. She couldn't even say it was mind-blowing—although it did hit the spot, or he did, so to speak. Instead, it was fumbly and messy and at times awkward, but it was fun. It was new and different and it woke her up.

When they kissed, it was hard and fast, with tongues sliding, exploring. She hadn't been undressed by a man in years. When she and Garret had sex, they'd both strip down under the covers and then turn to one another. But Will tore at her clothes, wrenched her sports bra up over her head, and leaned down to take one of her nipples in his mouth while the bra still had her arms trapped together above her head.

She elbowed him in the face when she tried to get his shirt off and he caught his watch in her hair. When he first went down on her, she was self-conscious about her lack of maintenance down below for all of three seconds before she was overcome by pleasure, and when she returned the favor, she experimented with her tongue in ways she'd never considered with Garret.

Their foreplay didn't last long and Will had barely pulled on the condom in time before he slid himself inside her and Poppy found herself digging her fingernails into his flesh as both of them moaned together.

Afterward, it was hard to know how she really felt about the entire experience. The first man she'd been with since her husband left her. Was she ashamed? Did she feel dirty? Or did she feel empowered? Fulfilled and content? She was a single woman—she had every right to sleep with whomever she wanted. But the question was, had he actually wanted her, or was he only interested because Annalise had painted her as an easy target?

As she gathered up her things, dressed herself in the dark, and crept from his apartment, Poppy found herself thinking of the man at the pub who'd tried to warn her. Did knowing Will's reasons for sleeping with her take away from the pleasure of what she'd just experienced? If she was honest, yes, of course it did. Didn't anyone want to feel desired for who they were?

But still, she'd needed what Will had given her. She'd needed it to open her back up to the possibilities of being with a man other than Garret. It was a new beginning. And that's why she'd forgiven Annalise for setting her up behind her back. That's why she'd chosen not to call her out on it.

In the cinema, as they waited for the previews to start, Annalise grabbed Poppy's cup of lemonade and removed the lid. "Here," she whispered, "special surprise for you," and she tipped in vodka from a flask she'd been hiding inside her handbag.

"Annalise!" Poppy hissed. "We're not teenagers.

We could just *wait* and go for a drink after the movie. I swear to God, I think you may have a problem."

"Yeah, maybe." She giggled before touching her cup to Poppy's. "Cheers," she said. "Pass the popcorn."

Two-thirds of the way through the movie, Emma Thompson was figuring out that her husband had bought another woman an expensive necklace and Annalise was whispering to Poppy that she ought to kick him in the nuts, when Poppy's phone started buzzing in her back pocket. She shifted slightly and pulled it out from under her butt to try to take a discreet look at the screen, then glanced sideways as she realized Annalise was doing the same with her own phone. Poppy saw that it was an NOP notification and pocketed it to check it later. Annalise was still looking at hers and a moment later she nudged Poppy.

"Bathroom," she whispered, and stood up, ducked her head low, and turned sideways to shift past her and along the row of seats.

Later that night Poppy remembered the notification and went to look for the message. But once again it had vanished.

The Imposter

It's possible she'd already taken it too far. She was connecting with these women on a personal level—commenting on their lives, offering advice—as if she knew what they were going through, as if she understood. When in fact, she had no right. But she couldn't leave. It was like she was involved in an online role-playing game. Single Lady. Child-free. Disposable income. Nothing holding her back, nothing tying her down. It was intoxicating.

Plus, she'd come here with a purpose, she had a job to do. So what if she'd gotten a little caught up in her role while she was playing along, gathering information? If she wanted to be good at her task, then getting involved to this extent was probably exactly what she needed to do.

And if she could have a little fun at the same time, then so be it.

PART TWO

Annalise

NOP MESSAGES

Inbox

Inga Fallon

This group is hideous. A friend told me all you do is bitch about us mums? Fuck you, we don't need your judgment. Bitter much? Get over yourselves and stop whinging. You'll get it one day. One day you'll have kids and you'll understand how hard it is. And I wish I could be there to tell you I told you so.

Chapter 9

Annalise wasn't overly concerned when the first message came through. At the time, she had no idea it was the start of something bigger. She was in the middle of coaxing Will into hitting on Poppy when her phone had lit up on the bar in front of her. She was so glad she'd decided to look straightaway, because it gave her the chance to get rid of it before Poppy saw it.

Poppy didn't need to read something like that—especially not when she was finally ready to move on from Garret tonight. It would totally ruin her mood, and then who knew when she'd be up for it again? As much as Annalise wanted to reply to this Inga woman and lay into her, instead she jabbed at the screen until she'd deleted the message and then blocked the sender from the group. How the hell did she get wind of their group anyway?

Once the message had been dealt with, Annalise had turned her attention back to Will. "I can tell you're into her. You've been making eyes across the bar for the past ten minutes. Be a man and step up."

"How do you know I wasn't making eyes at you?"

"Forget about me. I'm not your type, trust me."

"Funny. You look a lot like my type to me."

Annalise couldn't help but feel flattered. Her instincts were telling her to flirt. He was good-looking, the sort of guy she'd normally be happy to take to bed. Her body started to respond on its own. Her back arched ever so slightly. Her lower lip pouted.

"Is that right?" she said.

Will grinned as his gaze roved across her body. But then a tiny voice at the back of her head spoke up. *You were supposed to be doing this for Poppy.*

She stopped herself just in time.

Once her work was complete, Annalise hung behind for a short time to keep an eye on Poppy and Will and make sure they were hitting it off. She grabbed a spot near the doorway and filled in time writing in her notebook, before soon calling it a night. She cornered a cute staff member as she was leaving, making him promise to pass on her message to Poppy. His knees almost buckled when she whispered it into his ear. Poor guy couldn't have been any older than nineteen. He begged her for her number but she refused. He was too young even for her. She headed home, content in the knowledge that Poppy was finally going to get lucky.

Annalise had had Poppy pegged from the moment she met her. Poppy was a good girl. A good girl who worked hard and followed the rules. She dressed like she was older than she was: neat trousers with the pleat down the front. Flat shoes. Plain beige blouses. Her features were ultra-pronounced. Her eyes, nose, and mouth were all clustered together right in the center of her face. Huddled, as though they were protecting one another from the elements. And then her forehead, cheeks, and chin seemed to spread out from the features at the center. She should have compensated with a fringe and maybe some layers around her face, but instead she accentuated the wide-open space by tightly pulling her hair back—and she wore her hair the same, every single day. As soon as she had the opportunity, Annalise would have to convince her to change that.

Poppy was also great at her job. She had an incredible knack for knowing what things were about to go viral. "People think it happens organically," she told Annalise once, "and sometimes it does, but there's also a formula. A constantly fluctuating formula, but still a formula. It's art mixed with science mixed with psychology. It's beautiful." She was a little bit tipsy at the time.

When Garret had betrayed her, her pain had been obvious almost instantly. It was written all over her face. It was in the way her shoulders rounded. It was in the way the odd strand of hair started to creep out of her ponytail and fall across her face. It was in the lines that etched their way across her forehead and spidered out from her eyes. Annalise was hooked. She wanted to know more. She wanted to know what had happened to her and she wanted to save her.

Karleen's disloyalty meant Poppy had an opening for a new best friend, and Annalise's relationships had been so shallow for so long that she supposed she was looking for a way to settle down a bit. Sometimes Annalise wondered if that was why she started to get carried away with Lawrence. Was she secretly after something more? She didn't really think so. It was more that she just liked the way he always went down on her first.

All it had taken for Annalise to draw Poppy in was one of her trademark flirty smiles—the type she'd usually reserve for a bloke she wanted to bang for the night, but she'd had a feeling a little bit of flirting would work on Poppy. Sometimes that's what a new friendship between women was like—a touch of flirtatiousness. Mutual attraction. Didn't have to be sexual. Could be if you wanted it to.

The day that Annalise had told Poppy she'd join her soccer team was the same day that Annalise had first slept with Lawrence. It was only supposed to be a one-off, but somehow it hadn't worked out that way. It had started when Lawrence watched the conversation between Annalise and Poppy. He'd been turned on by the way the two women were flirting with one another. He might have thought he was hiding the hard-on beneath his trousers, but Annalise had sensed it, and when Poppy had left the break room, she'd walked straight up to him until their faces were barely inches apart and whispered, "I know you want me," before turning on her heel and walking away without waiting for his reaction.

He'd looked up her mobile number on the internal staff list and texted her within the hour.

If Annalise was completely honest, this tactic didn't work for her every time. Sometimes a man might find it too intimidating. Or maybe she might have read them wrong, misinterpreted their desire. But mostly she was spot on. And Annalise knew she was good-looking. Not in the traditional, symmetrical features kind of way, but in the big lips, big eyes kind of way. Like, they were almost too big—another fraction of a millimeter and she'd have a cartoonlike face, especially with such a small frame, the body of a twelve-year-old boy. But she knew how to make it all work for her. Catch her at certain angles and an onlooker might say she was an ugly redheaded duckling, but with the right lighting, the right hair, the right facial expressions, she knew she was hot as fuck. And it all came down to confidence anyway.

After Annalise left Poppy and Will together at the pub, she summoned Lawrence to come and meet her for a late-night rendezvous of their own.

Jess—Hey girls, would love to get some opinions on this short story I wrote this afternoon. Warning you now, it features explicit content—but then again, we're all grown women, so I don't see why anyone would have any issues with it. It's up on my blog— link below. Looking forward to your thoughts.

Viv—Wow, Jess, just had a quick read. Very . . . detailed! Some great imagery in there.

Annalise—HOLY SHIT!! Woman, you are a serious deviant! In need of a cold shower after reading that. You kiss your mother with that mouth?!

Bette—Not my cup of tea, I'm afraid. But well done for giving it a crack.

Chapter 10

Annalise found that it happened every now and then. A bloke couldn't accept that a woman was running the warehouse.

Poppy had just headed back upstairs after getting her failed night with Will off her chest. Most of the delivery guys knew Annalise, and just like her staff, she had their respect, because she demanded it from them, she forced it out of them. The truth was, Annalise had actually lied on her résumé to get this job. She loved being the boss of a bunch of men and she loved that some of them were in fact more qualified than she was. Besides, in her opinion, considering how many unqualified men held jobs above more capable women, Annalise was simply evening the scales.

It was the larger, beefier blokey-blokes who accepted

her the most readily. They were the ones who were quickest to guess she was stronger than she looked. They were the ones who didn't offer to lift the boxes down off the truck for her because "she wouldn't want to break a nail, would she?"

But it was inevitable that a man who didn't so easily accept Annalise's position would show up once in a while.

The new delivery guy was weedy. A short, skinny man in a baseball cap with a pinched face and a dirty, dirty porn-star mustache. As soon as he spotted Annalise walking out of the office toward him he started giving her the once-over. Eyes scanning up and down.

"What have you got for me?" she asked.

"Oh, I got plenty for you." He said it low and under his breath. Quiet enough that he could pretend she wasn't meant to hear it, but loud enough that she could. Annalise glared at him and his tone switched.

"You want to get your boss for me, love."

"I'm the boss down here, *love*. What's the delivery?"

He snorted. "No, sweetheart, I need the *warehouse* manager. Off you go and find him." He pulled a pack of cigarettes out of his back pocket and tapped the bottom to feed one out, and stuck it to his lower lip while he fished in his pocket for a lighter.

There were days when Annalise was in the perfect

frame of mind for someone like this. Days when she could say all the right things. When she could sass his arse from here to far North Queensland and back. And there were other days—far less frequent ones, but they existed nonetheless—where she just wasn't in the mood for this kind of shit.

She stepped forward and snatched the cigarette out of his mouth. "I'm the fucking manager down here and there's no smoking in my warehouse," she snapped.

A couple of her staff were sitting on top of some crates having a smoko break just a few meters away and the delivery guy scowled as he reached out for his cigarette.

"Oh yeah, and what are those boys doing over there? Playing the fucken flute? On the rag, are you?" he added, a glint in his eye as though he was pleased with his slight. "Gimme me ciggie back, sweetheart, before I start to get *eye-rate*."

Annalise squeezed her fist tight, crumbling the cigarette in her hand and letting the tobacco sprinkle to the concrete floor. She watched as his face hardened and his hands twitched by his side. He leaned in even closer.

"You better stop playing, girl."

"Why?" Annalise whispered. "You the type of man who likes to hit women? You the type of man who feels big if he can make a woman cry? The type of big man who only thinks a woman is worth anything if she's on her knees?"

She could feel the eyes of her staff on the two of them, watching as the hostility continued to grow. They knew Annalise liked to deal with dickheads like this on her own, but something about this guy was making the hairs on her arms stand up. She'd read once that goose bumps were a leftover reflex from when humans used to have fur all over their bodies. When you were scared and that fight-or-flight instinct started to kick in, the goose bumps caused the hairs all over your body to stand on end, to make you appear bigger to your attacker.

His voice became a low growl. "Who the fuck do you think you are? I'm startin' to think someone needs to put you and that tight little arse of yours in place." As he spoke his arm snaked around her waist to grab at her backside and he squeezed, hard, fingernails digging into flesh. It was meant as a demonstration of dominance and it caused bile to rise up in her throat. In a flash her knee was up, striking him sharply in the balls. In the meantime, the warehouse guys had jumped to their feet and were on their way over to step in, but the bloke was already doubled over in pain by the time her would-be saviors were around her.

"She's fucken crazy," he gasped, his hands pressed between his legs as he looked around at the guys and waited for their sympathy.

"She was easier on you than I would have been," said Bruce, one of the forklift drivers, who was built like a boxer. "You all good?" he added to Annalise.

"Fine," she said.

"I could have you up on assault charges," the driver shouted.

Annalise looked around at the others. "You blokes see me assault this nice gentleman here?" she asked.

"Nope. Saw this grub put his hands on property that doesn't belong to him, though," said Bruce. The others all nodded in agreement.

Then Annalise heard footsteps and she turned around to see Lawrence walking swiftly toward them. He'd been texting her all morning, making crude jokes about last night and trying to get her to agree to another tryst this evening. She'd ignored them. She wasn't doing it to be cruel, she was just trying to keep things low-key. He must have grown tired of waiting and decided to come and charm her face-to-face.

"What happened?" he asked.

"This dickhead tried to give her shit," said Bruce.

"What do you mean?"

"It's nothing," Annalise said before Bruce could

answer again. "Bruce, deal with this delivery for me, would you?"

Annalise grabbed Lawrence by the hand and started leading him through the warehouse stacks, past the spot where she and Poppy had hidden out that morning and all the way to a rarely used back storeroom.

"What happened?" Lawrence asked again. "Did he try to hurt you? Do I need to do something about that guy?"

"Don't be ridiculous," Annalise replied. "It was nothing, I can take care of myself."

"So what exactly are you dragging me back here for?"

"What do you think?" Annalise asked as she pulled Lawrence into the storeroom and closed the door behind them and shoved some boxes up against the door.

"Here?" he asked.

"Yes here," she replied.

She knew it was weird to drag him away like that in the middle of the day, right in front of her staff, when they could easily guess what she might be up to. Yes, it was her style to be sexually aggressive, but this was taking things one step further. All she knew was that the incident had put her on edge. She might have joked to the other guys that she had it all under control, she might have acted cool and calm and confident. She might have told them all she could take care of herself. But when that guy had invaded her space, for just a moment before he'd reached around to grope at her body, she'd thought he was about to do something else. And she'd seen another man's face, in another time. She'd seen the back of a meaty hand as it was lifted into the air, watched it as it swung down toward her. And it felt like an injection of adrenaline had coursed through her body.

Now Annalise was restless and full of pent-up energy and aggression, and Lawrence was going to help her let it all go.

NOP Messages

Inbox

Belinda Martin

The concept for this group is horrible. You should all be ashamed of yourselves. Women are supposed to support one another and build one another up. Not tear each other down based on our life choices. I hope you all take a good, long, hard look in the mirror.

Chapter 11

Annalise was wishing she had more vodka to get her through this crappy Christmas movie when her phone buzzed. She saw that it was another message to the NOP admin account. On her right, Poppy was looking at her phone as well. She tensed up and waited. But Poppy didn't open the message, she ignored it. Annalise pretended she needed to go to the bathroom and crept out of the cinema to take a proper look.

She found a seat in the foyer and checked it out. It was more of the same, but this time, some chick named Belinda had gotten wind of the group.

Once again, Annalise decided to go with delete and block. There was absolutely nothing wrong with NOP. Nothing wrong with what they were doing or saying. But how did yet another woman know about them? And why did these women all think NOP was so awful? It must have been due to their steadily increasing member numbers. The more members they had, the more chance there was of some woman joining NOP and spilling the group's secrets to a friend or a coworker—maybe just for the fun of sharing some juicy gossip about the new, exclusive Facebook group. But how could she figure out where the leaks were springing from?

She put her phone away and headed back into the theater to join Poppy for the remainder of the movie. At least the good news was that her friend still had no idea anyone was out there taking issue with NOP. And Annalise planned on keeping it that way.

Let's hook up tonight.

It was the following afternoon and the text message came through as Annalise was finishing up her work for the day. There were a few things that bothered Annalise about it. Number one—she usually instigated things with Lawrence. Number two—there was no question mark on the end of the message. She didn't like that he was trying to be all "commanding." There was only room for one alpha in this . . . well, you couldn't call it a relationship. In this . . . whatever this thing was. Anyway, the point was, they'd clearly established the fact that she was the one calling the shots. And number three—it was pretty damn presumptuous of him to assume she didn't already have plans this late in the day. Insulting actually. Oh, and one more thing—he was right upstairs in the office, he could have walked downstairs and asked her in person.

She had her "read" receipts on, which meant he'd know she'd seen the message. So Annalise purposely sat on it for a good ten to fifteen minutes, letting him sweat. Eventually she typed back a single-word message.

Doubtful.

His reply came back instantly.

Why doubtful? You know you want me.

She sent him an emoji of a face yawning.

Seconds later he sent a string of emojis: a red heart, a hand with the index finger pointing sideways, and then another hand making a circle shape followed by two more hearts. The message was more than clear.

Keep it classy would you? she flicked back.

Classy is boring. Blatant innuendo way better. Want a lift home?

Poppy gave her a lift home when she could, but she often worked late and Annalise didn't always want to hang around waiting for her, which meant taking public transport. She had to admit that tonight she wasn't particularly looking forward to heading to the train station and being crammed onto the busy platform with all the sweaty business suits.

You can give me a lift. But not saying you can come in.
Oh you'll want me to cum in.

She sent back a "sick" green emoji face.
He responded with a laughing emoji.
Dammit. Annalise knew it: he had her. She was flirting with him and she was going to take him home and screw him, and that meant he was going to have all the power.

She considered for a moment what this could be like if it wasn't all about who had the power. If it had nothing to do with playing complicated games or winners and losers. What if instead it was about telling the truth or saying what you wanted and when you wanted it? Or desire and kindness and seeing where things went?

But it just wasn't her.

In the car as they left the office, Lawrence tried to casually suggest they grab a bite to eat. Annalise knew what was happening—he was trying to turn it into an actual date.

"Not hungry," she said.

"Liar," he replied, "you're always hungry. I've seen you put away a double hamburger and chips and go back for a hot dog."

"When have you seen this?"

"Last year's office function for the launch of the new camera line."

"Yeah, well, you're not taking me out to dinner."

"Who said I was trying to take you out?"

"Lawrence, I see right through you."

"You're not as perceptive as you think. I'm just hungry. I'm going to stop somewhere and grab something to eat real quick. You can wait in the car if you want."

"Yeah, okay, sure, sure."

She thought she had him pegged when they turned toward the riverfront restaurants. "You can hardly call this a quick bite to eat," she began, but then he made another turn and another and next thing they'd turned into the carpark of McDonald's.

"Touché."

"Told you," he said as he parked the car and un-buckled his seat belt. "You want me to bring you back some nuggets or something?"

Annalise had to laugh. "I'll come in with you."

They walked inside and ordered separately, he didn't try to pay for her meal. Then he sat at one of the larger shared tables with a bunch of teenagers down the other end and Annalise took a seat opposite him.

Throughout their early dinner, they chatted about work, about soccer. He stopped with the lewd jokes and suggestive comments and Annalise was simultaneously caught off guard and put at ease. But the more they chatted, the more she shifted toward an understanding.

I don't feel that way about you, Lawrence. I just don't.

She loved his company. He made her laugh. He was decent in bed. He wasn't bad-looking. He could be a nice guy.

But she didn't feel *that* way about him.

It was a sad realization. She'd been playing this part for so long. This cool, easygoing, "I'm only here for the sex" role. And yet all this time, there'd been a small part of her that was half thinking, *Maybe I'm not just in it for fun. Maybe he'll find a way through. Maybe he'll wake me. Maybe I'll turn.*

So to know that he wouldn't turn her, that she

wouldn't wake, that maybe she never would, for anyone . . . it was sad. And the thing was, she didn't really want to break his heart. She wanted to be his friend.

When they were all done she went to the bathroom. When she came back to the table, thinking they were about to head off and wondering if it would be wrong to sleep with him tonight, she saw him waiting for her with three sundaes in front of him.

"I didn't know which flavor you liked," he said.

Annalise stood in front of the bathroom mirror and stared at her naked body.

"It wasn't about him," she whispered to her reflection. "It was about you. It was about you getting what you wanted, what you needed."

"What did you need, Annalise?" she asked, a little louder. The sound of sheets rustling made her fall quiet.

A low rumble of muffled music started to come through the ceiling and she looked up, tried to focus her hearing, figure out what Poppy was listening to up there. *Oh God, it was the Smashing Pumpkins'* Adore *album.* Arguably their saddest ever. Poppy hadn't listened to that since the very first days after Garret.

Pull yourself together, Annalise. This isn't you. You had a moment of weakness. A moment of hope. A moment of wondering if maybe you could make it work.

All over a fucking sundae. Forget about the sundae. The fact is, you can't create love where there is none. You want to turn out like Poppy? Listening to depressing music and pining for a guy who broke your damn heart?

Now you need to do one of two things:

One—go back to the way it was. Harden the hell up and keep using him however and whenever you want and who cares if you break his heart.

Two—call it off for good. Before he falls any further.

But how was she supposed to decide?

She picked a T-shirt up off the floor and pulled it on over her head, fished a pair of PJ shorts out of the wash basket, and stepped into them, not bothering to find underwear first.

Either way, Annalise, you don't hide in the bathroom after sex. This isn't you.

She strode into the bedroom and lifted one foot to prod at the slow-breathing lump under the covers with her big toe. "Up," she said. "Come on, up and at 'em. Up and at 'em and get out."

Lawrence rolled over and opened one eye to squint at her.

"Fuck you're a harsh bitch, Annalise."

"That's what my tombstone will say," she replied. "Here lies Annalise. She was a tough bitch. She fucked a lot of men and she never let them stay for breakfast. Now piss off, I have to go upstairs and see Poppy."

Lawrence sat up wearily. "You know, next time you call, I might not come running."

"Bullshit, you'll always come running. And if I remember correctly, you were the one who chased me today."

"I'm serious," said Lawrence as he lifted the covers to hunt for his underpants. "I do have some self-respect, you know."

"Ha! I've never seen it." Annalise turned away, pretending she was looking for his pants. But in truth she was hiding a stray tear that had sprung into one of her eyes. She squeezed them shut tight. Forced it away. Then she opened them again and spotted his pants on the floor. She picked them up between her toes and flicked them at him. "Hurry up. Actually, just let yourself out, will you? I'm going upstairs."

It was late, so she didn't think she needed to worry about running into anyone in her pajamas when she stepped outside her apartment door. Almost immediately the door opposite swung open and her neighbor charged out, pushing a stroller with a toddler wrapped up in a dressing gown. "Don't judge me," said the woman, a young mum with a strong South African accent who Annalise had met maybe once or twice before. "The only reason I'm taking her out this late is because she won't sleep."

Annalise shrugged her shoulders with complete indifference. She wanted to make it clear that she couldn't care less. "Um, all good by me," she said, unsure what the neighbor—what was her name again? Cynthia maybe?—was expecting her to say.

"Sometimes she's an angel. Tonight, she's the devil."

"Okeydoke," said Annalise, raising her eyebrows and bouncing on her toes, hoping Cynthia—if that was her name—wasn't going to want to keep chatting.

"Anyway, have a good night," said Maybe-Cynthia. She paused before adding, "I swear to God, you don't know how good you've got it."

Annalise left Maybe-Cynthia waiting for the lift and headed up one level via the stairs to knock on Poppy's door, once, twice, and then again harder, until the music was finally turned down. Poppy opened the door and stood back to let her in. She'd known who it would be.

"All right," Annalise said, "what's the deal? You haven't thrown up in the gutter in front of another random bloke, have you?"

Poppy laughed but Annalise could see she'd been crying.

"Nothing like that. Honestly, I'm all good."

Annalise pulled the door shut behind her and they both headed for the couches. Poppy sat down and curled her legs up underneath her and Annalise stood over her, sizing her up, wondering what had triggered the setback. "Is it because you didn't close the deal with Will?"

"Nah," she said, but a strange expression crossed her face when Annalise mentioned his name and she suspected it did have something to do with it.

"I'm just feeling emotional," she said. "I am allowed to relapse, you know? That happens."

"Relapse?" Annalise scoffed. "You're not a bloody cancer patient. Hasn't it been . . . you know, long enough now?"

Poppy threw her hands up in the air. "I don't know! I mean, it's been about five months but I'm not the expert on getting over your husband leaving you for your best friend. Either way, I do think you're allowed to keep feeling stuff . . . especially when you know that eventually, they're going to be bringing a new life into the world."

Ah, so that's what was bothering her.

"Yeah okay, but you've got time to prepare for that. We can make sure you're ready and by the time this baby's on the scene you're not going to care less. But for now, I just don't see the point in wallowing."

"Wow, you can be harsh sometimes."

"Can I? That's the second time someone's said that to me tonight."

"Tonight? Wait, did you have someone with you downstairs?"

Annalise looked away. "Yeah, no big deal."

"Lawrence?"

She nodded.

"And what made him call you harsh?"

"Just the usual. Me kicking him out after sex. You'd think he'd be used to it by now."

"Annalise, don't you think it's been going on long enough now that maybe . . . you know, maybe you could actually let him stay the night?"

"Don't you start on me. I get enough of this shit from him. Anyway, I came up here to talk about you."

"I swear I'm all good," said Poppy. "No rescuing required."

Annalise held her hands up defensively. "Okay, I'll drop it. But did you record *The Voice* tonight? Because I need something to do while I give Lawrence enough time to clear out."

"Of course I did, and of course I haven't watched it yet. You want a coffee?"

"Only if you put a shot of Kahlúa in it."

When Annalise got back downstairs to her apartment, Lawrence was gone, as she'd asked. But for once, as she climbed into the cold empty bed, a part of her— just the smallest part—was wishing he hadn't listened to her. She reached down to her bag that was sitting by the bed and searched through it for her notebook. The moment her fingers closed over the hard edges, she felt a sense of relief. Knowing she'd be able to pour everything out of her mind and onto the pages made her feel better.

Chapter 12

One day every week, Annalise doesn't drink. She figures it's pretty impressive—her level of restraint. People ought to hold a parade for her. One day out of seven when she doesn't consume alcohol. She knows that probably makes her sound like she's an alcoholic. If anyone asked her, though, she'd tell them that she's not. Because it's a choice. If she wanted to stop, she could. That's why she doesn't drink on Tuesdays. She's making a point. She can choose not to drink if she wants to.

On Tuesdays Annalise has a routine. She doesn't fuck men on Tuesdays. She comes home from work and changes into her leggings or shorts or track pants. Sports bra, singlet, trainers. She puts her soccer ball in her netted bag with the strap that goes across her chest.

She takes the stairs instead of the lift down to the ground floor of her apartment building. She jogs through the streets and down to the river. When she hits the grass, the ball comes out of the bag and she dribbles it along the riverbank. It's a challenge 'cause the grass is thick and there are weeds and rocks and muddy patches. Every now and then she almost loses it into the water. Maybe it teaches her bad habits—kicking a ball over rougher terrain instead of on the flat pitch—but it's awesome exercise. And then again, some of the local grounds they play on aren't that well taken care of, so maybe it's good for her game-playing skills.

After thirty minutes she reaches a concrete skate bowl. It's lit up by a couple of streetlamps, covered in graffiti and almost always deserted. Sometimes she wishes she had a board and knew how to skate. But she doesn't. So instead she uses it to train. She kicks the ball against the concrete sides of the bowl; she runs up and down the slopes. The ball echoes when it hits and bounces off at unexpected angles. More challenges. She goes hard until she hits the point of exhaustion and then she pushes herself some more.

If she thinks about having a drink, she kicks the ball harder.

If she thinks about calling Lawrence, or picking up

some random bloke for a one-night stand, she kicks the ball harder.

She doesn't stop until she physically must.

Not until her legs are jelly and her back aches and her chest is tight and burning.

The walk back to her place is painful but brisk. The thought of a hot shower spurs her forward.

Back at her place, she has a shower followed by a bath. Indulgent. Wasteful, she knows. But she needs to wash the sweat and grime off her body before she can lie down and soak. After all, who the hell wants to marinate in their own dirt? She fills the bath with Epsom salt and her torn muscles start to heal. A glass of wine would go down nicely with the bath, but she can refrain—because it's Tuesday. She drinks a Gatorade instead.

When she's done, she eats something simple for dinner—cheese on toast. Or a tin of baked beans.

But on a Tuesday night in early May, things went differently.

On that Tuesday night, she heard a thump from up-stairs.

The Imposter

She almost slipped up. Gave herself away. On the one hand, she'd grown so used to this fabricated persona that it came naturally to her. But on the other hand, she'd been a mother for so long that it was easy to fall back into old habits. *When my daughter was younger,* she'd started to write. *Holy shit!* she'd thought, clapping her hand to her mouth. *How did I almost write that?* Delete, delete, delete.

She started again: *When my niece was younger . . .*

PART THREE

Poppy

Chapter 13

Tuesday night Poppy put a scalpel through her hand.

She didn't do it on purpose. It wasn't an angsty teenage self-harm thing. Well, not entirely. She *was* being stupid, though. Stupid and self-destructive. Unfortunately, she had never been great with blood.

She'd been sitting on the floor in the lounge room and using the scalpel and a cutting mat to chop up some old photos for an album she was putting together for her mum and dad's anniversary. Her half-eaten dinner was on the carpet next to her—an open pizza box and a foil-wrapped stick of garlic bread. She was listening to the soundtrack from one of her favorite old films— *Dirty Dancing*—it was mellow enough to enjoy while she sipped on red wine and worked on the photos, but upbeat enough that Annalise wouldn't start banging on her ceiling to tell her to cheer up. She was feeling good. The previous night they'd won another game of soccer. Elle had put Poppy back into goals, where she felt at home again, while Annalise had been returned to striker and scored twice.

She took a break to scroll through Facebook on her phone and that's when she saw him. Garret. It was his face that caught her eye first. Obviously, they were no longer friends on Facebook, so she wasn't used to coming across his familiar features in her news feed. There was the initial shock, just at seeing him again—his round, cheery face, beaming out of the screen at her. And then there was the slow realization as she took in the rest of the photograph. The beige walls, the monitoring equipment. The hospital bed. She knew what this was.

And then she saw Karleen. Red-faced and sweaty. Strands of her curly hair sticking to her cheeks. A smile of pure unadulterated joy. Wrapped up in a pink-and-yellow-striped blanket in her arms was a squishy, wrinkled baby. All scrunched up eyes and mottled skin.

Why? Was her first thought. *Why am I seeing this! Why do I have to know that the baby is here?*

It was because they'd posted the photo publicly and

a mutual friend had commented. That's why it had turned up in her feed.

Okay, so what is this that I'm feeling? Why does it feel as though my body's just been coated in dry ice? I mean, it can't be jealousy, can it? Because I didn't want that. I don't. And I don't even want him anymore. I'm sure of it. I don't! So why am I reacting like this? What's wrong with me?

She started doing the calculations. What was the date today? Wasn't it far too soon for their baby to have arrived? That was why she was freaking out—because she wasn't ready. When did they split up? When did she arrive home to find the two of them waiting smugly at her kitchen table? How many months had it been? She counted on her fingers and her brain struggled to function, struggled to list the months in order. *January, February, March.* She chanted in that singsong tune she'd memorized as a child when she was first learning the names of the months. But eventually her mind slipped into gear and she had her answer. Karleen was already pregnant when they told her. And she would have been far enough along to have known. In fact, she would have been close to four months along. Was she showing? Had Poppy been so distracted that she hadn't even noticed a change to her friend's lanky body? *Four months*. The exact amount of time Karleen had said they'd been seeing one another. So, he'd knocked her up on day one, had he?

How could they not have told her? Hadn't they owed her that much? Hadn't they owed her the whole truth?

She tried to pick up her glass to gulp down some wine and that's when she noticed how much her hands were shaking. The red liquid sloshed over the edge of the glass and stained the carpet. She looked at the small pink marks and slowly, carefully, she got to her feet. She walked over to the kitchen bench and put down the wineglass. She searched through the cupboard until she found baking soda and then she took it back, got down on her hands and knees, and shook it over the stains. At first it sprinkled. A light dusting. But then she shook harder, until several small mounds of white powder formed.

She stared at them. She dipped a finger into one. Watched the small pile crumble. Pressed her finger into it. Focused in on the sensation of the cool, soft powder on her skin.

She spoke out loud to the empty room. "But . . . but why do they have to look so happy?" She hated the sound of her whinging voice, but for crying out loud, they shouldn't get to be happy, should they? They broke her heart. The two of them. They tore up her life, her world. They weren't supposed to be all full of joy. They were supposed to be miserable. They were supposed to fight with one another. What happened to karma?

And what about trust? Shouldn't there have been trust issues between the two of them now? Once a cheater, always a cheater, that's what they say. They built their relationship on the back of deception. Plus!— and she was on a roll now—why didn't they at least have the decency to play out their disgustingly happy life behind closed doors? Why did they have to flaunt it out in the open, right where she could see it? Right where they knew she'd end up seeing it?

And then there was wine. So much wine. All the wine. She gulped it down knowing she'd be vomiting in the morning. At some point, after the bottle was empty and her vision was doubling, she pulled up a chair at her dining table, opened up her laptop, and clicked back through to Facebook. She went to her happy place, NOP. But this time, she wasn't looking for friendly cheerful posts with positive reinforcement about her life choices. She was looking for the opportunity to tell some hard truths.

Who the hell else is DONE with the mothers of the world thinking they run the fucking joint? I'm talking about the women who get to park right next to the entrance at the shops in those special "parent's parking spots" just because they have a bloody pram. And they lose their shit if you park there for two seconds to grab a bottle of wine from the bottle-o or whatever (which may or may not have happened to me the other day). Why on earth do they even need those spots??! Or the women who think it's fine to let their kids scream in the middle of a restaurant when you're paying good money for a nice fucking meal and all you want to do is hold a conversation with your friends. Or the women who you work with who think they have the right to use their kids as an excuse to prioritize their own time above yours. Because I'm totally fed up with it. I'm sick of being nice and understanding and putting up with them judging me for my life choices. Ladies, I am PISSED.

The comments rolled in. She'd struck a chord with a lot of other members.

Nicole—*YES!! Me too. That's why I love this group so much. Because it's the only place I can completely escape all of that crap.*

Catriona—*Spot on. I've always wondered why shopping centers put in those "parent" parking spots. I mean*

spots for people with wheelchairs I get. Spots for the elderly I get. But being a parent isn't a disability, is it? It's
a choice. And my mum never needed a designated spot
to get me and my brother out of the car and into the
shops. Actually she always joked that having a spot far
away was best 'cause that was her only chance at fitting
in some exercise!

There were the odd comments where women weren't
quite as on board.

I don't know, said Bette, I think you're being a bit
harsh? I think it is pretty tough being a mum. Just because I never wanted to be one doesn't mean I don't
empathize with them.

While as usual, Jess only wanted to change the subject. Who cares! Seriously, there are more important /
fun things to worry about than a bunch of mothers who
have nothing to do with us. For example, I'm thinking
of creating an NOP spin-off group for other creative,
open-minded women who want to exchange amateur
erotic fiction. Is that something others would be up for?

But for the most part, people wanted to pile on. They
started to tell their own stories about dealing with the
parents in their lives:

Marns—My area manager didn't finish her work
'cause she left early to get her baby from day care, so I

*had to pick up the slack again this week. And she actu-
ally gets paid MORE than me.*

Carla—*Kid at my local café threw up on my shoes
last week, the kid's mum was too busy fussing over her
poor little diddums to bother apologizing to me. And
they were expensive shoes!*

Dianna—*My gym has started letting mums bring
their toddler into the morning yoga classes if they
can't get them into the crèche. It's very nice for them
and all—but it makes it a bit hard for me to center my
chakra when a high-pitched voice starts wailing that
they're bored and they want a milkshake.*

The posts filled Poppy with cruel hard pleasure. She
gulped down her wine as she relished in the hatred they
were all sharing for these nameless women. She put up
another post:

So why don't we do something about it, girls? I challenge all of you to stand up for yourself next time a
mother is using her "mum status" to get away with
something—you know, leaving work early, disrupt-
ing a yoga class, or letting her kid ruin a nice pair
of shoes or whatever. I want you to DO something
about it! Don't let the mum get away with that shit.
Stand up for yourself! I dare you!

It seemed like such a good idea at the time.

Later, when she'd run out of things to write on NOP, she came across a video on YouTube. She was mindlessly jumping from article to video to whatever mind-numbing thing she could find on the Internet, trying to take her mind off Garret and Karleen, when she found it. It was mesmerizing to her drunken brain. In the video, a woman had placed her hand on the table in front of her, spread out her fingers, and was stabbing the space between them with a knife. Slowly at first and then faster and faster.

Poppy knew it was a terrible idea to try it out for herself, but she did anyway.

The embarrassing thing is she hadn't even sped up yet when she plunged the scalpel right between the knuckles of her ring finger and her middle finger. At first she just stared at it, the handle wobbling as it stuck out of the back of her hand. There was no blood, and for just a moment—no pain. There was only a strange sensation of pressure. And then she pulled it out.

For another few seconds, it still didn't bleed. Then a small bubble of dark blood formed, and her brain caught up with her nervous system and there was a rush of pain. She panicked. The blood continued to bubble up out of the neat slice in her skin. It bubbled up and it dripped over. The more it flowed, the more her stomach turned. And the pain worsened. She had a bad feeling she'd hit something important. A vein? A nerve ending? An artery? She pushed back her chair and stood unsteadily. She ought to get something. A Band-Aid? Not big enough. A bandage, then. But did she have any? She caught sight of her reflection in the mirror that hung above her dining table. Earlier her cheeks had been flushed pink due to the alcohol. Now her face had turned sallow. There was a slick sheen of sweat across her brow. She tried to swallow but her throat felt as though it had closed over. The last glass of wine she'd downed at speed threatened to stage a return. Her brain clouded over and she reached out to grasp the back of the chair for balance but missed, her fingers closed around air. She tipped over, hitting the floor with a hard thud that jarred her shoulder. Her world turned black.

A few minutes later she opened her eyes to see Annalise's face swimming into view above her.

"Whatcha doing?" Poppy asked curiously, her voice coming out thick and slurred.

"That's an excellent question," Annalise replied. "See, Tuesdays are my night to myself. So I'm not overly happy to be here. But I heard a loud noise from my ceiling. And at first I thought, whatevs, it's probably nothing. But then I called your mobile and you didn't answer and so . . . here I am. Checking on you. Glad you gave me your spare key. Honey, what the hell have you done to yourself?"

Poppy tried to sit up and take a look but a rush of dizziness forced her back down. Her head was heavy and her body felt sluggish. *What did I do?* She tried to remember.

She closed her eyes and an image of the scalpel sticking out of the back of her hand appeared. *Ah, that's right.* She opened them again and lifted her arm so she could take a look at the damage. It looked like Annalise had wrapped the wound up in something. A rag? A tea towel? Whatever it was, it was stained red.

"I think I fainted . . . not great with blood."

"I think we have to take you into emergency," Annalise said. "Or at least the medical center down the road. I can't get the bleeding to stop, I think you hit something important. Your hand is shaking. Can you straighten your fingers?"

Poppy attempted to comply.

"Two of your fingers are still bent. That can't be a good sign. Can you sit up, slowly?"

"I think so."

With Annalise's help Poppy managed to carefully

make her way into a sitting position. "Hey, Lise," said Poppy as she paused to stop the room from spinning. "Why are you always the one taking care of me?"

"Because I never need help."

"But you must . . . sometimes. Everyone needs help sometimes."

"How about we focus on the injured one just now? Come on, let's get you up on your feet."

Annalise put an arm around Poppy's waist and supported her as they made their way out of the apartment. In the lift, Poppy tried again. "One of these days, you'll be the one in trouble. And when that day comes, I want you to come to me, you hear me?" Poppy leaned in close, attempting to make meaningful eye contact with her friend, but Annalise clapped her hand over her mouth, pinching her nose at the same time, and turned away. "Holy shit, Poppy!" Her voice came out muffled and nasal. "How much did you drink? Your breath could start a fire."

"Couldn't. Would need something to ig-ignite it."

"You know what I mean."

The lift shuddered to a stop on the ground floor, and before they stepped out, Poppy paused. All three walls inside the elevator were covered in mirrors, which meant Poppy could see both of them reflected, over and over. Hundreds upon hundreds of Poppys and

Annalises, repeated forever. Each and every Poppy, a drunken, disheveled mess. Each and every Annalise, a composed and capable friend, taking care of her charge. Poppy lunged away from Annalise and pressed her face against the glass. "In one of these . . . just one, I'm in there looking after you."

"Bullshit." Annalise took her by the arm and pulled her out into the foyer as the doors tried to close on them. "In every single one of them, I've got your back."

They ended up cabbing it the short distance to the local medical center, where the on-call doctor was irritatingly good-looking. It was humiliating to explain how she'd come to stab herself with a scalpel to a square-jawed, blue-eyed Adonis. Plus she was still a little inebriated, which meant her attempts at trying to sound sensible and sophisticated were failing miserably.

Luckily she had Annalise by her side ready and willing to humiliate Poppy herself.

"So it's like this," Annalise explained, "my girl here got herself sloshed, saw a pic of her ex on Facebook with the new partner, all happy shiny families in hospital with their new baby, and she–"

Poppy cut her off. "I wasn't sloshed first," she said, as though it was highly relevant. "I got sloshed *after* I saw the pic."

"Sorry, of course," said Annalise, "and then she decided to try the knife-between-the-fingers trick. Why did you do that again?" she asked Poppy.

"Video of it came up on YouTube. Looked like fun."

"Fun?" said the doctor. "Not my idea of fun."

"Yeah, well, we all got different ideas of fun, don't we?" said Annalise. "Maybe yours is dressing up in your wife's knickers and bra and a feather boa on the weekend, but I wouldn't judge you for it if it was."

For a moment the doctor looked horrified, then he burst out laughing. "All right," he said, pretending to wave up a white flag in defeat, "no judging here. And no, I don't dress up in my wife's knickers," he added, "because I don't have a wife." He winked at the both of them. "But a feather boa sounds like fun."

The rest of the consultation was a lot more relaxed, at least until he finished his examination and told Poppy he was concerned she might have suffered some long-term damage.

"Long-term?" she asked. "Seriously? But I'm a goalie, I need my hands."

"It's okay," Annalise interrupted. "Next Monday night is a bye for soccer, so you've got more time to recover."

But the doctor shook his head. "Long-term is well beyond a fortnight. There's no way you're using that hand to catch a soccer ball for the next few weeks, maybe even months. You've ruptured an extensor tendon and they're not quick to heal. I can stitch you up now with a local, it's a fairly straightforward procedure with a small incision so I can locate the ends of the cut tendon and reunite them, but it's followed by a lengthy period of rehabilitation. How long? I can't say for sure."

"Elle's going to kill me."

Chapter 14

At first Poppy forgot she'd even posted her challenge on NOP the previous night. But she was notified of a comment the following day and it all came flooding back, making her cringe at how nasty she'd been.

They were having their next NOP catch-up at a restaurant that evening, and apparently there were going to be ten women attending this time. It had all been arranged by Carla, and Poppy was feeling some trepidation as she and Annalise arrived. Would some of the women be less than impressed with the previous night's Facebook tirade?

They wove their way through the dining area and found the group sitting at a large round table by the fireplace. Poppy only recognized three faces—Kellie,

Jess, and Carla. The rest of the women were unfamiliar and they all introduced themselves one at a time. At first, Poppy tried to keep up with the names, but in the end she gave up and took her seat.

A waiter approached and offered wine and she tried to decline. After the previous evening she wasn't up for alcohol, but Annalise coaxed her—"Don't underestimate the hair of the dog"—and Poppy gave in. "Fine, just one," she said.

"Hey, thanks so much for arranging this," Poppy said across the table to Carla. "I've been a bit slack lately with getting members together."

"Not a problem," she replied brightly.

"Where's your friend you brought last time?" Annalise asked.

"Sophie? She couldn't get here tonight."

"Who's looked at the menu yet?" asked one of the other women whose name Poppy had already forgotten. "I'm leaning toward the beef cheeks."

"Yuck," said a redhead to her left. "Vegetarian here," she added. "I'm looking at the eggplant lasagne."

"Forget about dinner," said Kellie loudly, gaining the attention of all nine other women, "who else wants to talk about Poppy's massive rant on NOP last night?"

"Epic," agreed the redhead. "Swear to God, you

don't know how much I've been holding back with my posts because I wasn't sure if others would be on board with too much bitchiness. But now those gates are open, there is so much I want to get off my chest."

"Anyone completed the challenge yet?" another woman asked.

"Me!" exclaimed the beef cheeks fan gleefully. "Already did it today. I met one of my old high school friends for coffee in my lunch break. Every time we get together she shoves her phone in my face to show me photos of her kids and I have never been the least bit interested in seeing them, but I always act the part and ooh and aah over them. But not today! Today I pushed the phone away and said 'no thanks.' You should have seen her face!"

Poppy's stomach flipped. That wasn't what she'd meant when she set that challenge. She'd wanted people to stand up for themselves if they were being marginalized, not turn against their friends because they were bored of looking at photos. That was plain mean.

"Oh my God," said Jess. "Sweetie, I think you need to get laid if you've got that much pent-up frustration over a couple of photos. How did your friend react?"

"Well, she wasn't impressed, obviously. But I'm sure she'll get over it."

Poppy doubted that. She couldn't imagine Nolan being particularly forgiving if she refused to look at photos of his children.

"I did one too!" said a tall blonde who was sitting next to Carla.

"Oh yeah?" said Poppy, her voice full of nerves as she waited to hear what came next.

"I invented an appointment for myself this afternoon so my area manager couldn't leave before me to pick up her baby as per usual. I waited until I saw her about to pack up and I just said, all casual, 'Hey, Philippa, I have a doctor's appointment today, so I have to leave early.' And she was all put out and started to say, 'But what about the Finnigan proposal' and I said, 'You'll be all good to finish that, won't you?' And then I gave her this really sweet smile and said, 'You totally owe me after I wrapped up the Allacino job, right?' I mean what could she say? It was awesome."

Poppy felt relieved—that was actually fair enough. Why shouldn't she have a bit more give and take at her work? It was more in line with what Poppy had wanted to achieve with the challenge too.

A waiter approached to take their orders, and as they chose their meals, Poppy hoped the conversation would move on to something else.

The rest of dinner ended up being fairly uneventful.

Despite Annalise's attempts at plying Poppy with more wine and hinting she ought to hit on the cute waiter, Poppy managed to stick to only one and a half glasses, and she enjoyed the company and the fact that they stopped talking about mothers. One of the women did bring up Poppy's bandaged hand, asking her what she'd done to herself, but Poppy brushed it off as a "silly accident" and thankfully, the woman didn't push for more of an explanation.

As they were sorting out the bill—and arguing over whether they should split it evenly among everyone or have each person tally up how much they'd each spent and pay for their own meal—Poppy glanced sideways and saw Annalise's red notebook peeking out of her handbag. She was filled with an urge to reach across and grab hold of it so she could open it up and see what it was that Annalise was always writing about in there. But a moment later, Annalise had pushed it back deep inside the bag and zipped it shut.

Throughout the week, the nastier posts on NOP continued to grow with more and more members keen to take up (and expand upon) Poppy's original challenge.

Dianna—*I had a go at a family at my local pizza place last night because they were refusing to do a THING about their kid who was tearing around the restaurant, screaming his head off and almost tripping over the* *waitstaff. I actually think the waiters really appreciated me stepping in and saying something.*

Catriona—*So I have a stack of nieces and nephews, and all my sisters and brothers expect me to turn up to celebrate every little milestone and I don't think any of them has ever considered just how much money I have to fork out for gifts for them. Well, last week two of my nephews had birthdays, so when the fam-bam got together at the park to celebrate I decided to mess with them by giving one of 'em a card with fifty bucks in it and the other—the shitty one I once caught breaking a Christmas gift on purpose 'cause it wasn't the "right brand"—a card with only ten bucks in it. Totes hilare seeing them compare their spoils and the looks on their faces—priceless. Waiting to see if my sister (the one who has the shitty kid) is going to have the gall to call me out on it and if she does . . . well, who knows just what I might say to her.*

Nicole—*I was at the Pear and Fig with a few other women for a business meeting. This group of mums came in and I just don't understand why they would choose this café for their mother's group catch-up. There's so many other cafés that are more suited—you know, more space, more noisy, whatever. The Pear and Fig is known for being a corporate hangout. Anyway, I look over and as I'm watching this kid starts pull-*

ing one sugar sachet after another out of the container in the center of the table and he's opening each one up and tipping them all over the table. And the mum isn't doing a single thing to stop it. And I just thought, this is ridiculous. I happen to know the owner of the Pear and Fig and I know they work hard to turn a profit and things like sugar packets are one more expense that this mother was letting her kid completely waste for his own amusement. I'd had enough. I went over and let the mother have it. I'm sorry but I just couldn't let her get away with it. And you know what she did? She didn't clean it up, she just LEFT!

As the stories continued to pour in, there were clearly some people in the group who didn't like it. They lost a few members—women who said that wasn't what they thought the group was all about. To be honest, Poppy wasn't sure she blamed them. But there were others who loved it—they relished completing the challenges, they thought it was hilarious. The group was taking on a life of its own.

OMG! commented one woman on Catriona's post. *I have two nephews and I refer to one of them as "the shitty one" too! How funny is that. My sister would die if she knew, she thinks he's an angel.*

Another comment read, *Well, I have a thirteen-year-old niece who is the devil incarnate and, same as your sister, my brother thinks she can do no wrong. Yet I can tell she's the bitchy girl at school who bullies all her friends. What is it with parents and their inability to see past their kid's big blue eyes?*

If Nolan and Megs had a daughter next, Poppy couldn't imagine ever thinking about her niece that way, even if she did grow up to be a bit of a queen bee. She'd like to think if she had any concerns about her own niece, she'd be able to chat openly with her brother about it. But then again, maybe this woman was right— maybe her brother would be blinded by his daughter's "blue eyes" or whatever, and maybe it wouldn't be so easy to broach such a subject.

Either way, it was all hypothetical for Poppy, whereas the stuff happening on NOP was very real and very current and she wasn't sure she could put the lid back on Pandora's box.

It was one thing to bitch to each other. It was one thing to tell the world you don't want kids or you're just not a kid person or whatever. But to start waging war against parents? Well, Poppy supposed they were all just doing exactly what she'd told them to do.

"Say something," she'd written in that original post. *"Stand up for yourself."*

She should have deleted it the moment she was sober.

Annalise kept trying to reassure Poppy that it was all harmless fun. "So what if some of our issues are creeping out into the real world?" she reasoned. "Why shouldn't we be allowed to be honest about the way we feel?"

And then new challenges started popping up. Members who thought Poppy's idea deserved to be expanded even further.

I challenge you to choose a venue that's NOT kid-friendly for your next get-together with your friends or your family. When the parents within the group complain that it doesn't suit them, tell them you're done accommodating them!

Here's another challenge for you all! If you have to buy birthday and Christmas gifts for your friends' kids or your relatives' kids, it's time to tell the parents it's not fair and they need to cough up for it themselves! Because you're never going to have children, which means they're never going to spend the same amount of money on you, are they? I don't know about others, but I reckon I spend hundreds each year!

Poppy didn't know what to do. Should she put a stop to it? But how could she demand that other members refrain from setting challenges when she was the one who'd kicked it all off?

Others kept it fun and light, though. For instance,

Viv was somehow able to continue to tell stories about her annoying neighbors' kids that Poppy could relate to without being so harsh.

> Kids next door were having a screaming match this afternoon—something to do with Pokémon (don't ask because I can't explain it). It was driving me up the wall. Anyway, next thing their mother is banging on my door. I've barely opened it up before she asks, "DO YOU HAVE ANY WINE?" If she wasn't on the verge of tears I would have killed myself laughing. She snuck inside for a quick vino—not sure if her kids even noticed her missing—and I gifted her with the rest of the bottle to take home and enjoy later after the little monsters went to bed. It was a good reminder that even though I might find their noise annoying, it's ten times louder and more stressful for her.

Viv made Poppy empathize with her and she made her laugh at the same time. And to be honest, Poppy thought that was the kind of healing she needed, not this insidious poisonous joy the other women were sharing at someone else's pain.

But the worst thing was that sometimes a part of Poppy *would* want to join in with those nastier conversations. She would remember Garret and Karleen and everything they'd done to her, and she'd see the image of the two of them in that hospital room, holding that neatly wrapped package, and the same hatred she'd felt on the night of the scalpel would surge up inside. She wondered if she was no better than any one of the women on NOP who were turning nasty and cruel. If she saw Garret and Karleen in person, would she have to fight against the desire to say something horrible. *Your kid is ugly. I hope your kid ruins your life. I hope your kid screams the house down every single night.*

She didn't like finding that much hatred still inside of her.

Chapter 15

They were halfway through the next Monday-morning meeting when Poppy's phone started lighting up like a Christmas tree on the table in front of her. She placed a hand over the screen, and when the flashes continued through the gaps between her fingers, she flipped the phone facedown and tried to pretend nothing was happening, even though several other managers were glancing toward her with curiosity.

Meanwhile, across the table, Annalise started vibrating.

ERRRRGH.

ERRRRGH.

The buzzing sound from inside her jeans pocket was insistent and she shifted in her chair, pulled out her phone, and turned it off.

Now every manager in the room had their attention on Poppy and Annalise.

"What's made the two of you so popular all of the sudden?" Lawrence asked.

"Excuse me," Frankie said from the other end of the table, "but can we please stay focused? We've still got a few more items on the agenda to get through."

The moment the meeting ended, Poppy and Annalise escaped into another meeting room and locked the door behind them.

"All right," said Poppy, unlocking her phone to check her notifications, "what the hell is going on?" A second later, a wave of nausea washed over her. "This is all hate mail," she said, opening one message after another, her fingers fumbling, becoming more and more frantic as she checked each one. They were coming through to her personal Facebook account and appearing in the separate NOP admin inbox. She was being bombarded with angry messages. She couldn't keep up with them. They just kept coming. She read one aloud to Annalise: "'Who the hell do you women think you are? What gives you the right to judge us, to write these horrible things about us? You're all a bunch of nasty old bitches who deserve nothing but pain and unhappiness.' Why would someone say something like that to me?"

"It's me too," said Annalise. "I'm getting the same messages. Oh, Poppy, I'm so sorry, I should have said something sooner."

"What do you mean, said what?"

"We got a couple of these messages recently. But I deleted them and blocked the senders. I didn't want you to be upset."

Poppy remembered the phantom notifications. Now it made sense. "But why would it matter if you had told me. What difference would it make?"

"I don't know . . . But maybe we could have stopped it before it got this insane."

"How?"

"I don't know!"

Poppy was transfixed by her screen as the angry messages continued to flood in. She saw horrendous words and snippets of phrases flash up as Facebook gave her a taste of each message.

Fuck the lot of you.

Mangy cunts.

You Utter Bitches.

"Oh no," Poppy said suddenly.

"What is it?"

"I just got an email from my mum . . . look."

Annalise leaned over and they both read the email together.

Hello Darling,

How are you?

Listen, I feel awful to "cut straight to the chase," as they say, but my friend Edna just phoned me, and well, she was in a bit of a fluster. She said her daughter Susan told her about some "FACEBOOK GROUP" that she claims you're heading up and she seemed to think you were antimothers and making fun of mums like her Susie and well, she was just a bit hurt, I suppose. On Susie's behalf.

I reassured her of course that that doesn't sound like you AT ALL and that she must have her wires crossed, but well, like I said, she was in quite a state and so I thought I should at least "follow up," as they say.

I know you're recovering from your divorce and your dad had a big talk with me about how I need to lay off, so it's wonderful if you've found a bit of an outlet. But I did wonder if this group might have something to do with your new friend Annalise? And maybe that's where the mix-up has happened?

Much love to you and give me a call when you can to talk about this.

Mum X

They finished reading the email at the same time. "Bloody hell," Poppy said. "Mum's friend Edna and her daughter Susan don't even live in Parramatta. They live out Sutherland way. How did they come across it?"

"Maybe she has a mate here in Parra who told her about it. And by the way, you've never told me how much your mum clearly loves me."

"Annalise! Not the point right now."

"Okay, fine, whatever. Let's check the member posts, see what other people are saying."

They pressed their heads together as they clicked through into the group to check for updates.

"Damn," Poppy whispered, only a few seconds later.

It looked like a whole heap of their members were being targeted. There were countless posts and conversations among women within the group all discussing the fact that they'd been the recipient of nasty messages. And many of them said the messages had come from women who signed off as "proud members of MOP."

"So it's not just random mothers targeting us, it's all MOP women, then?" Poppy said.

Annalise read another one out loud. "Hey, girls, be careful what you say on here, I think someone in this group is *not* who she says she is. Someone *has* to be reading what we're posting here in NOP and passing it back to MOP, because I just got a message where one of my previous posts was quoted back to me, word for word. This group is private, so there's no way they could have seen it unless they were a member."

Poppy looked at Annalise. "Do you think she's right? Do you think one of our members is a mole? An imposter?"

Annalise nodded. "She has to be right," she said. "How else would they be able to see what we're saying?"

"I guess I stopped vetting members properly. So many women wanted to join, I got slack."

"This is utter crap," said Annalise. "We weren't actually doing anything to hurt them. They should just stay the hell out of our lives."

"That's not entirely true, though, is it? Annalise, this is all my fault."

"What do you mean?"

"I told people to stand up for themselves and our members got mean. They started letting mothers have it—out in the real world. No wonder these women are angry."

"Don't blame yourself. As far as I could see, no one stepped over the line. People were only being more honest, that's all."

"Check out our member count as well," said Poppy. "Last time I checked we were about to hit seven hundred. And that was even with the few women who dropped out because they didn't like the challenges. Now we're back down to five-fifty. A whole heap of women have been intimidated into leaving. That's not fair. Lise, what the hell are we going to do?"

"We're going to bloody well fight back."

"How?"

"Hang on. Scroll back up, what's that link Kellie's posted?"

They read the post together.

Kellie—Ladies, I think I've just discovered the reason why every mother in the area seems to suddenly have intimate knowledge of NOP. Click through to this article.

Poppy obediently pressed on the link and they simultaneously gasped when they saw the headline of the article published to the *Parramatta Gossip and News* site:

SHOTS FIRED!
LOCAL MUMS UNDER ATTACK FROM
NEW WOMEN'S GROUP

BY ANONYMOUS

When I was tipped off by a friend that a new local Facebook group had started up, I knew that I had to find a way to get myself on the inside. You might wonder why? Well, membership is restricted to one very specific group: NON-MOTHERS. And digging deeper: no men allowed, just women, but women who not only don't have children, but they also don't WANT children. Ever. They call themselves NOP (Non-Mums Online in Parramatta), perhaps out of jealousy that they were unable to join popular local community group Mums Online in Parramatta (affectionately named MOP). I'm sure they thought they were very clever coming up with that one!

Now, as a mother with two children, I am obviously not eligible, so I created a fake Facebook account. I joined the group, and to begin with, it was mostly friendly and harmless. But the mood quickly changed.

When I found out that the group's founder, Poppy Weston, was betrayed by her husband and her best friend who went on to have a child together, alarm bells started ringing. Was this about connecting women with a shared interest? Or was it really about getting back at Poppy's ex–best friend? Was it a defense mechanism after her husband took away her chance to have children?

I knew I had Poppy pegged right when she put

up an angry post that could only be described as a call to arms. Our fearless leader has had enough of the mums of the world "running the joint." She's decided it's time for the women of NOP to start standing up for themselves. To tell mums what they really think.

Now, I can't speak for any other mums out there, but as a mother of two little angels / monsters—I sure as hell do not feel like I'm running the joint. And the last thing I need is to start copping crap from other women who think I'm somehow ruining their lives.

I want to issue a warning to local mums: watch out for childless women in the shops, in restaurants, in cafés, or on the street who are raring to have a go at you if you so much as bump their ankle with your pram. Because the ladies of NOP are out for blood.

In the meantime, I'm still a member under my false name and I'm going to remain there until my cover is blown, because someone needs to keep an eye on these women. Good luck on the streets, mamas!

Poppy was livid. "Who the hell is this person?" she spluttered. "How does she know so much about me?

About us? Right down to the fact that Garret left me for my best friend?"

"I don't . . . I don't know," said Annalise. "I seriously don't get it. I mean, I guess I've bitched to some people within NOP about how much of a dick Garret is for the way he treated you . . . but I didn't think I went into that much detail." She looked guilty but Poppy was too caught up in her anger with the writer of the article to pay too much attention.

"And how dare she make those assumptions about my reasoning for starting the group! I was jealous of MOP? Please! And she thinks Garret took away my chance to have children? That I don't even know what I want? It's absolutely ridiculous!"

"I know," said Annalise, "it's horrible. And she claims she's still a member! We have to figure out who she is. We have to get her the hell out of our group."

"But . . . but how?"

"Let me have a look and see if there are any comments on the post where the article was shared. Maybe someone has an idea?"

Once again, they looked down at the phone together. Unfortunately, the comments were filled with women who were just as flummoxed as Poppy and Annalise, and members who were worried their previous posts on NOP were no longer safe:

Nicole—*If my best friend knew what I'd said about her kids—oh my God, that could tear our relationship apart. Jesus, I didn't really mean those things. I was just venting. Hamming it up for you guys as well. Also really hate the way the article keeps calling us "non-mothers" or "childless." I don't appreciate being defined by the absence of children. Besides, I'm not child-LESS, I'm child-FREE, thanks very much.*

Jess—*We need to know who it is in this group. Is she really still here? How did she become a member in the first place? I thought membership was tight! I thought I was safe to share with you guys. I know I come across as very open-minded, but I was actually only comfortable with discussing my sex life or sharing my erotic fiction with you all because I believed every-thing I said would stay within this group.*

Kellie—*If you've said something you don't want to get out, I suggest you go back and find it and delete it NOW. As long as the mole hasn't already screen-grabbed it, you'll be okay.*

Catriona—*Well, I'm already fucked, so thanks a fucking lot to whoever the hell it is on here who decided to attack us. My sister just phoned me crying because she saw a screen grab of a post I wrote here that had been shared on MOP. In it I complained a bit about her kids—the kind of thing I would never have said to her face.*

Poppy's anger turned to despair and she slumped down into a chair and began to cry.

"Oh, honey." Annalise wrapped her arms around her friend. "Please don't cry. That bitch doesn't deserve your tears. Don't give her the satisfaction."

Poppy tried to stem the flow of tears but she was so worked up that she was sucking in air, choking and spluttering like a heartbroken toddler. She wished tonight wasn't their bye at soccer. Even if it was giving her hand more time to heal, she would have loved to take all of her frustrations out on a soccer ball right now.

Annalise sat down next to her and snatched up her phone again. "I'm going to find her. I'm going to figure out who the hell she is."

PINNED POST

ATTENTION MEMBERS ** Please Read!
A note from the NOP moderators**

We're aware of the current hostility between some members of MOP and some members of NOP and we're working on a way to get it all sorted out ASAP. We're also working to see if we can get the *Parramatta News and Gossip* article removed. In the meantime, we're so sorry that some of our members have been targeted with abusive messages. We've definitely been copping the bulk of these messages too and we know how much it sucks. But please don't feel bullied into leaving NOP. We all know how great this group has been for connecting as women and supporting one another and just generally making new friends, and there's no reason to let a bunch of mums who've got the wrong idea about us put an end to those connections we've made. We'll keep you all updated on the situation. Thanks for your patience, Poppy and Annalise.

Chapter 16

Saturday morning, Poppy went down to her home ground to do some training. With everything that was happening with NOP, she needed a release, something to take her mind off the drama. Plus, with her injured hand she was going to have to be out on the field full-time during games, so she had to improve her fitness. The kids' games were on but there was an empty field where a bunch of spectators were kicking a ball around. She dumped her gear near the goalposts and took off for a jog around the edges of the pitch. The sun was warm on her back and it wasn't long before she'd taken off her jumper and tied it around her waist.

When Elle had pulled her out of goals during their first game, she'd been shocked to realize how hard it was to run for an extended period of time. She was sure she used to be much fitter than this. And actually, if she was completely honest with herself, she also used to *look* a lot fitter. Had her slightly rounded figure been yet another factor in Garret's decision to choose Karleen over her? But adding on a few extra pounds after getting married was normal, wasn't it? And it wasn't a fair comparison; Karleen had always had this amazing metabolism, meaning she could eat anything she wanted and never gain an ounce. It was the one thing Poppy had always envied of her. That and her curls.

Poppy had once complained to Garret about the fact that her hair had no body, said she wished it was more like Karleen's. They'd been lying in bed together in the darkness. Garret had reached out, stroked her face, and mumbled sleepily, "Nah, I love your hair. Karleen's is too big and poofy. She looks like Ronald McDonald. Yours is sexy."

Lies.

Poppy wanted to feel fit and she wanted to look it too. If she ever saw Garret again, she wanted to look hot. She wanted him to regret giving her up.

As she ran, Poppy tortured herself with thoughts of the last few days. So much for using the training to take her mind off her problems. Since NOP had come under attack from MOP, things had gone from bad to worse.

A lot of their members were taking things into their own hands. There was post after post with opinions from different women on how they should handle it.

Marns—*Can we please get someone into MOP? Start causing trouble from the inside for them! See how they like it?*

Carla—*A NOP friend told me the other day she overheard a group of mums at a café talking about us. They were calling us a bunch of middle-aged, bitter, twisted, barren bitches. She said she wanted to say something but she was on her own, so she decided not to engage. It really got to her, though, she left the café in tears. We need to do something about this, those MOP women are AWFUL.*

Nicole—*So! Any guess on who our mole is?!!*

Poppy shut down the last thread quickly. Of course she wanted to know who the hell the mole was—more than anyone else there—but she didn't want this to turn into a witch hunt. They'd already lost enough members because of this whole nightmare. She wanted to find the mole in her own way. She just didn't know how. She could hardly go through every single member one by one.

An image popped into her head. In it she was sitting in a dimly lit office with a woman opposite her, a bare wooden table between them.

"So you say you don't have kids, do you?"

"Of course I don't! I hate kids!"

"Oh yeah? So what's with the mashed bit of banana IN YOUR HAIR!"

She saw the woman slump forward to sob into her arms at the table. "They made me an offer I couldn't refuse! I got in too deep! I'm sorry!"

The idea amused Poppy enough to make her smile, which was nice for a change.

She'd also tried contacting the gossip site where the article was posted, begging to find out who wrote it and also for it to be taken down. But she was met with cut-and-paste responses.

Thank you for your email. We pride ourselves on giving our writers the option to be fully anonymous and to betray that anonymity would fly in the face of our guidelines.

Further to our previous response, please note that we have taken your feedback and concerns on board. However, on this occasion we have chosen to keep the article live due to community interest.

Annalise had been keen to further exacerbate things by pushing to make this an all-out war between the two groups.

"We should tell everyone to fight back. Get them to start PMing the MOP members the way they're spamming us. We can't let them just get away with this."

But Poppy had convinced Annalise to take a step back and give her some time to see if she could find another way to fix it first.

So far they hadn't provided any further updates to their pinned post from the other night, because Poppy simply didn't know how to deal with it. Should they shut NOP down and start fresh under a new name with tighter security around membership? Or ride it out and see if it would all blow over? Or maybe they ought to go with Annalise's idea and fight back.

It was all too much. And the entire thing was her fault for coming up with the idea in the first place. If only she hadn't posted that night when she'd been so hurt and so very drunk. And once things had escalated from there, she should have stepped in and said something. Stopped NOP from turning so ugly before it was too late.

The one positive was that so far, Nolan and Megs hadn't heard a thing about it and Poppy had been able to placate her mother by assuring her it was a misunderstanding. No one from her family had come across the gossip article. If they did, Therese would be unstoppable in her belief that Poppy *did* want children.

And Nolan would be hurt by the things she'd said about parents.

Poppy gave up on her laps. Her chest was starting to hurt and her legs were burning, so she headed over to the goalposts where she'd left her kit, thinking about what kind of drills she could do on her own. She supposed she'd start by taking the ball up and down the pitch and then maybe try a few shots at the goal.

She was dragging the ball back with her toe, when she realized someone was approaching from behind.

"Hey!"

It took a second for Poppy to place him, but then she remembered—it was the guy at the pub who'd tried to warn her off going home with Will a few weeks back. She supposed it wasn't that unusual to run into him there considering he was a member of the same club. But it was only kids' games on today, so it still took her by surprise.

"Oh, hello," she said. They stood awkwardly. What exactly was he expecting from her here? It wasn't like they were old mates. They'd had a brief conversation at the pub when she'd been completely drunk and had chosen to ignore his advice. What were they really going to say to one another other than "hey"?

"Doing some training?" he asked.

"Yep."

More awkward silence.

"Hey, I didn't ask you that night we met if you won your game."

"Yeah, just scraped in."

"And, ah . . . how about the rest of your evening? Score another win?" He raised his eyebrows at her and she glared back.

"Um. Not really any of your business, is it?" She sidestepped around him with the ball and kicked it halfway down the pitch so she had a good reason to sprint away from him and chase it down.

When she caught up with the ball and turned back around, though, she saw him walking toward her.

"Sorry," he began, but he said it at just the wrong distance away from her, so yet again there was an awkward silence as he realized he'd tried to start chatting too soon and had to jog the last few steps to catch up to her. "Sorry," he said again. "That was super weird. For some reason in my head I thought it would be funny, like break the tension or something. But as soon as I said it I realized it just sounded sleazy."

"What tension?" Poppy asked irritably.

"You know. The 'will they won't they' tension the two of us clearly have going."

"Are you completely deluded?" she said. "I don't know you. I don't even know your name!"

"Ah fuck," he said, looking down at his feet. "I did it again. Trust me, that sounded so charming in my head. I'm sorry, I'm terrible at this. I'm Jack, by the way."

"Poppy," she said reluctantly. "But seriously, what exactly do you think 'this' is?"

"Us flirting?" he said, a hopeful note in his voice.

"Oh!" She was caught completely off guard.

"Any chance you could forget like, *all* the dumb things I've said so far today? Seriously. Just wipe them from your memory. I feel like a complete dick."

Poppy chewed on the inside of her cheek. "Yeah, all right. But listen, I actually am trying to do some training. So . . ." She trailed off, hoping he'd get the message, but he grinned.

"That's actually why I came over. I saw you were training alone and I was checking to see if you wanted someone to train with you. You know—it's more fun if you have someone to pass the ball to . . . isn't it?"

She was about to decline, but goddammit he had such a hopeful puppy-dog look.

"Yeah, okay, fine," she said. "But no more of your hopeless attempts at flirting, right?"

"Scout's honor."

They ran back and forth the width of the pitch a few times, passing the ball between them without speaking, apart from the odd "sorry" called out when the ball was mis-kicked and caused the other to break their stride and chase it down. After a while they stopped and threw one another some high balls for headers, and then kneed it back and forth.

"How come you're down here this morning anyway?" she asked eventually, breaking the silence.

"I coach the under-eights. They had an early game and I was just packing up to leave when I saw you running laps. Recognized you from the other night and thought I'd come over and make a complete fool out of myself, 'cause that's always a fun thing to do on a Saturday morning. Actually, it makes for a perfect Saturday morning, seeing as my team got completely slaughtered as well and one of the dads had a go at me. So yeah, grand start to the weekend."

Poppy smiled for the second time that day. "Yeah, that sounds like a rough day. Hopefully the rest of your weekend will go better, eh?"

"Here's hoping. So why were you training alone?"

"Oh, I'm usually in goals, but I stupidly hurt my hand, so I'm trying to get used to being out on the field again."

"You're a goalie? Nice. What did you do to your-self?" He glanced down at the square bandage across the back of her hand.

Poppy regretted mentioning it at all. She was too embarrassed to explain, so she brushed it off in the same way as she had at the NOP dinner. "Just a silly accident. Come on, let's take some shots at the goal."

Jack asked for her number but she didn't give it to him.

A few reasons: to start with, he was weird. All that awkwardness with how they met and his terrible flirt-ing skills. And then there was the fact that he coached a kids' soccer team. Guess who must think that makes him perfect future daddy material? Or then again, for all she knew he could already have a kid on the team. She hadn't thought to ask. He probably thought he could melt her ovaries by pulling the kid card. And finally, she simply wasn't looking to meet anyone right now. Or anytime soon. Sorry, buddy—not happening.

The training was good, though. He did teach her one or two decent moves that she hadn't seen before.

That afternoon the twins were having a birthday party at one of those play centers. Nolan had assured Poppy it would be bearable, even for his child-hating sister.

"I don't *hate* kids, Nolan," she'd exclaimed, a note of hysteria in her voice as she panicked that perhaps he really *had* seen the article. "I'm just not a kid person."

"Well, either way, there's a quiet, grown-up area and they have good coffee—so it'll be bearable for all of us."

His voice had been kind, so she decided he hadn't seen anything and her secret was still safe.

Nolan's description of the center was a bit of an exaggeration. The place was a nightmare. A serious assault to the senses. Oh God, the noise. The noise and the colors, the sticky lino floor and the squeaky plastic chairs. The coffee was dishwater. Either Nolan had talked complete bullshit on purpose, or he had a very different idea of what was bearable for adults. The worst part was the sudden high-pitched screams from the frolicking children. Poppy felt as though she was in a horror movie, or a social experiment to test how much sensory overload a person could handle.

She was sitting eating leftover chicken nuggets and calculating the minutes until she could politely make her escape when she overhead her name.

"Actually, Nolan grew up there but Poppy still lives in the area."

She looked up and saw Megs chatting with another

parent, and Megs waved at her to move closer. Poppy obediently switched chairs to join in on the conversation.

"Laura and I were just talking about the social media blowup that's happening over your way," Megs said.

"Oh yeah?" Poppy hoped her voice sounded politely curious rather than slightly horrified.

"Have you heard about it?" Laura asked. "Apparently a group of women started up a Facebook page to rebel against a local online mothers' group and now there's some sort of big fight going on between the two groups, which is getting way out of hand. I heard that a woman from the new group gave a peanut-butter cookie to a kid in a restaurant because the kid was being too loud and she wanted to shut him up, but the kid was allergic and went into anaphylactic shock. The mother had to use an EpiPen on him. I mean really, in this day and age most people should know better than to hand an unknown child something with nuts in it."

"Oh my God," Poppy said, "was he okay?"

"Yeah, the mum acted quickly enough, he's fine. So, you haven't heard about any of this, then? Are you a member of the Parramatta Facebook mothers' group?"

"Poppy doesn't have children," Megs cut in quickly, and Laura looked momentarily embarrassed.

Then she said with a laugh, "Well, I guess that makes

you the smart one out of the three of us. No wonder you have such a nice top on. I could never get away with wearing white—it would last all of five seconds before it got smeared in Vegemite or apple sauce."

Poppy managed a smile. "Yep, definitely a bonus of not having kids."

Inside she was panicking. She hadn't seen or heard a thing about this allergic reaction story. And why were people from the Northern Beaches hearing about NOP?

"You still have plenty of time, of course," said Laura, reaching out to pat Poppy's hand.

Poppy shifted her hand away. "Not an issue," she said shortly. "I'm not going to have children."

"Oh, right," she replied. "Sorry, I shouldn't have brought it up. But listen, I've had friends with fertility problems, and with the right treatment, they were still able to conceive."

For fuck's sake. Was she for real?

"No, no," Megs interrupted, "Poppy doesn't *want* to have kids."

Poppy had to admit, she was kind of surprised. She and Megs had never really had much of a relationship beyond exchanging polite sister-in-law pleasantries. But there was a note of pride in her voice when she spoke instead of the usual judgment or disbelief that most people expressed.

"Right," said Laura. "Well, I am going to go and grab myself a muffin before I put my foot in my mouth anymore. It was nice to meet you, Poppy."

She got up and hurried away and Megs gave Poppy a sympathetic look. "Sorry," she said. "Laura's never had all that much tact. I bet you get that all the time. Other women making assumptions about why you don't have kids or feeling sorry for you because they think you must be pining for them. It must really suck."

Poppy was stunned. "Yes," she said, "all the time. Sends me insane. So, considering my own parents don't seem to get it, how come you're so perceptive?"

Megs leaned back in her seat. "It's not really hard to understand, is it? Don't worry, I'm working on your mum for you. Whenever she comes round to see the kids and drops comments about you having them one day, I drop my own hints right back. She'll get it eventually."

She paused before adding, "So are you a part of the other group? The one we were talking about in Parramatta?"

Megs mustn't have seen the article, then, otherwise she'd know full well that Poppy was a member. She tried to shrug in an indifferent sort of way. "Oh, you know, it's sort of meant to be an anonymous thing."

Megs shook her head. "Say no more," she said. "Just

be careful, okay? I've heard there's some really nasty stuff going on with that feud. I'm a member of a Northern Beaches online mums' group, and mostly it's pretty good. You know—helpful advice and that sort of thing. But even within the group the women can get bitchy at times. I can only imagine what it must be like between two opposing women's groups."

Poppy nodded. "All good, I'll be careful."

Soon after, she managed to escape the party. On the way home she wondered what Megs would think if she knew that rather than simply being a member of NOP, Poppy was actually the founder. Would Megs feel differently? Would she be disappointed in her? And also, she was going to have to see what she could find out about the story of the kid going into anaphylactic shock. That news had her rattled.

Tuesday morning at work Poppy went to see Paul and found Frankie's desk empty and his office door shut, the blinds drawn. She assumed they were both out at a meeting and had turned to leave when she heard a noise from inside his office and looked back. She stepped closer. She heard whispered voices.

What the hell? Were they seriously going at it right there in his office in the middle of the day? Poppy suddenly found herself wondering when and where Garret and Karleen had shared their secret trysts throughout those four months when he was cheating. Did they meet up during the day? On their lunch breaks? Did Karleen visit Garret at his work? His office was open-plan, he sat in a cubicle, so it's not like he could have pushed her up against his desk as Paul was probably doing right now with Frankie. Not unless they particularly enjoyed having an audience. Maybe they rented a room at a cheap hotel. Or climbed into the back of Karleen's car like they were teenagers.

Poppy was livid. How dare Frankie and Paul put their partners through that same humiliation and hurt that she had so recently experienced. And how dare they bring it all back to the surface for her. Enough was enough. Paul's wife needed to know what was going on.

She stepped quickly behind Frankie's desk and tapped her computer awake. Searching through Frankie's business contacts, she found Linda's number and scribbled it down on a Post-it note before hurrying back to her own desk.

Sitting down, she pulled out her phone and opened up her messages. But now that she was ready to say something, she didn't really know how to word it. She tried to imagine what it would have been like if someone else had told her about Garret and Karleen before they'd confronted her themselves. Would she have been less distraught hearing it from someone else? At least she would have gone into their little "meeting" prepared. But would she have trusted the information if it had come from an anonymous source? And would it have been more of a shock—receiving a random text out of the blue like that?

Poppy decided to put the question to NOP. At least it was something to distract everyone from the whole MOP mess. She would post the question, wait for at least five responses, and if the majority said do it, she'd do it.

Quick poll. Say you know two people are having an affair. Do you dob them in?

She tried—unsuccessfully—to distract herself with work while she waited. Eventually she checked back for comments and saw there were already about ten. She skimmed through them.

Marns—*Of course you do.*

Viv—*I'd want to know.*

Kellie—*Need to know more, depends on circumstances. Can you give details?*

Jess—*How do you know both couples don't have an arrangement in place where they're allowed to see other people? Opening up your relationship to other parties* can be a great way to keep things fresh. So it could be all aboveboard.

Dianna—*Absolutely. No excuse for cheating. Who cares about the circumstances.*

Carla—*You realize there's always two sides to every story, right?!*

In the end, the overall consensus was a resounding yes. They'd made the decision for her. It was the right thing to do. Linda deserved to know. Poppy hated the idea of another woman going through the same horrendous heartbreak she'd suffered. Hopefully Linda had a good friend she could turn to for comfort and advice. And hopefully she would confront Paul, not let him get away with it.

Poppy decided to keep it simple and straight to the point.

Linda, I'm so sorry to be the one to tell you this— but I'm an employee at Cormack and I think you need to know that your husband isn't being faithful to you. Again, I'm really sorry.

The second she sent it, she kicked herself. She should have checked if there was a way to block her number. Although maybe that only worked for phone calls? She wondered if she should block Linda's number now that the text had been sent so she couldn't call her and quiz her about what she'd said. Maybe she'd been too hasty sending that message. Maybe she'd made a terrible mistake. She jumped back up from her desk and headed down to the warehouse to see what Annalise thought about the whole situation.

Poppy found her directing one of her staff on a forklift and she waited impatiently for her to finish. When she was finally done, Poppy beckoned her over and they walked out onto the driveway to chat alone.

"So," Poppy said, "Paul and Frankie were at it again just now."

"What do you mean 'at it'?" Annalise asked.

"I mean I went to see him and his office door was locked and the blinds were down and—"

"Eww! That's so gross, in the middle of the day with everyone right there? You're kidding me?"

"So it got me thinking . . . don't you think Paul's wife should know what's going on?"

"What? Like you mean you want to tell her? You really want to get involved in that?"

"Um, that's the thing—I kind of already did . . . get involved."

Annalise closed her eyes and took in a deep breath. "Fuck's sake, Poppy, what have you done?" she said.

Poppy squirmed, embarrassed about her rash action.

"I take it you didn't see my post on NOP just now? Okay . . . so I stole her number off Frankie's computer and sent her an anonymous text."

"Shit. What did you say?"

"I just wrote that I was sorry but I didn't think her husband was being faithful to her. That was . . . pretty much it."

"And?"

"And what? That's all I said."

"*And* did you get any response back? Like did she ask who you were or how you knew or anything?"

"No, no reply."

"But she has your number now, what if she calls you, what will you do?"

"I don't know!"

"Well, you can't answer it. She can't find out you're from work, you could end up getting yourself fired."

"Oh."

"Oh? What do you mean 'oh'?"

"Well, I did sort of mention that I was from Cormack—I just wanted to lend the text some credibility, that's all."

"Jesus. And what about Frankie's husband? You took down his number and texted him as well?"

"Oh. I hadn't really thought about him."

Annalise raised her eyebrows. "So why didn't he get a look in?"

Poppy looked down at her feet, considering Annalise's question. But the answer was obvious. She hadn't worried so much about Frankie's husband because she couldn't relate to him in the same way as she did to Linda. When Garret and Karleen cheated, Karleen was a free agent. She was the archetypal "other woman." While Poppy was the scorned wife. Poppy had slotted Frankie neatly into the part of "other woman" and Linda took on Poppy's position. Frankie's partner didn't score a role. Poor bloke. Now that Poppy began to think properly about him, she felt a wave of empathy for the guy. He was just as hard done by as Linda.

"I just . . . didn't think," she said.

"Probably for the best," said Annalise. "I mean I'm all for stirring up a bit of drama, you know me. But I'm worried that you're potentially risking your job."

"So what do I do?"

"Leave it. Promise me you won't do or say anything else. Let's at least wait and see if she responds to you, then we'll figure it out from there. But if she does reply, let me know the second you hear from her, okay?"

"Okay," Poppy said. "Hey, by the way, I meant to ask—have you heard anything about a woman from

NOP giving a kid something to eat in a restaurant because the kid was bugging her and the kid having an allergic reaction?"

"Nope, haven't seen anyone talking about anything like that on Facebook. Why? Where did you hear it?"

"Just something someone mentioned. Don't worry about it."

A delivery truck came up the driveway and they both moved out of its way. Poppy recognized the company name on the side of the truck—it was a place Annalise had previously worked for.

"Here's one of your old mates," she said.

Annalise frowned back at her. "One of my old mates," she repeated. "What do you mean?"

"Didn't you say you used to work for Langum's Holdings?"

"No," she replied, "I've never said that."

"Oh," said Poppy, "I must have mixed it up with something else."

Poppy didn't know if Annalise was aware that she'd been part of the hiring process when she was appointed as warehouse manager. That was before the two of them had become such good friends. And the truth was, Poppy had picked up on a couple of discrepancies on her résumé—the dates Annalise had listed for the time spent at one of her past jobs didn't line up with that company having gone into liquidation. But Poppy hadn't thought too much of it—deciding Annalise was probably just padding out the time to increase her experience—and still put her forward as the best possible candidate to Paul.

But now, as Poppy sat back down at her desk, she crossed one leg over the other and jiggled them irritably. She pulled the elastic out of her ponytail and redid her hair, twice. What was going on here? The truth was, she didn't believe she had that company name mixed up. She was sure she remembered Langum's being listed on Annalise's résumé. She still had Annalise's documents on file, so she decided to look them up and make sure.

It didn't take long for Poppy to find the answer. She was right, and so now she had to question if Annalise had lied about more than that.

Poppy scanned the résumé, looking to see if anything else jumped out at her: graduated from Fairfield High School; completed a certificate in management studies at TAFE . . . studied at Sydney University.

Sydney uni. Sydney uni. Why was that tripping something in her brain? It clicked—the night they went to the pub after soccer, Annalise had been wearing a Macquarie uni jumper. Okay, so that wasn't such a big deal, was it? Wearing a jumper with a logo didn't really mean a thing. It could have belonged to an ex-boyfriend, or been borrowed from a friend.

But it bothered her.

It was her mum's fault. Therese's voice in the back of her head, questioning who Annalise was. Questioning where she came from. Poppy was annoyed with herself for never having asked. They were friends, it shouldn't have always been about her own problems and issues. Friendship was supposed to be two-way. So why didn't she know anything about Annalise beyond the woman she saw in front of her? Why had they never chatted about Annalise's childhood, her family? What had high school been like for her—had she fit in, had she liked university, had she kept in contact with any old uni friends?

Weren't these the kinds of things Poppy should have known?

All of a sudden Poppy was finding herself feeling more alone than ever in the NOP disaster. Because if she couldn't even trust her best friend—the woman who'd helped her start the group in the first place—who could she trust?

And if she couldn't trust Annalise, did that mean there was a chance the "imposter" within the group was even closer to home than she imagined? But that was ridiculous, wasn't it? Annalise didn't have any reason to betray NOP. They'd started the group together, they were on the same side. It didn't make any sense.

Then again, she'd thought she and Karleen were on the same side. For a moment, she felt a pang of longing for her old friend. Not the Karleen who'd betrayed her, but the one she'd loved way back before she'd even met Garret. The one who held her hair back so she could be sick after she had five Midori Cream cocktails on her eighteenth birthday, even as she scolded her for drinking too much. The one who helped her study for her final high school exams: "You're smarter than you think you are, Poppy, you just have to concentrate." The same girl who once had a crush on Nolan, and Poppy had fantasized about how wonderful it would be to have her best friend become her sister-in-law.

But next she saw Karleen sitting at her kitchen table, telling her she'd fallen in love with her husband. And the longing in her heart dissolved.

Thank God Nolan had always thought Karleen was a pain in the arse.

Poppy wriggled back into the large, soft chair, then leaned forward again to examine a spot on her chin in the mirror. Blackhead, she concluded before sitting back once more. Where did that come from? Maybe she should book in for a facial sometime soon. She had to admit, the treatment at this hairdresser so far was the best she'd ever received. An apprentice was bringing her a proper espresso, plus she'd been asked which hand cream she'd prefer for her complimentary hand massage.

The appointment had been set up for her by Annalise a couple of weeks back.

"You need a change. I think you should do something radical," Annalise had said. "Get an undercut with patterns shaved into it! Dye it blue!"

"Are you kidding me? You could get away with shaving the side of your head, I'd just look like I'd been in a terrible accident or had brain surgery."

And they'd both fallen about laughing. But that was before everything had blown up with NOP. And before Poppy had started to have her doubts about Annalise.

She still hadn't asked her about the lies on her résumé. Poppy didn't know how to bring it up without it seeming like she was ambushing her, but she knew she'd have to say something eventually. This wasn't the kind of the thing you could simply ignore.

She didn't know the hairdresser Annalise had booked her into. Poppy had never been the type of person to have a regular stylist. Usually she ducked into one of the discount "Cuts Galore" salons for a quick trim and left it at that. But Annalise had made the Saturday-morning booking and assured her she'd heard great things about the place.

She decided that when her hair stylist came over, she was going to throw caution to the wind and tell her she did want something radical. Something brand-new! As long as it didn't involve clippers, the stylist could have free rein. Well . . . as long as she told Poppy what she was going to do before she did it.

A young woman with a long plait hanging over one shoulder finally approached and stood behind her, catching her eye in the mirror. She introduced herself as Wendy, and Poppy picked up a southern American twang to her voice.

"So sorry to keep you waiting but your stylist wasn't feeling great, so we've fallen a bit behind."

"That's no good. I hope she's okay?"

"Not to worry, she'll be fine. Now, what are we doing for you today?"

"I need a change," Poppy said, a slight wobble to her voice. "Something completely different."

She was waiting for Wendy to turn into one of those stylists you saw on television makeover shows, brimming with ideas and excited to have a blank canvas to work with. But instead her shoulders sort of slumped.

"Oh yeah?" she said, not a hint of enthusiasm in her voice. "So, what kind of a change do you want?" As she waited for a response she absentmindedly pulled Poppy's hair tie out and started running her fingers through her hair, fluffing it out.

"I don't . . . I don't know," she said falteringly. "I was hoping . . . you might . . ." She felt silly and stopped short, unsure of what to say. Maybe she should just ask for a shampoo, blow-dry, and her usual centimeter off the ends.

Poppy noticed a guilty expression cross the stylist's face.

"A big change!" she said, and it was clear she was forcing an excited note into her voice now. "That's a great idea. We can do that. Cut, color, style—the works. Let me grab some pictures we can flick through and get an idea of what you do and don't like."

Ten minutes later they had a plan. Well, Wendy had a plan, Poppy wasn't entirely sure she'd completely followed as she'd flicked between magazines, hair color charts, and an album of photos of previous clients.

Next thing she'd run off to mix color and Poppy had no idea what was coming next. What was it about hairdressers that made her lose all of her assertiveness and turn into a meek schoolchild?

A younger apprentice came over to do her hand massage while she waited for Wendy to come back with the color.

When Wendy returned, Poppy nervously cleared her throat and asked carefully, "Sorry . . . which color did we land on?"

Wendy winked at her in the mirror. "Trust me," she said, "you'll love it."

For most of the coloring process, Wendy worked in comfortable silence, her face filled with concentration as she painted on the color and wrapped sections of Poppy's hair up in foils. But just as she was finishing, she let out a sudden sob that made Poppy jump.

"Are you okay?"

Wendy bit her lip, she looked embarrassed. She piled the last section of colored hair on top of Poppy's head, peeled off her gloves, and set a timer. Then she pulled a spare chair across and sat down next to her.

"Sorry," she said, and her voice choked up for a second. Poppy waited.

"It's really stupid," Wendy continued. "I shouldn't be letting it get to me—it's one of those things that keeps running around and around in your mind, though." A tear escaped and she wiped her cheek with the back of her hand. "You don't need to hear about it. It's totally inappropriate for me to be acting like this with a client." She stood up ready to move away, but Poppy caught her arm.

"I can listen. If you want to talk."

Wendy sat back down quickly, as though that was exactly what she'd been hoping for.

"It's this group I'm in," she explained. "An online mums' group."

Poppy's chest tightened. "MOP?"

"Yes! Are you a member?" she asked hopefully.

"No." Poppy decided not to elaborate on why.

"Well, I only joined recently," Wendy continued. "I have a two-year-old and someone told me it was a great place for new mums to get advice and meet other local mums, and I didn't have a mothers' group because I only moved here recently from overseas. Plus . . ." She paused, looking like she wasn't sure if she wanted to say the next bit. Poppy gave her what she hoped was an encouraging smile.

"Plus, I've been dealing with . . . postnatal depression. So pushing myself to get out of the house, to go and make friends . . . it's been difficult."

Poppy nodded and stayed quiet to let her continue.

"So at first it seemed really nice, but then the moderators of the group put up this warning notice about this other group—this non-mums group that was supposed to be full of women who hated everyone in MOP. And I was all like, oh okay, whatever, that doesn't really affect me, does it? But then I got invited to take my son out on a playdate with a few other mums I'd been chatting with on MOP. We went to this café here in the center—the Pear and Fig—I don't know if you know it? I don't think it was a good choice, to be honest. Not really enough room for all our prams and a bit too cool or trendy or whatever for a group of babies and toddlers to be crawling about the place. I had my little boy sitting on my lap, and I was talking with the other mums and I wasn't paying attention to what he was doing, and next thing I look down and realize he's opened, like, eight sugar packets and tipped them everywhere."

Poppy's stomach dropped. She already knew this story.

"I was about to start cleaning all the sugar up," Wendy continued, "and one of the other mums starts laughing and saying how cute Henry is—that's my son—and next thing, I realize these three women at another table—no kids—are staring. They're all shaking their heads at me in this real judgmental way like I'm the worst mum in the world for letting him do that. One of them gets up and walks over to us. 'Let me guess,' she says. 'A little MOP gathering, is it?' And then she goes on about how us mums always think we own the place and we can do whatever we want and she says she knows the owner and she's going to get kids banned from the place because all they do is make a mess and ruin everything, and apparently, my kid opening sugar packets was the last straw!"

Wendy paused and shook her head. "Sorry, you probably think I'm insane, like why am I all teary over this, right? But it's just that this was the first group of mums I'd met since I moved here and now I feel too embarrassed to see them again, 'cause they'll probably think I'm a terrible mum for letting my kid do that, and 'cause I've single-handedly gotten us banned from the Pear and Fig, and it's all so stupid because it's over something like a buck-fifty worth of sugar or whatever, and the most humiliating part is . . . I took off. As soon as it all happened, I was just so taken aback by the way this woman was talking to me that I just . . . I just left. So even if those mums didn't care about Henry tipping the sugar everywhere or the café banning us or whatever, they aren't going to want to hang out with me again because they must think I'm a basket case."

"Oh God, that sounds horrible. But . . . how do you know this has anything to do with the online group of non-mums?" Poppy asked, even though she knew full well it had everything to do with NOP.

"The woman told us they were members of NOP and that they were done putting up with our shit."

Poppy cringed inwardly and felt a sense of self-loathing.

She hesitated, trying to decide the right thing to say, but Wendy suddenly stood up. "Sorry, I shouldn't have been dumping all of this on you. Anyway, your color's got to stay on for another thirty minutes, you've got some magazines there to take a look at, and I'm just going to leave you to it."

With that, Wendy hurried away and disappeared out the back of the shop. Poppy sighed. She picked up one of the magazines and flicked idly through the pages, not taking in any of the pictures or stories in front of her, but instead thinking hard about what she might be able to do to help Wendy.

As she turned the pages, an idea began to form. What if she popped down to the Pear and Fig herself to ask them if they really did have an issue with what Wendy's kid had done? Just because the NOP woman had claimed she'd be able to have children banned didn't mean she'd managed to actually follow through. Hopefully Poppy would be able to reassure Wendy that it wasn't all as bad as she'd thought.

Poppy hopped up from her chair and strode out of the salon. She'd never in her life walked out of the hairdresser with foils in her hair and a cape over her clothes.

She knew plenty of women did—to go to the bathroom or maybe order a coffee—but she'd always preferred to stay hidden until she was completely done. Today, she didn't care. She was angry with herself for causing this woman so much hurt and she wanted to fix it. All of it.

She knew she must have looked a state when she burst into the café, cape flying, hair sticking up. She asked for the manager and explained Wendy's story.

"Are you kidding me?" he responded when she was done. "We have absolutely no intention of banning mums and I couldn't care less about a few packets of sugar. Look," he added, leaning in to whisper conspiratorially to Poppy, "I know the women you're talking about, the ones who made a fuss about that group of mums last week. Yes, one of them is an old friend, but she doesn't speak for me. They like to think this place is their corporate hang, but the truth is, mothers' groups make up sixty percent of my business. Trust me, you'll never see the day that we start turning away parents. So, if that mother is a friend of yours, you can tell her from me, she's welcome back here anytime."

Poppy was thrilled. That was the best response she could have hoped for. She couldn't wait to reassure Wendy. She returned to the salon and took her seat, picking up one of the magazines again to pass the time until Wendy returned.

By the time she reappeared—a good five minutes after the timer had buzzed, Poppy hoped her color hadn't been left on too long—Poppy was practically bursting to tell her what she'd done.

She was stopped short, however, by the expression on Wendy's face as she strode up and looked down at the back of Poppy's head. She wasn't upset again, and she wasn't smiling either. Instead her face was scowling.

"Time to take these out," she said, her voice clipped. She tugged roughly on one of the foils, pulling Poppy's hair hard as she removed it. "Yes," she said, "color's ready. Over to the basin." She stood back and pointed, her words more a command than an invitation.

Poppy stood up hesitantly. "Um, Wendy," she said carefully, "is there something wrong?"

Wendy glared back at her. "No," she replied. "Nothing at all. Could you hurry, please? I have other clients I need to get to after you."

Poppy was stung. What could have happened since Wendy had left her to make her turn so completely? She made her way obediently over to the basins and took a seat at the first one.

"Not that one!" Wendy snapped. "The next one over."

Throughout the entire wash it was more of the same. Wendy tugged and pulled at Poppy's hair as she ripped out one foil after another and Poppy was too shocked to speak up about how much she was hurting her. When she rinsed out the color the water was too hot and she skipped the conditioning head massage altogether.

Poppy was almost in tears, wondering what she could have possibly done wrong, by the time they returned back to her spot in front of the mirror.

"How do you want it cut?" Wendy asked, a nasty glint in her eye as she picked up the scissors.

"Wendy, really, could you please tell me what I've done wrong?"

"You know what, if you really want to know, then sure, I'll tell you. While I was out the back I was chatting with one of the girls—the one who was feeling sick—and guess what? Turns out she knows you. So we're chatting away and then she tells me that you happen to be the founder of NOP. Isn't that interesting? Bet you were having a good laugh to yourself as I told you how much those women had hurt me—all along you were one of them."

"What? No! That's not it—"

Poppy was cut short, though, as Wendy grabbed a handful of her hair and hacked it away. It was too much. Poppy wrenched her head out of her reach. "Hey! No!"

Her raised voice caught the attention of another stylist, who hurried over to see what was happening. As soon as she saw the back of Poppy's head, she gasped.

"Oh God," said Poppy, "what does it look like back there?"

"Um," said the stylist. "Just give me one minute." She pulled Wendy away by the elbow, and after a few tense words, Wendy vanished out the back and the new stylist returned to Poppy.

"I am so sorry about this. I'm Sonya, the manager here, and I promise you, I'm going to fix this."

It took the best part of an hour but eventually, Sonya was all done. She comped the service to make up for Wendy's treatment, and while Poppy's hair was the shortest and darkest it had ever been, she had to admit, Sonya had done an amazing job salvaging it.

She just wasn't sure she really deserved it.

Chapter 17

S he waits too long before making a move. She's going to need to make her decisions a lot faster in the game," Annalise said, jogging lightly on the spot to warm up her legs.

"I know, it's driving me crazy. Last time Jen went in goals for that half game she did a great job. But for some reason tonight she seems way more nervous."

Poppy turned away, she didn't want to watch anymore. It was their first game back after the two-week hiatus due to a bye followed by a forfeit, and their match was set to start in twenty minutes. Elle was coaching Jen, who was going into goals. Poppy tentatively touched the scab that had formed on her left hand. *Maybe I could manage . . .*

"I know what you're thinking." Annalise raised her

eyebrows at Poppy. "You can't. The doc said it would need longer than this. Why don't you go over and give Jen some tips?"

"I tried. Elle's still too pissed with me. She sent me away with a single look. Woman is fierce."

"I'm fiercer," Annalise said.

"All good, I should be warming up anyway. I'm still not used to all the running, much prefer staying inside my little box."

"Come on, we'll do a lap of the pitch together."

They took off at a light jog. Annalise was wearing the same Macquarie jumper and Poppy wondered if she should try to broach the subject of the gaps in her résumé with her. She didn't know how to begin, though, so instead she decided to tell her about the incident at the hairdresser. Annalise had already complimented her on the new hair and praised her for being bold by going so short. But Poppy hadn't mentioned Wendy yet.

"So I saw firsthand the results of a NOP/MOP altercation out in the real world the other day," she said as they ran.

"Oh yeah? What happened?"

She began to outline the story for Annalise, sticking to the important details because she was running out of breath. By the time they'd finished their lap and they stopped by their gear to stretch, Poppy had just got up to the part where she'd stuck up for Wendy at the café and was about to get to the good bit—returning to the salon only to find that Wendy had turned on her—when Annalise interrupted.

"So you took her side?" she asked.

"Well, it's not really about sides, is it? It's not a primary school fight. She was upset and I helped her out." Poppy lifted one foot to her backside to stretch her quads, resting her hand on Annalise's shoulder for balance. "But anyway, that's not the point," she said.

Once again, Annalise interrupted her. "Helped her out by having a go at the NOP girls who'd 'upset' her?"

Poppy could feel Annalise's shoulder tighten underneath her hand. "I didn't have a go at them," she said.

"No, I don't mean directly. I mean behind their backs. You were like, bad-mouthing them to this hairdresser chick, right?"

"I didn't agree with what they'd done." Poppy swapped legs and this time she balanced on her own.

"Why not?" Annalise was reaching down to stretch her calf muscles. "I mean, isn't that what NOP was supposed to be about in the first place? Women like us taking the world back from all those mummies who think they own it and have the right to do whatever they want?"

"No. Not exactly. It was about *connecting* women like us, not warring with mothers." Poppy stopped stretching and put her hands on her hips, watching Annalise, waiting for her to lift her face so she could read her expression. "You know how I feel about the way the group has turned since I put up that stupid drunken post."

"Yeah, I know how you feel, I'm just not sure I agree with it. I mean the whole reason we needed our own place was because mums like that were driving us crazy—noisy kids in restaurants; kids like the one whatsername mentioned on NOP recently, the one that threw up on her shoes and the mum didn't give a shit. Or the mum who changed her baby's nappy on a fricken table in a café." Annalise straightened and stared at Poppy now. Her face was hard and angry. Poppy hadn't seen that expression before—not directed at her anyway.

"Yeah, I guess," Poppy said slowly, carefully, "but only to a point. I mean, yes, we wanted to be able to whinge and bitch about crap like that, but we weren't supposed to start confronting them."

"Why the hell not?"

"So you think a woman deserves to be confronted just because her kid tips some sugar on a table?"

"Yes, I do! Because even though a little bit of sugar might not seem like a big deal, it's representative of something bigger. It's representative of a whole society of women who think they can get away with whatever they want because they're the all-holy untouchables. They're mothers."

"Annalise, I'm sorry, but that's not why I created NOP."

"*We* created NOP. Together. Besides, when you first came up with the idea it was less about women being all pally-pals with one another and more about you being pissed at there being some secret club that Karleen was going to be a part of and you couldn't be."

"This doesn't have anything to do with Karleen!"

"Bullshit. It has everything to do with Karleen. And you were a hell of a lot feistier back when you came up with the idea than you are now."

Bloody hell. She knew Annalise was a big supporter of the women on NOP, but she still expected her to have more empathy than this once she heard about what Wendy had gone through—once she'd heard what it was like from the other side.

"All right," Poppy said, "well, what about the thing with the kid who had an allergic reaction? Are you on NOP's side on that one? You think that woman had every right to give a child food without checking with the parents first?"

"Actually, I looked into that one. I found a news story

on it. That had absolutely nothing to do with NOP, it happened in Adelaide about six months ago, before we'd even started the group. But the story's doing the rounds on social media again now. And I'd say someone from MOP has decided to twist the details to use it against us."

"Oh," Poppy said, "I didn't know."

Annalise shot her a look of superiority that grated on her, and all of a sudden she found herself blurting out the question: "Hey, I thought you went to Sydney uni."

"Huh?"

"Your jumper," she said, "you're wearing a Macquarie uni jumper. But I thought you went to Sydney uni."

Annalise gave her a funny look. "No," she said, "I went to Macquarie. But we've never even talked about where I went to uni anyway, so I don't know why you thought I went to Sydney."

Their argument was cut short then—Elle was calling them over for a pregame chat. Several other players gave them sideways looks as they jogged over; Poppy hadn't realized how many of them had been listening in as the two of them had argued. Obviously, Annalise didn't know Poppy had seen her résumé. Or maybe she'd filled it with so many lies she'd actually forgotten she'd ever put Sydney uni on there. Either way, something really strange was going on. And it was too late to tell her the rest of the Wendy story now as well.

Weirdly enough, the game was the best Poppy had played in a long time. It could be hard to tell which way it would go when you were worked up. Would it throw you off? Cause you to make unforced errors? Or would it fuel you and push you harder than ever?

Apparently for Poppy, tonight it was fuel.

For Annalise, it was the opposite. She was way off her game and the more mistakes she made, the angrier she got. Elle took her off at halftime and didn't sub her back on for the rest of the game. Poppy saw Elle trying to talk to her every now and then, but it looked like Annalise wasn't in the chatting mood. Meanwhile, Poppy scored one goal and set up another. Jen shook off her nerves and once again did brilliantly in goals. They finished up winning 3–1.

When the whistle blew and they were shaking hands with the other team, Poppy looked over just in time to see Annalise's back disappearing over the hill.

As Poppy was packing up her gear, Jen tapped her on the shoulder. "Hey, is this yours?" she asked. She held up a slightly tattered red notebook and Poppy instantly recognized it.

"It's Annalise's," she said. "Must have fallen out of her bag. I'll give it to her at work."

Jen handed it over and Poppy stared down at it, filled with the desire to read it. Annalise might have said she just kept work notes in there, but Poppy could tell it was much too important to her to be simply a few scribbled warehouse orders or anything like that. She figured the only reason Annalise had even managed to drop it tonight was that she'd stormed off so quickly. However, Poppy resisted the urge to open it and instead stashed it in her own bag.

She looked over at the field next to theirs, where another game was being played. It was a men's game—Parramatta vs. Guildford. She stood watching for a minute, to see how Parra was going. She told herself it had nothing to do with Jack, but she couldn't help scanning the players' faces, checking to see if it was his team. If she did spot him, it would only be to let him know she'd tried out one of his suggested moves in the game tonight and it had gone okay for her. That was all.

He didn't seem to be there. It must have been a different side. She started to head off and had reached the end of the field when she heard a voice call her name. She looked around and realized it was Parra's goalie shouting at her. She squinted and saw that it was Jack. She hadn't realized he was a goalie.

He gave her a wave. "Wait," he called out. "Two minutes!"

He turned his attention back to the game as someone from Guildford broke through the back line and
started bolting toward him with the ball. The Guildford player had beaten the last defender and it was down
to striker and goalie. Poppy watched to see how Jack
would do. So far, he was holding his ground. If it were
her, she would have come out a bit, cut down on the
angle.

The Guildford player took his shot. Jack dove. It was
a great dive, he put his body fully on the line. It was
just in the wrong direction. The ball went in. A minute
later, the whistle blew for the end of the game.

Jack jogged over to her.

"That one was completely on you," he said as he
reached her. But there was an embarrassed look on his
face; she could tell he didn't like missing that save right
in front of her.

"On me, was it?" she said. "I have to say, it was a
very dramatic dive."

"Yeah, shut up. I made my move too early. You saw
him feint with the left foot, though, didn't you?"

"Must have missed it."

"Must have had your attention fixed on someone
else." He raised his eyebrows.

"Don't flatter yourself. And anyway, how was that
my fault? You were the one calling out to *me*."

"Yes, well, you walked by very distractingly. I like your new hair, by the way, it suits you."

Poppy couldn't help smiling at the compliment before shifting the focus back onto Jack. "I didn't know you were a goalie."

"Didn't think it would be fair of me to tell you."

"Fair?"

"Yeah. Makes girls weak at the knees when I tell them I'm a goalie. It's an unfair advantage. The goalie's the star of the team."

Poppy raised her eyebrows. "Is he, though?"

"Unequivocally. Your team did well tonight."

"You were watching?"

"Glanced over when I could. Saw you put one away."

Poppy couldn't avoid feeling pleased he'd seen her score. "Hey, tell me something," she said, unable to help her curiosity. "How come you coach kids' soccer? You have a son on the team or something?"

"God no, I don't have kids. No, no, it's my community service after I got out of jail for murder."

"WHAT?"

"Kidding! You really think they'd put a convicted murderer with a bunch of kids? I have a nephew on the team and my sister asked me to help out because she knows I'm such an *incredible* player." He grinned at her, paused and added, "Hey, why don't you come for a drink? A few of us are heading up to the pub now." He paused. "Where's your friend, the one you were with . . ."

He trailed off and Poppy finished for him, "The one I was with when you first met me—the one you don't like?"

"I didn't say I didn't like her. I don't even know her."

"She's already gone. Rough game for her tonight."

"Well, I can keep you company. Coming?"

Poppy hesitated, considering his offer. But if she went, what then? Maybe things would progress, maybe they'd start dating. At some point, there would have to be a conversation. *Do you want kids one day? Because I don't.* Maybe he doesn't either. He did look horrified when she asked him if he had kids. But who knew what that really meant? And maybe if she fast-forwarded a couple years ahead, she'd be going through the exact same pain that she just suffered after Garret's betrayal.

Nope. She opened her mouth ready to decline, but before she had the chance Jack said, "Fantastic," as though she'd just agreed.

"Huh," she began, but he cut her off. "I'll see you up there in ten. Or do you need a lift?"

"No," she said, "I've got my car but—"

He was already backing away from her. "Just grabbing my gear, see you soon." He turned and jogged away.

Poppy wandered slowly toward her car, wondering what she was going to do. Turn up and meet him as he was apparently expecting? Or just stand him up?

Five minutes later she entered the pub, once again wishing she was dressed in something other than her soccer uniform. She slipped into the bathroom before seeking out Jack and his teammates, and at least ran her hands through her hair in front of the mirror and tried her best to fix it up a bit.

Eventually she decided she wasn't going to look any better and headed back out to find Jack. It took her several minutes to spot him, and when she did, she realized the reason she'd had so much trouble was because he was sitting alone in a booth.

"I thought you were going to be here with a group," she said as she approached the table and slid into the booth opposite him.

"They all bailed on me," he said, shrugging. "So I guess I'm lucky you didn't stand me up too."

"I guess so."

"Can I buy you a drink?"

"I ordered one while I was looking for you. Bartender's bringing it over."

"All right, but the next one's on me. I did kind of coerce you into turning up."

Poppy laughed. "Yes," she said, "you did actually. I was planning on saying no."

"I know you were. I could see it on your lips. That's why I didn't give you the chance."

Poppy felt an involuntary tingle at the thought of Jack watching her lips and immediately tried to shake it off. *Take it easy.*

"And why were you so keen to get me here?" she asked, unable to stop a flirtatious tone from creeping into her voice. So much for taking it easy.

"Because I wanted your advice about something."

"Oh." Poppy felt the tingle vanish. "What about?" she said, nodding her thanks to the bartender who had just delivered her beer.

"About goalkeeping, of course. You saw my abysmal dive tonight. I need tips, woman!"

The tingle returned and Poppy found herself laughing again. "Oh, really?" she said. "And I thought your stuff-up tonight was supposed to have been all my fault for distracting you?"

"Well, yes, there was that. But a guy can always use a few more tips." Jack picked up his own drink and raised it to Poppy in a cheers, and she clinked her glass against it.

They fell into easy conversation about each of their games that night, about how their teams were doing in the competition and how long they'd played soccer. Then they shifted seamlessly to other topics, but not the usual "what do you do?" or "where are you from?" Instead they talked about politics (first Australia and then they moved on to the current state of America), where to find the best coffee (Jack argued that an Italian restaurant across the road from his apartment building held that title, Poppy claimed it was the one near her work), and their favorite teachers from primary school (Mr. Bamford for Poppy, Mrs. Walsh for Jack).

When Jack offered to buy the second round, Poppy switched to a Coke. She wanted to keep a clear head. She was enjoying chatting with Jack and she didn't need alcohol to keep the conversation flowing.

Later, when the pub was starting to empty out, Poppy wondered if Jack would expect her to want to head home with him, as he'd seen her do with Will. But instead, he kissed her on the cheek, checked that she was right to drive home ("I've only had one beer!"), and said good night.

She wasn't sure if she was disappointed he hadn't tried it on, or charmed that he was so much more of a gentleman than Will. She was walking to her car when she heard her name being called and she turned around to see Jack heading toward her.

"Sorry," he said, "I just realized I don't have your number, which means I might not be able to track you down again—and it was your turn to buy the next round when we finished up."

"You're really going to keep score?"

"Nope, I'm not. But I needed an excuse to see you again. How about dinner next Saturday night at the Italian place I was telling you about? My shout?"

Poppy smiled. She reached for his phone and typed her number into it. "Let me think about it," she said.

Later that night, once Poppy was home, she was unpacking her sweaty soccer socks and shin pads when she came across Annalise's notebook. What she really ought to do was head straight downstairs, knock on Annalise's door, and return it to her. She might already be wondering where it was. But what if the contents of this notebook could give her answers? Answers about why Annalise had told all those lies about her past.

What if she just took a peek?

What if she just read a few pages?

She sat cross-legged on her bed, opened it up and began to read.

17 March

It's funny that people don't have a clue what I'm really like. I wonder if you would have known . . . had you been given the chance. Most of the time I feel like I'm cut off from reality. Trapped inside my own head. Buried beneath a thick layer of insulation. Muffled. Muzzled. Sometimes I'll find myself examining my own actions, my own words, with the curiosity of a polite but concerned stranger, while still behaving as though there is absolutely nothing wrong. I make jokes with strangers. Maybe the girl behind the counter as she froths the milk for my cappuccino. Maybe the bartender at the local pub. I can make them laugh with genuine delight in their eyes, even while inside I'm aching.

I shouldn't complain to you. I have no right. But who else is there for me to tell?

Do you want to know something I find strange? I find it strange how memories work. The fact that I can forget something that happened just the other day, or what I ate for breakfast this morning, and yet I can still have a memory from my childhood of the inside of a walnut-brown cot, of a voice singing quietly, "It's raining, it's pouring, the old man is snoring . . ."

That memory was from before it all changed. It's

the only one I have of the life that could have been. The life that should have been, had he not come along and ripped the two of us out of that world.

People don't realize it when they meet me. They don't know about the constant narrating bitch inside my head. Judging my every move, every decision. Speaking over the sound of my own voice. Reexamining conversations. Telling me I'd done it wrong. Telling me I'd misinterpreted.

Sometimes I can silence that voice. The meds helped, even the psychologist for a little while. But it didn't last. She kept probing. She wanted to know about my childhood. I suppose she could sense that something was there, but I didn't want to talk about that. I saw no need. Digging all of that up would just make it worse. Plus, she wanted me to do things like "practice my mindfulness, challenge my negative thought patterns. Perform some self-love." I spat out my water when she first said that one. I thought she was talking about the kind of self-love I'd normally do in the shower. Apparently not.

It was all bullshit. It didn't help.

Poppy did, though. Poppy is my distraction. My outlet. Fixing her, fixes me. You know what I mean? Even if, technically speaking, I'm betraying her—every day I betray her. But I don't mean to.

Poppy looked up from the pages. *Every day she's betraying me?* What the hell did that mean? Since that first moment when the idea of Annalise as the imposter had crossed her mind, she'd dismissed it. It simply didn't make any sense. But now she had to consider it again, didn't she? Because what else could she mean by "betrayal"? Then again, there was a lot more to take in here within these pages. The memories, the negative self-talk. There was so much more beneath the surface with Annalise than Poppy had ever realized. She read on.

26 March

I keep hearing the Tardis everywhere. It's this blue police telephone box from *Doctor Who.* Bigger on the inside. The Tardis has this very specific sound when the Doctor starts it up. A sort of *woob-woob-woob-woob.* I hear it underneath the sound of a trolley being pushed through the supermarket. Inside the vacuum cleaner. Behind the coffee machine at the café. Underneath the water in the ocean.

It was my favorite show when I was a kid. Watched it with a cushion on my lap. When it got scary, I'd hold the cushion up in front of my face and hide behind it till everything was all right again.

The sound of those Daleks' voices still makes my skin crawl. Not that we were supposed to watch TV. Weren't even supposed to have a TV actually. But there was one—in his private quarters.

Sometimes, when he came back, he would run the palm of his hand across the screen to check for static electricity so he could tell whether or not we'd been watching. But Tiana always knew to wipe the static away with tinfoil when we were done. Tiana was the eldest, so she was the one who decided what we watched when the opportunity came up—and *Doctor Who* was her favorite, so *Doctor Who* was what we watched.

What the hell does it mean? The fact that I keep hearing the Tardis everywhere. Is it the obvious—a metaphor for escape? I don't think so. I think it just means that these days I watch too much television. *Doctor Who* is available on Netflix now, so I've been watching it again. I have this weird love-hate relationship with the show. You see, I love it, but it takes me back to the worst time of my life. It takes me back to hell.

I watch it now and I think, why am I torturing myself? But it's tinged with happiness, isn't it? So I watch.

24 April

Once I helped this little old man onto an escalator. He was so tiny! His wife was flustered, she'd stepped on and then looked back and realized he was having trouble. I often forget that old people were once young. I see them as characters in a story. Sometimes they're there for comic relief. Sometimes for a moment of tenderness, of fragility.

I took his arm and helped him on and you could tell he was embarrassed but grateful. When we reached the top, the two of them wanted to chat. The problem was, the more we spoke, the more I fell in love with the two of them.

Why couldn't you be my nan and pop? Why couldn't you adopt me as your own?

But eventually they started to get uncomfortable. You see, they might have wanted to chat at first, but even they had their limitations when it came to talking to a complete stranger. And every time they tried to leave, I'd engage them in conversation once again. I wanted them to stay. I wanted them to sit down and have a cup of tea and some raisin toast with me. I wanted to make plans.

I took it too far, I know that. I shouldn't have tried to take her by the arm. It was different when I was helping him onto the escalator, the physical contact was justified. But the look in her eyes. She was afraid of me. She was confused. And that's when their granddaughter turned up.

Where the fuck were you when your pop was trying to step onto the escalator? You weren't here. You weren't here for them.

You could see her eyes darting between the three of us, weighing it up. Trying to figure out who the hell I was. She was twitchy. She was reaching out for me, she was about to take hold of my arm and pull me off of her grandmother. And I guess that's when I knew my grip on her arm was too tight.

I probably left her with bruises. Purple gray on withered skin.

That's not what was supposed to happen. They were supposed to fall in love with me too. Because it's not fair, is it? Why shouldn't I have a family? Why shouldn't I have a nan and pop who love me unconditionally? Why couldn't I have had that all my life?

You must hate me.

26 April

He bought me a sundae.

9 May

There's this scene in an old eighties cult movie called *The Lost Boys* that I like to think about sometimes. A gang of vampires takes the lead character, Michael, to a railroad bridge and one by one they jump off the edge. Michael looks down to see that they're all hanging by their hands off the railings below. He climbs down and hangs with them, and then he realizes a train is coming.

When the train goes overhead, the bars they're holding on to are rattled ferociously and they all shake violently until the vibrations force them to let go and fall into the mist below.

Sometimes I think that's what my body needs.

To be shaken so intensely that eventually all I can do is let go.

Poppy snapped the notebook shut. She'd read too much. Way more than she'd intended. She was breathing hard and a tear slipped down her cheek. Poppy had taken a look behind a curtain that wasn't hers to lift. She shouldn't have opened it. She should have given it straight back. She needed to talk to Annalise, ask her directly for the truth about her past, not find out about it this way. But at least she knew now that she was right about Annalise lying. She replayed the words in her mind: *Even if, technically speaking, I'm betraying her—every day I betray her. But I don't mean to.*

She put the book under her pillow and decided to find a way to slip it back into Annalise's bag without her ever knowing it had been missing.

Kellie—How's everyone going with the whole NOP / MOP battle? Any more fallout from private posts being spilled to the public? Or do we think the mole has slunk off now? I've noticed people don't seem to be sharing so much personal goss on here lately. Hope we can get back to normal soon. I'm kind of missing my daily NOP fix.

Nicole—I get the feeling that whoever she is, she's still here. Don't ask me why, maybe my Spidey Sense is tingling!

Viv—I miss the way it used to be too. Did you guys notice that Catriona is gone? When this all first blew up, she posted to say she was screwed 'cause her sister saw one of her posts. She must have decided to quit the group. Such a shame this is happening.

Chapter 18

The following morning, Poppy waited by her car for Paul to come and meet her. They were supposed to be heading out to the shops to take a look at fidget spinners—the latest craze that had swept across the country in such a sudden wave that even Poppy hadn't seen it coming. Sometimes that happened; sometimes the most unexpected thing took off and there was no rhyme or reason to it and no way you could have predicted its instant popularity. They wanted to see how many different places were stocking them, have a chat to a few vendors about how well they were selling, and figure out whether it was too late to jump on the bandwagon and ride the final waves.

While she waited, a text came through from her mother.

It's almost the end of May and we haven't done our FAMILY DINNER yet this month. What night is good for you, darling?

Poppy typed back a short reply: *I'm going to have to skip this month. Too much on at work. Sorry.*

The truth was, she didn't want to see Therese now that she knew Annalise was hiding things from her; she didn't like the idea that her mother might have been right all along. Earlier, Poppy had slipped down to the warehouse and shoved the notebook in Annalise's bag while she was distracted with a delivery. The desire to read more when she'd woken that morning had almost overpowered her. To read those pages was a violation and she couldn't do it. She would find a way to get Annalise to talk instead. She'd figure out what had happened to her friend to cause her so much pain and she would help her through it. And at the same time, she would find out how exactly it was that Annalise was betraying her. She just didn't know how she was going to do any of that yet.

Now, as Poppy began to think Paul had forgotten all about her, and she was considering heading inside to knock on his office door, she looked up to see Frankie walking toward her. Poppy frowned. "Where's Paul?" she asked.

"He told me to tell you he can't make it. Last-minute conference call with some overseas manufacturers."

"Which overseas manufacturers?"

"Not sure," Frankie said. "But he's asked me to come with you in his place."

"It's fine," said Poppy. "I can check it out on my own."

"Yeah, well, he wants me to come with you. I might actually be useful, you know? I've seen the fidget spinner craze go absolutely mental at my kids' school. Both my kids have one."

Poppy headed round to the driver's side while Frankie hopped into the passenger seat. They were both silent on the drive across the bridge to the city. Every now and again Poppy sensed that Frankie was about to strike up a conversation—she kept hearing the intake of breath, as though she was steeling herself to speak, seeing her shoulders lift out of the corner of her eye. But each time nothing would follow. After a while Poppy started to wonder if it was actually some sort of nervous tic.

At the shops they strode through the center, stopping at different outlets and temporary stands. They took it in turns quizzing the shop owners or attendants, passing their questions off as those of interested customers.

"My daughter wants one of the rainbow ones. Do you get those in often? Do they sell out quick?"

"Do you find the light-up ones are very popular? I'm trying to decide which one is best for a gift."

One stall holder proudly told them that he ordered in five hundred a day and was sold out by 4 P.M. every afternoon. The things were everywhere: tobacconists, newsagents, supermarkets, gadget shops, and department stores.

Between shops, Poppy and Frankie only spoke briefly to exchange thoughts on where they should head next or how they were faring on their mission. Often Frankie would try to extend the conversation further, but Poppy always shut her down with a one-word response. She wasn't interested in friendly chitchat with someone who was having an affair. Hopefully it had ended. There had never been any reply from Linda, so Poppy didn't know for sure.

After a good hour of research, Poppy concluded they were too late—the market was already flooded. Even with their quickest business setup they'd be coming to the party at the tail end. She doubted it would be worth their while. Better to try to predict the next toy craze for when this one burned out.

Her feet were hurting and she noticed Frankie waning next to her as they walked through the center. "Ready to call it?" Poppy asked.

"Probably a good idea," said Frankie.

Poppy felt her phone buzz in her pocket and she slowed down to pull it out. The message was from a number she didn't recognize.

So . . . on for dinner Saturday? was all it said.

She felt an instant warmth wash over her. She hadn't meant to play hard to get with Jack when she'd told him she'd think about dinner, she just wasn't sure if it was what she wanted. There was definitely chemistry between them. He was attractive, he was friendly, and he was easy to talk to. But her heartbreak at Garret's betrayal still felt fresh. It was coming up to six months now. At what point would it stop hurting? She looked back up, considering what she would reply, and the air seemed to vanish from her lungs.

Garret and Karleen. They were walking through the center directly toward her, pushing a pram in front of them. Poppy froze. Frankie took one or two paces before realizing she was no longer beside her and turned back to see why she'd stopped.

Poppy's face must have given her away because Frankie's voice was slightly alarmed as she asked, "What's up?"

"N-nothing," Poppy stammered. She shoved her phone in her pocket and looked around, frantically searching for somewhere she could escape. They hadn't spotted her yet and she wanted to keep it that way. "We haven't checked in here," she said, waving her hand at the shop to their left.

"It's a shoe store," Frankie said. "They won't sell fidget spinners."

Poppy ignored her and pushed past another shopper to make a dash inside. But then she heard a voice: "Poppy!"

Frankie caught her arm. "Hang on," she said. "Someone's calling you."

How dare they? How fucking dare they call out to me like we're still good friends? Surely they'd want to pass her by and pretend she didn't exist just the same as she did? Not Karleen. She obviously still thought they could reconcile. She was steamrolling toward Poppy while Garret trailed behind. At least he had the decency to look uncomfortable.

"Oh, Poppy, I'm so glad to run into you," said Karleen as she reached them. "I almost didn't recognize you—your hair is just so . . . different! But listen, I really feel like this is fate."

Fate? *Fate! Was she insane? This wasn't fate! This was a nightmare.* So far, Poppy's mouth had remained snapped shut. She couldn't trust herself not to explode in a string of expletives. But it was getting weird—Frankie looking curiously between the two of them; Karleen waiting for her to respond; Garret shuffling his feet like a schoolboy who'd been caught chewing gum in church.

Poppy opened her mouth to say . . . something . . . anything, but Frankie spoke over the top of her.

"Cute boy," she said. "What's his name?"

Karleen did a double take. The baby in the pram was covered in a pink blanket. She had one of those flower headbands on her bald head. She was wearing a pink cardigan. No one could have mistaken her for a boy.

"She's a girl," Karleen said, a look of pure annoyance on her face.

"Oh my God! Sorry!" said Frankie. "I didn't realize! Boy, you really have to pink this one up to stop people getting confused, don't you? Don't worry, I'm sure it will get easier when she grows some hair."

Karleen was clearly lost for words. She turned to Garret as though expecting him to step in and say something, stand up for their daughter, but he was still refusing to look up.

"Well," said Frankie, "so nice to meet you but we have to get back to work. Big cocktail function this evening at Darling Harbour, special guest, can't say who, but . . ." She leaned in and whispered, "Adele's in town, you know?" She winked at Karleen. "No rest for the wicked!"

She sidestepped around the pram and Poppy followed her, starkly aware of the fact she hadn't said a single word throughout the entire exchange. As they passed, Garret finally lifted his head. *I'm sorry,* he mouthed at her, then he added in a whisper, "Your hair looks fantastic."

They were almost back to the car when Poppy finally spoke up. "Frankie," she said, "what *was* that?"

Frankie grimaced. "Did I take it too far?" she said.

"Are you kidding me? That was amazing. How did you know?"

"It's probably not what you want to hear, but you know how people gossip in the office. I heard about what happened with your ex and, well . . . the way you reacted when you saw them, I figured that had to be them." She paused. "That *was* them, right? Your ex and his new partner . . . your old friend?"

"Yes, that was them. Her office is near here. They must have come into the city to show off the baby to her work mates. Ugh, I can't believe how good she looked."

"You thought she looked good? You're kidding, right? Her makeup was caked on a mile thick to try and hide the massive bags under her eyes. She looked awful."

"Really? I can't believe you came up with the whole Adele cocktail-party thing!"

"I know what it's like when you have a new baby. You're all wrapped up in yourself and you think you're so special, but I thought they needed to be reminded that other people are still out in the world having an awesome time. You think they bought it?"

"Karleen is a massive Adele fan and I saw the jealousy on her face. They totally bought it."

"Good!" Frankie sighed with relief. "I know we don't know each other well. But I really hate cheaters and I kind of thought they deserved everything I gave them and more."

At the mention of the word "cheater" Poppy was snapped back to reality. She stopped grinning at Frankie and hopped into the car. But as they drove back to the office a thought occurred to her. What if Annalise had been wrong about Paul and Frankie from the beginning? Would someone who was having an affair really have the gall to come right out and say they hated cheaters? She wished she could talk to Annalise about it. In fact, she'd love to tell her the whole story of how Frankie had handled Karleen and Garret. But first she needed to sort out everything else with Annalise. And that was going to take time.

Later that afternoon, an invite came through to the admin account of NOP from a local women's shelter. The shelter was running out of funds and as NOP was a group of local women, they thought they might be interested in booking a few tables at a fund-raising event they were holding on a cruise in the harbor in June. Poppy wasn't sure that the members of NOP would really be up for a big night out, considering recent events. She'd stayed off NOP for the last several days. Since the horrible incident with Wendy, NOP wasn't giving her the same comfort it once had. Notifications were piling up: messages from members wanting to know if the mole had been found, and stories about continued altercations with MOP members. But Poppy hadn't been able to bring herself to deal with any of it. Besides, the members of NOP were all grown women, they could handle themselves. However, she thought she should at least pass the invite on—after all, it was a good cause.

The response surprised her. Members put their hands up for spots right away that evening and Poppy realized she was going to have to attend herself. It would be odd if the founder of the group didn't show up. She hoped she and Annalise would have everything sorted by then, it would be nice if they could attend together.

She forgot all about the message from Jack until much later that night as she was climbing into bed. And when she did remember, she saw an image in her mind. An image of Jack walking toward her through a shopping center one day, pushing a stroller in front of him. A different woman by his side.

So how was she going to respond to his message? With a yes or with a no?

The Imposter

She knew she should cancel her account and get out. They were on the warpath looking for fake members. Any day they might check out her account, sift through the posts, realize her timeline didn't actually go back that far, that it was pretty bare. Notice she didn't have many people on her friends list. All the red flags that would tell them it was a fake account under a fake name.

But then again, with several hundred members, what were the chances they'd choose to look into her? Plus, things were careening out of control and she was sort of loving it. She was reveling in the chaos she'd created. It felt good, after so long hiding her true self from the world, after so long playing the part of the perfect mum, to instead simply cause destruction and mayhem. She was stealing private posts from NOP and secretly passing them on to other MOP members. She even contributed fabricated stories about altercations between the women of NOP and MOP, to make it appear as though the situation was way worse than it was. Screw them, screw the lot of them. They'd brought it all on themselves.

PART FOUR

Annalise

Chapter 19

Yet another Tuesday night was ruined. And this time she didn't even make it out her apartment door with the soccer ball. She was about to step into the hall when the door opposite hers was flung open and her neighbor—what *was* that woman's name again? Sydney? Cynthia? Something along those lines—practically launched herself at Annalise. She was dressed in some sort of uniform—white shirt with pin stripes and a leaf-shaped logo on the front that Annalise didn't recognize.

"Oh, thank God," she said, "I was hoping you'd be home. Listen, I know we don't know each other well but I need to ask you a favor. A huge favor. Hugest. It's asking a lot and you're probably going to think I'm a terrible mother but I have no other choice."

Annalise stared back at her. *Was she going to get to the point anytime soon?*

"I'll owe you," she continued, "big-time. And I'll pay you, of course."

"Cynthia," Annalise said, taking a stab at her name, "what are you on about?"

"Oh, sorry," she said, "I haven't asked yet, have I? Can you babysit for me?"

She must have seen the look of horror on Annalise's face.

"I know!" she said. "I know, I know, and I would never ask, but my sitter canceled on me last minute, and I've tried everyone else I can possibly think of and no one is answering my SOS messages or returning my calls, and the problem is, my boss told me if I call in sick one more time that's it, I'm done. Annalise," she pleaded, "I need this job."

Annalise had to admit she felt bad for her, she honestly did, but a close friend would have trouble convincing her to babysit for them, let alone a virtual stranger. Although at least she knew her name.

She was starting to shake her head, ready to throw her hands up and tell her it wasn't her problem, and besides, she had plans for the night. She needed this time to herself out in the crisp night air, pounding the ball as hard as she could, processing everything that was going on at the moment—her argument with Poppy, the online war that was showing no signs of waning. But then a tiny figure appeared behind the neighbor's legs and peered around at Annalise. Big, oval-shaped eyes looked up at her from under a too-long fringe.

Annalise was picking up on something in her expression. What was it? Was it hope? Was she hoping Annalise was going to say yes? Or was Annalise imagining it? It could be she was hoping she'd say no. Could be she just wanted her mama to stay home with her.

Either way, Annalise didn't get the chance to answer. Because next thing, her neighbor was grabbing her handbag off a shelf inside the doorway and slinging it across her body, all the while babbling about how thankful she was and how she would make it up to her and she was *leaving*!

"Wait, Cynthia! I haven't even—"

"It's Beth, by the way," she said, "not Cynthia. And this little cutie patootie here is Harmony. I'll be back by eleven and everything you need is on the kitchen counter. Thank you, thank you so much. You're a lifesaver."

And with that she kissed Harmony on the top of her head, whispered, "Mummy loves you," jabbed at the lift button and stepped inside the elevator and was gone.

Annalise stood still, sort of shell-shocked. *But,* she thought, *but I can't do this for you. And it's not just because I don't know what I'm doing with kids.*

A nasty feeling washed over her and she felt a flash of anger at Cynthia—oops, Beth—for putting her in this situation. For a second she considered scooping up Harmony and taking the stairs to try to beat Beth to the ground floor, but Harmony turned away and toddled back inside the apartment. Annalise's shoulders slumped. There was no getting out of it now. She needed to push those nasty memories and thoughts away. Forget about it. She checked her watch, it was 8 P.M. Beth had said she'd be back by eleven. All she had to do was get through the next three hours and then she could be back in her own apartment and she wouldn't let Beth get away with this again.

She followed Harmony inside and closed the door behind them. She picked up the instructions off the kitchen bench:

Dear Annalise, thank you for being my savior tonight.

What the hell? She already *knew* she was going to get her to babysit!

I know you're not a kid person and I know to-night is going to suck for you but I honestly had no other option. FYI, Harmony is eighteen months old, which means she thinks she's in charge of the world and that she can do anything and everything on her own. She can't. She's still a baby.

She's already bathed and in her nappy and PJs for the night and she's had her dinner. All she needs is her bottle of milk (instructions under the bottles next to the fruit bowl, over there to your right). And some cuddles and maybe a story and a lullaby (if you're up for it?) and pop her in her cot and she'll go right to sleep.

I can't afford normal sitting rates—although I get the feeling you wouldn't know what they are anyway? Ha! But I thought maybe it's fair if I just give you half of whatever I earn tonight?

So I know I told you I'd be home by eleven—I lied. I won't be home till about one. Sorry. Thought you might not let me leave if I told you the truth. There's a lasagne in the fridge you can have for your dinner if you want? It's homemade and I've been told I'm a pretty good cook.

Thank you again. See you later. Please don't punch me in the face when I get home.

> *Beth (not Cynthia. I've been trying to tell you for the past year that my name isn't Cynthia.)*

Despite her anger, Annalise had to smile at the end of the note. So Beth had a bit of sass about her, did she? Well, at the very least she could respect that. Though she wasn't too happy knowing she was now here for five hours instead of three.

She looked over at Harmony, who had sat herself down in the middle of the rug in front of the blank television.

"So," said Annalise, "I don't know if I'm impressed with your mum for her ingenuity or furious with her for tricking me into looking after you. I'll tell you what," she added as she wandered over and sat down on the couch in front of her, "if I were you, I'd be pretty pissed at her for giving me a name like Harmony. Oh shit, I'm probably not supposed to swear in front of you, am I? Probably shouldn't have said shit just now either, should I?"

She tipped her head to the side, watching Harmony's face. "Or do you not even know what I'm saying? What age do kids start talking? Can you speak?"

Harmony stared blankly back at her.

"*Sprechen Sie Englisch?*" Annalise tried. "*Parlez-vous anglais?*"

A hint of a smile appeared at the edges of Harmony's mouth and she let out a tiny chuckle.

"You making fun of my German and French, woman?"

She giggled again.

"You try and do better," Annalise said. "Hey," she added, "what time do your kind go to bed? Like, when can I banish you to your baby cage and turn on the TV? Your mum better have Foxtel, or I'm gonna be pissed. Oops, sorry, I did it again, didn't I?"

Harmony pointed a chubby finger at Annalise. "Again," she said, her tone firm.

"Oh! So you *can* talk. Again what? You want me to swear some more? I don't know, now that I know you can speak, I guess I shouldn't say things like shit or fuck or whatever in front of you, should I?"

"Again," she repeated. Her brow creased. "Again!"

"I know what you want," Annalise said. "You want me to speak another language again, don't you? Well I'm sorry, kid, but my phrases are limited. Let's see, I can order a croissant in French . . ." She put on her best French accent and said, "*Je voudrais un croissant s'il vous plaît.*"

Harmony burst into a fit of giggles, much bigger than the last time. Jeez, it didn't take much to get this kid's sense of humor going.

"And I can order an orange juice if I'm in Germany," she continued. *"Ein orangensaft bitte!"*

More peals of laughter. This time Harmony tipped backward onto the rug and lay on her back, her body rocking with delight. She reached up and grabbed hold of her toes.

"More!" she commanded between giggles.

"¿Qué estás haciendo en mi cabeza?" said Annalise. "That's Spanish, by the way, it means you're doing my head in. Are we done with this game yet?"

"More!"

"But I'm running out of things to say!"

"More! Again! More!"

Annalise had to admit, Harmony's laughter was kind of contagious. She gave in and went through her entire repertoire of foreign language phrases again. And then again. After the fourth time through, the kid's laughter seemed to be finally abating to mild amusement and Annalise figured she could give it a rest.

"Right," she said, "what are two single ladies going to do for the rest of a Tuesday night?"

She got up and wandered around to the kitchen to

see about Harmony's bottle. She supposed she should give her her milk and put her to bed.

Turns out that was the most naive thought she'd ever had in her entire life.

More fucking lies from Beth. This kid *did not* want to be put in her cot. Every time Annalise even tried to approach the cot with Harmony, she screamed blue murder. Didn't matter if she carried her or led her by the hand. Didn't matter if she spoke German or French or Spanish—apparently all of those phrases had completely lost their charm. She made a mental note to learn some new phrases before she saw her again and then shook her head at herself. *What the actual fuck? I don't need to learn any new phrases 'cause I'm not planning on ever doing this again.*

Eventually she gave up altogether on getting Harmony into the cot or even into her bedroom. "Fine," she said, "you win. If we watch TV together, will you sit with me and not do that super-annoying ear-piercing screaming shit anymore?"

"Shit," Harmony said with a firm nod.

"Ah crap, I knew I shouldn't have sworn in front of you."

"Crap," she said.

"Stop it!"

She plonked Harmony on the couch and sat down next to her to turn on the television and see what she could find. Oh God, was she going to have to go PG on this now too? She flicked through the stations— thankfully Beth did have Foxtel—and tried to settle on an old episode of *Modern Family*.

But within seconds there was a loud grumble from her left.

"What?" she asked. "It's a family show! You can tell 'cause it has the word "family" in it. Look, there's even a little girl in it."

Harmony grumbled again and reached out to pat the remote control.

Annalise sighed and started flicking again. She tried stopping on one family-friendly show after another, but each time Harmony patted the remote and waited for her to keep changing channels. "I swear to God I'm not watching something animated," she said, "or some Teletubby shit or whatever."

"Shit," Harmony said again. "Up," she added.

"Up?" Annalise asked. "You're already up. You're up on the couch. How much higher do you need to get?"

"Up," she repeated.

"You're already up," Annalise said, an irritable tone creeping into her voice.

"UP!"

"The only thing higher than where you are now is on my lap and I don't want you on my lap, okay?"

Annalise could have sworn that Harmony rolled her eyes in response and she was impressed by the tiny kid's level of sass. Then Harmony flipped over onto her tummy, slid herself backward off the couch, and toddled over to the cupboard under the television. She opened up the cupboard door and started running her fingers along the spines of the DVDs like she was a customer browsing in a shop. She found the one she was after, pulled it out, and brought it over to place in Annalise's lap.

"Up," she instructed.

Annalise helped her climb back up next to her on the couch again. She looked at the DVD on her lap. It was called *Up*. She felt foolish.

"Sorry," she said. "Wait, this is a cartoon!" But she couldn't be bothered arguing, it would be easier to put the damn movie on.

Ten minutes later she was a sobbing fucking mess.

She'd never seen an opening of a movie as sad as this damn thing. Watching the cute little boy and his girlfriend grow up, get married, start getting ready for a baby, and then WHAM. No baby. No happiness. And next thing, the woman's dead and the little boy is a grumpy old man and Annalise is left devastated.

"How is this your favorite movie?" she wailed at Harmony, who was staring wide-eyed at the screen, clearly not one bit emotionally affected by the story. "Have you no heart?"

They kept watching, and as the movie went on, Harmony started to lean into Annalise. First it was just an elbow placed carelessly on her knee. Then her head resting on her arm. Then she started to snuggle in a little more and a little more.

Eventually, somehow without Annalise noticing, Harmony had managed to clamber her way onto her lap, her head resting against Annalise's chest, her hair tickling her chin. Her warm, compact little body felt nicer than she'd expected.

More tears started to flow, but this time it had nothing to do with the movie.

"Ah, Harmony," she murmured through silent tears. "What have I done?"

She looked down and realized Harmony was sleeping.

Annalise woke up with a start, momentarily confused about where she was, who was in her bedroom? Leaning over her, touching her shoulder. The fear flipped her stomach, causing an abrupt bout of nausea to rise up within. Then she remembered. The nausea dissipated as quickly as it had appeared. She wasn't in bed. She wasn't even in her own apartment. She was next door, in Beth's. Harmony was asleep on her lap and Beth was above them, looking down at Annalise with this big weird grin on her face.

"I knew it!" she whispered. "I knew you were a big softy underneath it all. Look at the two of you."

Annalise glared back at her, and all of a sudden the weight of the warm body against her own felt suffocating. Too hot. Too heavy. She needed to get her off, off, off.

"Here," she hissed, "take her, would you?"

Beth scooped up her daughter, her face changing. "I'm sorry," she whispered, "I know it's a lot later than I said—"

Annalise cut her off. "Whatever. Just don't ever expect me to do this again." She stood up from the couch and headed for the front door.

"Wait a sec! Your money! Let me just put Harmony down in her cot."

Annalise didn't wait for her to come back out from Harmony's room.

Chapter 20

Saturday morning, Poppy asked her out for brunch. Annalise had never been a brunch person. And the two of them hadn't spoken all week since the argument at soccer. It was easy enough to avoid one another— Annalise stayed hidden down in the warehouse and Poppy didn't leave the office upstairs. But she didn't like things being this way between them, and while she would have preferred to catch up over a few drinks rather than a weird half-breakfast half-lunch nonsense meal, she agreed.

Poppy met Annalise at her apartment door, and they walked to a café overlooking the river in silence, apart from the odd perfunctory comment about the weather or work, or the annoying guy who lived one level up from Poppy and liked to practice on his drum kit at highly inconvenient times like 3 A.M. on a Wednesday.

At the café, after they ordered their food—poached eggs on sourdough with smashed avocado and goat cheese for Poppy; a bacon and egg roll with barbecue sauce for Annalise—Annalise looked across the table at Poppy, waiting for her to speak first, but she had a feeling Poppy was doing the same, so she bit the bullet.

"You had some pretty decent moves at our last match."

She saw Poppy's face glow despite the fact she was trying to remain modest. "I had a good game," she said, and Annalise laughed at her.

"You can't do modest," she said. "You're so fucking proud of yourself!"

Poppy laughed as well. "Yeah, okay, okay," she said. "But come on, I've been in goals for so long, I didn't expect to be any good out on the field."

"Listen," Annalise said, deciding to take the lead, "I've been thinking about that whole hairdresser story you told me. I guess I can understand why it had you so worried. Things have really turned to crap with NOP, and I suppose having our members out there hassling mums adds fuel to the fire."

"Yeah, it really does," said Poppy.

"So I get it. I get why you've been upset with everything that's happened."

"Thanks, Annalise, it means a lot to me that you understand where I'm coming from."

"We can fix it, you know? We can fix NOP, get it back to the way you thought it was supposed to be," she said, even though she didn't exactly know how.

"I don't know if we can," said Poppy. "The problem is, it's taken on a life of its own."

"We'll find a way," Annalise said, because it was the best she could offer.

"Oh, by the way, did you see NOP members have been invited to a fund raiser on a boat next month? It costs ninety dollars per head, but quite a few of the girls have already said they're interested. Do you want to come?"

"Drinks on the harbor? Sure, why not?"

"You know what? I never told you the end of the hairdresser story."

"There's more?"

"There's a LOT more."

Poppy described how Wendy had turned on her and Annalise listened with growing amazement.

"Holy shit," she said when Poppy was done. "I can't believe that little fucker did that to you. That's awful."

"I know. Although if I'm entirely honest, I kind of think I deserved it."

"What do you mean you deserved it?"

"Well, she wouldn't have been so upset in the first place if I hadn't caused NOP to start picking on parents."

"Poppy, you went out of your way to make it right for her. Besides, you weren't the one who went up to her in the café, were you? And you didn't force the women who did. They acted on their own."

"I guess. I wonder who it was that told her about me being a part of NOP."

"Hang on," said Annalise "Your appointment wasn't meant to be with someone called Wendy." She grabbed her bag and searched around inside it for her wallet.

"Oh yeah," said Poppy, "she did say someone else was feeling unwell when I arrived."

"No, no, Poppy, you don't get it, I know who told her."

"What? Who?"

Annalise pulled a business card out of her wallet and held it up to show Poppy. "This is who you were supposed to see."

Poppy read the name and stared back at Annalise, perplexed. "Sophie," she said. "So? I don't know what this means."

"Sophie came along to a NOP get-together, a little

while back. She handed out these business cards. That's why I booked you with her—I thought she'd be good! I completely forgot that's who you were supposed to see when you first told me about Wendy. Sophie must have dobbed you in to her."

"But why would she do that? Wouldn't that be admitting to Wendy that she was a member too?"

"Not if she's our imposter! Not if she's the one who wrote the article."

"Oh my God. Do you think she could be?"

"I think it's worth checking out."

A waitress delivered their food and they thanked her distractedly, too caught up in the drama to think about eating.

"Have a look on Facebook," said Poppy. "See if she's still part of the group."

Annalise started searching and had found her within seconds. "Yep," she said. "Still a member."

"Go to her profile, see what you can find."

"I'm already doing that."

Annalise scrolled through Sophie's account. "I see photos of her out to dinner, photos of her rock climbing with some guy . . . oh, that's her husband, I think. Oh my God! There's a pic of her here with a kid! Wait, no, it's her niece, she's got her sister tagged in the photo. I don't know, Poppy, it's all looking pretty legit . . . not like a fake account that's been thrown together to sneak into NOP. She has over three hundred friends and her timeline goes back for years and years. I don't think she's a mum."

"Oh. Well, there's still something weird going on, right?"

"For sure," said Annalise, putting down the phone. "I reckon we should visit her at her salon together and confront her about the whole thing."

They turned their attention to their food now and slipped back into easier topics as they concentrated on filling their stomachs.

"Hey," said Poppy as she sawed away at a very dense piece of sourdough toast. "I had a sort of date after our last soccer game."

"What? Why didn't you open with that? What do you mean a 'sort of date'?"

"It's hard to explain, but he's a soccer player from the Parra men's side, so it was really just a drink after the game. But he wanted me to have dinner with him tonight."

"And are you going to?"

"No. I chickened out. I'm not sure if I really want to *meet* someone. You know what I mean? Shouldn't I stay single for a while? It's only been six months. Isn't that what you're supposed to do after a serious relationship ends?"

Annalise smirked. "Oh yes, and you should also go trekking through Tibet and *find* yourself. No, honey, you're supposed to do exactly what you want to do. If it feels right to date someone then do it. As far as I'm concerned, six months is plenty. If it feels right to fuck randoms, then do that. But don't try to follow some supposed rule telling you how to live. What's he like anyway? Is he nice? Is he hot? Is he good in bed?"

"Annalise! I haven't slept with him. We just had one drink," said Poppy. "And yes, I think he's nice . . . he seems nice. And good-looking, I guess."

Annalise tried to press her for more information but she changed the subject. "You want to know the best thing about brunch?" Poppy said.

"What's that?"

"You can have champagne with it if you want. Fancy a mimosa?"

"God yes."

Poppy ordered their drinks, and by the time they'd finished their food, they'd had two each. A little later, they progressed to wine—"It's pretty much lunchtime now anyway," Poppy said—and before they knew it they'd turned brunch into a boozy afternoon.

There was a lull in conversation and Annalise caught Poppy staring at her.

"What?" she said. "Do I have something in my teeth?"

"Annalise, why did you lie to me?"

"What do you mean?" she asked, taken by surprise. "Lie about what?"

"About your past. About everything," said Poppy. "I was on the hiring team when you got the job as warehouse manager. I knew you'd made some stuff up on your résumé, but I didn't care. I thought you deserved the job anyway. But the other day, when I asked you about your jumper . . . you'd lost track of your lies, hadn't you?"

Annalise felt a jolt. *Shit.* She did her best to keep her face composed as she responded. "Excuse me? Lost track of my lies? What are you on about?"

"You messed up. You forgot you'd put Sydney uni on your résumé. The other day I realized you've been wearing a Macquarie uni jumper. I thought you'd just tell me it belonged to a friend or whatever, but instead you told me you went there."

Annalise thought fast. "What makes you think I didn't go to both universities but just left Macquarie off my résumé?" she countered.

"The problem is, I went back and checked out some

other stuff. You even lied about your high school. Who does that? What's the point? You lied about everything. That truck that was dropping off a delivery the other day, the one I asked you about—their company name was on your résumé."

All right. Annalise knew she was caught out. She could stop with the indignation. But that didn't mean Poppy needed to know everything, she could still keep this all under control.

"Okay, fine," she said, "I lied. But it's not some big conspiracy. I was just trying to catch a break, okay? And I'm doing fine as manager, so who cares?"

"I care! It's not about Cormack, it's about me knowing nothing about your past. We're supposed to be friends. So what's your deal?"

"My deal? Okay, first of all, I don't have a 'deal.' I'm just me. And for the record, it's not like I've lied directly to you, I lied on my résumé. I didn't know you when I did that, and I never even knew you had anything to do with hiring me. But since then, you've never actually asked me any questions about my past, so I've never lied to you."

"Well, I'm asking now."

"Yeah well, you're going to need to be a bit more specific than that. What exactly is it that you need to know?"

"Where did you grow up?"

"Queensland."

"So why name a Sydney high school on your résumé?"

"Because I didn't go to high school."

"Why not?"

"Homeschooled."

"Okay, so homeschooling is legitimate. Why not just put the truth on your résumé?"

"People don't trust it."

"And did you go to university at all?"

"No."

"What about family? We're always talking about my family—my parents driving me crazy and my brother and my nephews, but we never talk about yours."

Fuck. Poppy was firing questions at her like she was in a police interrogation.

"Must make you feel like a great friend. The fact that you've never bothered to ask."

"Exactly! I feel terrible," said Poppy. "So talk to me about it. Do you have brothers or sisters? Are you close with your parents? Do they live up in Queensland still?"

Enough was enough. She'd thought she could handle this. She thought she could stick to simple answers and get through it. But she couldn't and she didn't want to and she shouldn't bloody well have to. The bacon and egg roll was sitting heavy in her stomach and the mimosas sloshed around it.

"You know what? I don't want to do this. I don't like the way you're interrogating me. I was happy to come out to brunch with you because I wanted to move past our argument at soccer, but I don't need this shit. I'm done."

Annalise stood up from the table and swayed on the spot. She hadn't even noticed that all the champagne and wine had made her light-headed. She righted herself, snatched up her handbag, and strode out of the café without bothering to offer to split the bill. Poppy didn't call out after her.

Chapter 21

Tuesday nights were sort of ruined for Annalise. She'd lost her momentum. Too many interruptions and she just couldn't get back into her usual routine.

On this Tuesday night, though, no one was stopping her. Annalise started to change into her gear to go train alone like normal but then she stopped. There was a bottle of red on the benchtop and it was calling her name.

Fuck it, she thought. *I can drink on a Tuesday night if I want to.*

It didn't help that she and Poppy were fighting. Annalise had skipped the Monday-morning meeting yesterday, sending one of her staff to take her place instead, and at soccer last night, she and Poppy had pretty much ignored one another. Elle had tried to ask her what was wrong at the end of the game; in fact she was a lot gentler than usual—she didn't even pull Annalise up on a fumbled pass that cost them a goal. But Annalise had faked a headache and taken off.

Yes, okay, she had lied, Poppy had a right to be annoyed, but that didn't mean she had the right to interrogate her.

Annalise changed into pajamas. She poured herself a drink and ordered pizza. When the knock on the door came, for a second she thought it was going to be Beth, as she hadn't buzzed the pizza guy upstairs. But it turned out someone else must have let him in downstairs.

She paid him for the pizza, and before she shut the door, she caught herself looking across at Beth's door, wondering if it was going to open. Wondering if she was going to appear. If she was going to ask for her help again. Of course Annalise would tell her no . . . but she still stood waiting. Wondering.

Beth had slipped ninety dollars under her door the morning after she'd babysat. Annalise had picked it up and shoved it into her wallet. But she hadn't spent it yet. It had stayed tucked in a pocket of her wallet and hadn't been touched again. She couldn't say why. Or maybe she could say, but she didn't want to be tempted. Because if she went there, there was no coming back.

Beth didn't come out. And eventually Annalise took her pizza inside.

When she finished eating, she went looking for her notebook. She hadn't written in it for a while, which was unlike her. She checked her bedside table, her kitchen bench, her handbag. She couldn't find it and she started to panic. Where had she seen it last? She couldn't think straight. She spotted the backpack she'd taken into work the other day and searched through the contents inside. The notebook was stuffed between a folder and a clipboard with crumpled delivery slips. *Thank God.* She opened it up, turned to a blank page, and began to write.

30 May

Do you want to know something that worries me sometimes? You probably don't. You probably want me to stop this. To leave you be. But I need to talk to you. I think you know why.

Here's the thing that worries me—that I might have been doing something really basic in completely the wrong way for my entire life. And I think, what if someone notices one day? What if they spot me doing this really simple thing—like making pasta or filling a car up with petrol or offering someone a hug or a kiss on the cheek when I ought to be shaking hands—and they give me this look, like, what are you doing? And slowly I realize, I've got it wrong. I've always had it wrong, but I never knew. And how could I not have known?

It's because of the way I was brought up. I wasn't taught any of those basic, ordinary, everyday things, was I?

No. Instead I was taught about worship. I was taught to worship him. And I was taught how to keep secrets. Filthy, disgusting secrets.

And I was taught to hate. I was taught to desire one thing only: escape. I knew I should take others with me. I knew that I shouldn't go alone. But how was I supposed to make it happen? How was I supposed to do the right thing?

Chapter 22

It wasn't the nicest place to do it. The floor was sticky and Annalise didn't want to think about what had made it that way. The smell of feces was barely covered up with citrus air freshener. It was 2 A.M., and this setting seemed like a fitting place for her to conclude her ruined Tuesday night.

She'd fallen asleep on the couch after drinking alone in her pajamas and woken with a start to find her mouth dry and the television flickering silently in front of her. She didn't know what made her think of it, it was as though she'd plucked the idea from her dreams. No, that wasn't true. The thought had been edging its way to the surface for the last couple of weeks, it was only that she'd been ignoring it. Willing it away. But as the pepperoni pizza churned in her stomach, she knew it had reached the point where she could no longer pretend the signs weren't there. She had to know for sure.

She'd thrown on clothes, a jacket, and a beanie and walked swiftly down the road to the twenty-four-hour chemist. Inside, the shock of the harsh lights made her pupils constrict and she squinted as her eyes slowly adjusted. She found the family planning section, grabbed the first test she saw, and took it up to the register. She waited for the middle-aged man behind the counter to judge her: A tired woman with couch-cushion creases on one side of her face and a fleck of pizza sauce in the corner of her mouth buying a pregnancy test at almost 2 A.M.

But he didn't react, he scanned the box, accepted payment, and passed back her purchase as though it was nothing more than a pack of chewing gum.

She was going to walk back home and take the test in her apartment, but halfway there she detoured into a service station and asked the young girl inside for the key to the bathrooms around the back. The key was attached to a large wooden board. "Make sure you bring it back," said the girl.

"How could I forget?"

Now she paused in front of the scratched and worn sheet metal that hung on the wall as a substitute for a mirror. Her mottled reflection looked back at her. She remembered standing in front of her bathroom mirror that night after she'd slept with Lawrence, before kicking him out. She remembered how she'd tried to remind herself she was powerful, that she was in control. She didn't feel powerful now. She didn't feel in control. She hated that girl for her pathetic attempts at being tough.

This time as she looked at herself, she felt only guilt.

This was her mistake. She was responsible for her own body. She should have been more careful. And she knew what the answer was going to be. She'd known it well before she'd walked down to the chemist and made her purchase. Well before she stepped inside this dark and dingy bathroom. Well before she squatted above the stained toilet seat and peed on a small white stick.

Her period had been late before, she'd never really been especially regular, that's why it didn't tip her off right away. So what had tipped her off? She supposed it was the way she'd been acting. Getting confused about things. Losing her temper . . . more than usual. Hormonal. Being so weird about that whole thing with Harmony next door. Arguing with Poppy. Slipping up. Playing soccer so badly. And of course, those flashes of nausea that had hit her on and off over the last couple of weeks.

It was all enough to tell her that there was something going on.

This test would just confirm it for her.

She finished counting out the three minutes. She picked up the stick. One line. She waited. She might have known the truth, but still she willed the second line to remain invisible. It ignored her pleas. It swam to the surface. Tears fell and she slammed her fist against the metal on the wall in front of her.

How could she have been so foolish?

Now she had a choice to make.

But really, there could only be one answer.

Chapter 23

1 June

Sometimes I wonder about telling a complete stranger the whole truth. Instead of a person I actually know. And I don't mean talking to a professional either. I mean an elderly man I meet on a park bench. Or the woman sitting next to me on the bus. Or the teenager who's lining up behind me to order fish and chips.

I imagine how I might tell my story. In a whisper? Or a shout?

I imagine how they might react.

They'd be horrified, of course.

Annalise hadn't told anyone her news yet. It was two days later and she was doing paperwork at her desk, checking off deliveries and sorting out invoices that needed to be sent upstairs to accounts. The secret weighed on her like sandbags dragging a body down to the ocean floor.

Things were still more than strained between Poppy and her, so she couldn't confide in her friend. Although even if they *had* been getting on like a house on fire, this wasn't a secret she'd want to take to Poppy, considering they'd bonded over a shared desire to *not* have children.

And she wasn't ready to tell Lawrence either. Not yet. At least she knew he was the father. Not too long ago it would have been difficult to work out, but lately he was the only one she'd been sleeping with.

And she hadn't done a thing about it. No trip to the doctor or family planning clinic to talk through her options.

She was sort of ignoring it, to be honest. Although at least it was putting an end to her drinking problem. Yeah okay, she'd known it was a problem, all along she'd known it. But at least she was giving it up now, when it mattered. At least she cared enough to do that one thing.

Would she tell Lawrence first? Did he have a right to know? But why? It was her body, wasn't it? Why did she have to tell him about something that was going on with *her* body?

Because it's a part of him.

Fuck that. Fuck him.

And then something happened that changed everything. Something that was going to give her the opportunity to reconcile with Poppy.

She found out Frankie's secret.

Frankie was careless. Annalise went to her desk looking for a warehouse clearance form she was supposed to have had Paul sign and return to her. She couldn't find Frankie or Paul, but she needed that form. She was searching the desk when she knocked the mouse and Frankie's screen lit up.

When she glanced at it and saw Facebook open on the screen, at first she was smirking at the fact that Frankie was just as bad as everyone else, slacking off at work. But then she saw the name at the top of the page. She wasn't logged in as Frankie Macchione, but as "Viv Fairweather." Annalise knew that name. She knew it well. One of the original, earliest members of NOP. One of their favorites.

It took her a second. She blamed the little cells that were converging in her belly. They were making her slow. *Why is she logged in to Viv's account?* The synapses in her brain sparked and she understood. Frankie *was* Viv. She was the mole. She was the one who had been bringing NOP down from the inside.

That's when Frankie's mobile phone started ringing on her desk. Who the hell leaves their phone sitting on their desk anyway?

She should have just let the thing go to voice mail, but she was so angry and she wasn't thinking and she snatched the thing up and answered it. She took the message with the blood running through her body, pounding in her ears. She would pass the message on later, when she'd simmered down. But first she needed to go and talk to Poppy. This was going to fix things between them. This was going to put things right. They'd have a common enemy.

By the time she realized she hadn't passed on the message, it was too late.

Frankie's kids had already gone missing.

PART FIVE
Frankie

Chapter 24

The first time Frankie truly understood the dynamic between Poppy, Annalise, and herself, it hurt. It was earlier on in the year—late summer—and she overheard them talking about her behind her back at work one day. It would have been funny how discreet they thought they were being when they had their private little chats, if it wasn't for the fact that what she'd overheard was so damn hurtful.

That morning during the usual watercooler chatter, someone had mentioned in passing that Annalise was joining Poppy's soccer team and that they still needed more players. At that stage, while they'd never been particularly friendly with her, Frankie still thought she might be able to bring them around. She thought they were just the kind of people who played it cool, who took a while to open up and show their nicer side. She'd played on a mixed indoor soccer team with a few friends a couple of years back and she thought it could be fun to do something for herself for a change.

She ran into Poppy in the ladies', and as they stood side by side at the sink, she casually said she'd heard that Poppy played on a women's soccer team. Poppy had given her an irritated sideways look, as though she was bothering her just by speaking to her. "So, do you need another player?" Frankie had asked. "Because I–"

She'd cut her off. "Nope. Team's full up."

Frankie was taken aback by just how abrupt she'd been. It wasn't as though they were mates but she didn't think she'd ever done anything to offend her. Later Frankie headed down to the warehouse to check on a delivery for Paul. She'd been almost at the bottom of the staircase but she'd stopped when she'd caught her name. It was Poppy's voice, she was down there chatting with Annalise.

"So Frankie cornered me in the bathroom today," she was saying.

Cornered her? How had I cornered her? I'd been standing next to her and asked her a question!

"She wanted to join the soccer team."

"Did she?" Annalise had exclaimed. "Ugh, I hope you said no."

"Of course I did. God, I couldn't stand to have to see her out of work hours as well."

Frankie had wanted to leave. She didn't want or need to hear any more. But she was afraid that if she started back up the stairs, they might hear or see her. She didn't want them to have the satisfaction of knowing their words had affected her.

So she stayed and continued to listen. She didn't get it at first. She had never done anything to them, so why did they have such hostile feelings toward her? She soon realized she wasn't the only one they were bitching about. And every woman they complained about was a mother.

They whinged about Martha and Jodi both getting their Christmas leave forms in *so early* last year, about Steph asking if she could come in earlier in the mornings to knock off in the afternoon in time to pick her kids up from school.

"As if she'll be getting any work done at six A.M. while she's waiting for everyone else to get in! Trust me, she'll be kicking back with her coffee and scrolling through Facebook for three hours. Having kids is like some kind of free pass to do whatever the hell you want," Poppy had said while Annalise made noises of agreement.

And then they came back to Frankie. "Did you see

Frankie's face at the last meeting when she said she'll be in late this Friday after her kid's dance recital or whatever the hell it was? She looked so smug and self-satisfied."

Frankie was furious. She had *not* looked self-satisfied, thank you very much! *They* were the ones with the superior smirks on their faces during staff meetings. Rolling their eyes as soon as anyone mentioned their schedules. To be honest, Frankie thought they'd be disappointed if someone didn't give them the satisfaction of being right.

She had wanted to stomp down those last couple of steps, burst out into the warehouse, and shout, "Screw you two. Like either of you have a single idea what it's like to have children!"

For God's sake, if they wanted to guarantee they scored the annual leave days they wanted, then why didn't they make the effort to put their forms in early like everyone else? And yes, of course Steph would probably spend the first few hours of her day looking through Facebook if Paul agreed to her request to change her work hours, but that had nothing to do with her being a mother, that was just because she was bloody lazy. *Everyone* at Cormack knew that.

Besides, there were plenty of other mums there who

worked damn hard—herself included. If Frankie left early to pick up the kids, or took the day when one of them was sick, she had to catch up on all her work at home that night after they were in bed. And for every occasion that she took time off to go and see her kids get an assembly award or run in the cross-country, there were about fifteen more events she missed. Just the other day her youngest daughter, Hayley, had asked her why she never came into the classroom for parent helping like all the other mums did. While her eldest, Coby, was starting to complain that he was too old to go to the After-School Care Club and that his mate Scott's mum let him walk home on his own.

And all Frankie wanted to do was shout, *I'm doing the best I can! And for crying out loud, why don't any of you ever ask the same things of your dad?*

So, she knew that Poppy and Annalise looked down on her. That they judged her.

Frankie had to admit, she gave it back. She was angry, so she used her position to get back at them. She cut in line at the nearby café. She ordered in the type of milk and biscuits that she liked for the office kitchen.

Not long after, Frankie overheard them down in the warehouse once again—she'd taken to heading down those stairs with very soft steps, just in case. This time they were whispering about this new Facebook group they'd started up and Frankie's curiosity was piqued. After a bit of searching, she found the group and checked it out.

> NOP is a closed group for women without chil-dren.
> PM one of the moderators for more information or to request an invite to join.

Frankie wanted to know more. She already had a fake Facebook account all set up. She'd opened it up a few years back when she was checking an ex-boyfriend's profile out of curiosity. She made a few tweaks and used it to submit a request to join NOP, and she was able to join straightaway as one of their earliest members.

Frankie quickly learned that this was Poppy and Annalise's way of whinging about other women—about women like her. But here she was, able to be a fly on the wall and see exactly what Poppy and Annalise were like outside the context of work. Even better, she could join in. She could have perfectly friendly, chatty con-versations with the two women who despised her, and they had absolutely no idea who they were conversing with.

It gave Frankie a weird voyeuristic pleasure.

She was also a member of MOP, had been for a long time. Her sister Lucy was one of the moderators of the group and she'd pushed her to join. She'd love Poppy and Annalise to meet Lucy. If they thought Frankie was the typical soccer mum, they'd be blown away by Lucy. She was the perfect parent. She married into money and didn't have to work, which meant she could be there for anything and everything her children needed. She was also studying journalism, because once her kids were older she wanted to be able to get back into the work-force. If she wasn't Frankie's sister, Frankie would probably hate her. No. That wasn't true actually, because here was the thing about Lucy—she was also *nice*.

MOP could be impressive in the way it drew a community of women together. Because in among all the incessant, repetitive posts about when you should stop giving your child a dummy, or cloth nappies versus disposable, or the pitfalls of fussy eaters or nonstop tantrums, there was also this wonderful sense of camaraderie.

Once, a mother had posted a late-night plea for formula for her baby because she'd run out and couldn't leave the house, and five different women had all flown into action, dropping off several spare tins to her home. It was a beautiful thing to see unfold.

And when Hayley had been obsessed with the Woolworths animal collector cards and desperate to get hold of a ringtail possum card to complete her set, Frankie had popped a request up in the group, and a mother from just two streets away had responded within two minutes that she had a spare and would be happy to drop it into her letterbox the next day. Hayley had been delighted, and for once Frankie had felt like she was a kick-arse mum.

On the other hand, there were also times when MOP could suck the life right out of her. Recently, Frankie had gone to MOP to vent about life as a working mum after Poppy and Annalise had made her feel awful for taking some time off to go along to a school event.

Does anyone else struggle with the nonparents at their work? I've got a part-time office job and a DD6 and a DS10 at home and I'm sick of being judged by the single women here who get pissed off anytime I have to leave early or take time off for a school event or whatever. And by the way, I always catch up on my work after hours, plus my boss is fine with it, so what the hell does it even have to do with them? Anyway, sorry—just wanted to share and see if anyone else is dealing with the same sort of stuff. It's getting me down today.

All she had been after was a bit of "Chin up love, you'll be right"—some validation that yes, it was tough, but yes, she'd get through it. She should have known it wouldn't be that simple.

The first comment was great.

Yes! I'm with you 100%! I work in retail and not only do I have the 18-year-old high school or uni students getting pissed off with me if I nab the best shifts to fit in with my kids—'cause apparently their homework is more important than me being home in time to tuck my babies in at night—but I also have the older women, who should understand 'cause they're actually mums as well, but it's just that their kids are all grown up—but instead they want first pick of the shifts 'cause they've been working there longer!! Feel like I'm the enemy in my own workplace. SUCKS! Chin up, Mama!

She'd scrolled to the next comment.

I'm lucky enough to work in a family business, so I get to pick my own hours, but I can imagine your struggle. So sorry. Hugs.

It felt good; the tension melted away.

But then a comment stopped her short.

Don't take this the wrong way hunnie. But I just don't get why ppl even have kids if they're not gonna stay home wit them in those early yrs? I mean, if you make the choice to work for whateva reason—fair enuf, but don't whinge about it if the rest of the world isn't bending to make life easier 4 you. Sorry you're having a rough time, but that's just my opinion on it. If you want to spend the time with kids, quit your job and B there for them.

There was a reply below it.

Are you KIDDING me? Not everyone can afford to stay home with their kids!!

And then another.

Sorry, but that's a little judgmental. Some mums need jobs to make money to, you know, actually FEED their children! LOL!

And one more.

I actually agree with this. You're either a SAHM or a working mum. If you're a working mum, you have a responsibility to your workmates, your boss, your career, to give it your all, not to keep slacking off and using your kids as an excuse to take days off. You're the one who prioritized career over family, so now you have to follow through.

Frankie had wanted to hurl her phone across the room.

She really wished she'd stopped reading before she'd gotten to that comment.

So there it was, the ugly side of MOP. Maybe she shouldn't call it that. Maybe it's not ugly, people having their own opinions. They had every right to, didn't they? But why did they have to say those things when they knew they were just going to make you feel like shit?

That's where NOP came in. A completely different vibe. Everyone within NOP was on each other's side, and the reason was that they all had a common enemy: mothers. There was no reason for the women in NOP to tear one another down, because they were too busy tearing down the women of MOP.

What had begun as a fun game, a chance to spy on Poppy and Annalise, turned into something else altogether. Frankie realized that she enjoyed taking on this different persona. Becoming Viv was like a drug to her. She got to cast off everything that currently defined her as "Frankie"—mother, wife, PA. She envisioned a fantasy job for herself, she talked about fake dream holidays that she'd taken and more that she was planning. She invented hobbies and chatted in a way that was outside of her own comfort zone. It wasn't that she wished she didn't have the life she had—she adored her family, she'd never want to give them up—but getting to pretend to be someone else was intoxicating.

Frankie had heard how some actors could be shy and introverted until they stepped onto a stage and became someone else. That's what this was like—she was stepping onto a stage.

But then in May those two worlds collided.

It was her sister Lucy who alerted her to the news. She was working at her desk when an iMessage popped up in the top right corner of her screen.

Check out the Da-RAMA happening on MOP right now!

Frankie opened up Facebook and clicked across to the group. While she waited for the screen to load, she typed a message back to Lucy.

What's going on? Kids were so shitty with me yesterday BTW. Couldn't come and watch special performance at assembly. Apparently it's unforgivable.

The reply pinged back almost instantly.

Tell 'em to pull their heads in. You're an awesome mum. Call me later and tell me more about it. But for now take a look at the pinned post from one of the other moderators at the top of MOP and you'll see what I'm talking about.

The group page finally loaded properly and she saw the post Lucy was talking about and started reading.

MOP Moderator—Some of you might have read an article (link in comments below) about a new local women's Facebook group that was apparently inspired by yours truly. Or should I say "ours truly"?! Because obviously MOP is a movement that has grown to be a part of all of us. This new group is called NOP and it was started by a local woman who was upset when she discovered she couldn't join MOP because she's not a mother. I know they say imitation is the sincerest form of flattery, but come on! Oh, and can I interrupt here to say that we can and do have some nonmothers within our fold!! Sometimes pregnant women join, so that they can get some advice prebaby, and we have on occasion approved women who are having trouble conceiving. SO, there was no need for this woman to feel excluded. #JustSaying

Anyway, according to the article, this new group is very much EXCLUSIVE to nonmums. (How's that for a bit of exclusion? Can you say IRONY?!) The main issue with NOP is that they use it to BITCH and WHINGE and COMPLAIN about US!

However, the good news is that the person who wrote the article is one of our very own members. So that means we have our own little spy who will continue to keep an eye on things.

Unfortunately, some of this animosity between MOP and NOP has also spilled out into "the real world." A few members have told me they've been confronted when they've been out and about with their little ones by NOP members who are keen to judge their parenting. Really nasty stuff.

Therefore, I want to issue a bit of a warning to you all. It sounds to me like the women in this group are quite hostile. So please watch out for women who are looking to engage us mums in unnecessary arguments. Don't let them pull you in—it will just ruin your day. And remember, the likelihood is: They're JUST JEALOUS of us! Hopefully this group will fizzle out (their member numbers are about 10 percent the size of ours) and we won't have any more incidents. Chin up to anyone who has been personally affected by the NOP group, and remember: This too shall pass!

Peace and love.

Frankie was totally captivated. *So.* Someone else in NOP was a fake member like her? She wondered who. She texted Lucy again.

Oh wow, that is a bit of drama!

The dots flashed up, telling her Lucy was composing a reply.

Another message popped up, this time from her husband, Dom.

Hey if you do grocery shopping tonight use the St. George credit card instead of the CBA one. Okay?
Sure thing.

Frankie made a mental note. Meanwhile Lucy came back to her.

I know!! All very interesting ☺

Frankie leaned back in her chair and rubbed her chin. Was this going to cause her problems? Would her fake profile be in jeopardy if Poppy and Annalise started trying to figure out who had infiltrated the group?

She glanced around to make sure there was no one nearby, then she leaned forward again, switched across to her fake Facebook account, and checked in to NOP to see if there'd been any posts about this whole MOP thing on the other side. She hadn't logged into NOP for a few days, so she might well have missed something important.

She was about to start scrolling through the page when a notification popped up in the top corner of her screen. It was an email from Paul. The subject line was just:

See you in my office, please.

She hopped up immediately and strode in through his door.

"Close it behind you, please."

Frankie shut the door.

"Just flick the blinds closed too, would you?"

"Paul," she began, gently, carefully, "people will . . ."

"Please."

She closed the blinds.

Every day Frankie questioned if she was doing the right thing.

Chapter 25

It was the usual afternoon juggle—picking the kids up and remembering which day it was and therefore where to actually head to collect them. Frankie had a real mix of things set up to cover their care. Two days a fortnight they were at the on-site public school care. One afternoon they were picked up by the Kids Club van and taken to a private center, and wherever possible, either her sister Lucy helped her out or Mandy, another mum at the school. But she still had to constantly coordinate different people, call in favors, and sometimes leave early and pick them up herself when she could. The frustrating part was that Dom didn't have to be a part of the organizational hell. He just did his nine-to-five job and came home at the end of the day.

The kids were at another mum's house today. And Frankie wasn't proud of the fact that she didn't really know this mum as well as she should in order for her to have her kids in her care. Okay, she didn't know her at all. But she'd been stuck that afternoon after a friend had pulled out last minute, and that friend had offered to connect her with this other mum, Chelsea, who she assured Frankie was brilliant—very responsible, had kids at the school, great parent, great person, and would be happy to help out. Frankie had felt embarrassed asking for a favor from someone she barely knew, but she'd had no other choice.

Frankie rang the doorbell and waited for Chelsea to answer. The second the door opened, Frankie recognized her, and kicked herself for not putting the name to the face sooner. It was the mum from the school parents group who'd guilted her into volunteering for the upcoming athletics carnival. Frankie had said no at first, when Chelsea had approached her—for God's sake, she had a job! Couldn't these people understand that? But the look of judgment that had crossed Chelsea's face . . .

"I know, I know, it's tough—I get it, I do," Chelsea had cooed at her while Frankie nodded along, thinking, *No, you don't, you don't get it at all because you're a stay-at-home mum and you have the time to turn up to any school event you want to! And I bloody well respect that, I honestly do! But you don't respect my choices, do you?*

And she was right, because Chelsea had continued on: "It's just that everybody else is juggling things too and we do all need to take our turn, you know? You couldn't make it to the school disco, could you?"

So Frankie had let herself get guilted into it. And the whole time the voice in her head was screaming, *How many more pieces of myself can I give away?*

"Frankie," Chelsea exclaimed now as though they were old friends. "So, great to see you. Your two little munchkins have been absolute angels for me this afternoon. Come in. Can I get you a drink?"

Frankie's first thought as she followed her through the door into her immaculate home was that Chelsea and Lucy could be best friends. Actually, no—Lucy had genuine kindness in her heart, she would never have pushed her into volunteering for the carnival like Chelsea had. This woman was all fake. Fake platinum-blond, dead-straight hair (had to be hair extensions as well). Fake tan. Fake nails. But the designer clothes were genuine. Frankie would love to be able to afford an outfit like the one Chelsea was wearing.

"Um, no, I'm fine, thanks, though. I'll just gather up their stuff and we'll get out of your hair."

"Honestly, it's no trouble, you're not in my hair at all. I was going to sneak in a cheeky glass of wine before I start cooking dinner. Sure you don't want to join me?"

Frankie hated people who called a drink "cheeky." What was so cheeky about it? Are you underage? Are you skolling vodka at 9 A.M.? No. You're an adult having a glass of wine in the late afternoon/early evening. Act like it.

"No, really, I'm good," she said, and started calling for the kids.

"Now," said Chelsea as Coby and Hayley appeared and started packing up their school bags, hats, and jackets, "Hayley mentioned you hadn't had time to work on the Australian animals project with her, so we just made a little bit of a start on it together. Show Mum," she instructed, and Hayley proudly lifted up the cardboard to show Frankie.

She swallowed. She'd had no idea Hayley was supposed to be doing some sort of animal project. "Oh, wow," she said, forcing the enthusiasm into her voice. "That looks fantastic, Hayley." She paused and added to Chelsea, "You shouldn't have. We would have got to it eventually."

"Yes, well, it is due tomorrow, and I just thought the two of you will end up staying up till midnight if you try to do the whole thing tonight, and you know how kids get if they don't have enough sleep. Turn into little terrors for the teachers."

The criticism of her parenting was clear. And right now Frankie didn't care that she'd saved her a stack of time on the school project tonight. All she wanted to do was rip up that poster and start fresh with her daughter. But obviously she'd never do that to Hayley.

She forced out a thank-you and got the hell out of there as fast as she could.

It was times like these when Frankie especially felt the loss of her parents. They would have made fantastic grandparents, Frankie's mum and dad. They would have loved to step in and help out with Coby and Hayley, and Frankie wouldn't have taken advantage of them too much either. Well, at least she liked to think she wouldn't have. But she and Lucy had lost their mum to a stroke when they were in their late teens. And then their dad passed away when they were both in their twenties. Some relatives had offered the romanticized notion that their father had died from a broken heart. If they thought this would somehow be a comfort, they were wrong. It was diabetes that had killed their dad— plain and simple. And Frankie found the idea that he'd succumbed to his grief and chosen to leave his two daughters offensive.

These days, Frankie and Lucy didn't talk about their parents often.

Dom wasn't coming home until late that night. The kids were in bed, the animals project had been finished off, and Frankie had filled her stomach by grazing off the kids' plates, along with a few "cheeky" glasses of wine. She wanted to unload on Dom, tell him all about Chelsea and how she'd shown her up and judged her, but as far as Frankie knew, he hadn't even left the office yet.

She wandered restlessly around the lounge room, sipping her wine, on the one hand enjoying the peace and quiet, and on the other hand half wishing the kids hadn't fallen asleep so obediently on time tonight, just so she could have someone to chat to.

They were outgrowing their home. The kids didn't have their own space. There was only one small single living area for the four of them to share, and their bedrooms were barely big enough for a bed, a bookshelf, and a wardrobe. The kids both needed their own desks so they could keep their homework more under control, instead of spreading it out across the dining room table or the kitchen bench, and constantly losing important sheets of work. And a second living space would be great for them to chill out away from their parents once in a while, instead of having to retreat into their bedrooms if they wanted to escape them. And okay, if she was entirely honest, Frankie would much prefer to watch an episode of *Grand Designs* or listen to music in the afternoon while getting dinner ready, instead of having to put up with episodes of *Mister Maker* or *Ben Ten*—depending on which child won the battle for the remote.

Coby would also love a dog. Plus a yard big enough to play with the dog. Hayley didn't like dogs, but if they got one, it would be good for her . . . But all they had out the back was a four-by-four-meter courtyard with a patch of grass so small you could maintain it with a pair of nail scissors.

They had a five-year plan: a schedule to get them out of that town house and into their dream home, with a big yard and maybe a swimming pool. They'd plotted out how much they needed to save to make it happen and estimated how much they'd be able to sell this town house for at the end of the five years, based on average growth for the area. It was definitely viable and they were currently coming up on two and a half years. Halfway there. Frankie often caught herself daydreaming about what their next house might look like, wondering if they'd be a different family in a different house. More organized. More relaxed. More loving to one another. Could a house do that to you? It was probably wishful thinking, but then again, personal space could surely do wonders for relationships, couldn't it? Both between husband and wife and parents and children.

When Dom finally arrived home at close to eleven, all hopes of Frankie unloading on him were quickly dashed. The first thing he said when he came through the door was, "Did you use the CBA card the other day when I asked you not to?"

Frankie stared at him, irritated by his tone, and by the fact that he hadn't even bothered to greet her before launching into an accusation. He'd always been blunt. He came from a massive Melbourne-based Italian family and he'd grown up learning to be loud, outspoken, and to get straight to the point in order to be heard.

She had to stop and think what he was on about for a minute, but then she remembered the message he'd sent. It had come through right when she was finding out about the scandal between MOP and NOP and it had completely slipped her mind. When she'd shopped for groceries later that night she hadn't even thought about it when she swiped her card at the checkout.

"Oh yeah, I guess I did. Sorry. Was it really a problem?"

He grunted and dumped his bag down before crossing the room straight to the kitchen. "If it wasn't a problem I wouldn't have asked in the first place," he said. He opened the fridge and stood scanning the contents. "What are we having for dinner?"

"Catch-and-kill-your-own night," Frankie replied. "I ate with the kids. What's the issue with the CBA card anyway?"

"Problem with the bank," he said, running one hand through his dark curls and messing them up. "A transfer that failed. Forget about it, I'll sort it out. So you've eaten?"

"Yep. Well, sort of."

"Any ideas on what I can have?"

"I don't know. You're a big boy. You'll figure it out."

She took her glass of wine and headed upstairs to the bedroom, where she climbed onto the bed and sat against the pillows. She didn't feel like staying downstairs with Dom when he was being so irritable. Especially not when she'd been hoping to complain to him and get his sympathy. And if she was completely honest, she was also hoping for that sympathy to turn to sex. They seemed to be going through a bit of a dry spell lately.

Sometimes she wondered if Dom still found her attractive. She thought she had a plain, average, normal face. She wasn't stunningly beautiful, but she wasn't ugly. Her chin didn't jut. Her nose wasn't pointed or hooked or turned up or long, but it also wasn't a cute little button either. Her eyes weren't too close together or too wide apart. Her face wasn't heart-shaped, her hairline didn't dip into a widow's peak. Her ears didn't stick out. She guessed that's what she meant by normal. No special, defining features.

Her mother was Sri Lankan and she'd been born with silky brown skin—so maybe that was her special, defining feature? Maybe that's what made her beautiful to Dom?

Did other men look at her? It was something she wondered about all the time. She wondered about it more often than she probably should. She wasn't a very good feminist, was she? She pretended to be one. There were videos on social media of women walking through a city to demonstrate how hard it was for a female to put up with the attention: the catcalling, the comments, the propositions. Sometimes they called the men out on it, or they threw out clever, smart-arse responses.

Frankie knew how she was supposed to react to these videos—she was meant to be appalled by the behavior of the men. She should have been fist-bumping the air when the women shut them down.

But secretly, she'd find herself wondering why men didn't pay her that kind of attention anymore. She was jealous of those women.

Was it because she was too old for that now? Was she even attractive anymore? Did anyone glance at her and check for a wedding ring? Did anyone look her up and down? Or was she simply invisible?

She decided to try Lucy for some sympathy instead. She put her wineglass down on the bedside table and typed out a text on her phone.

So this mum who looked after the kids this afternoon did Hayley's school project with her.

The reply came back immediately.

Score!
    No! Not score. Annoying. She was showing me up.
    Umm, sorry? How was she showing you up?
    By proving she's a better mum than me. That she's more on top of things.
Rubbish! Count it as a win, NO ONE likes doing homework with their kids.

Frankie had to admit, she could see how it sounded from Lucy's point of view—like Frankie was being a spoiled brat. But she couldn't seem to convey the way

Chelsea had spoken, the way she'd seemed so smug about it . . . that comment about keeping kids up too late and making life harder on the teachers.

Frankie decided to drop it and move on to something else. For a second she considered asking Lucy one of the questions that they always avoided. *How much do you still think about Mum and Dad? How much do you miss them? What do you think they would have thought of our kids?*

But instead she wrote:

Dom is in a terrible mood tonight.
Rough day at work?
I don't know. Didn't ask.
Communication babe! Key to a good relationship!

Okay, maybe she wasn't in the mood for Lucy tonight either. Frankie shut down the conversation with a quick *Thanks, good idea, heading to bed now,* and turned to Facebook instead. She hadn't checked back to see what was going on with the whole MOP/NOP drama and she wondered if anything more had happened. She scrolled through the various posts about the back-and-forth between members of each group. This was the exact distraction she needed.

Tuesday of the following week, Frankie had to work late again and once more she was stuck for what to do with the kids. She wished Dom's parents lived up here in Sydney instead of down in Melbourne. One thing she knew—she wasn't asking Chelsea for any more favors.

She sat at her desk and tried to figure out what to do. *Why does this have to be all on me?* Why couldn't Dom step in and help out for a change? It wasn't like he didn't have enough sick leave saved up. She gave him a call.

"What's up?" he asked when he answered.

"I need you to pick up the kids this afternoon," she said.

"What?" he said. "Why would I be able to do that? I'm at work!"

Frankie couldn't believe how incredulous he sounded at the mere suggestion he leave early in order to take care of his own offspring.

"I know that," she said, "but I'm sure you can leave early just this once. For crying out loud, it's not as though you've *ever* done it before."

There was silence for a moment then he took her by complete surprise. "Okay," he said. "It's no problem. I'll get them."

"You will?"

"Yep. Don't worry. See you later tonight."

Frankie hung up the phone in a slight daze. It was such a complete one-eighty. Maybe he'd heard the desperation in her voice? Having his support in this way felt like such a lovely change. Was that all it took? The simple act of actually asking for his help? If that was the case, she ought to ask more often. Maybe the only reason he never offered was because he had no idea how hard it was for her.

Oh, bugger, she thought then, he's not going to have a clue where to meet them or what time or anything.

She texted some instructions to him and got back to work.

On the bus on her way home, Frankie couldn't help herself. She sent Dom a message to make sure it had all gone fine and that he hadn't forgotten to get the kids. A response buzzed back. It was a selfie of Dom, Coby, and Hayley, beaming up at the camera. She smiled as she stared at the image. Coby and Hayley were both fair-skinned like Frankie's dad, each with a light dusting of freckles across their noses. And Hayley had inherited Dom's dark curly hair. Neither of them looked like Frankie, though. Apart from maybe Coby's eyes. Sometimes when she was out with the kids she caught

people looking at them, and suspected they were trying to work out whether or not she was their biological
mother. In the picture, Dom looked hot with his collar
turned up and a sexy glint in his eye. Coby was poking
his tongue out—he never liked to smile for photos, but
Hayley was grinning toothily out of the phone at her.

The phone dinged again and she thought it was another message from Dom.

It wasn't.

It was from Paul's wife.

Chapter 26

Frankie hopped off the bus at the next stop and called Dom. She kept her voice light and breezy. "Hey, babe, I know you've already done me this massive favor of leaving work early to get the kids and I was about to head home, but . . . a few of the girls at work want me to have a quick drink with them tonight. Do you mind? You good with the kids?"

Before he could answer, Frankie gabbled on, "I wouldn't ask, but you know how hard it's been getting the women here onside, so I don't want to turn them down now that they've finally asked."

"Of course." His deep voice with its thick Italian accent came back warm and reassuring. "I'm fine with the kids."

Frankie closed her eyes, saw the picture of the three

of them all grinning up at her, and felt a hard pang of guilt at lying to him.

"Hey, Frankie," Dom added, "just do me a favor and remember to use the St. George card this time, would you, and, uh . . . try not to put too much on it. The issue with the CBA card means that now the St. George account is almost maxed out."

"Absolutely," she said. "I won't forget this time."

Once she'd hung up, she ordered an Uber, and within five minutes, she was heading back in the same direction the bus had brought her. Waste of money—it was a shame Linda couldn't have texted a little earlier, before Frankie had gotten so far away from North Sydney. Linda wanted to meet at a coffee shop on MacArthur Avenue. She wouldn't say in the message what it was about. But Frankie could guess, and there were butterflies dancing up a storm in her stomach as the Uber driver took an agonizingly slow route through the traffic to the city.

At the café she spotted Linda in a far corner, her dark hair pushed back by a pair of sunglasses, her fingers absentmindedly tapping on the tabletop as she waited. She'd picked an isolated table, away from the rest of the patrons who were clustered nearer the front, enjoying the last of the sunshine. Frankie made her way through the café and took a seat opposite her.

The expression on Linda's face confirmed her fears.

"It's gotten worse, hasn't it?" Frankie reached across the table to touch Linda's hand.

Linda opened her mouth to speak but a waitress appeared next to them. "You need a menu, or is it just drinks?" she asked, a friendly smile across her face.

"I'll take a flat white with one, please," said Linda.

"Skim cap," Frankie said, eager for her to leave them be.

"Anything to nibble on?"

"Nope," Linda and Frankie said in unison.

Then Linda added quickly, "Thank you, though." She was always polite like that.

The waitress left and Frankie looked at Linda, willing her to talk.

"It's not that," she said. "It's this." She pushed her phone across the table and Frankie read the text message on her screen in confusion at first.

Linda, I'm so sorry to be the one to tell you this— but I'm an employee at Cormack and I think you need to know that your husband isn't being faithful to you. Again, I'm really sorry.

Frankie was flabbergasted. "Paul is *cheating* on you?"

Linda gave her a pitying smile. "Frankie," she said, "no, darling, Paul's not cheating . . . this text is about you. Someone thinks the two of *you* are having an affair."

"But . . ." Frankie stopped for a second, trying to get her brain around it. It fell into place. "Oh my God, you're right!"

There was a beat and then they both started laughing hysterically. They laughed for a good few minutes before they were able to regain their composure, and when the waitress put down their coffees, she gave them a quizzical, amused look.

"I needed that," said Linda, stirring her coffee and smiling. "I really did. Sorry," she added, "I didn't mean to be so mysterious with getting you here and everything, but I wanted to let you know straightaway. If there's someone at Cormack who's watching closely enough to start to think something is going on—well, even though they've come to the wrong conclusion this time, they might come to the right conclusion next time."

The amusement cleared from both of their faces and Frankie nodded. "I guess you're right. It's not good, is it?"

It was six months previous that Linda had first called Frankie and asked to meet because she had something important to discuss. She'd cut straight to the point that day. "Paul's been diagnosed with early-onset Alzheimer's," she'd said. The bottom line was that Paul and Linda didn't want anyone to know just yet. Only a year prior to that he'd floated the company on the stock exchange. Soon after there'd been a falling-out between Paul and two members of the board. Paul had been trying ever since to claw back a majority shareholding of the company. But when the symptoms had begun to worsen, he'd realized he only had a short time frame in which to get the company back under his control before it was discovered that he was no longer capable. All he wanted was to have enough control that he could ensure the company remained intact. And Linda had wanted Frankie's help. "Paul trusts you," she'd said. "So you're the only one in the company that he's comfortable with knowing the truth, at least until he gets these legal issues sorted out. Once it's all fixed, he'll make an announcement and relinquish the director's position to someone else. But in the meantime, we need you to look out for him. Shelter him from difficult decisions or tough meetings wherever you can. Run interference, calm him down when he's confused, whatever you can do to help hide our secret."

At the same time, Linda would be working with lawyers, trying to find a loophole, a way to get back majority shareholding. They'd been hopeful it wouldn't take too long to sort out, and Linda was apologetic that she was asking so much of Frankie, expecting her to lie to everyone else in the company, as well as Dom.

"The fewer people who know the better," Linda had explained, "and as Dom works for CT&T . . ."

She had a point. Cormack sometimes did business with CT&T. If Dom accidentally let something slip over a beer with workmates one Friday night, it could get back to the wrong people.

Now as they sipped their coffees, Frankie asked Linda if she was at all worried when she got the text. "Like, just for a second? Or did you put two and two together straightaway?"

"No, I wasn't worried. Wouldn't matter if he was completely lucid, Paul could never cheat on me. He always joked that he didn't understand how adulterers coped with more than one woman. Plus, I should have expected it. The amount of time you have to spend in his office, one-on-one, settling him down and reassuring him, it's amazing no one's come to this conclusion sooner."

"Yeah, that's true. I was in there for hours today, actually. He came over all paranoid. He wanted me to look up all this random stuff about one of our competitors

on his computer for him and he wanted the door locked
and the blinds drawn. It must have looked suspicious
from the outside."

Linda hesitated. "So you think he's getting worse,
Frankie?"

"Oh, um, I don't know."

"It was the first thing you said when you got here.
You thought that was why I needed to see you. Tell
me honestly—are we running out of time to get this
company stuff under control?"

Frankie reached for Linda's hand again. "Maybe,"
she said softly. "Hey, what if he takes some leave? Pretend the two of you are off on some tropical vacation for
a few weeks, and in reality, you just stay home, see if
you can get it sorted once and for all. I mean, Jesus, how
much bloody money have you already spent on those
lawyers? Surely they must be ready to make a move—
they're bleeding you dry."

"It's not a bad idea, to get him out of there," said
Linda. "But my worry is that once he's not there, not
in his normal routine . . . I don't know, I just think that
maybe he'll deteriorate faster than ever. Sometimes
I think it's the act of getting up at the same time each
day, getting ready for work, eating the same breakfast,
catching the same train . . . all of that is what steadies

him. On the other hand, some days I'm terrified he's going to step onto the wrong train and end up somewhere up the Blue Mountains or something like that, that he'll get confused, forget who he is, where he lives, and I'll never see him again. I have this dream—this nightmare—where he's wandering lost through the bush and he's calling out my name and I can't get to him, and it makes me feel sick. Sometimes I even follow him to the station, watch to see that he heads to the right platform, gets onto the right train. But he'd be so offended, so embarrassed, if he ever knew."

"I wish there was more I could do," Frankie said. "I've got a day off coming up later this week for the kids' sports carnival. Should I skip it?"

"Don't be silly, you're already going above and beyond for us. And you have a young family. I hate that we're putting all this extra stress and pressure on you. But anyway, that's not the point today, we need to figure out what we're going to do about this 'Good Samaritan' who thinks Paul and you are cheating. Do you have any idea who at the office would be likely to want to dob you in to me?"

The answer came to Frankie immediately and she couldn't believe it wasn't the first name she'd thought of when Linda had showed her the message. *Poppy.* And goddammit, she should have seen this coming. Poppy had posted in NOP just the other day asking for everyone's advice on whether or not she should dob someone in who was cheating. But it had never occurred to Frankie that Poppy could have been referring to her and Paul. Even worse, Frankie had commented on that post! *I'd want to know,* had been her advice.

But before she could answer Linda's question, Linda's hands suddenly flung up to her face. "Oh shit, Frankie," she gasped, "I just realized—what if this person texted Dom as well?"

The skin on Frankie's arms prickled and she rubbed them roughly. Linda was right. What if Poppy had? Dom had been acting so unusual today. So much nicer than normal. Was it because he was trying to play it cool? Did he think he could catch her out by making her relax?

And even worse than that, the thing was—she really had lied to him. It might not have been as bad as having an affair, but still. She wasn't being honest with her husband. All of a sudden her deception felt all the more wrong.

"I have to go," she said. "I have to get home and find out."

Linda nodded. "I'm so sorry, Frankie, if this ends

up making your life even harder. I feel awful. Go. Call me when you can and let me know how it goes with Dom. I'll figure this out."

Frankie wasted yet more money on another Uber back home—she didn't want to wait for the bus. She climbed out of the car and faced their neat, blue-and-white town house, then she hesitated at the front gate. How should she handle this? Obviously, it would be weird if she asked him straight out whether or not he'd received a random message from an employee at Cormack today. She guessed she just had to act normal and see if Dom showed any signs that he'd been contacted.

She let herself in the front door and Dom stuck his head around from the kitchen. "You're home earlier than I expected."

"Yeah, it didn't end up being such a big deal after all. One or two drinks and everyone was already calling it a day."

"Where did you go?"

Frankie had the answer ready to go. "Top Deck bar, not far from work."

"Much to drink?"

"Nah, just a cocktail."

"Cocktail? Those things are such a rip-off. Why don't you just drink beer?"

Well, at least that was sounding more like the Dom of late, worrying about her spending too much instead of encouraging her to go out.

"I didn't feel like a beer," she replied.

His phone dinged and he pulled it out of his pocket to look at it. Frankie's body went rigid—was that Poppy texting him right now? But then he looked up at her and said, "Did you catch an Uber there and back again?"

"Yep," Frankie said. They shared the same account, which was why he was seeing the notification of the bill on his phone.

"Why didn't you take the bus?" he asked.

"I'd only just missed one coming home and the cocktail was sitting a bit funny in my stomach, so I didn't feel like waiting around. Actually, I'm still feeling a bit off. I'm going to take a shower."

Frankie ran upstairs before he could say anything else, the guilt weighing heavily on her shoulders as she went.

Chapter 27

Frankie could feel the sweat trickling down the center of her back and soaking into the waistband of her jeans. Why the hell did she wear jeans anyway? Because she didn't like her legs in shorts. Still, she should have ignored her body image issues in favor of comfort. Even though it was almost winter, the sun was glaring and her jeans felt hot and tight and stiff. Dumb choice.

Sad. That's what Donald Trump would say: wore jeans under the hot sun at the sports carnival. I will investigate this dumb choice. *Sad.*

She looked up just in time to realize that the next heat of kids was taking their positions ready for the race and she wasn't even looking at her stopwatch. She reset it and hit the start button just in time as the starter gun went off and the children came tearing toward her, little arms pumping, chests puffed out, chins up, red-faced.

Shit. Which kid was she supposed to clock again? She picked out one in a yellow bib, hoping she had the right one, and prepared to stop the timer as he reached the finish line. She hadn't expected her job to be this stressful! And the other parents all took it so seriously. It wasn't the Olympics, but they bloody well acted like it could have been. Frankie wanted to give them all winning stickers. Okay, she got why that was wrong— you can't give them a sense of entitlement. They have to know that the real world includes winners and losers. She just hated the look on their faces when they stared up at you, all hopeful, waiting to see if they'd earned a sticker or a ribbon or whatever, and you had to send them on their hot, sweaty, deflated way.

Maybe it was because she never won any races as a kid.

"Mum! Mummy! MUM!" Frankie knew you were supposed to recognize your own child's voice, but it took her a good few seconds to register that she was the "mum" being hailed. She turned around to see Coby running over to her, a bit of a skip in his step. The fact that he'd let a "Mummy" slip out told her how excited he was.

"I won," he said, breathless as he came to a stop in front of her and held out the handwritten ticket he was meant to take over to the marshaling table and exchange for a blue ribbon. "Did you watch me? I told you to watch. It was just over there—my race? It was the long distance. Did you see me come in?"

Frankie hesitated. She'd completely missed it. And wasn't that supposed to be the whole point of taking the time off work—to actually experience the joy of watching her kids racing? But instead she'd been stuck in the one spot, with no shade. Most of the other mums had brought sun umbrellas—one or two even had beach tents for their toddlers to play in while they watched big sis long-jump or high-jump or whatever. But not Frankie—she was under the searing sun in her stupid hot jeans, watching child after child who were of no significance to her whatsoever.

"Yes!" she said to Coby, deciding to throw caution to the wind and pretend she'd seen him—he'd never know. "I almost missed it because I was timing a race over here, but I looked across just in time to see you win!"

Coby stared at her. "You saw me come in first?"

"Yes! Saw you out in front!"

"No, you didn't. Because Trent crossed the line

before me. It's just that he got disqualified 'cause he started before the gun. That's how I won. If you were watching, you would have seen me come in second."

He gave her a well-perfected "I'm not mad, I'm just disappointed in you" look and Frankie kicked herself for getting caught out. She was about to try to explain her way out of it but her phone started ringing and she jumped on the distraction.

"Hello?"

There was a pause. Then heavy breathing. Then quietly, so quietly it was hard to hear with the sounds of the carnival around her, a voice: "Frankie?"

"Paul?"

"Yeah. Frankie. Um . . . I think I need . . ." His voice started to drop in and out. She could only catch half words. "Might be . . . don't know . . . could maybe? . . . not lost . . ."

Frankie pushed the phone hard against her ear, felt the sweat building up on the screen. "Paul, what is it? What's up, I can't hear you properly."

At the same time another mum's face appeared in front of her. "Mrs. Macchione?" she said at full volume, as though the phone pressed against Frankie's ear was nonexistent, while also completely overdoing the Italian pronunciation. "The next race is about to start. You need to be ready to time on lane six."

Frankie glared at the woman and thrust the stop-watch at her before turning away without bothering to explain. "Paul, I'm sorry," said Frankie. "I missed it again. Tell me what's up?"

"I went out," he said. "Just for lunch. I'm not lost, I just don't know where I am. Could you . . . maybe, could you help me? Linda's not . . . I can't . . . I don't know . . . I can't reach her. It's not that I'm . . . I mean, I don't need help. But could you sort of . . . could you fix it?"

Oh God, he sounded so strange and confused. The complete opposite of the normal Paul—the Paul she used to know, when she first started working at Cormack, before any of this began. When he was just that little bit arrogant and overtly opinionated, plus a tiny bit flirty, but not enough to be creepy. Basically a funny, nice boss.

"Okay, Paul. Don't worry, I'm coming now, okay? I'm coming to find you."

"I'm not lost," he repeated, and his voice sounded petulant, like a small indignant child.

"I know, Paul, that's okay. I need to get something from the shops anyway, so it'd be nice to meet you for a coffee. Is there somewhere nearby you can sit down and wait? A bench seat? Tables and chairs?"

There was another long pause. Muffled noises and

then his voice came back again. "I can wait for you here," he said. "On this chair. If that's what you want."

"That's great. I'm hanging up now. I'll see you soon."

Frankie shoved the phone back into her pocket. She was confident she knew where he was. There was a shopping center close to the office—it was huge and mazelike so it was no wonder he'd become confused. She knew as well that Linda had packed him lunch so he wouldn't have to go anywhere, but he'd obviously forgotten. Once upon a time a walk across to the shops for lunch had been part of his daily routine. Sometimes he slipped back into old habits.

Coby had been waiting for her, listening in on the conversation.

"Are you *leaving*?" he asked. The look on her face answered his question before she could. "Mum, I haven't even done the shot put or triple jump yet. And there's going to be finals after lunch. Will you be back for the finals?"

At the same moment Hayley seemed to materialize from nowhere. "Mummy, where have you been. You haven't been watching me *all* day!"

"She has to go," said Coby. "She's leaving."

Christ. It was like she was walking out on them for the rest of their lives.

"Mummy!" Hayley squealed. "You can't leave, you told me you'd watch me. You *promised*. If you go, that breaks your promise, and if you break a promise then you have to *die*."

Frankie crouched down in front of both of them, took in a deep breath, and steadied her voice. *It's not the end of the world, she told herself, it's not, it's not, it's not. I'm there for them when it counts. One day, they'll forget this even happened. I'll be there when it counts. I'll be there when it counts.*

"I'm sorry," she said. "I'm really, really sorry. But there's an emergency at work and I have to go. But I'll come back, okay? As soon as I get it all sorted out, I'll come back and I'll try my best to be back in time to catch the end of it all, okay? I'll try my absolute best."

Thankfully an announcement came across the oval from a PA system, telling all the children to rejoin their class groups for lunchtime. "Listen," she said, "you have to go back to your teachers and your friends now anyway."

"You were going to have a picnic lunch with me," said Hayley. "That was a promise too. You're breaking two promises. That's double dead. You'll get double dead now."

"Hayley! Stop saying that! Contrary to what someone's been filling your head with, breaking a promise is *not* in fact punishable by death, okay? And when you're a grown-up and you have a job, you'll get it."

Hayley at least let Frankie hug her good-bye, but Coby pulled back out of her reach and Frankie headed off to her baking oven of a bus with a heavy dose of mum-guilt dragging her shoulders down. And once again she felt the injustice of it all. Neither Hayley nor Coby had even asked about whether or not their dad could take time off work to come and watch them. It was like there was this unspoken rule where mums were expected to be flexible, were supposed to be able to get out of work and be there for them, but for some reason there was no expectation at all on dads to do the same.

Once more, she longed for her parents. They would have loved to have come along with a couple of fold-out chairs and watched the kids race.

Thirty minutes and several questionable amber lights later, she parked at the shopping center and strode quickly through the car park and inside. She dialed Paul but it rang a few times before going to his voice mail.

"Hey, Paul!" She kept her voice bright and casual as she left him a message. "Just here to meet you for a coffee. Can you call me back? It's Frankie," she added, just in case, and then, "Just redial the last number you called, okay? I'm checking where to come and find you."

She made her way through the center, trying to keep the rising panic at bay as she phoned him again and again and he still refused to answer. Should she call Linda? But she'd just be worrying her, and he was probably hanging about somewhere in a food court or a café and all would be perfectly fine and she would have stressed her out for nothing. Especially considering Linda had told her about that dream the other day.

But another voice at the back of her head was arguing. Because what if this was a bigger deal than she'd first thought? What if she'd got it wrong and he hadn't actually fallen back on old habits and come here? What if he'd got on a bus or train or something and he was somewhere else altogether? And now he wasn't answering his phone. What if he'd gotten himself into some serious trouble? Started an argument with someone who didn't understand his condition? What if he wasn't indoors? What if he was actually outside somewhere? It was *hot* today. Paul wasn't an *old* man, but he was older, and if he got himself lost and he didn't have any water and he was in that searing sun somewhere . . .

"Frankie!"

She spun around on the spot and all at once her heart

jammed against her ribs. It was Paul, striding toward her, a look of surprise on his face to see her. "What are you doing here?" he asked as he came to a stop in front of her. "Weren't you supposed to be at your kids' sports day or something like that?"

Frankie was too relieved to feel frustrated with him.

She was sitting up in bed that night, her laptop on her knees, checking through the schedule for next Monday. She wanted to have it done now so she didn't have to work over the weekend. She'd made it back to the carnival in time to be tasked with the job of packing up the marshaling table. Chelsea had hurried over to her while she was folding down the legs of the table.

"I noticed you couldn't hang around today, so I grabbed *great* photos of your kids for you," she'd told her cheerily, while the mum who'd tried to get her off the phone when Paul had called kept throwing her dirty looks.

Hayley and Coby hadn't forgiven her all night. She was grateful they were both in bed and fast asleep before Dom had come home, so she hadn't been "dobbed in" for missing out on half the carnival. She knew if they'd said something, all she would have had to do was tell Dom she'd been called into work—but she was feeling more and more guilty about keeping Paul's secret from her husband. She really needed to tell him. She needed to stop lying.

She was sick of looking at work stuff. She switched across to Facebook again and started scrolling through some MOP posts when she came across one that had her choking with laughter.

Hello, ladies, I have decided to share a story with you to lighten your day . . . however, be warned, this story draws a fine line between making you laugh and making you puke. It's not for the weak-stomached and it's not to be read while eating. Prepare yourselves. Strap in. I'm about to admit to you the most humiliating thing that has ever happened to me . . .

STOP NOW IF EATING!

So, I was unwell with a bit of a stomach bug for a few days. A few days of being trapped at home, close to the bathroom. On the third day, I was starting to feel better. No more running to the toilet, stomach not gurgling so much. I started cleaning the house, getting back on top of things. I took a shower. I got out of the shower and dried myself, wrapped my hair in my towel, and walked naked to my room. On the way into my room, I paused. I felt the growing need to fart. No need to worry!

I'm better now! It's just the sweet release of some gentle gas. Nothing to write home about. I released. I felt something more than gas. Something liquid. I looked down in horror and there it was on the floor. It had splashed up onto my feet. I stood frozen. Miss Six approached down the hall, asking me a question. "DON'T COME DOWN HERE!!" I shrieked at her. She stopped, looked at me in confusion. "MUMMY'S NOT WELL!! MUMMY'S NOT WELL AT ALL! STAY AWAY!" She backed away from me. I still stood frozen. What was I going to do? It was ON MY FEET! But there was nothing for it, I had to get to the toilet, it wasn't over. I made the dash on tiptoes, all the while shouting at the children, "STAY DOWN THAT END OF THE HOUSE. DO NOT COME DOWN HERE!" I finished in the toilet as quick as my disgusting body would allow me. I cleaned my feet. I raced back down the hall, trying to avoid my previous footsteps—ready to clean up the horror that awaited me. I stared at the floor. It was gone. Completely gone. I gaped stupidly, but where . . . but how? And then I saw him. The dog. The dog had cleaned it up for me. "OH MY GOD YOU DISGUSTING CREATURE!! HOW COULD YOU EAT THAT?" The dog stared back at me, unperturbed. He sauntered over, paused, and licked the doorframe. "IT'S ON THE DOORFRAME?

OH GOD WHAT IS WRONG WITH ME? WHAT IS WRONG WITH YOU?! GET OUT!! GET OUT, GET OUT, GET OUT!"

I spent the rest of the day recleaning the house, reshowering myself, and disinfecting everything. I ran to the toilet anytime there was even the hint of a fart.

And that my friends, is my finest hour.

P.S. The dog was fine.

By the time Frankie finished reading she was crying with laughter. That had to be the most horrendous story she'd ever read. She had to share this with the girls on NOP, they'd love it. She took a screen grab of the story, blotted out the fact that it was a MOP post, and then logged in and shared the image.

People started commenting on it almost immediately.

OMG, where did you get this story? That is priceless!

That is the most revolting thing I've ever heard. Why am I not surprised it was a mother who decided to share that story with the world via the Internet?

I'm glad she shared it, I haven't laughed that hard in a long time. This thing needs to go viral! I'm going to share it on another page, I know some other people who could use a good laugh.

Oh no. Frankie hadn't thought about the possibility that NOP members might want to share it somewhere else. There was a rule within MOP that you were never supposed to screen-grab anyone's posts. But she'd hidden the name at the top of the post so no one would know who it belonged to, and there'd be no way for anyone to figure out Frankie had been the one to steal it in the first place. She started to feel a bit guilty. Perhaps she shouldn't have shared it so readily.

Dom appeared in the doorway and Frankie snapped her laptop shut. She didn't want him to glance at the screen and see anything about NOP. She wasn't sure how he'd react if he knew about her secret online identity, but she doubted he'd be too pleased that she was pretending their children didn't exist. It would be difficult to explain why being Viv gave her so much pleasure without it seeming like she didn't enjoy being a mum. Of course she loved being a mum. She just also liked taking this chance to escape that role.

His eyes narrowed and she realized she'd been a bit too obvious in her attempt to hide what she'd been doing. She smiled widely at him. *Too much teeth! Tone it down!* "Coming to bed?" she asked.

"Yeah, long day," he said. He headed into their en

suite and Frankie reopened her laptop, logged out of her secret Facebook account, and then closed it again and placed it by the bed.

"Hey, Frankie," Dom called from the en suite, "is this price on your shampoo in here for real?"

"What do you mean?" she called back.

He stuck his head out from the bathroom, holding up her shampoo bottle in one hand and conditioner in the other. "The price stickers," he said. "Are these seriously thirty-five bucks a pop?"

"Yeah, I guess, if that's what they say on them."

"Jeez, they saw you coming," he said.

"They're the ones I always buy," she replied. "My hair's a nightmare without the proper salon stuff."

He huffed and disappeared into the bathroom again and Frankie felt a hint of irritation. Why was he suddenly questioning her hair products?

After a few minutes he returned and climbed into bed next to her. "Coby was telling me tonight he's joining the school rugby team," he said as he shuffled down under the covers. "How much is that going to cost?"

Frankie propped herself up on her elbow to look at him. "Dom," she said, "what's with all the money questions lately? First I get in trouble for using the wrong credit card, now you're at me about my shampoo. What's the issue?"

"No issue," he said shortly. "I'm just trying to keep an eye on things. I'm the one who deals with all the bills around here, you know."

"Yeah, because you like dealing with finance. It's your *thing*."

"Okay, so that's what I'm doing. Dealing with the finances, that's all."

"Well, there's no extra cost for the rugby team. It's an in-school activity and he wears his normal sports uniform, so you can stop worrying about it. Just be happy the kid is finally interested in a team sport."

"Yeah, yeah, that's great," Dom said distractedly, turning over to face the other way and switch off his lamp. "I'm just making sure we're still on track for your dream house," he added. "Night."

Frankie put her head on the pillow and lay awake, staring at the dark ceiling. *Your dream house*, she repeated to herself. *I thought it was supposed to be our dream house.*

Chapter 28

Frankie should have known it was too good to be true.

But the thing is, Paul was *completely* lucid when he materialized from his office on Thursday morning, looking so pleased with himself, practically bouncing on his toes. He clapped Frankie on the shoulder and asked her to take a quick walk outside with him.

"I'm feeling the need for a bit of fresh air."

"Sure thing. Fresh air sounds great."

It had been almost a full week since the incident that had pulled her away from the sports carnival and he'd actually been really good all week. Barely any strange comments or vague looks. Well, apart from his funny turn on Tuesday—the day he was supposed to go looking at fidget spinners with Poppy. Even if he hadn't said a few odd things that morning, she still would have accompanied the two of them to the shops to keep an eye on him. But in the end, she thought it best to leave him safe in his office, chatting away on the phone with Linda, and she'd taken his place with Poppy.

That shopping trip had been interesting. Walking alongside Poppy and thinking to herself, *I know you. I know the real you. You've complained to me about your parents not understanding your life choices. I've encouraged you when you were out trying to pick up guys. The two of us are friends, and you have no idea.*

Sometimes hearing Poppy and Annalise's side of the story through NOP made Frankie feel more empathetic toward the two of them, made her want to forgive them for the nasty things they'd said about her. Other times she'd catch them looking at her with utter disgust, and she'd remember that Poppy had tried to out her to Linda for an affair that wasn't happening, and she'd stop feeling so forgiving.

But when they'd run into Poppy's ex and his new partner and baby, Frankie saw Poppy's anguish and she couldn't help herself. She had to stand up for her.

Now Frankie and Paul walked one block down from the office, crossed the road, and headed into Watt Park. Once they were in the park, they meandered along, quietly at first, and Frankie wondered as they walked what Paul was thinking, whether he was confused, if he was wondering where they were or what they were doing out there. Or if he was still with her. But then he spoke and it turned out he was fully lucid.

"I really appreciate how you've been helping me these last few months, Frankie. I know it's put a lot of added strain and stress on you and I haven't liked doing that to you. But I do think I can at least make it up to you a little. Linda and I were going through the company finances together last night and we've earmarked an amount as a bonus for you, to show you just how much we do appreciate your help. It'll be about fifteen percent of your salary. We can run it through with your next pay run."

Frankie was thrilled. With Dom's constant chatter about money these last couple of weeks, a bonus would be fantastic. And it was startlingly lovely to hear Paul sound so much like his old self.

"Paul, you have no idea how perfect your timing is. This is fantastic, thank you so much. Fifteen percent? Are you sure? That sounds generous."

"Yes, I'm absolutely sure. The extra effort you've put in more than warrants it. And the other good news is that we've almost got the ownership issues all sorted out, so we'll make an announcement soon about my condition and you won't have to keep covering for me."

"Paul, that's wonderful."

She realized the look on his face had taken a sad turn. "Not that I'll be happy to lose you as my boss," she added quickly. "I just mean, surely it will make things easier on you as well, right?"

He nodded. "Yes, you're right. It will."

She never thought to ask him to put the offer in writing.

That night Frankie made sure the kids were in bed early. She cracked open one of the nicer bottles of wine and ordered dinner for her and Dom from their favorite Thai takeaway place. She was looking forward to telling him that he could stop pestering her about silly things like the cost of her shampoo. *Hmm, maybe best not to open with that.*

Somehow, her bright and breezy manner irritated Dom the moment he walked through the door.

"What's with all this?" he asked, indicating the neatly set table. They usually ate in front of the television.

"Thought it might be nice for a change."

He seemed instantly suspicious, "Why are you being so . . ."

"So what?"

"So . . . cheerful?"

"I can't be cheerful? I have nice wine, an attractive

husband, and a massaman curry from All Thai-ed Up on its way."

"The expensive place?" he said, sounding irritated. "What's the occasion?"

"I have news!" she half shouted, well aware that she sounded slightly frenzied, but unable to help it. She was so desperate to rally, to stop him from ruining this great news with his new ultranegative attitude.

Dom stared back at her. His eyes slowly widened. "Shit! You're not pregnant, are you?"

Frankie glared back at him. "Do I look pregnant to you?" she snapped.

"Uh . . . no?"

She chose to let that go . . . for now. "No, I'm not pregnant. I'm getting a bonus from work—a big bonus!"

Dom's brow knitted. "A bonus?" he said. "What for? Don't most companies do bonuses at the end of the year, at Christmas?"

"It's for all my hard work," she said, refusing to let his suspicious tone affect her, even as a voice in the back of her head was nagging at her. *What if he did get a text from Poppy that day? What if he was still wondering if she was cheating on him with Paul?* She pushed the voice aside. "But the point is," she said, "more money means we're one step closer to our dream home, right?"

He nodded. "Yeah sure, of course, babe." But he

didn't sound nearly as excited as she'd hoped. "Congratulations." He stepped in and gave her a kiss on the forehead. "It's great news," he said, and she could tell he was trying his best to inject some enthusiasm in his voice, but wasn't quite pulling it off.

Frankie pulled back from him. "Dom, is everything okay?"

"Of course," he said. "Let me go and change. I'll be right back."

He headed off upstairs and Frankie was left feeling completely deflated. She'd thought this news would have made his night. She also looked down at her stomach and poked at it. She hadn't put on any extra weight lately, had she? No, she bloody well hadn't, Dom was just being a typical male.

"Remind me whose idea it was to play squash?" Frankie asked George from accounts as they picked out their hire racquets and headed down to join the rest of the staff.

"Some new person in HR," he said. "Apparently, he's right into team-building exercises. I don't think this is going to be the last."

It was Friday afternoon, and there was really far too much work to do to have almost the entire office down the road at the squash courts for the afternoon. Somehow the request from HR had slipped past her straight to Paul and he'd approved it without thinking through the consequences.

"How is squash team building?" she asked. "Isn't it all about getting on the court and thrashing your opponent?"

"I think you can play doubles, can't you?"

"Jeez, it'd be crowded on the court, wouldn't it? Still, you'd think a proper team sport—like netball or soccer—would make more sense." She spotted Poppy and Annalise at the back of the group, although surprisingly they weren't standing side by side, which was highly unusual. Frankie wouldn't have minded a game of soccer with them on the opposing team. It would be nice to show them they weren't the only ones who knew how to kick a ball.

"Oh God," said George as they got closer, "look, Steph and Martha both have all their own gear. They're going to take this so seriously."

"Excellent," Frankie said, "this is going to be a blast."

They were split up and sent to their various courts and Frankie found herself facing Linda. So much for the team-building element—they were playing one-on-one.

"How'd you get roped into coming along to this?" Frankie asked as they made their way onto the court.

"I dropped by the office the other day and Marcus conned me into coming along," Linda replied.

"That must be the new guy who planned this whole thing. I haven't even introduced myself to him yet."

"Too busy, huh?" she asked sympathetically as she took up her position and prepared to serve the ball.

"Exactly," she said, and was caught off guard as Linda hit a perfect serve and she had to dart sideways in order to return it.

Linda hit the ball back and Frankie took a swing and completely missed it. "By the way," she said as she walked to the back of the court to retrieve the ball, lowering her voice in case other staff on the adjacent courts could hear them, "I just wanted to thank you for the bonus. I'm beyond thrilled. You don't even realize how perfect the timing is."

Linda took the ball from her. "What bonus?" she said, and served the ball with perfect accuracy yet again. "What are you talking about?"

Frankie hit it back and struggled to chat while concentrating on the game. "Paul told me yesterday about my bonus that you two agreed on," she said between breaths. "It's such a great surprise."

Linda loped forward elegantly, somehow able to keep up the conversation without losing her breath or breaking her stride. "I'm sorry, Frankie, but I have no idea what you're talking about."

She smacked the ball with surprising strength, but this time Frankie didn't even try to return the ball, instead letting it fly past her ear, hit the glass behind her, and bounce to the floor. She let her racquet hang by her side as Linda picked up the ball and turned to face her.

"But . . ." said Frankie, "he was definitely completely himself when we spoke. I'm certain of it. And he told me you two had worked out the finances together. And that everything was about to be sorted by the lawyers too."

Linda shook her head. "Oh, darling, he was way ahead of himself. Of course we've talked about giving you something once this is all sorted out to show you how appreciative we are of your help. I mean, you're doing a lot of overtime, and that's while trying to look after a family as well. But he shouldn't have promised you that. Not yet. Cormack's not in a position to pay you a bonus right now. And it's still the kind of thing the board needs to approve. We can't run this past them at the moment, not until we have everything under control."

"Oh," Frankie said, unable to stop the disappointment from showing on her face. She couldn't believe she was going to have to tell Dom her windfall was a lot further off than she'd thought.

"I wish I could give you better news, Frankie. I'm sorry, I really am, but there's no bonus coming—not right now."

Chapter 29

It was a whole heap of things that led to the worst afternoon of Frankie's life. Just one little thing after another. One choice. One mistake. One wrong move.

Leaving her phone on her desk.

Not checking the voice mail on her work phone the moment she got back to her desk.

Assuming that everything was fine. Assuming that the afternoon was going the way it was supposed to go. But nothing ever seems to go to plan when you're a mother.

The first lucky break was when she sent Mandy that text message. At least that way she found out that something was wrong. Otherwise she might not have realized for hours.

Hey, thanks again for picking the kids up today. Any

chance you could remind Coby to keep working on his speech for science?

The reply came straight back.

Didn't you get my messages?

But before she had a chance to ask what she meant, the phone started ringing in her hand. It was Mandy.

"I left messages, one on your work phone . . . another with one of your coworkers. I couldn't get the kids today. Oh my God, she promised she would pass the message on."

"What do you mean? So wait, you don't have the kids?"

"No, I don't!"

"But then . . ." Frankie looked at her watch. Classes had finished forty minutes ago. Why hadn't the school office called her to ask who was picking up the kids?

"Don't panic," Mandy said. "They'll be waiting at the office, I'm sure of it."

"Okay, I have to go," Frankie said, "I have to call them."

She hung up and dialed the school. The recorded message kicked in. She left a garbled voice mail. "This is Frankie Macchione. Is anyone still there in the office? I've just found out my kids weren't picked up today— Coby and Hayley Macchione. Are they there at the office? Can someone please call me back urgently?"

She hung up and stood frozen for a moment. What was she supposed to do next? Start calling around to their friends, figure out if they'd gone home with someone else? But if anyone else had taken them, wouldn't they have let her know?

Frankie snatched up her handbag. She needed to get to the school. She had to find them. Her phone started ringing again and she looked down to see the school calling. *Thank God.*

She answered it. "Yes?"

"This is Renee from the office. I'm sorry, Mrs. Macchione, but Coby and Hayley aren't here. Myself and Mr. Tiller from maintenance are going to do a sweep of the school now, check if they're waiting somewhere for you. But listen, are you sure someone else hasn't collected them for you?"

"I don't know!" Frankie said, aware that she sounded like the worst mother in the world. "Mandy Quick was supposed to take them home today but apparently I missed a message from her telling me she couldn't, so now I don't know."

"Okay, stay calm. I'm sure they're fine. We'll start checking, you call around your school mums' network and see if someone else has them for you. I'll call you back in ten."

Frankie hung up once again, feeling more afraid

than ever. She looked up to see Poppy and Annalise striding toward her determinedly.

"Poppy! You drive, don't you? Can you please give me a lift? My kids didn't get picked up from school like they were supposed to and now I don't know where they are. I need to get there as quickly as possible."

They both stopped short, staring at her for a moment, maybe taken aback that she would ever ask either of them for help, considering their relationship. But Frankie knew Poppy, she knew what she was really like. She'd seen her other side through NOP. She'd seen how compassionate she could be—provided she wasn't spiraling because of that idiot ex. Plus she knew how much Poppy had appreciated the way she'd stepped in and stood up for her when they'd run into said ex and his new partner at the shops. Poppy owed her for that one.

"Yes," Poppy said, seeming to find her voice. "Of course I'll give you a lift."

Annalise had turned a funny shade of gray. At the time Frankie thought she was actually worried about her children. She knew better afterward.

Annalise came with them in the car. She sat quietly in the back while Poppy drove, weaving between the traffic at high speed, God bless her, and Frankie made calls. She phoned parent after parent, trying to track down the kids. She tried Eve, who lived a few doors down, and Eve ran up the street to check the house for her. The kids didn't have their own keys, but Eve made sure they hadn't walked themselves home and weren't sitting on the front porch waiting for her. Frankie then tried Lucy in case she'd somehow picked them up for her. She hadn't.

They were almost at the school when Frankie realized she hadn't even called Dom yet. Now she felt like an awful wife as well as a terrible mother. What was she going to tell him? He needed to know—even if they were perfectly fine at a friend's house and it was all just about to be okay, he needed to know what was going on. Frankie would want to know.

She dialed his number and waited for him to answer. Voice mail. She left a shaky message: "Call me as soon as you get this."

Hopefully by the time he heard her message and called back it would all be okay. She would have found them.

As they pulled up to the front gates of the school, Frankie's phone rang again. It was the school office.

"I'm here," she said, breathless, "here at the school. Have you found them?"

"I'm so sorry, Mrs. Macchione, they're not here. Are you *sure* they're not with another parent? At a friend's house?"

"I've called . . . I've . . . I've tried everyone," she said as she climbed out of the car and strode toward the office. Renee met her out the front and she hung up her phone to speak to her face-to-face.

"I've tried everyone I can think of," Frankie continued. "I don't understand, where could they have . . ."

She was getting so confused. All she wanted was to see those two kids walking toward her. She'd lost Coby at the shops once, when he was a toddler. Hayley had barely flickered into existence in her stomach at the time and she'd been in a clothing store in a large shopping center. Coby was toddling in and out of the clothing racks while she browsed. She kept thinking she ought to stop him from doing that. He still had jam on his chin from his sandwich, he was probably going to make the dresses sticky. But he was having such a fun time and she was tired.

She stopped paying attention to him for what could have only been twenty seconds. She was so sure of that. The problem was that she spent too long searching among the clothing racks all around her, because she was certain that any second he would pop out and surprise her. She never thought that he'd have run off out of the store. But by the time she realized, she'd given him far too much of a head start.

When she dashed out of the shop, she didn't even know which way to turn. Up toward the movie theater? Or down toward the food court?

And all that she wanted was for him to just appear.

That's all she wanted today. She wanted Coby and Hayley to both appear.

Obviously, she found Coby back at the shopping center that day. A security guard helped her and within minutes he'd taken a message over his radio. A small boy had been spotted by some staff at a jewelry store, he was sitting on one of those little shopping center rides. It was a good sixty meters from the clothing shop where she lost him.

She remembered that she cried and she thanked the jewelry store ladies a lot. And she hugged Coby very, very tightly. Later she wondered if those women were all judging her. If they all thought she was a terrible mother. And she wondered what her own mum might have said. Would she have been cross with Frankie for losing her grandson? Or would she have laughed and reassured her that it happened to all parents?

Today, however, even though Coby was much, much older, even though the two of them were so much more capable and responsible than a three-year-old, it felt worse. Frankie didn't know why. Was it because the world was a scarier place these days? Or at least it was if you believed social media and the news. Was it because of all the stories she'd read over the years of people who disappeared without a trace?

"Do we . . . when do we call the police?" Frankie asked Renee.

Renee looked back at Frankie, the mention of the police seemed to frighten her. She pushed her glasses up her nose, "Um," she began, "I guess now we should . . ."

"Hey, Frankie, what's going on? Is everything okay?"

Frankie swung around to see Chelsea striding toward her, looking smart and capable as usual. She was the last person Frankie wanted to see right now and she didn't have the time to deal with her.

Renee answered before she could. "We've got a bit of a situation going on here. Frankie's kids didn't get picked up as they were supposed to and now they're . . ." She obviously didn't want to say the word "missing," but there was no point pretending it wasn't happening.

"Missing," Frankie finished for her.

"Oh God, Frankie," Chelsea exclaimed. "I stayed late to help out with band practice, but unfortunately I didn't see your two. What can I do to help? You've obviously already done the ring around to their friends to see if someone else has picked them up for you?"

Frankie nodded. She appreciated the fact that Chelsea at least gave her the benefit of the doubt that she'd be smart enough to have done that much.

"And are the police involved yet?"

"We were just about to . . ." said Renee.

"All right, that's good," said Chelsea. "You make that call now. The sooner they know what's going on, the better. Frankie, I'm going to get on my phone and start getting our own search under way for you. There's an online mums' group I'm a part of—MOP. They'll help us to get a bunch of local mums out on the streets. Don't worry, we'll find them. It's only four P.M. They can't have got too far."

Frankie didn't bother to tell her she was also a member of MOP. She was happy for Chelsea to be the one to coordinate the search—she didn't think she had the mental capacity to do it herself.

Frankie realized that Poppy and Annalise were still there; waiting by Poppy's car, they looked to be having a tense, quiet conversation. A moment later, Poppy strode over to her. "We'll start searching the streets for you. Tell me your address, we'll drive between here and your home looking for them. Are there any shops or parks that they like to go to sometimes after school? Anything like that we should check?"

Frankie gave Poppy the details and showed her a couple of photos of the kids from her phone. "Hayley's backpack is bright pink," she added as they headed for the car. "Oh, and Coby will probably be playing with his fidget spinner, he never puts the thing down."

She watched them drive away with a silent prayer that Poppy and Annalise would be her saviors that day. That they would find her kids for her. Meanwhile, Renee called the police and Frankie dialed Dom again. He needed to know what was going on.

PART SIX

Poppy, Annalise, & Frankie

Chapter 30

They were both quiet as Poppy reversed out of the school driveway and turned the car down Williams Street to start the search. But eventually, Annalise spoke up.

"I fucked up, Poppy. I really fucked up, didn't I?"

Poppy shoved the knuckle of her index finger into her mouth, her other hand on the steering wheel. Annalise could tell she was biting down hard. Her chest heaved as she sucked in air. "Look," Poppy said eventually, "yes, it's bad. It's really bad. But I'm sure they're going to turn up. We just need to find them. We need to find them and everything will be okay again. She doesn't ever need to know you had any part in this, okay? We'll fix it.

"Annalise," she continued. "Just one question. I . . . I have to ask. You didn't do this on purpose, did you?"

"What? What do you mean, on purpose?"

"I mean you didn't do it because of one of those stupid NOP challenges, did you? You know, 'make the mums stay at work later' kind of thing."

"No! That's not what this was. I made a mistake, that's all. I literally forgot to pass the message on."

"Okay. I just wanted to check. Don't worry, we'll find them. We'll find them and everything will be fine."

Poppy drove slowly down the road, her eyes scanning the footpath, and Annalise tried to focus and do the same on her side of the road.

Annalise didn't make a habit of crying. In fact, she could probably count on one hand the number of times she'd let tears fall down her face as an adult—including watching that stupid movie with Harmony recently.

But right now she felt like crying. She wanted to cry about everything. About her horrible mistake that had led to Frankie's kids going missing. About the secret she was holding inside right now. About the truth of her past that she still hadn't confessed to Poppy.

She had gone to Poppy that afternoon to tell her what she'd found out about Frankie. It was going to bring the two of them back together, she'd thought. It was going to be the focus of their attention and she'd use it to find a way to make Poppy forget about her lies. Or she'd come up with more lies if she needed to. Either way, they would put all that rubbish behind them.

Poppy's face had flushed red when Annalise told her what she'd seen on Frankie's computer screen. "Bloody hell, I was starting to like that woman," she'd said.

Annalise had been surprised by that. What did she mean she was starting to like Frankie? Since when?

They were going to confront her together. But then Frankie had dropped her bombshell. Her children were missing and instantly Annalise knew it was all her fault. She'd admitted her mistake to Poppy while they were waiting at the car just now. Poppy had stayed calm. "We'll fix it," she'd said. "We'll find them ourselves. They can't have gotten far."

Now, as they drove from the school to Frankie's house and then turned around and backtracked, Annalise started to panic. Why the hell hadn't they found them yet? When they were close to the school yet again, she suggested they split up. "I'll go on foot," she said. "Maybe I'll see something or hear something if I'm out of the car?" She felt like she was grasping at straws, but the car was suffocating. "You go and try the park Frankie mentioned."

Annalise had only taken a few steps when she saw it

on the ground. The metal edges caught the sunlight. A fidget spinner.

It didn't mean anything, did it? Anyone could have lost that. It wasn't necessarily his. She picked it up and felt the cool shape press against her palm. Maybe it was, maybe it wasn't. But it didn't feel like a good sign.

She walked back up to the school. She was going to have to show it to Frankie.

Dom finally answered the phone on the third call. His tone was irritable when he picked up, but Frankie didn't give him the chance to grumble at her.

"The kids are missing," she blurted.

"Missing? What do you mean missing?"

"I mean there was a mix-up with school pickup and they're . . . they're just gone."

At first he tried to calm her down, tried to reassure her, offered all the same solutions that everyone had already suggested before him. "A friend must have them." "Could your sister have picked them up?" "Aren't they waiting at the school office?" "Did they walk themselves home?"

Frankie snapped at him, "You think I haven't already thought of all that?" She felt guilty and softened her voice. "They're *properly* missing, Dom. You need to get here."

"I'll be there in five," he promised. She didn't stop to ask how he thought he could get there so quickly when his office was at least half an hour away. She was just glad at the thought of him being there, of having his help. He was their father. She would push the burden onto him. The blame, the guilt, the responsibility of finding them. He would do it. He would find them for her.

Once she was off the phone, she looked back at Renee. "Do I have to wait here for the police or can I start searching myself? What am I supposed to do?"

But Renee was still on the phone herself. She covered the mouthpiece and whispered to Frankie, "Hang on, I'm finding out."

"Listen, Frankie," said Chelsea. "I can imagine you want to get out there and search for yourself, but right now you're probably better off here, coordinating everything and hearing back from anyone that's out looking. Everyone is going to want to report back to you, plus the police will need to talk to you. I know it's hard, but try to hold on. I know we're going to find them—the word's out on MOP and there's a bit of a modern-day phone-tree-style thing happening through Facebook. People tagging in other mums who they know live close by. Others are already out on the streets searching. I bet we'll have good news any minute."

She pulled Frankie into a hug then, sudden and firm. It took her completely by surprise, and Frankie realized that Chelsea's smothering embrace was more of a comfort than she'd ever have expected.

"It's going to be fine, Frankie, I can guarantee it." And the conviction in her voice combined with the warmth of her hug made Frankie think she'd judged her far too unfairly, right from the beginning.

Then she saw Annalise walking toward her. And she hated the expression on her face. She hated it with every fiber of her body, because she knew it meant bad news. This wasn't supposed to happen. Poppy and Annalise were supposed to come back with good news. They were supposed to come back with the best news, they were supposed to bring her kids back to her.

Annalise opened her hand to show Frankie as she got closer. She recognized it instantly. The red, green, and yellow patterns. Coby's fidget spinner.

"Is it . . . ?" Annalise started to ask.

"It's his," Frankie said, snatching it from her. "Where did you find it?"

"Not far from the back school gates," she said, "in the gutter."

"The gutter?" Frankie said. And that word— "gutter"—it took on such an ominous sound. What was his prized possession doing in the gutter? Her heart broke for Coby, wherever he was, whatever had happened to him, he must have noticed he'd lost it, he must be wondering where it was.

"Poppy's still driving around searching," Annalise said. "But I thought I should bring this to you. I'll . . . I'll keep looking."

She turned to walk away and Frankie's phone buzzed in her hand. She looked down at it, willing it to be good news. It was a text message from Paul. She didn't have time for him right now. She didn't have time for whatever crisis he was having or whatever thing he was confused about. Her family needed to come first this time. They needed to come first all the time.

The phone rang then, and she saw that this time it was Mandy. Frankie guessed she was only calling to check in and see if they'd been found, but she answered it hopefully. Had the kids somehow turned up at her house?

"Frankie, have you got them?" Mandy asked when she answered.

"No, not yet," Frankie said, managing to stop herself from shrieking at her, *Why couldn't you have just got them like we planned!*

"Oh God, I'm so sorry! Listen I've got someone coming round to watch mine so I can get out there and help look for them. I still can't believe that woman . . . Annalise, I think her name was, I can't believe she didn't pass on the message to you. I *told* her it was important."

Frankie's brain clouded over and she found herself looking up at Annalise, who was obviously waiting to see what the news was before she set off to look again. No wonder she and Poppy had been so happy to help—it was Annalise's fault that anything had gone wrong in the first place.

Frankie finished the call with Mandy and stepped closer to Annalise. "You took the message?" she said. "You were the one who was supposed to tell me Mandy couldn't get my kids today?"

Annalise's face twisted. "I did, but I didn't mean—"

"Really?" Frankie said. "Are you sure you didn't mean it? Because I know about your group and I know about your challenges. Are you sure you weren't completing a little NOP challenge for yourself? See if you could get a mum stuck at the office instead of running off to collect her kids?"

"What? No! God no! That's not what happened. This wasn't intentional."

Frankie stared at her, hard. Then something clicked. Annalise wasn't surprised at all about the fact that she knew about NOP or the challenges. And she and Poppy had been on their way to talk to her before she'd told them her kids were missing.

"What were you and Poppy coming to talk to me about today?" she asked, her voice sharp.

"It was . . ."

Frankie saw her resolve give in.

"I'd just told Poppy about your fake profile," Annalise admitted, "about you being the mole in NOP. I'd seen it on your computer."

Chelsea was suddenly by Frankie's side, her shoulder pressed up against her. A physical gesture of support, but she remained quiet, letting Frankie speak.

"Right," Frankie said, "and now you're trying to tell me that you neglecting to pass on the message was an accident? You weren't trying to get back at me? Fucking hell, Annalise, if anything, *anything* happens to my kids, it's on you."

Her phone buzzed yet again in her hand. It was the same message from Paul, reminding her to open it. Annalise looked across at the screen.

"Yeah, well, maybe you should look a little closer to home if you want someone to blame," she said. "If you weren't screwing the boss maybe you'd have more of a handle on your kids' schedules."

"Excuse me?" Chelsea interjected, still superglued to Frankie's side. "Is now really the time?"

Frankie wanted to launch herself at Annalise, attack her, strangle her. "I'm NOT screwing Paul," she yelled.

"Then why is he texting you?" Annalise spat back.

"I don't fucking know!"

Frankie jabbed at the phone to open the message, ready to shove it in her face, presuming it would be some inane work-related question. And then she was going to tell Annalise to get the hell away from her and let her focus on finding her children. Dom would be here any minute, and once he arrived, she'd know what to do again.

But instead the message caught her by surprise.

Just remind me, is Coby lactose intolerant? Or is that my imagination?

Frankie stared at the text, perplexed. Why was he asking her that right now? What did that have to do with anything? God damn Paul and his confused mind. As she looked at the screen, another text popped up.

Wanted to make sure before promising the two of them an ice cream.

Her hands shook. She almost dropped the phone. Did this mean . . . did Paul have her kids?

She dialed his number immediately and waited while it rang, turning her back away from Annalise. Chelsea remained by her side, waiting to find out what was going on.

"Hey!" Paul answered brightly. "You didn't need to call, I only wanted to make sure."

"Paul," said Frankie, trying her best to keep her voice steady. "Are my kids with you? Do you have Coby and Hayley?"

"Yeah, of course," he replied. "I took them out to Balmoral to keep them entertained until you were ready. So where did we land on the ice creams? I didn't want to ask Coby direct in case it disappointed him if he couldn't have it."

"I . . . but . . ." A thousand questions were running through her mind. How did he have them? Why did he have them? And more importantly, were they really there? Were they really okay?

"Can I talk to Coby, please? Now?" she asked, and she couldn't keep the impatience out of her voice.

"Okay, sure."

She heard muffled noises, Paul's voice calling out, "Your mum wants to talk," and then heavy breathing and Coby's voice. "Hi, Mum."

"Oh Jesus," she said, and she started to cry. "You're okay."

"Um, yeah. Why wouldn't I be?"

She shook her head despite knowing he couldn't see

her. "I was just . . . it's nothing, I was just worried," she tried to explain. "And your sister is with you too?"

"*Ye-e-eah.*" Coby drew the word out slowly, as though he were answering a crazy person. "Obviously."

"Okay, good. That's good. Put Paul back on, would you? Wait! Coby, before you go, I've got your fidget spinner, okay? In case you were worried about it."

"Did I lose it? Okay cool, thanks, Mum."

Paul's voice came back on the line.

"Stay there," she told him. "Dom is picking me up in a minute and we'll come straight over to you, okay? Don't go anywhere, promise?"

"No problem, we were going to hang about here for a bit anyway. Listen, Frankie, are you okay, you sound distressed? I told you I'd collect your kids for you, after I tried to pick up my voice mails from the wrong message bank and heard the one from your friend. Did you forget?"

"No, Paul," she replied, "I didn't forget. I'll see you soon," and she hung up the phone, still not having answered his question about Coby—who wasn't and never had been lactose intolerant.

"I didn't forget," she repeated to herself as she lowered the phone from her ear. "You just never told me."

This couldn't go on.

Annalise was pretty sure she was almost as relieved as Frankie when she heard that the kids were okay. She was still angry with her, angry that she'd been playing the part of Viv all this time. Angry that Frankie really believed she could have made that mistake on purpose. Once she knew they were fine, Frankie had looked at Annalise with such disgust in her eyes as she told her to leave her alone.

"And just by the way," she'd added, "I might have been in your stupid group under a fake profile, but I'm not the only one. Someone else wrote that article. So good luck sorting that mystery out."

Annalise had walked away from her and called Poppy to tell her to stop searching and come and pick her up from the school. "They've found them. It's over. They're fine."

She burst into tears.

By the time Poppy had circled back to pick her up, she'd managed to stem the flow of tears down to a trickle, but she knew her face would be red and raw. Poppy pulled over and Annalise climbed in, keeping her head down.

"I know, honey," Poppy said, when she saw her face, "I know." And she reached out to hold her hand, staying parked on the side of the road. "But listen," she continued, "it's all worked out in the end, okay? You can forget about it, she doesn't ever need to know you didn't pass on the message."

"She knows," Annalise said.

"Oh. Well, she knows about your mistake and we know about her secret."

"Yeah, well, she knows we know about that as well, and she claims she didn't write the article. Not that she had an explanation for why she was ever in NOP in the first place."

"Probably went in there to have a laugh at us. I'm curious to go back now and reread everything that Viv ever posted. So where were her kids anyway? A friend had them?"

"Paul had them."

"Paul! Are you kidding?"

"Nope. But she claims they're not having an affair either."

"Right," Poppy said slowly, "you know what I think, I think there is something really bloody weird going on with that woman. And whether or not she was passing our info or screen-grabbing our posts back to MOP, either way she betrayed us. I can't stand thinking about her pretending to be someone else all that time, pretending to be our friend. Pretending she was one of us when she's not. She's a mother, she doesn't get us. She can't get us."

Annalise stayed quiet.

"Come on," Poppy said, putting the car into gear and turning on her indicator, "let's get out of here. You want to go home or you want to go out for a drink?"

Annalise considered the offer and then remembered that she wasn't allowed to drink. "Um, just home, please. I think I want an early night."

On the way to Balmoral, Frankie confessed. The thing that surprised her was that Dom did too.

He'd arrived at the school just minutes after she had told Annalise to get out of her face. His terrified expression as he walked toward her had made the tears start falling again, which meant she had to quickly reassure him that they were happy tears, that she'd just found out where the kids were.

Luckily Renee had still been on the phone with the police, so she was able to immediately let them know it was a false alarm. Chelsea had called off the search and Frankie had thanked her profusely for all her help, before hopping into Dom's car to race over to Balmoral as fast as they could, despite the peak-hour traffic.

"I have to tell you something," she'd begun as Dom weaved his way through the cars.

"So do I," he said.

"Me first," she said firmly. "I've been keeping something from you and I'm so sorry and I wish I never had. But I've realized that you and the kids come first. There shouldn't be any secrets between us."

"You're sleeping with Paul," he said. And his voice sounded utterly resigned.

"What? No! Fuck, why does everyone think that? Oh God, Poppy did send you an anonymous text, didn't she?"

"Poppy? The woman at your office you're always complaining about? What does she have to do with this? What text?"

"You didn't get a message telling you I was cheating?"

"No."

"Well, why did you think I was having an affair?"

"Because you're always working late and you spend so much time with Paul. And 'cause . . .'cause we never have sex anymore." He looked embarrassed. "It seems like lately, you're not really into me in that way. I've got this damn gut starting to stick out and I can't blame you for not liking the way I look, but—"

Frankie cut him off. "Dom, I am definitely not sleeping with Paul. I'm not cheating on you with anyone. I love you."

"Oh," said Dom, and she noted the twinge of hope in his voice. "You're not?"

"No. I'm not. But I have been helping him keep a secret from Cormack. He has Alzheimer's. Linda and Paul asked me if I would help them cover it up until they could get some ownership stuff sorted out. The only reason I didn't tell you is because I was worried you might accidentally mention something to some of the guys at drinks after work or something. But it's been putting this extra strain on me. Half the time I'm doing his job for him and trying to fit it in with the kids and everything. That's why I've been doing so much overtime. I feel like maybe today would never have happened if I was more on top of things. Paul's intentions were good, he knows how busy I've been, and he probably thought he could take some of the pressure off by helping out—he used to get along great with the kids when they were little and I'd bring them into the office sometimes. But picking them up without my say-so—it's not on. And if his illness wasn't the big secret that it is, then none of this would have gotten so out of control."

Dom reached one hand out and placed it on her knee. "Don't feel so bad," he said, "this wasn't such a big lie . . . more of an . . . omission, really. And he's a good bloke, so the kids will be fine with him. I'm just glad you're not sleeping with the guy."

Frankie let out a small laugh. "Well, I'm glad that makes you happy."

"If I'm entirely honest," he continued, "I'm trying to react my best because I don't know what you're going to think of me when I tell you what I have to say."

"Jesus," she said suddenly. "Are *you* having an affair?"

"No, no, nothing like that," Dom assured her. "But I haven't been honest with you either."

She stayed quiet, waiting to see what he had to say.

"Maybe you noticed . . . maybe you've been . . . picking up on hints? I haven't been good lately, my mood. I'm sorry, I kept thinking I would fix it myself so you wouldn't need to worry and I'd get back to normal and none of it would matter. But it's not fair to you—not fair to you or the kids, for me to be acting like this."

Frankie couldn't help but interrupt him again. "Wait, does this have something to do with all that money stuff you keep bringing up lately?"

"Yeah, it does. I lost my job."

"Oh, babe!" Now she reached out to put her hand on his leg, wishing she could hug him properly.

"I'm so sorry, Frankie."

"Honey, don't be ridiculous, you don't need to be sorry."

But he still wouldn't let her comfort him, his leg felt stiff under her touch. "Yes, I do. I haven't been working for over two months now. I've been lying to you all this time."

She was stunned. "Over two months? Why? Why wouldn't you just tell me?"

"Because. I needed to find a new job. I needed to have the problem fixed before I told you. But the thing is, if I'd been honest, you could have leaned on me to take care of the kids. I could have picked them up this afternoon, but instead I was . . ." He trailed off and she could hear the shame in his voice.

"Instead you were what?" she asked.

"Sitting in the pub drinking."

Frankie felt a twinge of disappointment. "Is that what you've been doing—all this time? Every day?"

"Not every day," he said, "I've had some interviews, but not many. Only two, actually. And I've been sending out applications. But like I said, I didn't want you to know, so I had to leave the house at the same time every day, pretend that I was going to work. But I had nowhere to go . . . so I ended up at the pub. I had some severance pay, but I knew it wasn't going to last long."

"Well, definitely not if you were spending it in the pub every day." She couldn't help herself. The sting of him telling her that her hair products were too expensive when he was off drinking in the pub all that time was too much.

"I know," he said. "It wasn't my plan. It's not what I wanted to do. But I just felt like I needed the drink. Needed it to make me feel . . . less."

"Feel less what?"

"No, I mean it made me feel less of anything. I didn't want to feel."

Frankie sighed. "We both screwed up."

"Guess so," said Dom. They turned onto Military Road and hit traffic. Even though she knew the kids were supposedly safe, she was still itching to get to them. What if Paul got confused again, lost track of them?

"Try the backstreets," she suggested.

Dom took the next turnoff and weaved his way through the smaller streets. Frankie glanced sideways at him; he'd always had this amazing sense of direction. If she tried to turn off the main road to avoid traffic, she'd end up completely lost.

But Dom drove with confidence, feeling his way. It was sexy.

"No wonder I've got this gut," he mumbled. "Too many beers."

She reached across and jabbed at his belly. "You're

kidding, right? You look fine. You know what's stupid? I thought you didn't find me attractive anymore."

"Why would you ever think that?"

"For one thing, you thought I was pregnant."

"I didn't think you *looked* pregnant. You were acting so crazy when you said you had news and it's all I could think of. I was terrified of having another mouth to feed."

"And it didn't occur to you that we hadn't had sex for ages, so being pregnant would be a tad impossible?"

"Oh yeah. Good point."

"So you do still find me attractive?"

"Of course I do! You're my gorgeous wife. Everyone always tells me I'm batting above my weight with you. But it's hard to be in the mood when you're feeling so . . ."

"Ashamed?"

"Yes."

"You don't need to, you know? You have nothing to be ashamed of. People lose their jobs. It happens, it's part of life. But what you're supposed to do is lean on your partner and let them help you through it. Same as I should have done with all my work problems. I'm going to put an end to this rubbish with Paul and Linda, tell them I can't keep this up. You know that bonus I told you I was getting? Linda reneged on it. I mean she told me I'll still get it eventually, but not anytime soon. And I'm starting to wonder if it's ever going to happen, if they really are going to get this crap with the board in hand."

"Are you sure?" Dom said. "Because I can help you out more, take some of the pressure off at home so you can cope better at work."

"Yeah, I'm sure. But give me a week or two to make sure I've got a few things sorted for them before I tell them."

"Okay, no problem."

"And hey, listen, we'll find you a new job together, okay? I'll help you get your résumé back in order. I'm betting you didn't even bother to update it before you started sending it out."

Dom scratched at his chin. "I didn't think it was so bad."

"Jeez," she said, "no wonder you've only had two interviews. I'll have people begging to get you in the door."

When they finally arrived at Balmoral Beach and spotted Paul and the kids, Frankie had a hell of a time stopping the tears from starting up again. She wanted them to fly into her arms, shouting "Mummy! Mummy!" like they used to when they were small, but of course Coby was far too cool for that these days and

Hayley was too distracted by the sand castle she was building. But it didn't stop her from squeezing them tight.

As soon as Annalise entered her apartment, she leaned against the door, waited until she was sure Poppy's steps had faded away upstairs, then she turned straight back around and went out again.

She couldn't sit at home that night. She knew that if she remained alone, her own thoughts might drive her insane. She'd had enough of falling to pieces. She needed to keep moving, keep her hands busy, keep her body working, keep her brain on something—anything else. She caught a train into the city. She liked the idea of being surrounded by life. By people and noise and busyness—and she needed more than Parramatta could offer her.

What if I did make today happen on purpose? her inner thoughts questioned.

Shut up. Shut up, shut up, shut up.

What if a part of me was trying to get back at her, trying to make her pay for what she'd done?

Just be quiet, just leave me in peace.

She pulled her notebook out of her handbag and placed it on her lap. But she couldn't find a pen. She leaned forward and tapped the girl who was sitting in front of her on the shoulder. The girl looked irritated as she pulled out her headphones and turned around to face Annalise.

"Sorry, do you have a pen?" Annalise asked.

The girl stared back at her as though it was the most incomprehensible request of all time.

"*No,*" she said, and she turned back around and re-placed her headphones.

Annalise sat back. On another day she might have given that chick hell. Not today.

"Hey," said a voice from across the aisle. Annalise turned. An older man smiled at her. "Here," he said, holding out a pen.

Annalise reached across and took it with a smile. "Thanks," she said.

1 June continued

Would you like to know something the world is ob-sessed with these days? The world is obsessed with tiny moments in time. Snippets of life that go viral. And the life cycle of these moments keeps getting shorter and shorter. Something new appears. It builds up and it builds up and then whack! It's mas-sive. The white and gold dress. Or blue and black if you're insane. Planking. Bottle flipping. The ice bucket challenge. Dabbing. The two down-to-earth blokes from Queensland who videoed themselves stopping a guy who was trying to break into Oporto's. The mum at the races who got super drunk and stripped down for a nudie run.

We get obsessed with these people or these trends. We post and we share and we comment. And then one day, it's over. We've moved on. It's forgotten. They're forgotten.

But what happens to them?

And what if they went viral for all the wrong reasons? What about the person who goes viral for dressing up in black face for a party and maybe they didn't know that it wasn't okay? Maybe they didn't mean any harm in it. Maybe they weren't taught that basic fact of life: black face is WILDLY offensive—never, ever do it.

And so they get torn to shreds on social media. They receive death threats. They lose their job. Two days later, we forget about them. We move on with our lives. But what happens to them? How do they move on with their life?

How do I move on with my life?

I made a mistake. A terrible mistake. But you already know that.

In the city, Annalise wandered aimlessly at first. She ended up in Darling Harbour, walked around the edge of the water to Cockle Bay Wharf, and discovered that the Sydney aquarium was open late tonight. She'd never been. Not as a child, not as a teenager. Not once in her life had she been to a zoo, an aquarium, a wildlife park, or anything like that.

She bought herself a ticket and started wandering through the dimly lit corridors. It was quiet; she only passed the odd person here and there. Not the crazy nightlife she'd originally intended on surrounding herself with tonight. But the calmness of the setting soothed her heart and she found that the angry voices in her head quieted.

She took a seat in a darkened viewing area in front of one of the floor-to-ceiling underwater glass windows. She couldn't see much movement in the water at first. And then a large dark shape began to glide lazily toward her. As it came closer, it turned and began to drift back and forth in front of the window.

"What are you?" she asked quietly. The body shape was like a dolphin, but the nose was like a walrus or even a hippo. She stood up to read a caption on the wall with a description of the creature. A dugong, she learned.

"What are you doing up so late?" she asked the dugong. And she walked closer to touch her fingers to the glass. The creature swam down to meet her, brushed its nose against the glass. "Do you like it here? Or do you miss the ocean? Or were you bred here in captivity? Do you ever think about escaping?"

She turned and rested her cheek against the glass. "I do."

Chapter 31

Poppy had expected that Annalise might not turn up to work the next day. And then throughout the weekend, she understood why she continued to avoid her. But on Monday, Annalise still didn't show up at work.

Obviously, Poppy had been trying to check on her. Phone calls and text messages had all gone unanswered, until she'd knocked on her door on Sunday night—and then a message had appeared on her phone, which she suspected was simply sent to get her away from the door. And probably to stop her from kicking it down in case she thought Annalise was passed out drunk in there or hurt or something.

Sorry, I'm fine. Just busy, can't talk.

On Monday afternoon, Poppy texted her again to ask when she would come back to work.

I'm trying to cover for you, but people are wondering where you are!

But Annalise ignored it.

She tried once again: *Guess I'll see you at tonight's game.*

She was confident she would see her at the game. Annalise didn't skip soccer—she loved it too much. Even when they were fighting, or if she was having a bad game, she still loved playing.

But she didn't turn up to soccer either.

"Where's your mate?" Elle asked as Poppy laced up her boots.

Even though Annalise had been part of the team for several months now, Elle still referred to her as "Poppy's mate."

"Um, I'm not sure if she's coming tonight."

"Why not?"

"She hasn't . . . been well."

It was the best Poppy could do. How could she explain everything Annalise had been through of late? The arguments they'd had over NOP; being the cause of Frankie's kids going missing; being interrogated by the person who was supposed to be her closest friend. Poppy had completely stuffed up at that brunch. Her plan had been to casually bring up stories from her past and then ask Annalise about her own history. Instead she'd panicked and blurted it out: *Why did you lie to me?* She shouldn't have come on so strong, firing questions at her, demanding to know about her past.

Poppy didn't even care anymore that Annalise had lied to her, she just felt guilty for having invaded her privacy by reading the notebook. She wanted so badly to figure out how to get Annalise to open up to her in the same way she did when she wrote in those pages. There was such incredible pain in those written words, and the line about how she'd somehow betrayed Poppy didn't even seem to matter anymore. Who knew what she meant by that, it could have been anything. Maybe she was simply referring to the fact that she'd lied about her schooling and past jobs—nothing more.

Poppy couldn't believe she'd ever suspected Annalise of somehow being the imposter within the group. And Annalise had looked so proud when she'd come to her and told her that she'd discovered that Frankie was Viv. Poppy supposed it was lucky that they had never ended up confronting Sophie and Wendy at the salon. Now that they knew Frankie was the imposter, she didn't trust her word that she hadn't been the one to write that article. Why else had she ever been a member? Poppy accepted that she might never understand why Sophie had turned Wendy against her.

Either way, it was clear when Annalise brought the information to Poppy that she was planning for it to bring the two of them closer together, and obvious that she desperately wanted to fix all the problems with NOP for Poppy.

But then Frankie's kids were missing and Annalise was devastated that she hadn't passed on that message. Poppy believed her when she said it wasn't intentional.

When Poppy had driven them both back to the apartment block after the children were found, she'd tried over and over to find the right way to reach Annalise, to help her to open up and to reassure her that they were still close friends. That secrets and lies could be forgiven. But Annalise didn't want to chat and Poppy couldn't force it.

"It's not like her," Elle said as she helped one of the other players tape up her ankle ready for the game. "At the beginning of the season she played with bronchitis. You couldn't get her off the pitch if you tried. She wouldn't even take a break when she copped an elbow to the skull and you could tell she was seeing stars. She must be really sick."

Poppy avoided answering and slipped her shin pads into her socks. "I guess," she said eventually.

"Yeah, well, next time tell her to let me know before the game if she's not going to show, would you?" said Elle, her moment of concern vanishing as quickly as it appeared.

There was another game going on next to them, but it wasn't Jack's team. Poppy felt a pang of regret at having declined his invite to dinner. She did like him. Quite a lot actually. And she wanted to see him again, wanted to know if there might be something between them. But at the same time, she wasn't ready—she was too afraid, which meant dating wouldn't be fair on either of them. So far, he hadn't pushed for a rain check.

She told herself she didn't care. Told herself she didn't want to see him.

Told herself it wouldn't matter if she never ran into him ever again.

But she knew these were all lies.

Chapter 32

5 June

There's a lesson I want to share with you: there is more value in a mirror than most people realize. Taking the time to stare at your own reflection is an opportunity to look into your soul. I'm not even kidding. I know it sounds ridiculous. But let me explain. If you step out of the shower, slick back your hair, wipe the steam from the glass, and then stop still and simply look, you know what you'll see? You.

Your face at its rawest. Your eyes. Your nose. Your lips. Your ears, your cheeks, your forehead, your chin. You can explore it to its greatest depths. Every wrinkle. Every freckle, every blemish. The flecks of color in your irises. The dryness of your skin. The way your nostrils flare when you breathe in sharply. The way one eyebrow reaches up higher than the other when you yawn.

There are parts of you that you'll love. Parts that you know so well. The curve of your petite ears. Your eyelashes. Their length. Their color.

There are parts that you'll hate. The jut of your chin. The length of your neck.

But beyond that, you'll see yourself. You stare long enough at yourself in a mirror and you'll stop seeing the physical features. You'll see your personality. Your history. Your mistakes. You'll see the flaws inside. Again, there'll be parts you'll love and there'll be parts you'll hate. You'll dig up memories. Memories that make you ashamed. Memories that make you proud.

You'll see the moment you picked up the bird from the side of the dirt driveway with the broken wing. Tucked it inside your jacket. Took it back with you, hid it from everyone. Placed it in a shoe box with a soft tea towel for comfort. Tried to nurse it back to health.

You'll see the moment you stole a pair of sunglasses from the corner store while the woman behind the counter gave you a friendly smile. You'll feel the frame of the glasses pressed against your skin, hidden up the sleeve of your jumper.

But then again, you won't get to experience any of those things, will you?

It didn't take that long for Annalise to pack up the essentials. She'd rented the apartment fully furnished, so there wasn't really that much in the place that belonged to her. Everything she owned could usually be condensed down to one backpack if needed.

Although she admitted she had settled quite a bit there. She'd started to acquire a few new extra things that she normally wouldn't bother with. Most of that would end up in the Dumpster behind the building.

She didn't make the decision straightaway. There were a few days of lying in bed all day until the sun set. Getting up, making it as far as the lounge, and lying there until it was time to return to bed. She was hardly eating because she wasn't hungry.

But once she'd decided what she was going to do, she found some energy. Enough to shower. Enough to start gathering her stuff together.

She avoided Poppy, ignored most of her messages, shooting back the odd reply only when she knew she needed to in order to get her off her back.

When there was a knock at the door on Wednesday

night, she assumed it was Poppy. She stood still in the middle of the lounge room, trying to decide what to do. She hadn't planned on saying good-bye. She'd intended on just leaving the following morning. But did she at least owe her the courtesy of knowing?

The knocking was insistent, so she gave in and opened the door.

It wasn't Poppy. It was Elle. Annalise was taken aback. Seeing her out of context threw her. She was dressed in tight jeans and a low-cut black top. Annalise had only ever seen her in footy shorts or tracksuit pants and a jersey. Her hair was out as well, instead of tucked away under a baseball cap. It was long and ringlety and a lighter shade of red than Annalise's own hair, a sort of golden auburn.

"Elle!" she said, stunned. "What are you doing here?"

"Came to check on you," she said. She pushed past her and came inside without waiting for an invitation. She looked around the apartment and her eyes swept seamlessly across the backpack, which was leaning against the lounge. She didn't react. "First you were off your game for a couple of matches and then a no-show Monday night. Not like you."

Annalise felt irritated that she could be so single-mindedly focused on her team above all else.

"Yeah, well, I've had some shit going on," she replied.

"I figured. You got something to drink?" Elle said.

"I'm kinda busy," Annalise said, but Elle wandered through the lounge room and across to the kitchen, where she opened the fridge, as though Annalise hadn't even spoken.

"Not much in here," she said. She crouched down, found herself a beer, and stood up. "You got a bottle opener?"

"Twist top," Annalise replied.

Elle opened up the bottle and took a swig. "I take it you don't want one?"

"Why do you assume that?"

"Because you're not well." Then she very obviously stared at Annalise's stomach before raising her eyebrows and taking another swig.

Annalise grimaced. "Yep. I'm not great, so it's probably better if you—"

Elle cut her off. "Stop trying to kick me out."

"But I don't really get what you're doing here," Annalise said, exasperated. "We don't even know each other that well."

Elle feigned a knife to the heart. "Hey, that cuts deep. I've been coaching you all year."

"Yeah, but all you've ever said to me is "pass" or

"drop" or "pull back," or "shut down that fucking player before I lose my shit!" It's not like we're besties or anything."

Elle took another sip of her drink. "Never too late though, is it?"

"It kinda is."

She looked at the backpack again. "So, you're leaving?"

"Yeah. Tomorrow."

"That means you're skipping out on the rest of the season."

"Seriously! Is that all you think about? Your soccer team? You really think I'm going to change my plans for a game?"

Elle put her beer down on the kitchen benchtop and crossed over to Annalise, standing directly in front of her, much closer than Annalise expected.

"No," she said, "I wasn't expecting you to change your plans for a game." She hooked her index finger in the belt loop on the side of Annalise's jeans and tugged on it, pulling her closer still. "But I was thinking I wasn't done getting to know you yet."

Annalise felt her heart rate pick up. Was she . . . was Elle . . . hitting on her?

She'd been hit on by women before, but it had never been like this. There had never been this much friction between herself and the other person. Usually she was happy enough to flirt back, more for the fun of it than anything else. It was nice to be hit on. It was good to feel wanted, desired. But she'd never really felt anything for another woman.

This, though. This was different. It was strange because she'd never even looked at Elle that way. She wasn't sure if she even knew she was gay—the thought had never occurred to her because she'd never had any reason to think anything about Elle beyond what she was like as a coach.

So the sudden sparks between them were throwing her for six. She didn't know how to react. She'd lost her usual sense of calm and smoothness. For the past week, she had barely thought about drinking because she'd felt too sick to even contemplate alcohol. But right now she wished she could down a couple of shots of tequila.

Elle held her gaze for several more seconds and then she let go of the loop on her jeans and stepped away before turning to pick up her beer again. Annalise was left to wonder if she'd completely fabricated the entire thing. Then Elle walked back over to her, took her by the hand, and pulled her across to the couch.

"Just talk to me," she said. "Tell me what's going on. When you've told me what's happening, I'll go. I'll leave you be, I promise."

"You're . . ." Annalise paused, lost for words. "You're . . . odd," she said.

Elle laughed and nearly choked on her beer. "Odd," she repeated. "Not the reaction I was necessarily hoping for. But okay, we'll start with odd and see if I can work my way from there to awkward and then maybe charming, okay? Seriously, talk to me."

"What do you want to know?"

"Everything."

And so that's what Annalise did. She told her everything. Well, *almost* everything. She started with the group. She explained about Poppy's idea and how she wanted to help her get past Garret's betrayal. She told her about Lawrence and how she hated herself for leading him on for so long when she wasn't and never had been in love with him. She told her about the group turning bad and the war starting up between MOP and NOP. She told her about Frankie and how she'd taken that message and not passed it on, and about how afraid she'd been that something really terrible might have happened to her kids and it would be all her fault.

And then she told her about discovering that she was pregnant—which somehow Elle had already guessed—and that she felt like such an idiot for letting it happen, and that she couldn't bring herself to tell Poppy because the truth was . . . she wanted to keep it. She was terrified, but she wanted to have this baby. And she knew Poppy was going to be so hurt.

She wasn't actually sure she even knew herself that she *did* want to have the baby until she spoke the words out loud to Elle. But somehow, the words had just come to her: I want to keep it. And as soon as they left her lips, she knew it was the truth. Had she been lying to Poppy all this time when she claimed she never wanted children? She couldn't be sure. All she knew was that some sort of maternal desire had kicked in and taken hold of her—hard.

As she'd spoken, she'd kept her face down, not wanting to look at Elle, not wanting to see how she reacted to anything she had to say. But now she looked up at her and saw something unexpected. She'd either thought she'd be judging her, considering how much she'd unloaded, or else she'd have an expression of pity on her face. But there was something else there. Amusement? Did she find Annalise's problems—her life—amusing?

"Why do you look like you're about to start laughing at me?"

"I don't," Elle replied. "I'm just smiling because I'm kinda thinking, *That's it?* That's the whole story? I mean sure, you've been through some stuff, but it's all manageable. So, what's with taking off? And where are you going anyway?"

"Um, I don't really know."

"You don't know why you're leaving or you don't know where you're going?"

"Both."

"*Riiiight.* You really are a hot mess, aren't you?"

"Thanks."

Elle shuffled across the couch, closer to Annalise. She placed a hand on her knee, her other arm was on the back of the couch. "Well," she said, "you're in luck. Because I'm a mess too. So, that means the two us have an opportunity. An opportunity to help each other out."

"How are you a mess? You're the most together person I know."

Elle laughed. "You're kidding, right? You haven't noticed my anger management issues? You don't think there's shit going on in my own life that I'm putting on you guys when I take you to task for stuffing up in a game? Everyone has problems, Annalise. But the nice thing is, it's usually much easier to sort out someone else's issues than your own."

She paused. "You do realize that half the time when I'm coaching you guys, I feel like I have no idea what I'm doing and I'm terrified you're all going to figure that out and call me on it?"

"No way that's true. You're always one hundred percent sure of your decisions."

"Nuh-uh. Remember the first game when I pulled both you and Rowena out of the front line at halftime? Shuffled the entire team around?"

"Yep. I remember."

"You want to know why I did that?"

"Why?"

"It was because I was seriously losing my mind just being around you. I had this huge crush on you from the moment you first turned up to training. And to start with, I felt like I was fawning all over you, telling you what an amazing striker you were and whatever else. And then I was like, oh my God, I need to play this cool. Next thing I know, I'm creating utter chaos on the field and I was on the sideline thinking, *What the hell did I just do?* Thank God Poppy set up that goal right at the end, because afterward I could pretend like that was my plan all along."

"You're kidding? Everyone on the team thought that was the best tactic ever when we won. You're telling me it was a fluke?"

"Complete fluke. That's why I put you straight back up front the following week. And then you had that horrible game after we all heard you and Poppy arguing over something. And I subbed you out and kept trying to talk to you, but you wouldn't have it. I was going crazy! I wanted to say something, to tell you how

I felt, but I didn't even know if you would be . . . you know . . . interested in women. But ever since then, you haven't been yourself and I've been wondering what's going on with you and if you were okay. And I figured, look—even if you're not the least bit interested in me in that way, I still care about you. So I figured I'd come here tonight and check if you're all right, and just be honest with you. No more guessing games. I like you, Annalise. So what do you think about that?"

Elle was leaning in close again and once more Annalise's body was fizzing. A desire to grab hold of her and pull her close overcame her.

"I don't know," she whispered, "I've never even . . ." And she found herself leaning in farther still, her words drifting away, her mind fogging, her heart pumping.

Elle closed the final gap between them and their lips met. Her lips were soft and her kiss was gentle and slow. Elle reached for Annalise's body and Annalise reached back. Their legs tangled. They kissed harder, harder and faster, and Elle's hand was under Annalise's top, cupping her breasts, and then her lips were on her neck and they were pressing their bodies together and Annalise thought, *This . . . this is what I've been waiting for.*

It was several hours later. They'd made their way from the couch to the bed, and now, as Annalise lay there awake in the dark, she realized she was so comfortable in Elle's arms that she was on the verge of falling asleep.

But the usual doubts started creeping in. *This isn't you. You don't fall asleep in anyone's arms. You don't relax and you don't give in.*

She shifted away from Elle abruptly and sat up, facing away from her and toward the wall.

"That was fun," she said, continuing to look at the wall. Her voice had taken on a cooler tone.

"I thought so," Elle replied.

"Onetime fun," she said. "But I don't have sleepovers." She turned back around and tried to look at Elle, but struggled to meet her eyes. "So . . . you're going to need to . . ." She trailed off, expecting her to get the drift. But Elle didn't start to scramble for her clothes.

"I'm going to need to what?" she asked, her own voice just as cool as Annalise's.

"Go," she finished.

"Is that right?"

"Yeah, well, I'm sorry, but like I said, I don't do sleepovers. You think we're going to braid each other's hair or something?" She stood up from the bed and moved away. "This doesn't change my plans. I'm still leaving tomorrow. I'm going to take a shower. Just let yourself out and shut the door behind you."

She didn't wait for a response, instead walking

swiftly into the bathroom and closing the door. Inside, she turned on the shower taps straightaway. She needed the noise to cover the sound of her tears.

Why had she done that? Why did she treat people this way?

Was she ever going to change?

She spent a good twenty to thirty minutes in the shower, using up all the hot water. She wanted to make sure she'd given Elle plenty of time to get dressed and leave.

When she finally emerged from the steam-filled room, she took one step toward the bed and stopped. There was still a shape there under the covers. Was it Elle? Or were the sheets just crumpled in a way that made it look like she was there?

The shape moved. Elle rolled over and faced her. "You think you can get rid of me that easy?" she said.

"Oh, thank God."

Chapter 33

As much as she was confident Annalise wouldn't turn up to the fundraiser, Poppy had still knocked on her door on her way downstairs to the waiting Uber, one last try to convince her to come out and join her. But there was no answer, and she couldn't hear any movement from inside or see any light coming under the door. Annalise had now missed an entire week of work with no explanation. Poppy had the strangest feeling that she was never going to see her again. It didn't make any sense, she had to show up eventually—she had a job, she lived one floor down from her, she couldn't hide forever. But it was just this sense of foreboding, and she kept thinking, *I've lost her.*

The boat was much larger than Poppy had expected. There was a huge open deck with fairy lights strung across it and inside, and a function room with at least forty tables and a stage down one end of the room.

Poppy scanned the chart at the doorway to see where the NOP tables were, and her finger stopped over the name of another table: *Mums Online Parramatta. MOP.* She didn't know why she hadn't expected this. It should have occurred to her. They were another local community group full of women, and they'd been around way longer than NOP. Of course they would have received an invite.

She checked the location of their tables and her stomach clenched when she realized that the NOP and MOP tables were quite close to one another.

A part of her wanted to storm right over to them and let them have it. They were the ones who had started all of this. If they hadn't taken such offense to NOP and assumed they were all out to get them, then none of the back-and-forth between the two groups ever would have happened. But at the same time, Poppy knew much of the fault was with NOP. They'd provoked. They'd taken things further by letting their members get carried away with the challenges.

It would be smarter to just stay away from them.

She made her way through the room to one of NOP's tables and looked around at the faces already seated. Annalise wasn't one of them. Kellie and Jess were sitting side by side, and there were several other women she didn't know. Poppy claimed a chair for Annalise by slinging her handbag over the back of it and took a seat next to Kellie.

Annalise guessed Elle's encouragement was the reason she decided to pull herself together and turn up on Friday night. Enough hiding. Enough running. She needed to tell Poppy the truth. The truth about her pregnancy and the truth about her past.

But she knew the right thing was to tell Lawrence first. Along with Poppy, he'd called her several times throughout the week, asking if she was okay. He'd sent texts asking if she needed him to "nurse her back to health" followed by winking emojis. He obviously assumed she was home sick with the flu or something like that. She'd ignored all of them. On her way to the boat, she called and asked if she could drop by to chat.

"Sure! See you soon, babe!" The excitement in his voice made her feel like she was about to kick a puppy, and she hated herself for how she'd led him on.

Telling Lawrence was so much harder than she thought it would be. She didn't know how to open. She didn't know how to make sure he didn't get his hopes up. She didn't want him to think this meant something for the two of them, because it didn't, at least not in the way she knew he would want it to. Yes, they were going to be connected now, but only as friends, friends with a shared responsibility. That was it, nothing more.

He already had the wrong idea, though, when she asked him to meet her out the front of his place. He obviously thought she must have been there for a trip to the bedroom. She had to catch his wandering hands more than once as they sat down on his front steps to talk.

"Listen, Lawrence," she began, and then, "stop!" as he leaned in and tried to pull her close. He pulled back abruptly.

"What's up?" he asked.

"There's no easy way to say this," she said. "And I'm sorry to spring this on you . . . but I really should have already told you. I'm pregnant."

Lawrence stared at her and she could see he was trying to take it all in, trying to figure out the right way to respond. "You're joking," he said eventually.

"No joke."

"Is it mine?" he asked.

"It is." She could hardly be offended by the question considering how much she used to throw it in his face that they weren't exclusive, that she was more than happy to sleep around.

He remained guarded, but she could sense that there

was a tinge of excitement to his voice when he spoke next. "So, what does this mean?" he asked.

"I'm so, so sorry," she said again, "but it doesn't mean anything for us in terms of . . . in terms of a relationship. I just don't feel that way about you. But I do want you to be a part of this baby's life—as much as you want to be. If you're willing, we'll be in it together, but only as friends, nothing more."

Lawrence reached out and placed a hand on her knee. "Yes, but . . . but you *do* have feelings for me, I've seen it. And this"—he motioned toward her stomach—"this can only bring us closer together."

"No, Lawrence," she said, and as gently as she could, she brushed his hand away from her leg. "I think . . . I think I could be in love with someone else."

"So there is someone else," he said, his face changing, turning ugly with anger. "Which means you don't really know if it's mine. So maybe you're just playing me? Maybe you're messing with me, or you want to get money out of me?"

"No!" she said, hating seeing him this way. "That's not it. The other person, it's all really new, and well, to be honest, it's kind of impossible for her to have gotten me pregnant."

"Her?" he said.

"Yeah, her."

"Oh shit, is it Poppy?"

"No! It's not Poppy. Poppy's only ever been a friend to me."

"So . . . you're telling me you're gay?"

"I don't know! This is all brand-new to me. All I know is I have feelings for her. Strong feelings. I really am sorry, for the way I've treated you . . . the way I . . . took advantage of you."

Lawrence fiddled with his watch and turned away to look out across his dark front lawn. "Nah," he said, and Annalise was relieved to see that the anger had dissipated as quickly as it had spawned. "You didn't take advantage. I always knew where I stood with you. I just . . . hoped, that's all." He looked back at her and smiled then—a sad sort of smile. "But if I'm not even on the right team, what hope did I ever have?"

The cab pulled up near Darling Harbour quicker than Frankie expected and she still wasn't altogether sure if she wanted to be here. Of course it was all for a good cause, but she wasn't sure she was up for a night with a bunch of women from MOP. But Lucy had talked her into attending, and she couldn't sit in the car all night letting the meter tick over. She paid the driver and climbed out, then crossed the road and headed down to the wharf to find the right boat.

On board she found her table and was about to take her seat, when she saw a familiar face across the table and did a double take. "Linda! I didn't know you were part of MOP." *Although why you would be considering you and Paul don't have children,* she added silently, but she figured it would be a bit rude to say that out loud. She'd never asked why the two of them didn't have kids.

Linda smiled back. "I'm not really. A friend asked me to take her spot when she couldn't make it last minute. It's for a good cause, so I agreed."

Lucy appeared next to Frankie then, looking stunning in a sleeveless, brightly colored knee-length dress. "Yay!" she said happily. "You showed up!"

"Of course I showed up," Frankie said crossly. "If I say I'm going to do something, I do follow through with it, you know?"

"Yes, yes, of course you do, sweetie. Now, I'm not sitting next to you, sorry, I'm a few seats away. But there is another MOP member coming who has kids at your school, and she'll be next to you, okay?"

Frankie felt a wave of affection for her sister. Typical Lucy, always playing the mother. Even before they'd lost their parents she'd been that way.

The lights were dimming, and Poppy was thinking she needed to accept the fact that Annalise wasn't going to make it in time, when she felt a hand on her shoulder. She turned around to see her friend looking down at her.

Poppy couldn't keep the grin off her face. "You made it!" she said.

"Yep. Listen, I'm so sorry for ignoring you these last few days."

"Here, sit down." Poppy motioned to the chair she'd saved but Annalise remained standing. "Could we . . . could we go for a walk? I need to talk to you."

Poppy furrowed her brow, the look of sadness in Annalise's eyes worried her. She was about to agree, but someone started tapping a microphone at the front of the room and everyone fell silent.

"It's okay," Annalise whispered, taking her seat, "we'll wait for a break."

"**As you** can all see, we're making a move away from the wharf, so I hope everyone has their sea legs ready!" announced the woman who'd taken up the microphone and addressed the room.

Annalise looked across to a window and saw the landscape begin to glide by as the boat reversed out and slowly began to turn. She felt her stomach churn, and she stared down at the table and tried to ground herself.

"You okay?" Poppy whispered.

"Fine!"

Annalise was feeling encouraged by Poppy's kindness—she wasn't angry with her for freezing her out these last few days, in fact, she seemed happy to see her. She just hoped she was going to remain as understanding once she'd told her everything she needed to say.

A waiter appeared behind Annalise and leaned across with a champagne bottle to fill her glass. She covered it with her hand. "No, thanks." He indicated the wine-glass instead and held up a red wine bottle in his other hand. She shook her head. "I'm good," she assured him.

The MC up the front started welcoming everyone.

Poppy gave her a sideways look. "Are you *sure* you're okay?" she whispered.

Annalise nodded.

Kellie leaned across Poppy. "Never thought I'd see the day when this one would turn down a free drink," she hissed, jerking her thumb at Annalise and winking at Poppy.

God, did she really drink that much that one night saying no meant everyone went into shock? Plus, could you really call the drinks free when they'd already chipped in ninety dollars per head?

"I'm not in the mood," Annalise hissed back.

Poppy now leaned in too. "Hey," she whispered, "you should know there's a whole heap of MOP women here tonight."

"Of course there is," said Kellie. "I assumed that's why you wanted to book us some tables, so we could *represent!*"

She fell quiet as several other women across the table shot them a look.

Serious? Annalise mouthed back at Poppy.

"Serious that they're here," Poppy hissed, "but no, I didn't plan it that way!"

Great, thought Annalise, *one more complication to an already complex night.*

Poppy picked up her wineglass and took a large sip and Annalise twisted around in her chair to look at the other tables. She felt the skin on the back of her neck prickle and realized that just a few meters away, three women were all giving their table some major stink eye. She whipped her head back around and breathed in deeply. Could she really deal with this tonight? Maybe she shouldn't have come after all.

Frankie thought there were far more whisperings and mutterings around the table than there should have been, considering the official proceedings of the night had begun. Shouldn't they all wait until the MC stopped talking? There would be plenty of opportunities for chatting throughout the night.

She caught a snippet of the conversation between two women seated between herself and Linda.

"Can you believe they even had the gall to buy three tables? Let alone any!"

She was curious. "Who?" she asked, leaning in on their conversation.

"NOP! They're just over there."

Frankie spun around in her seat and scanned the faces. Her gaze landed on Poppy and Annalise, who were leaning into one another, having their own whispered discussion.

Right, so Annalise who hadn't even turned up to work all week could suddenly show up for a night out on the harbor. Wasn't that nice for her?

"Frankie!"

She turned back around, surprised at the volume at which someone was exclaiming her name when everyone was trying to stay quiet.

It was Chelsea, pulling out the chair next to her own to take a seat. Ah, so this must be the school mum that Lucy had mentioned.

Chelsea lowered her voice. "Had to head to the ladies' first and steel myself by popping a few antinausea pills—never been good on the water," she said. "Anyway, good to see you."

"You too," said Frankie, and found that she really did mean it. She was still feeling extraordinarily grateful toward Chelsea for the way she'd helped her when the kids were missing.

It suddenly occurred to Frankie to wonder if the woman who'd written the article about NOP could be here tonight—the other imposter in the group. As she wondered, her eyes locked with Linda's and Linda tipped her glass a fraction in a silent cheers. Frankie lifted her own in response.

The MC wrapped up her welcome and the noise began to swell around the room as waiters weaved their way between the tables delivering starters.

Poppy turned to Annalise. "You want to go outside on the deck somewhere to chat?"

Before Annalise could answer, a group of NOP women from one of their other tables seemed to materialize around them.

"Oh my God, Poppy," said one who she only vaguely recognized from one of their NOP nights out. "I can't believe it!"

"Can't believe what?" Poppy asked, looking up and

feeling slightly irritated by the way they were all shut-
ting her and Annalise in, their faces shining with excitement.

"Carla!" the woman practically shrieked.

Beef Cheeks, Poppy suddenly thought, that's who
she is—the woman who ordered the beef cheeks last
time they went out. She still couldn't think of her name,
though, and she didn't think the woman would appreciate it if she started referring to her by her menu
choice.

"What do you mean? What about Carla?" she asked.

"She's at one of the MOP tables," said Beef Cheeks.
"She has to be our mole."

"What?" Poppy stood up to look past them all but
she couldn't spot Carla.

"Where?" she asked. "I don't see her."

"She's changed her hair, that's why you don't recognize her. It's really short now and heaps darker. Plus,
she's wearing really thick glasses. Must have had contacts
in when she came out with us. We nearly couldn't tell it
was her either."

Poppy looked again and this time she zeroed in on the
woman with short dark hair, and concentrated on her
face. They were right. It was Carla. Had she chopped
off all that long, beautiful hair just to disguise herself?
And then it occurred to her—was the long hair the dis-

guise? Was she wearing a *wig* when they met her? No wonder her hair had seemed so glam and lustrous!

At the same table, she saw another familiar face: Frankie. Right, so that made sense, the two imposters were friends. And Frankie must have known who had written that article all along. She sat back down and looked sideways at Annalise, who stared back at her, looking uncharacteristically horrified, rather than fired up as she would have expected.

"Carla's probably not even her real name!" said Beef Cheeks, and Poppy found herself wanting to ask her why she was so damn happy about all of this.

"Sorry," said Annalise, interrupting them all and standing up, "I have to run to the bathroom." She pushed her way between the gaggle of women, and Poppy wished she could follow her and make sure she was okay, but the faces were still all staring down at her expectantly.

Annalise strode down the side of the boat to reach the stairs to the upper deck. She needed fresh air. Her head was spinning. She couldn't say if she normally got seasick because she'd never been on a boat before. Like the aquarium, this was her first time.

Upstairs she stood still and grasped the railing. She looked out over the black water, drinking in the chilled air. After a few minutes, the stirring in her stomach settled a little and she glanced around to see Frankie coming up the stairs. As soon as Frankie saw Annalise she spun on the spot to head straight back down.

"Wait!" Annalise called.

Frankie paused, her back still turned. This was going to be another chance for Annalise to clear the air. Another chance for her to work her way toward a fresh start.

"What do you want?" Frankie asked.

"Please, Frankie, I just want to talk to you."

Frankie finally faced her. "Um, now's not really good," she said.

"Please," Annalise repeated, "I really need to say this."

She saw Frankie's face start to relent and she took a couple of steps toward her.

"Okay," Frankie said, and folded her arms. "What is it?"

Now that Annalise had her attention she realized she was going to have to actually speak. She hesitated, and Frankie cut in, her voice clear and cool. "I'm surprised to see you out and about, by the way. Poppy's been keeping us all updated at work about how sick you've been."

She felt a rush of gratitude to Poppy. Believing that she was going to run away had meant she hadn't bothered to call in sick or explain her absence in any way. It meant a lot that Poppy had covered for her, even though she'd continued to resolutely ignore her attempts at contact.

Annalise took a deep breath and ignored Frankie's slight. "I wanted to tell you how sorry I am," she said, "for not passing on that message to you. I swear to you, I didn't do it intentionally, and it had nothing to do with a NOP challenge or getting back at you for being a fake member or anything like that. But I was careless and I truly am sorry. Poppy and I . . . we've never been nice to you. We've always judged you and made certain assumptions about you that weren't fair. I'm hoping that we could maybe . . . start fresh."

Frankie looked more than a little taken aback. She stayed quiet for a moment and then her eyes opened wide.

"Annalise," she said, "why have you been so sick all week?"

Frankie had to admit she was pretty shocked to receive the apology from Annalise. She'd never heard her speak with so much compassion. She'd only ever known her as the rough, sweary warehouse manager who didn't take shit from anyone and didn't care what anyone thought of her. Who put away beers and hamburgers like a person twice her size and had brought that group of blokes in the warehouse under control within days of starting her job at Cormack.

Something had changed. And then it clicked. Annalise didn't have a drink in hand. It was rare to see her out at any event without a beer or a shot. Annalise had been away sick all week. Annalise seemed different.

Frankie's eyes flicked down to Annalise's belly and she saw her hands instantly cover it up. "You're pregnant, aren't you?" she said.

"How does everyone keep working that out?"

"Just a hunch," Frankie replied.

"Listen, please don't say anything in front of Poppy. I haven't told her yet and I think it's going to break her heart."

"Why would it break her heart?"

"You're kidding, right? You were in NOP. You saw firsthand how much it means to her. And we were in it together. Considering how badly she reacted to your betrayal, how do you think she's going to feel when she finds out about me?"

"But you can hardly call this a betrayal, can you? You fell pregnant! It's not like you were lying to her all along."

"Yeah, well, there are . . . there are other factors . . . But anyway, the thing is, I promised her that this wasn't what I wanted, that I had no interest in ever having children, same as her. But now that it's happened, well, I want it."

"And you really think she'll blame you for that? For changing your mind?"

"I don't know. I just know she's going to be hurt. And she's already been hurt enough. So, don't say anything until I've had the chance to tell her myself . . . please?"

Frankie nodded. "Okay, fine. I won't say a word."

"I better go back in," said Annalise. "There was drama happening at the table when I took off. Apparently, the person who wrote the article outing NOP is here tonight, sitting at your table actually."

"Really? Shit, that is some drama. Hey, Annalise, thanks for saying what you said. I appreciate it."

Frankie watched Annalise head back down the stairs and then took her spot at the railing, not in any rush to return inside herself.

"You okay there?" said a voice from behind her, and she turned around to see Linda approaching.

"Oh yeah, I'm fine. Just escaping the noise for a minute."

Linda came and stood next to her and they both looked out across the water toward the Opera House.

"Not a bad view," said Linda.

"Absolutely."

Frankie had booked a meeting for Monday with both Paul and Linda to talk about the part she was playing in keeping Paul's secret. She was going to finally tell them she couldn't help them anymore. Not at the expense of her family. Should she say something now? But no, this wouldn't be the right place to do it. Then she remembered what Annalise had just told her: the imposter who wrote the article was sitting at her table tonight. What if it was Linda? What if she'd lied to Frankie just now when she'd claimed she was here tonight filling in for a mate. What if she was playing both sides, like Frankie had been?

She decided to ask her straight out.

"Hey, Linda, are you the one who wrote the article about NOP?"

Linda tipped her head sideways to look back at Frankie. She paused then said, "Um, what's a NOP?"

Immediately Frankie realized It was a dumb thought. Of course it wasn't Linda, it made no sense. She laughed. "Right, sorry. Never mind, obviously not you."

"Not me. I'm glad I've got you alone, though. I know you're probably already planning on chatting about this at our meeting on Monday, but I'm going to preempt you, if you don't mind."

Frankie waited.

"I'm so sorry, Frankie," she said. "So sorry for the pressure we put on you. I've been selfish."

"No, you haven't," Frankie tried to interrupt.

"Yes, I absolutely have, and I need to say this. We took advantage of you. I was so caught up in trying to keep things safe for Paul, in trying to hold on to the company. What we should have done was accept the truth that he wasn't well and been up-front about it, not created all these secrets and lies and made you a part of it all."

"I didn't mind," Frankie tried again.

"There's more. Paul was right about giving you that bonus. We did have the money and we didn't need to pass it by the board either. But again, I was being selfish."

Frankie felt a jolt. "What do you mean?"

"I mean I wanted to hold on to the money in case we needed it for Paul—for legal bills or medical bills. But I'm going to set things right. We're going to make the announcement about Paul and he's going to step down from the director's position, and you're going to get your bonus ASAP. I feel horrible, I actually used Paul's illness against him. After you told me at that squash game that he'd promised you the bonus, I convinced him he'd made a mistake because he was confused, and that he was wrong about the money being available."

"Oh."

"I'm going straight to hell, aren't I?"

Frankie didn't respond immediately, torn between the desire to comfort the woman who'd become her friend over the past few months and the hurt that she felt at having been betrayed in that way. Especially when she and Dom actually did need the money. She swallowed. "I found out last week that Dom lost his job two months ago and has been lying to me about it all this time."

"You're kidding! Oh God, I feel terrible. I'm so sorry."

Frankie sighed. "It's okay," she said. "I mean, if you're going to set everything right, I guess there's no harm done."

"I am. I definitely am." Linda stared out into the darkness. "I feel like I'm losing him, Frankie," she said. "All the pieces I thought I knew, they're just not there anymore. For the first time the other morning, for just a minute . . . he didn't know who I was. He didn't know his own wife."

"That's awful," said Frankie, because she didn't know what else to say.

"**We have** to go and confront her!" It was Kellie who was chiming in now.

"I . . . I don't know . . . maybe now isn't the time . . . the place." Poppy had the feeling she wasn't going to be able to avoid a confrontation, though; the group of NOP women surrounding her had grown and everyone had an opinion.

"I can't believe she has the nerve to be here. To just sit over there like she wasn't hanging out with us a few weeks back. I can't believe I asked her if she'd like to join my husband and me for a threesome," said Jess.

"Wait, what?" said another member.

"It makes sense now, doesn't it?" said Kellie, ignoring Jess completely.

"What does?" Poppy asked.

"The way she was always asking questions! Asking us why we chose not to have kids or how we felt about stuff. She was interviewing us for her bloody article."

The other members' voices all tumbled over one another.

"Oh my God! She was Sophie's friend, wasn't she? Sophie was her way in! That's how she must have found out about us in the first place! She sold us out to her journalist friend!"

"But didn't Carla bring Sophie on board?"

"Is she definitely a journalist, does anyone know that for sure? Or was it just a one-off blog piece about us?"

"Well, we're not going to know unless we go and *talk* to her."

They all fell silent then and moved aside. Two new women were standing in front of Poppy now, both with their arms folded. One was just pregnant enough that you could tell. The other was super skinny and wearing a silky cocktail dress that clung to her slight frame.

"It's Poppy, isn't it?" said the one on the left—the pregnant one, stepping forward.

"Yes."

She pulled out Annalise's chair and sat next to Poppy. The other woman remained standing. The rest of the NOP members backed away a little, pretending not to listen when they clearly all were.

"I'm Yasmine," said the pregnant woman. "And this is Leanne. We're both a part of MOP, Leanne's one of the moderators, actually. We thought it might be good for us to talk."

Kellie stepped back in again. "Hey, anything you want to say to Poppy you can say to all of us," she said, her tone aggressive.

"Kellie," Poppy said, "it's fine." She didn't want this to turn into something too big. She looked back at Yasmine and Leanne. "So how exactly is it that you know who I am, when I don't know you two from a bar of soap?"

"We know quite a bit actually," said Yasmine.

"Considering you're from MOP, then it would be nice to know how that is," said Poppy. "Because NOP isn't for mothers, just like MOP isn't for women like me."

"You know that's exactly what I take issue with," said Leanne. "You never even bothered to check if you could have joined MOP before you started your own group. If you had, you would have found out we're actually perfectly happy to accommodate some women without kids."

"*Some,*" said Poppy. "Some women without kids. Let me guess, just the ones who are planning on joining your ranks but aren't pregnant yet, or can't get pregnant or something like that? Well, what about the women like me—the women who have no interest in ever having kids? I really doubt you'd want us to join. And you know what? We don't want to anyway. That's why we made our own group."

"You made your own group so you could harass and intimidate mothers," said Yasmine.

"No, that's not what NOP was for and it's not what it's about. You're the ones who turned it into a battle between us and you. You're the ones who put some fake member into our group to spy on us. Presumably that's how you know who I am?"

"We didn't *put* her into your group, she chose to join on her own because she was curious. She just happened to already be a member of MOP, and when she saw what was going on, she decided to do something about it," said Leanne.

"Besides," added Yasmine, "even if it wasn't for her, I would have known who you are. Because I used to be a part of NOP too."

"Oh, for God's sake, is every member of MOP also a mole in NOP? What the hell?"

"I wasn't a mole! I was a part of NOP legitimately. I couldn't have kids, and I believed that I didn't want them, and I loved being a part of your group. But then I fell pregnant, and instead of congratulating or supporting me or letting me stay a part of this group where I'd formed a close network of friends, you booted me out and blocked me without even bothering to explain why. It bloody hurt! So I joined MOP and I got to know the women there, and they supported me and became my friends."

Poppy stared at Yasmine. She thought back to that day, down in the warehouse with Annalise, when she'd read the excitable post on NOP. When she'd known that any day she'd hear about that same excitable news from Karleen and Garret when they had their baby, and she'd thought, *I don't want to be happy for you, I really don't.* And she'd just wanted to shut out people like her. She'd used Yasmine as an example—*This group isn't for people like her!* And yes, maybe she'd gone about it the wrong way. But at the time, she'd thought that was the best choice.

She really didn't know how to respond.

Annalise arrived back at the table to find Poppy in the middle of a heated discussion with two strange women and she immediately felt that familiar desire to protect her. Right from the moment she'd become her friend, that's all she ever wanted to do.

"What's going on?" she asked, stepping in and eyeing the woman who was seated in her chair.

"Well," said Poppy, "this is Yasmine and Leanne from MOP, and you know what? I actually don't know what they came here to talk to me about. I don't know what it is that they want from me."

"I just want to understand why you're doing it," said Leanne. "I want to know why you think you have the right to harass women just for being mothers, just because they made a different choice from you."

"We . . . we weren't," Poppy said, and Annalise could

hear the desperation in her voice. "That's not what our group was about. NOP was a chance for women like us to connect over things like how easy mothers have it, how many advantages you get in the world. Things just got . . . out of hand."

"And it wouldn't have escalated any further if you lot hadn't started bombarding us with abusive mail." Annalise stepped in.

"Well, it definitely didn't seem that way to us," said Yasmine. "What about the woman who gave a cookie to a kid and he ended up being allergic to it? That was off the back of one of your horrendous challenges."

"No, actually, it wasn't. That story had zero to do with NOP," said Annalise. "I checked into it when it started doing the rounds. It didn't even happen in this state and the people involved had nothing to do with either group. Someone decided to take the story and use it as a way to paint us as evil. And I'm betting it was one of your members who spread that rumor. So, can you get out of my chair, please?"

Yasmine stood up next to her friend. "This is going nowhere," she said, giving both Poppy and Annalise a derisive look, and she was about to turn away, but Leanne stood still.

"I need to say this," she said. "You honestly think you guys are the ones suffering some great injustice in the world? You really think mothers are the ones getting special advantages? Are you kidding me! Have you ever been told, 'We didn't mention the manager's position to you because it's much longer hours and we know it wouldn't suit you as a mum'? Because I have. Have you ever been kicked off a bus because your kid threw a tantrum and the bus driver said he was too tired to deal with a mother who couldn't control her damn kid? Because I have. Have you missed out on holidays, or said no to that gorgeous leather jacket because you know you need to save your money for school uniforms, or been glared at in a café by a bunch of middle-aged women judging your every move—because I've had all of these things happen to me. And yes, yes, I chose to become a mum. This is my path, and maybe that means I have to wear the consequences of everything that comes along with it. But I don't see why it means I have to give up on my career. Or why it means I have to put up with the daily judgment of people who don't know me and don't know my kids and yet they think they could do better. And you think you have it bad? FUCKING SPARE ME."

The two of them turned away and headed back to one of the MOP tables.

The NOP ladies all erupted in conversations.

"Can you believe them!"

"Way to go, Annalise—can you *please* get out of my chair—classic!"

"God, they were awful. No wonder we had to start our own group, can you imagine the self-righteous posts they must put up in theirs?"

Annalise put a hand on Poppy's back. "You okay?" she asked.

Poppy smiled, picked up her wineglass, and took a large sip. "Yeah," she said, "I guess." She kept her voice low and Annalise had to lean in close to listen. "It's just that . . . they're not wrong. We really did start harassing mothers. Annalise, I don't know how this is all going to end."

"You know what?" said Annalise. "I think we should go and talk to that mother-effing Carla bitch. Or whatever her real name is. She has a lot to answer for in all of this."

Frankie was relieved to find a full glass of champagne waiting for her when she got back to her table. After the "deep-and-meaningfuls" she'd been through with both Annalise and Linda, she needed a drink and a break from the drama. Chelsea welcomed her back with a big smile. "Still no entrées have made their way to our neck of the woods yet," she said cheerfully, "but I assume we'll get fed eventually."

"You know what?" said Frankie. "As long as they keep the drinks coming, I'm happy."

Chelsea laughed. "With you on that one, especially with the heat we're getting from the NOP chicks over thataway." She jerked her head and Frankie looked over to see both Poppy and Annalise standing up and making a beeline toward them.

"Oh God, what now?" Frankie said. Then she remembered Annalise's comment about the person who wrote the article being seated at her table. She looked back at Chelsea and gasped, "On no, it's you, isn't it?"

"What's me?" Chelsea asked.

Poppy and Annalise reached them and Frankie was ready and willing to defend Chelsea. Even if she had caused a lot of trouble by writing that article, Frankie owed her one after the way she'd helped her out with her kids. She stood up. "Listen, girls," she began. But Poppy stepped past her, and then past Chelsea as well.

"Hi, Carla," she said.

Frankie did a double take. "What?" she interrupted. "That's not Carla, that's Lucy!"

Lucy stayed seated, her manner cool and calm as she looked up at Poppy and Annalise. "Hi, girls," she said.

"Lucy!" Frankie said. "Are you kidding me? You wrote the article?"

"I can't believe you didn't pick it up, sis. I totally knew that was you pretending to be Viv in the group."

"You did not!"

"Um, yeah, I totally did."

"Wait," said Poppy, "this is your sister? Okay, wow. Why am I not surprised?"

"Hey, I didn't know she was in the group!" Frankie looked at her sister. "Why didn't you tell me?"

"Well, why didn't you tell me?"

"Because . . . well, I don't know. But I had a good reason for being there."

"So did I."

"What? Just to get a story? You're not even a proper journalist yet!"

"Yeah, well, it was good practice."

"It was a shit article," said Annalise, "just by the way."

"Thanks."

"You realize you completely ruined our group?" Poppy cut in. "You stirred up so much trouble for us."

"No, no, Poppy. You did that all by yourself when you went on your little drunken tirade and showed your true colors."

The lights dimmed again and the MC started calling for people to take their seats again.

"You are unbelievable," said Annalise.

"No, *she's* unbelievable," said Lucy, thrusting a finger at Poppy, "to think that she could get away with all the trouble she's caused."

They were all ignoring the MC and none of them seemed to notice that the room was quieting around them.

Frankie stared at her sister in amazement then reached out and batted at her hand. "Stop pointing. Sit down!" she hissed.

"No! I'm not going to sit down. These two women need to understand that they have no one to blame but themselves!" Lucy stepped in closer to Poppy and Annalise, and her voice reached a feverish pitch as she screamed right into their faces. "You stupid, childish girls, playing your ridiculous little games!"

Frankie could see flecks of spit shooting forth from her mouth. The entire room was silent, even the MC had stopped calling for attention. All eyes were on the confrontation happening in the middle of the room.

"Lucy! Stop!" Frankie tried again, but Poppy spoke over the top of her.

"I KNOW!" she shouted in reply. "Don't you get it? I know that I fucked up! I hated how it all turned out, but that was never what our group was meant to be about! It all got out of control!" Her voice cracked on the last word.

There was a pause and the entire room seemed to tip slightly sideways and for a second Frankie thought she was having a dizzy spell. Then she realized it was the boat. Annalise grabbed hold of the back of Chelsea's chair and Lucy stumbled. Poppy somehow held her balance.

The MC spoke up again. "Sorry, everyone, but I need you all to sit down, please. I've just been informed a larger ship passed by a little closer than expected and we've hit a large wave from their wake. That should be the worst of it, but I still need you to take your seats. The waitstaff will resume dinner service momentarily."

Frankie reached out for Lucy's arm. "Please," she begged, "sit down, would you?" Her sister finally complied and Poppy and Annalise both turned away to head back to their own table.

"Excellent," said the MC, clearly relieved to see that the argument had been broken up. "I'd now like to introduce our next speaker of the night . . ."

Chelsea nudged Frankie. "That was insane," she whispered. "Are you okay?"

"Yeah, I'm fine," Frankie murmured, "but I don't know what the hell has gotten into my sister."

Poppy and Annalise sat down as quietly as they could. Poppy kept her eyes low. She was mortified by her behavior and she didn't want to see the expressions on any of the faces around them. A hard lump had formed in her throat and she clenched her teeth together. *Don't cry, don't cry, don't cry.* She desperately didn't want to cause yet another spectacle by bursting into noisy tears on top of everything else.

At first, Poppy wasn't listening to the speech, she couldn't—she was too caught up in her own problems to focus. But the seriousness of the words penetrated her consciousness, and when she did tune in, all thoughts of NOP were immediately thrust from her mind as she listened.

". . . when you're in that sort of situation, it's easy for other people to judge," the woman was saying. "They look at you and they see that you have kids and they say, well, why wouldn't she just leave? They think that you're selfish. That you're a bad mother. But what they don't know is that it isn't that simple. You question every decision you make. If I leave, will he track us down? Will he take it out on the kids? How will he make me pay? Plus not everyone has somewhere to go. I didn't. I had no family nearby. No friends. Not one. And that's because he orchestrated it to be that way. He wanted me to feel isolated. He wanted me to believe I was worthless." The woman's voice choked up and she paused for a moment and looked down at the floor.

The entire room was dead silent. There were no more nasty looks shooting between the NOP or the MOP tables. Everyone was focused on the woman up the front.

"However, I got a bit of a lucky break. A school mum suggested I join this local Facebook group for Parramatta mums in order to meet people. Through this group, I started to form local community connections. Eventually, I asked the moderators of the group to post an anonymous query on my behalf. I asked if anyone else had been through what I was going through and how they broke that cycle. I was so afraid when that post went up. I was ready for the judgment to start. I was ready for the perfect mums out there who would call me out for putting my kids' lives at risk. But what I wasn't ready for was the level of compassion I received. I wasn't ready for the number of women who were willing to share their own personal stories. These women gave me hope. They told me about a new women's shelter that had recently opened its doors here in Parramatta, and within two weeks, I had a plan. I had a way out. The volunteers at Safe Haven were absolutely incredible. They made me feel human again. They gave me back my dignity, they showed me that I was worth something. And for that I can't thank them enough. Now, while I know you've all already dug deep to book a table here tonight, it would be great if you could continue to dig deep because Safe Haven is now in need. Without a serious boost to their funding, they're not going to be able to keep their doors open, and that would be an absolute tragedy."

Poppy glanced sideways at Annalise and wondered if she was feeling the same way that she was. In a word: humbled.

The woman out front finished her speech to thunderous applause. Now that there was another break in proceedings, Annalise took the opportunity to excuse herself. "I'll be back in five," she said to Poppy, and hurried away from the table.

She wanted to take Poppy aside now and confess her secret. She wanted to do it as soon as possible, before she lost her nerve. Or before any further drama with MOP got in the way. The only thing was, that speech had hit her hard.

As the woman had spoken, all she could see standing in front of her was her mother. The woman's dark hair had morphed into waist-length red locks. Her eyes had turned piercing blue and she'd been speaking directly to Annalise. *It's easy for other people to judge,* she'd said. *They think that you're selfish, they think that you're a bad mother.* Toward the end of the speech, Annalise's stomach had started cramping and now she headed to the bar, hoping that a fizzy drink might help ease her discomfort.

It was true. She did think her mum was a bad parent. She always had. *Why can't we just leave, mum? Why can't we run away?* But was it the same for her mother as it was for this woman who had spoken? Did her mum have those same fears? Was she terrified that he would track them down? That he would make them pay if they escaped?

Did she refuse to leave because she was trying to protect her?

It was a romantic notion, the idea that her mother loved her so much that she stayed simply to protect her. But it was also unlikely. She was obsessed with him. Brain-washed. That was why she stayed.

What if she had been part of a mother's group along the same lines as MOP back in those days, before she met him? Social media might not have existed, but community groups did. What if she'd had that same sort of network, the support of friends who might have seen the signs before she was drawn in by his lies? Women who might have stopped her, talked sense to her. Women who might have saved both of them. Could things have been different?

As Annalise stepped up to the bar, she straightened her shoulders and lifted her chin. *Stop it*, she told herself. *There's no point running over and over the past when there's nothing you can do about it now.* She squashed the memories back down and waited to be served. But as a bartender caught her eye she was hit by another one of those stabbing cramps and she leaned forward and grabbed at her stomach. *Ouch!* The pain was getting sharper and a wave of nausea swept over her. She grimaced at the bartender and gave a small shake of her head to indicate she'd changed her mind, then turned and headed for the bathroom instead. Was this really nerves? Or maybe it was morning sickness. She quickened her pace.

In the bathroom, she pushed her hands against the sink and leaned forward to let her forehead rest against the cool glass of the mirror. For a moment, she flashed back to that service-station bathroom from a week and a half earlier, remembered looking at herself in that sheet metal and feeling so afraid and lost and unsure.

She was still afraid, but at least she felt like she had a way forward now. At least she knew what she wanted.

Frankie watched as Chelsea filled up her glass for her, having snatched a bottle off a passing waiter and refused to give it back.

"Okay," said Chelsea, "talk to me. What was all that about?"

Lucy had disappeared from the table the moment the speech had finished, so Frankie felt free to chat with Chelsea about her sister. Plus, the constantly refilled glass was helping to loosen her tongue. She explained her part in the entire MOP/NOP debacle as best she could from start to finish, but it involved plenty of backtracking as Chelsea tried to follow.

"*So, wait, you were already working with some people from NOP?*"

"*And who was Viv? Oh, you were Viv. Right, got it.*"

"*But Lucy was Carla. Why did you all keep changing your names?*"

When she was done, and Chelsea seemed satisfied she understood everything, they both fell quiet for a minute as Frankie took another large gulp of her drink and Chelsea looked deep in thought.

Eventually, Chelsea spoke. "Okay," she said, "so you might have started out in this group as a bit of fun and to one-up those girls at your work, but it turned into something more for you. It was an escape."

"Yes."

"Because you were finding life as a working mum hard?"

"Yes."

"And you thought people like me, stay-at-home mums, we had it easy?"

"Ye—wait, what?"

"It's okay, Frankie. You know how you said you could see the way those girls looked at you at work, how you thought they judged you? Well, I could tell the same thing about you. I could see the way you judged me. I knew you were pissed off when I asked you to help out at the carnival."

"Oh." Frankie didn't know what to say. She wanted to argue, to tell her she'd misunderstood, but it wouldn't be the truth and she was getting too drunk to form a coherent argument anyway.

"Honestly," said Chelsea, "it really is fine. I get it. There's a few of us mums on the Parents and Citizens' Association who cop that kind of shit all the time. And you know what happens with us? People don't actually even ask us if we're free when it comes to organizing or helping out with school events. They just assume. They just count you in. It's always, oh, Chelsea can do that, she doesn't work. Oh, Chelsea will run the Mother's

Day stall. Chelsea will run the Father's Day stall. Chelsea will organize the fun run. You know what? Just because I don't work, it doesn't actually mean I have all the time in the world. Or that I don't want to take a bloody break! I have three kids. Between them they do activities and sports five afternoons a week. My eldest is a swimmer. A good swimmer. Like, she might make it to the Olympics one day. That means five A.M. training in the morning before school. My husband takes the fact that I don't work as a given that I'll do everything, I mean everything with the house and the family. I'm busy! So once in a while I want other mums to step in and pull their weight when it comes to volunteering for school stuff. Is that too much to ask? When the school puts out a note asking for parents to volunteer, do you know how many people actually respond? We're lucky to get one parent per class. Because everyone thinks someone else will do it. It can be really disheartening."

Frankie was blown away. Helpfully, Chelsea topped up her drink for her again.

"Chelsea," she said, "I'm really sorry."

"Forgiven," Chelsea said lightly. "I just wanted the chance to share my side with you. So, when you say that there's this big 'us and them' war going on between mums and nonmums, it kind of makes me think, maybe people just need to sit down and talk. Share their side of the story. A little understanding and a little empathy could go a long way."

Frankie nodded.

"And as for your sister, sounds to me like she has a serious chip on her shoulder. You mentioned you've always seen her as the perfect mum, right? Well, have you ever asked her how she sees herself?"

Poppy had gone looking for Annalise when she ran into Yasmine outside on the deck. She thought about what Yasmine had said earlier: "Instead of congratulating or supporting me, you booted me out. It bloody hurt!" She was right. It wasn't fair.

Poppy stopped right in front of her and stared her in the eyes. "Yasmine," she said, "I'm sorry. We shouldn't have kicked you out of the group. It was a dick move."

"Yes," said Yasmine, "it was. I really liked you guys."

"I was being childish. I was hurt by my ex, who was having a baby, and I thought that to keep NOP as my safe place, my happy place, I had to shut out anyone that was different. Anyone who wanted something other than what I wanted. I was selfish, really, really selfish."

"And an arsehole," said Yasmine, and she folded her arms tight.

"Yes, and an arsehole."

"You know, I actually really miss some of the girls I became friends with through NOP."

"Listen, you probably wouldn't want to . . . but if you want to rejoin, you're welcome to."

Yasmine unfolded her arms and looked down, one hand absentmindedly caressing her pregnant belly. "Maybe," she said. "You accept people with dual citizenship? Or are you going to expect me to give up MOP as my country?"

Poppy laughed. "Half of our fucking members seem to have dual citizenship anyway, so what's one more?"

The cramps worsened, her stomach clenched and unclenched. Her body started to heat up. Annalise splashed water on her face. Out of the corner of her eye, she clocked two women walk into the bathroom and head to the mirrors to fix their makeup. Annalise turned away from them and hurried into a stall, closing the door firmly behind her, to try to compose herself. She didn't want a couple of strangers staring at her, thinking she'd had too much to drink.

Inside the stall, more spasms forced her to double over in pain.

This isn't normal, she thought. This isn't nerves and this isn't morning sickness. This is something else altogether. And then she felt it, a dampness in her underwear. She tugged at her dress and pulled down her pants to see. There was blood. Dark, red streaks of blood.

Another cramp hit and this time she dropped down to her knees and wailed.

Frankie found Lucy at the bar, doing shots. There were several full shot glasses in front of her, along with an alarming number of empty ones.

Neither of us is going to be sober enough to have this conversation, she thought, and she pulled up a stool next to her sister.

"Talk to me," she said. "And give me one of those shots, would you?"

"What do you want me to say?" Lucy asked. But she obediently slid a shot across to her sister.

"Tell me what's going on with you?"

Lucy sniffed. "I don't want to talk about it." She sounded like a sulky teenager.

"Too bad. You have to. Start by explaining how you ended up as a member of NOP in the first place."

Lucy threw back another shot.

"And also tell me how the hell you got all these drinks at once! Where's the responsible service of alcohol?"

"I slipped that guy back there a hundred-dollar note. He was happy to give me as many as I wanted."

"Jesus. You're not drinking them all, okay? You'll end up needing your stomach pumped."

Lucy reached for another glass and Frankie blocked her. Lucy tried to bat her hand away, Frankie grabbed at her wrist and they descended into a hand-slapping battle, reminiscent of their childhood. Frankie was the tiniest bit more sober, so she prevailed and Lucy finally gave up.

"I'll let you have the next one when you answer my question." Frankie poked her tongue out at her sister and shot one herself.

"*Fine.* I heard about NOP from a parent at school who had a sister in the group. I thought it sounded interesting and I was trying to learn to "think like a journalist," as my lecturer keeps saying. I had an assignment coming up and I thought it might make for a good story. So, I made up a fake name and a fake account and I joined."

"How'd you join so easily? Didn't they notice your account was brand-new?"

"They mustn't have checked it. I think they were at the stage where it was really starting to take off, lots of new members. Anyway, soon after, I got invited to a get-together in real life."

"And you actually went along?" Frankie couldn't help but feel impressed by how brazen her sister was.

Anytime she'd been invited to any event, her alter ego "Viv" had politely declined. Although she never would have got away with it, as Poppy and Annalise would have recognized her on the spot.

"Yeah. You remember my old friend Sophie from uni? I convinced her to sign up too so I'd have some backup. She never had kids, so she was able to be a genuine member. You want to know the most embarrassing part?"

"Yes."

"I actually wore a disguise when I went along. In case one of them ever saw me out and about with the kids."

"You're kidding me! What kind of disguise? Did you put on a little fake mustache and a bowler hat?"

"Shut up! No. But I did wear a wig. Stop laughing at me!" Lucy paused. "I'm having another shot now, and if you try and stop me I'll punch you in the arm."

Frankie picked up two glasses, handed one to her sister, clinked their glasses together, and they both threw them back.

"What are we drinking, by the way?" Frankie screwed up her face. "It's not exactly pleasant."

"It's called a Kick in the Balls. Tequila, whiskey, and a liqueur."

"That explains it."

Lucy touched a finger to her lips. "Did you know that Mum used to love tequila and Dad loved whiskey?"

Lucy was only four years older than Frankie, but every now and then she would come out with some tidbit of information that took Frankie by surprise. She shook her head.

"They were never big drinkers or anything like that. But I can remember a night around the kitchen table just after I turned eighteen . . . the three of us doing shots together."

"Where was I?"

"Can't remember. A sleepover at a friend's house? You would have only been fourteen, so they wouldn't have wanted to do it in front of you. Mum drank both of us under the table."

Frankie smiled. She wanted to continue their conversation about NOP and the article, but she also didn't want to stop talking about their mum and dad.

But a shadow crossed Lucy's eyes.

"So anyway, I infiltrated their stupid group, and at first, I didn't think there was much of an angle there after all, until all of a sudden Poppy went on this hate rant and I decided it was going to make for a brilliant story. I wrote my anonymous article, which stirred things up even more. After that happened, Sophie started to feel uncomfortable about the group. She didn't like the way the women were behaving. Next thing, Poppy turns up at her salon for a haircut, but Sophie was out the back 'cause she had a headache. Then, when the hairdresser who was covering for her joins her out the back halfway through the cut, Soph starts gossiping with her about how Poppy started up NOP, not realizing the other hairdresser had actually already had some kind of big altercation with NOP. Apparently the hairdresser lost it at Poppy when she went to finish her cut."

"Wow. I didn't hear about that. Okay . . . so I understand why you wrote the article. But when you were yelling at Poppy and Annalise back there, you sounded so . . . offended by them. Like you'd taken it really personally. What was that all about?"

Lucy spoke quietly. "I don't know."

"Yes, you do."

She looked away and reached for another shot. Frankie stopped her again, but this time her touch was gentle. "Tell me the truth," she said.

A tear slid down Lucy's cheek. She faced her sister. "I think I was trying to self-destruct," she whispered. "You don't understand what it was like. I went into the group thinking it was all about wanting a story, but then it wasn't that. Because I became this different person.

I liked being Carla. I liked pretending I wasn't a mum anymore, because if I wasn't a mum, then that meant I wasn't failing as a parent."

"Failing? Are you kidding me? How could you ever think you were failing? You're the most amazing mother I know. The perfect mum. The super mum!"

The moment Frankie said the words "super mum," Lucy flinched. "You really think that about me, don't you? Don't you realize how much it drives me up the wall that you think of me that way? Don't you get how much pressure it puts on me?"

Frankie pulled back, frightened by her sister's anger. "I didn't . . . I didn't know. But I swear, it's only because you honestly are incredible as a mum, so much better than me."

"I'm NOT! What kind of a mum jumps on Facebook and wishes away her children?"

"Me! I do! I was exactly the same on NOP. I loved having an alter ego. I loved pretending to be someone else."

"You're just saying that to try and make me feel better."

"No, I'm not. Look, I joined to spy on the 'mean girls' from work, but I stayed because I loved it. How did you know Viv was me anyway? How could you tell?"

"You told a cute story about giving your neighbor a bottle of wine but I'd already heard that story direct from you—only it was the other way around, they were the ones who gave you a bottle when you were at the end of your rope."

"Ah."

"What made you decide to share it but reverse the roles?"

Frankie shrugged. "I'm not sure. I guess maybe it was nice playing the part of the person who has it all together instead of the one who needs to be rescued."

"The hero. I get that. For me, though, the more I enjoyed playing the part of Carla, the more I hated myself for it. But I couldn't stop. So instead I decided to tear the group apart."

Frankie thought back to the words Lucy had screamed at Poppy earlier. *You stupid, childish girls, playing your ridiculous little games.*

It wasn't about them at all, Frankie realized. Lucy was angry at herself.

"You know I have all the same problems with my kids as you do with yours?" Lucy said. "But I keep it behind closed doors. I play the part of Happy Little Families when in truth I argue with my kids just like you do. I lose my shit and I yell at them. Sometimes I open a bottle of wine the second they get home from school, just to make it through the afternoon with their constant nagging."

"But why wouldn't you just tell me these things? Why keep it all behind closed doors?"

"Because ever since Mum and Dad died, it's been on me to protect you. I'm the one who's supposed to be there for you, not the other way around. I'm the one who's meant to have it all together. You don't need to hear about my problems."

"Lucy! That's ridiculous! I'm your sister, of course I'm meant to be there for you. It's supposed to work both ways."

"Can I tell you something?"

"Anything."

"I've been on antidepressants now for over a year."

Frankie slid off her stool, stepped closer, and wrapped her arms around her big sister. "Oh, Lucy," she said, "I had no idea."

Lucy began to cry into her shoulder and Frankie rubbed her back.

"Frankie," said Lucy, pulling back a bit, "do you miss Mum and Dad?"

She nodded. "Yes. I miss them a lot."

"Me too."

Poppy couldn't find Annalise anywhere. It occurred to her to check the ladies' bathroom. When she walked in, she almost immediately turned around to walk back out again. Leanne, the woman from MOP, was in there. She might have cleared the air with Yasmine, but she wasn't ready to try to explain herself to someone else.

But as soon as Leanne saw her, she spoke up. "Oh, thank God," she said. "I need help. I think the woman in this stall is sick but I can't get her to open the door. I didn't want to leave her and I've been waiting for someone else to come in."

Poppy hesitated. "So should I go and ask for help . . ." she began, but then she heard the moan from inside the stall and stopped still. It didn't sound like the drunken cry of someone who was feeling a bit under the weather. It sounded like an anguished cry from someone who was really, really not okay.

"What's wrong with her?" Poppy asked.

"I don't know. I can't make sense of what she's saying."

The voice spoke. "Poppy?" she said, her voice full of tears. "Is that you?"

"Annalise! What's wrong, honey, what's going on?"

It sounded like she was about to respond but instead she let out another shriek of pain.

"Open the door," Poppy said. "Let us help you."

"I . . . I can't," she whimpered. "I can't reach, I can't get up. If I move . . . If I move I might make it worse."

Leanne exchanged a terrified look with Poppy. "Make what worse?" she said.

And before Poppy had the chance to respond, Leanne had dropped down onto her belly on the damp tiles, and was commando-style crawling her way under the door to get to Annalise—not even pausing to worry about her silk cocktail dress. A moment later, the lock clicked from the inside and the door swung open to reveal Annalise curled up in a ball on the floor, her knees tucked into her stomach, tears streaming down her face. Leanne was crouched next to her, hands on her shoulders.

"What's happened?" Poppy looked at Leanne. "Do you think it's food poisoning or something?"

But Leanne pointed down at something on the floor. Poppy realized it was Annalise's knickers that she must have kicked off, and she saw the bloodstain.

"Is she pregnant?" Leanne asked.

"Pregnant?" Poppy exclaimed. "She couldn't be—" but she stopped short as Annalise tipped her tearstained face toward her and their eyes met.

"Yes," Poppy said. "Yes, I think she is."

"Then she might be miscarrying," said Leanne.

"Come on, let's move her out of here so she can lie down properly."

They both tried to gently take hold of Annalise's arms, but she cowered away from them. "No," she cried, "no, don't move me, don't make me move. I have to stay still, I don't want it to come out of me, I don't want to lose it. I can't. I can't lose this one as well."

Poppy didn't register the strangeness of her words. *This one as well.* She was too busy panicking. She was too busy hurting for her friend, she couldn't stand to see her in so much pain, so distraught.

"We have to, honey," she said, "you can't stay in here. We have to get you to a hospital." She looked at Leanne. "Wait, what are we going to do?" she asked. "We're in the middle of the harbor, how are we going to get help?"

"Shit, I don't know," Leanne replied. "But I'm going to run out and get my phone while you stay with her. I'll call triple zero. They'll tell us what to do."

She stood up and hurried toward the door.

"See if you can find someone else on board to help," Poppy called after her. "A doctor or a nurse or something."

Left alone, Poppy managed to gently ease Annalise out of the small compartment and lay her down on the tiles of the bathroom floor, resting her head on her lap and stroking her face. "It's okay, Lisey," she said, "it's going to be okay, we're getting you help. You're going to be okay."

"I'm not," Annalise cried. "I'm not okay. This is my punishment." And she let out another wail as her body twisted in pain.

"Punishment? Punishment for what? No, no, honey, you're not being punished, you're going to be fine, I promise you."

"My punishment for hurting everyone. Frankie. Lawrence. You. I lied to you, Poppy. I've been lying to you for so long."

"Sweetie, it's okay, you don't need to worry about that. I don't care that you didn't tell me you're pregnant. It's fine, it's so fine. Forget about it."

"Not that," she said, and she turned her face into Poppy's lap and cried out again as another cramp took hold of her. "About me. About who I am. I lied about so much."

"I don't care about your past. I swear to you, I don't. You're my best friend and all you need to worry about is getting better. Just hold on, okay? Help is coming."

Oh God, where was Leanne? What was going on out there?

"I have to tell you this," Annalise sobbed, "I have to tell you the truth."

She twisted again and tipped her head back so she was looking right up at Poppy.

"I was already a mum," she said. "I've been betraying you from the beginning. I was always an imposter in your group. I lied about everything."

Then she rolled back onto her side again, her head slipped off Poppy's lap, and she only just caught hold of her in time before she might have smacked her head on the hard tiles.

Poppy's brain was racing with what Annalise had just told her, but she had to put it aside. She had to ignore it and focus on her right now. Focus on getting her better, focus on getting her through this. She could worry about what she'd told her later.

The door swung open and Leanne burst back into the bathroom, flanked by two other people who immediately rushed in and knelt down on either side of Annalise.

Annalise didn't know why it mattered so much that she told Poppy the truth then and there. Maybe it gave her something else to focus on?

She couldn't say all of it out loud, though. As much as she wanted to, beyond that one simple admission, the words wouldn't come, so she closed her eyes and sifted through her memories, and she relived the story in her mind.

When Annalise was still a baby, her mother met a man. A man who she found so intoxicating, so mesmerizing, that she dropped everything to follow him. Maybe Annalise should be grateful that she didn't drop her too. That she didn't leave her behind. That despite her love for this man, she still loved Annalise, enough to take her too. But perhaps it would have been better if she had left her behind. She could have had a different life.

What really mattered is what did happen. She took Annalise with her and her life changed so completely from what it could have been. This man that she followed lived in a compound in the middle of the bush outside of Hope Vale in far north Queensland. That was where he led his cult. Annalise never knew if her mum regretted her choice once she settled into life there. She didn't know if she was disappointed to discover that she wasn't the only one he loved, or the only one who loved him.

On the one hand, one might think the fact that Annalise grew up knowing no different meant she would have been happy there. But she wasn't. She could never be. She hated him. She hated the way he looked at her and the other girls. She hated the way he drew her mother's attention away from her.

And the older kids told her stories. Some had moved there when they were older, so they knew about the outside world. God, how Annalise wanted to be a part of that outside world. She wanted to meet other people. She wanted to live a different life. She wanted to escape. From the moment she knew she could have a different life, she wanted to escape.

There were a few of them who plotted and planned. She didn't know how serious the others were, or how many of them were just playing out fantasies they never thought would come to fruition. But Annalise believed it. She knew her place wasn't there. She tried to tell her mum that she wasn't happy, that she wanted to leave. But her mother wouldn't listen.

She was fourteen when she finally made it out. There had been failed attempts before that, and each time she failed, he would punish her. And her mother would let him. Each time she let that happen, Annalise's hopes of her mum coming with her would diminish, further and further.

In the end, it was just Annalise and one other person who left together—a lanky fifteen-year-old boy named River. They hitched a ride all the way down to Bris-

bane and made their way in and out of shelters; sometimes they slept on the streets, sometimes they squatted
in abandoned buildings. He was the one who she fell
pregnant to. She thought they were in love. She thought
the two of them could find a way to live, find a way to
raise a baby together. And she thought she would be
a different mum. A completely different mother to the
one who had loved that man more than her. She didn't
know if her mother ever looked for her.

But she was just a kid! She wouldn't have known
how to look after a baby. She was kidding herself. They
were camped out in an abandoned warehouse when
she gave birth to her baby. River helped, but she knew
he was terrified. He wasn't ready to become a father.
Somehow, they got her out alive, even though they had
no clue what we were doing. They cleaned her and cut
the cord and Annalise hugged the baby close to her, and
she fed her just as she'd seen the women in the compound do with their own babies. They named her Opal.

River lasted four nights before he vanished. He was
way out of his depth. Three nights after he left, Annalise woke in the early hours of the morning to find her
baby blue. She'd fallen asleep with Opal in her arms but
she realized she must have rolled on her as she slept.
She tried to bring her back. She tried to revive her.

"Don't die, don't die, don't die," she said over and over again as she massaged her chest and breathed into her mouth.

But she was already cold.

She never had a chance of bringing her back.

She wrapped her up in a blanket and she walked. She walked and walked until her heels were rubbed raw and blisters appeared on her soles. She left the city and she continued on through the suburbs, past darkened red-brick bungalows with neatly mowed lawns and curtains drawn tight.

When she laid her daughter to rest, she wanted to say a prayer, but she didn't know any.

So instead she asked the earth to take her. She asked Mother Nature to love her.

She didn't ask God. She didn't know God.

And then she ran.

She told herself she would start over. That she would be a different person. A person who didn't deserve love or a family. A person who just lived one day to the next. A person who simply got by. She stole things. She invented things about her past. A primary school, a high school. As she grew older—a uni degree if she needed it for a job. Fake credentials, fake work experience. She slept with people. Sometimes her lies worked, sometimes someone checked her out and caught on to the lies. And so she'd move on to somewhere else and try again. She was good at charming people, good at talking her way in.

She did write to her daughter, though. Letters with no address, letters that could never be sent. But she did write them. Opal became her conscience. She shared her deepest, darkest thoughts. She confessed to her when she knew she'd done wrong. When she pretended to be happy, to be fine, Opal was the one she told the truth. What Poppy didn't spot when she snuck a look at that red notebook were two words, *Dear Opal,* scribbled on the inside front cover:

8 June
When you walk the streets instead of catching the bus or taking the train, the world is a different place. Because you notice the smaller things. The tiniest of details. A dent in the side of a letter box. A dilapidated side gate. A gutter with overflowing leaves.

A mound in the earth in the middle of the bush that shouldn't be there.

That shouldn't exist.

Frankie was sitting with her arm slung around her sister's shoulders when she heard that there was a medical emergency. For a minute, her mind jumped to Linda. She hadn't seen her all night since they'd talked about Paul and about the mistakes she'd made. Where had she been all this time? What if she'd stayed out on the deck after they'd spoken? And there was that big wave as well! What if she'd fallen overboard?

But no, there was Linda, back at their table, drinking alone. Frankie admonished herself for being overly dramatic.

Then the rumor reached Frankie and Lucy that a woman in the toilets was suffering a miscarriage.

Not Annalise, she thought as she remembered how she'd looked at her just an hour earlier when she'd told her how much she wanted this baby.

There was nothing Frankie could do to help. Aside from the fact that she was far too drunk to be of any help to anyone, apparently there was already a nurse in there looking after her and paramedics were on their way via water taxi.

When the paramedics arrived and they were making their way back toward the waiting water taxi with Annalise, Frankie pushed her way through the crowd and caught Poppy's arm. She gave it a squeeze and Poppy took her hand and squeezed back. Then they were gone.

The mood on the boat was subdued as it cut through

the water on its way back to the harbor. The rest of the speeches were canceled and people milled about, finishing drinks, chatting quietly. Somehow, Frankie, Lucy, and Chelsea found themselves sitting at a table with a mix of NOP and MOP women.

A woman named Leanne, who'd apparently been the one to first find Annalise, had a damp dress and a tear-streaked face. Frankie heard she'd crawled under the toilet door to get to Annalise.

Another woman—a member from NOP who was the nurse who'd gone in to help until the paramedics arrived—was sipping a bourbon, the ice clinking against the glass. No one was chatting, everyone was quiet.

Suddenly Lucy spoke up. "I wrote the article," she said, a little too loudly, her voice slurred. "The article about NOP. I wish I hadn't. I'm sorry."

Another woman chimed in. "Why do women do this?" she asked. "Why do we tear each other down? Why don't we support one another?"

"Because we're all still the bitchy girls who picked on one another in high school?" someone suggested.

"No," said someone else, "it's because we're all too caught up with our own problems. Our own shit. And we forget that everyone else has their own shit going on too."

A woman across the table stood up. "Hi," she said,

"I'm Kellie, and I've been a member of NOP for four months."

Everyone laughed.

"I loved it because I felt like I was a part of something. And because whenever I got together with my family, I felt like the odd one out because all my sisters and brothers have kids and it was nice to stop being the odd one out."

She sat down and a woman in a red floor-length gown to the left of her stood up.

"My name's Georgia and I've been a member of MOP for two years. When my daughter was first born, I went to MOP for everything. I asked about feeding, I asked about sleeping, I asked about cracked nipples, I asked about baby monitors and formula and nappies and anything that came up. The women on there were my saviors and I love them for it."

Frankie stood up, swayed a little, grasped the table for support, and spoke. "My name's Frankie but the NOP ladies would know me as Viv. I was a member of both groups and I saw the good and the ugly from both sides. Sometimes the members from MOP helped and supported me, and sometimes they judged me and made me feel like a terrible mother. Sometimes the NOP women were kind and understanding about mums and sometimes they were arseholes. No one is perfect. And no single group is perfect either. But I do think we can all do better for one another. A little empathy is all that's needed."

A woman who looked a little nervous stood up next. "Hey, guys," she said, "I'm Dee, and I was actually supposed to give a speech tonight. I was really nervous about it and I'm finding it hard enough just talking in front of all of you. I'm not a member of either of these groups you're talking about. But I've overheard a lot about them tonight and I think I've got the gist of what's going on. So I just want to say, I was a victim of domestic violence. I'm no longer a victim. Now I'm a survivor. But unlike the other woman who spoke tonight, I don't have kids. Now, from the perspective of a nonparent, I respect the idea of having a space for women who aren't mums to get together and connect. I could have used it a few years ago. But as another option . . . why not merge the two groups? Why not just make it a community of women? Simple as that?" She chewed on her bottom lip. "Might be good. Might not work. Just my two cents," she added.

There were nods and murmurs of agreement from around the table, and soon after, the women broke off into their own smaller conversations and the moment had passed. Frankie felt like they were on their way toward a change, though. Nothing major. It wasn't like women were going to stop judging one another overnight. But maybe the "them and us" mentality was starting to break down . . . even just a little.

When Frankie arrived home, Dom was waiting up for her. He put the kettle on as she came through the door and made them a cup of tea each. She noticed the house was tidier than when she'd left earlier this evening. Nothing amazing, but she could see he'd made an effort, which was nice.

She told him about the evening. About Linda's promise that the bonus was coming after all, and that by her calculations, it would see them through long enough that he had a few more months before he had to find a new job.

She told him about Annalise as well, and how angry she'd been with her for not passing on that message. But now all of that seemed so irrelevant. The kids were fine, it had all been okay. There was no point in holding on to that anger. And now she just wanted for Annalise to be all right.

Later, when they went to bed, Frankie checked her phone before she turned out the light and snuggled her way into Dom's arms. She saw a post on MOP's Facebook page from Leanne.

Evening ladies,

I know it's late, so most of you won't see this until tomorrow, but I felt the need to post it now, tonight.

This whole thing we have going with NOP? It's time for it to end. Several MOP members went along to a fund-raiser event tonight and met quite a few of the women from NOP. In fact, I met the founder of NOP and confronted her. I was angry with her for starting up that group and for setting out to hurt mothers. We argued, we couldn't seem to see eye to eye.

But later on, the two of us worked side by side to help someone. To help another woman.

And I realized that the two of us were just the same. Two women, trying to make it through. Trying to be there for the people we loved the most. Trying to find our way.

We have MOP as a place for mums to connect. A place to support one another. A place to meet and make new friends, share advice, exchange ideas. And you know what NOP is? It's a place for these other women to connect. So why shouldn't they have that? Yes, many of them said or did nasty things, but so did many of us.

So, right now, right here, I'm calling for an end

to this. No more fighting. No more messages of hate. I'll be extending the olive branch to NOP and I hope that all of you will too. There's room enough for all of us.

Good night.
Xx

PART SEVEN

Three Months Later
Spring

Chapter 34

Poppy was back in goals. Back where she felt like she belonged, for the grand finale of the season. So much for that doctor and his prognosis that her hand might never be the same. It was perfectly fine. The slightest twinge here and there, but otherwise more than capable of allowing her to catch a high-speed soccer ball. Okay, so she'd let one goal in today. But she'd made plenty of decent saves as well. And they were up 2–1 with ten minutes to go. All they had to do was hold them off until the whistle blew and they'd take home the win.

She looked over at the sideline. Elle was pacing back and forth, shouting instructions at the team. She was stressed, the team had missed a few opportunities to score and widen the gap, and Elle wouldn't like the game being this close. Plus her star striker was sidelined. But she wasn't as fired up as she could have been. Probably because every now and again, she'd lean down to chat with Annalise, who was sitting in a foldout chair, cheering them on, and whenever she spoke with Annalise, Elle's face would glow.

It had turned out that Annalise wasn't having a miscarriage on the boat. At first it had seemed like the worst possible news. One of the paramedics had taken Poppy aside and warned her that if she was losing the baby at this early stage, there wasn't going to be anything that could be done to stop it. But as the water taxi had taken them back to the harbor, the cramps had lessened. The bleeding had stopped. Afterward, at the hospital, the doctor had simply said, "Sometimes these things happen during pregnancy. It was only a very small amount of blood. Could be stress. The cramps might even have been from something she ate." All she could really say was that Annalise ought to take it easy throughout the rest of the pregnancy, just in case, but as far as she could see, everything was progressing normally.

Lawrence was also taking the situation really well. Most of the time. He made at least one more attempt once Annalise was back at work to win her back. But then he met Elle when she came to have lunch with Annalise. He took one look at her and said, "Yeah okay, I get it. I'd fall for that chick too." Since then he'd thrown himself into preparation dad mode. He was keen to share custody with Annalise and she was more than happy with that arrangement. "Might be a bit of a weird family," she'd said, "but it's still a fuck-load better than what I grew up with." It was nice for Poppy to see sweary, honest Annalise back on form.

She never told Annalise that she'd read any of the pages in her notebook. Annalise had opened up to her about her past and she was slowly becoming more and more vulnerable with her emotions. That was more than enough, and Poppy didn't want to hurt or embarrass her by telling her what she'd read.

The other thing she had chosen not to tell Annalise was about the call she'd had with Garret recently. She'd decided to keep that one all to herself. He'd phoned out of the blue, and when she saw his number on her screen, Poppy's first instinct was to ignore. But instead she'd taken a deep breath in and she'd answered.

"Poppy! Sorry . . . I didn't really expect you to pick up. Assumed I'd get your voice mail."

"Yeah, I know, I didn't think I was going to answer either."

"Thank you . . . for taking my call. I appreciate it.

Anyway, I wanted to just check in with you . . . see how you are. Karls and I, we treated you so badly and I really hate that we did that to you. Looking back, we should have handled it all differently. I mean, obviously— not cheating would have been a start, but the way we ambushed you with the news, it was wrong. How are you?"

Poppy had stayed quiet, considering his question. How was she? Really, honestly, deep down, how was she? If she searched inside for that person who'd sat across from her partner and her best friend, for that person who'd felt the shock of betrayal, the loss of a great big chunk of her heart, then sure, it still hurt. The sting was still there. But not in the same way anymore. It wasn't as sharp, it had dulled around the edges.

"You know what Garret?" she said eventually. "I'm fucking awesome."

"Oh. That's . . . that's great."

"And I'm glad that you got what you wanted. I really am."

There was a pause and she heard an intake of breath.

"You know what's funny?" he said.

"What?"

"I'll never really know what I did want. She fell pregnant the first time I slept with her. I mean, I love our baby girl, of course I do. But I'll never know for sure what I would have chosen had I been given the choice. I know Karleen was cruel to you as well, when we told you the news, but honestly, she's not a bad person. It's just that she was insecure. I think she could tell that I still had my doubts and she was terrified that you'd see through it all. That you would stop me from leaving. Sometimes I envy you. I envy the way you've always been so certain of what you want."

"I wouldn't worry so much about that, Garret. I reckon things turned out the way they were meant to."

Poppy looked again at the sideline and realized someone else was hovering not far from Annalise and Elle, watching the game. It was difficult to tell from this distance, but she was pretty sure she recognized his shape. Jack. They'd had coffee last week after she'd texted him and asked if he'd like to meet up. He'd written back within minutes:

Um . . . YES! (and here was me thinking I'd struck out with you). Can't believe you left me hanging so long. Name the when and where.

The date had been nice. Good, easy conversation. Great coffee, which Jack admitted was on par with his Italian restaurant.

"So when should we go there so I can try it out?" Poppy had asked.

"As soon as possible," he'd replied.

When they'd finally stood up and made their way reluctantly out of the coffee shop, Jack had taken hold of Poppy's hand and held it as they crossed the road to her car. He walked her around to the driver's side and she was saying good-bye and turning to open the car door when he gently pulled her back to face him again, cupped her face in his hands, and kissed her softly on the lips. It was the kind of kiss that made her body tremble and her knees almost give way.

It was the kind of kiss that made her think, *This really might work between us.*

Chapter 35

Annalise didn't tell Poppy everything.

She told her about her childhood. About her mother and the cult. About the boy she escaped with and that he was the one she fell pregnant to.

But not everything can be shared. She let her make her assumptions about that pregnancy. Poppy had heard her in the bathroom utter the words "not again."

There was no need for anyone to know she'd carried that baby to term. No need for anyone else to know she'd failed that baby at such a tender, innocent age. No need for anyone to know about her secret in the bush.

2 September

Dear Opal,

Are you tired of me telling you these stories? These theories? These nonsensical thoughts?

Do you wish that I would just come right out and say what I need to say to you?

That I would tell you what I should be telling you, every single day?

But if I say what I need to say, does that mean I'll stop writing to you?

You've been here for me for so long. Which is the opposite, isn't it? I'm supposed to be there for you. I was supposed to protect you.

I'm sorry, Opal. I'm so sorry for the way I failed you.

I'm sorry and I love you. With all my heart.

I always will.

I'm waiting now. Waiting to meet your new baby brother, and while I wait, I can promise you this: I will love him fiercely and I will take care of him the way I should have taken care of you. And one day, when Elle and I have grown old together and it's my time to leave this world, I'm going to join you wherever you are and the two of us can keep watching over your little brother together.

Now, as Annalise watched her team from the sideline, she jiggled one knee up and down and chewed on her fingernails. She wanted to be out there with them. Elle strode past her, shouting instructions at Rowena, and Annalise caught hold of her hand. "Chill," she said. "They've got it in the bag."

Elle squeezed her hand in response. "Yeah, I know. I'll feel better when the whistle blows though." Elle kissed the top of her head and then jogged off down toward their goal end.

"Hey, brought you this."

Annalise swiveled around in her chair to see Jack standing behind her, holding out a hot dog. "Poppy said you'd probably be starving by the end of the game."

She stood up and took it off him. "Thanks, you just finished playing? How'd you guys go?"

"Lost in overtime." He shrugged. "Next year. How's this game going?"

"Up by one. They'll take it home." Annalise took a bite of the hot dog and looked sideways at Jack while still keeping an eye on the field. "So, this your way of getting in good with the best friend?"

"Absolutely."

"Good start." She paused. "Just don't break her heart. You'll be all good by me."

There is always a huge collection of wonderful people behind the scenes who help bring a book to life and, as such, I'm usually terrified that I will forget to thank someone integral! So, I'll do my best and if I forget you, please know that I *do* appreciate your help and/or support.

A huge thank you to everyone from HarperCollins Australia, William Morrow in the USA and Michael Joseph in the UK—including, but not limited to: Anna Valdinger, Carrie Feron, Maxine Hitchcock, Katherine Hassett, Shannon Kelly, Dianne Blacklock and Matilda McDonald. You've all made such an incredible impact upon this book and for that I am truly grateful.

Thanks also to my extraordinary agent, Pippa Masson at Curtis Brown, as well as Sheila Crowley at Curtis Brown UK.

As always, much love to Steve Menasse, Maddie Menasse, and Piper Menasse—I'm very, very lucky to call you lot my family.

I'm extremely grateful to everyone who answered my questions on all sorts of different subjects, from school mum dramas to hand injuries and paramedic procedures—thank you Catherine Reynolds, Ian Hutchings, and Sabeeha Toynton.

A great big thank you to Jaclyn Moriarty for reading an early copy and giving me kind feedback, and also for suggesting that if I just made one small change it would be perfect, but then never ever getting around to telling me what that one small change was.

Hilarious, right? Okay, you can tell me now.

HARPER LUXE

THE NEW LUXURY IN READING

We hope you enjoyed reading
our new, comfortable print size and found it
an experience you would like to repeat.

Well – you're in luck!

HarperLuxe offers the finest in fiction and
nonfiction books in this same larger print size and
paperback format. Light and easy to read, HarperLuxe
paperbacks are for book lovers who want to see
what they are reading without the strain.

For a full listing of titles and
new releases to come, please visit our website:

www.HarperLuxe.com

SEEING IS BELIEVING!